PRAISE FOR

ON EART

"Weird and sweet... Like a 2020s *White Noise*: loud and colorful Americana with a sprinkle of apocalyptic doom—plus cats. It takes aliens (or an Emily Jane) to help us see our society for the bizarre, sugary, microplastic-poisoned dream it is."

—Edgar Cantero, *New York Times* bestselling author of *Meddling Kids*

"Heartfelt, witty, and secretly romantic... A delightful and poignant story about what it is to be human and what we owe each other."

—Christina Lauren, *New York Times* bestselling author of *Love and Other Words*

"Like a science-fiction novel that runs in the margins of I Can Has Cheezburger? memes."

—*Scientific American*

HERE BESIDE THE RISING TIDE

"A fascinating read that grabs you from the very first page and straddles a few genres in order to create a story that's unique and utterly heartwarming. It's a little bit women's fiction, a little bit *Stranger Things*, but it gave me the hopeful, aching sense of wonder that I got from watching *E.T. the Extra-Terrestrial* the first time. Loved every page!"

—Ruby Dixon, *USA Today* bestselling author of *Ice Planet Barbarians*

"Jane juggles the fantastical with the ordinary, and readers will relish this clever, heartfelt story about friendship and family."

—*Booklist*

"Emily Jane is a storyteller unbound by genre."

—Rebekah Bergman, author of *The Museum of Human History*

BOOKS IN THE BRANCHES TIMELINES

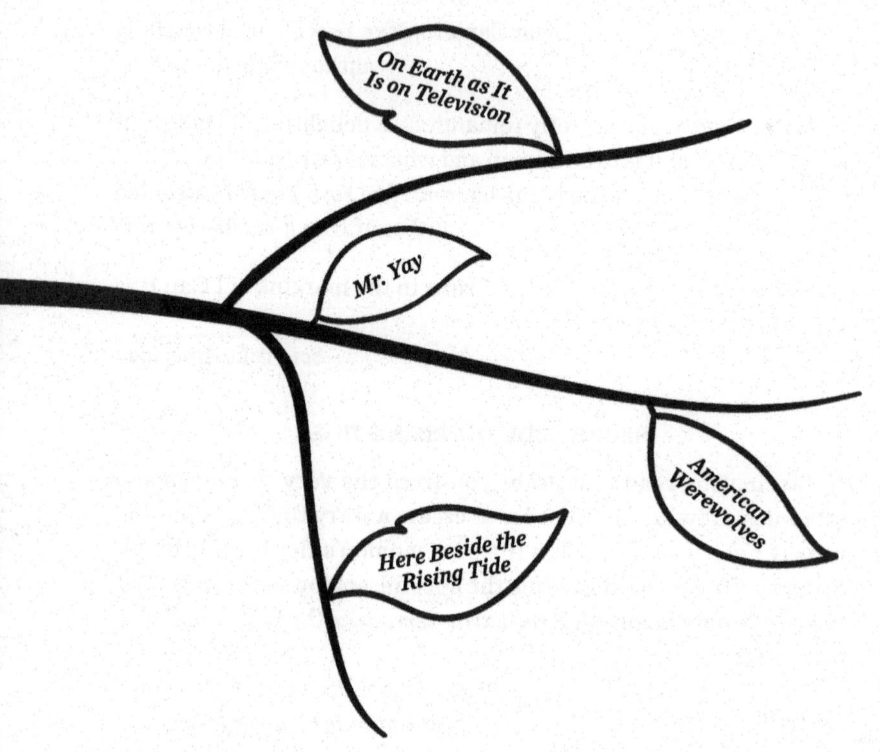

A NOVEL BY

EMILY JANE

HYPERION AVENUE
LOS ANGELES NEW YORK

First Edition, June 2026

10 9 8 7 6 5 4 3 2 1

FAC-004510-26085

Printed in the United States of America

Designed by Amy C. King

Illustrations by Faceout Studio, Amanda Hudson and © Adobe Stock

Library of Congress Control Number: 2025948138

ISBN 978-1-368-11604-6

Reinforced binding

The authorized representative in the EU for product safety and compliance is Disney Trading B.V., Asterweg 15S, 1031 HL, Amsterdam, The Netherlands

email: DCP.DL-EU.bookscontact@disney.com

www.HyperionAvenueBooks.com

for Delux

IN THE BEGINNING, THERE WAS RAP

Damn, yo,
This boy's tasty
That's what they say
When they hear me drop the bass line
I ace mine
Ain't ever gonna waste time
Facin' all those haters
Who think music's just a pastime
No. Yo, I can feel it in my soul
Bring the light, bring the love
And music makes 'em go—
It makes Me.

IN THE BEGINNING

"BRADFORD! EARTH TO BRADFORD! Turn that crap down! It's not even music. I swear. If I have to tell you one more time, those speakers are going straight in the trash!"

He turned the volume down, then off.

He cupped his small hands over his ears, to block out their voices. Only his own soft voice remained.

Silent, he whispered out loud. *Silent like a starfish.*

THEN WAY LATER

THEY NEVER stayed silent.

"What did I tell you, Bradford? You drop out of college? What do you think will happen? Your life will amount to nothing."

Except they were wrong.

Except by then, he was better at blocking them out.

Like he could hear music playing, even when it wasn't.

WINTER SOLSTICE

BRADFORD AND THE DOG

MAYBE THIS RANDOM DOG was why he dreamed of the dog. Him and the dog on a boat, waves sloshing all around them, water the color of a blue raspberry slushy. A pod of dolphins swam alongside the boat, except the dolphins were also dogs. Dogphins. A man rode one of the dogphins. He wore a denim jumpsuit and a fat gold chain. He waved and said, *We're making it stronger!* The Dream Dog gave a thumbs-ups, even though he didn't have thumbs. The Dream Dog wore a captain's hat.

Bradford had seen this dog before. This dog got to captain his own ship. The dog decided when to set sail. Which port. What they ate next. No one said, *C'mere boy. Roll over.* No one said he had to be a Good Dog.

Maybe he was a good dog, but that was beside the point.

This Random Dog had a cold wet nose. It used the nose to wake him up.

Not a good-dog move.

Bradford opened his eyes. A dog's eyes stared back. The dog's eyes were glossy brown, and way too fucking close.

"What... the... fuck," Bradford managed to say, before his brain caught up with his eyes and mouth. He scrambled back, into the corner of his bed, up against the peeling wallpaper.

"What the *fuck*."

The dog's tongue slopped out. The dog's bright pink tongue had two black spots, and later he would name these spots Zoey and Ernestina. But right now, the spots were both called: *What the fuck*.

The dog was a pit bull type. A full-bred pit bull? Unknown. Bradford hadn't majored in dogs at Canine Academy. It had the stocky bod of a pit. The I-will-crush-you jaw. Floppy triangle ears. Its fur was sleek, dark brown with a white tuxedo.

The thing was, Bradford Pierson didn't have a dog.

The thing was, Bradford Pierson lived in a studio apartment on the third floor of an old building on the boarded-windows-and-graffiti side of downtown, with a big sign in the lobby that said NO SMOKING—NO PETS.

In case the sign wasn't clear enough, the month-to-month lease that Bradford had signed in exchange for a key to that craptacular apartment said *No Pets* in at least two places and then went on to specify all the animals a pet might be. He couldn't even have a fish or a hamster.

Ironic, given the building had rats in the basement and cockroaches in the walls.

But Rules were Rules. Just like his dad always said. *Son, the Rules are the Rules. You can't just pick up your golf ball and drop it in the hole.*

Bradford had tried to tune out the Dad Platitudes and get on with his life, and yeah, maybe in his heart he'd always wanted a dog, but he didn't have the cash to feed a dog or deflea a dog or get the bones and treats that a dog deserved.

He didn't own a dog.

This Random Dog seemed to disagree. It stared at him like, *You know you want to feed me now. Let's take a walk. I know I'm a good dog, so you don't need to say it.*

It stared at him like it knew him well, and why was he getting so weird about their morning routine?

Technically, it was afternoon.

Bradford inched around the side of the bed. He slipped out. He walked over to the sink. The dog trotted after him, tongue out, goofy smile.

"Dude. *Dude,* stop. You're freaking me out."

He turned on the faucet. It gurgled out some brown water for a minute before turning clear. He filled a glass, drank. The dog sat. It stared up at him.

"What, you want water?"

The dog didn't answer.

"Fine. But I'm warning you—I know it tastes bad, but you better not spit it out. This isn't a resort. Dogs don't get bottled water."

Bradford opened the cupboard. On the shelf, next to the bowls, was a bag of dog food.

"What . . . the . . . fuckity fuck . . ."

He reached for the bag. Value-Kibbles. Lamb flavor.

"Really? That's what you like? Lamb flavor?"

The dog barked once.

"Shhhh! Shut up! You can't bark in here! You tryin' to get me kicked out?"

The dog gave a pathetic whimper. Oh, woe is hungry dog.

Bradford filled one bowl with food and another with water. He set them on the floor. The dog scarfed down the kibble. It slurped up the water. It got water all over the floor.

Bradford shook his head.

This dog.

It followed him around the apartment, even though there wasn't much apartment to follow him through. Just a box with two dirty windows, a kitchenette, a tiny bathroom tiled in pastel pink and blue. There was one dresser, which Bradford had found discarded on the street, a couch abandoned by the prior tenant, and an air mattress that claws could easily pop.

"Hey, you!" He turned to the dog. "Yeah, you. You better not get on my bed. That's *my* bed. Capisce?"

Bradford had paid for the bed himself. He had moved to the dorm from his parents' house. He hadn't asked for his parents' help, because he was doing this himself. Whatever *this* happened to be. He didn't want their strings. Their guilt. Their disdain.

He had, as a child, wanted a dog. He drew a picture of said dog on the front of his letter to Santa. He was nine. He had, he thought, been good enough at least, despite what anyone said. He had good grades and washed his dishes and made his bed. He didn't set fire to ants with a magnifying glass or pour salt on the garden slugs for fun.

He had found the letter to Santa in the trash, crumpled up, beneath a sprinkle of coffee grounds. He dug it out, brushed it off, and stuck it in the mailbox. But he forgot about postage, and no dog ever came. Until now.

"What? Why do you keep staring? Why are you following me around? Bozo."

On his heels. Would not leave him be. That damned tongue with its two black spots.

Then it occurred to him that, of course, the dog wanted to go out. And if he took it out, it would be out instead of in here threatening his lease.

He didn't own a leash because he didn't own a dog. But whoever this shitty apartment belonged to—*not him*—had dog food, so maybe they had a leash, too.

Oh, damn. They did.

Right there, hanging from a nail by the front door.

"This is fucked up," he told the dog. "You get that, right? You and me, we're not a thing."

The dog had a collar, plain blue, nondescript, no name or address tag. Bradford clipped the leash to the collar. But he couldn't just march out the door, down the stairs, past the NO PETS sign in the lobby. He and the dog would have to sneak out.

In his closet, he found an old hiking backpack that looked big enough to fit a pit bull–type dog. He picked up the dog. He slid the dog, hind legs first, into the backpack. This Random Dog didn't struggle. It hung limp, like it knew how this worked. Like it rode in this backpack *all the time*.

Bradford buckled the top, leaving a gap for the eyes and snout to peek out. He put the backpack on.

"Damn. You weigh like a thousand pounds. You need to chill on the dog food."

He opened the window. Cold air plowed through. He had forgotten his coat. He took off the backpack and set it on the couch. The dog didn't try to escape.

He put on his coat, shoes, and hat. He checked his pants

pockets. His phone and wallet were both still there, where he had left them. He checked his phone: *2:19 p.m., December 21.*

He had not jumped forward in time to a magic, dog-filled future, so far as he knew.

Bradford strapped on the dog-backpack. He stepped out the window, onto the fire escape. He climbed down the ladder, one floor, two floors, ready for each rusty step to crack beneath his weight, which was, his dad said, *not appropriate for a man his size*. This was a generous translation of Helena Pierson's words: *Grotesque,* his stepmom had said. Not to his face, but in earshot. *Disgustingly fat.*

Yeah, but no. He was not. He straddled the line between standard-fat and chubby. Big-boned. *Impressively boned,* Tommy had said once.

He tried to embrace it. His parents had named him Bradford Pierson III. But screw them, he was Fatty Bratty.

Bradford—or Bratty—hopped down from the last ladder rung. He shoved his frozen hands in his pockets. He walked around the building, to the street. The sky was drizzle-gray. The ground was damp and littered with cigarette butts and broken bottles. Cold wind whistled through the boards that covered the windows of the building across the street.

"Festive as fuck," Bratty said, remembering the date. December twenty-first. The winter solstice.

"He has to go," Bratty told the receptionist at Happy Paws Veterinary Clinic. "I mean, he's all right. But I have no idea where he came from. He just showed up. And I can't have pets. So can I just, like, leave him here?"

"Um, no," the receptionist said. "Sorry. We're just a vet. We don't take strays."

"Oh. You know where I can take him? 'Cause like I said, I can't keep him."

"Hmm." The receptionist looked at the dog head poking out of Bratty's backpack. "Yeah. So. The thing is... he's a pit bull."

"Yeah. So? I mean, is he?"

"Looks like a pit bull to me," the receptionist said. "And most of the shelters don't take pit bulls."

"Oh. That's... What, they're like, anti–pit bull?"

"That's just their policy."

"So they're prejudiced against pit bulls."

"Yeah, I guess so."

"So what, they just turn them away? Or—"

"Um, not exactly...."

The receptionist didn't want to say it. But Bratty knew exactly what she meant.

"That's fucked," he said.

"Yeah. Yeah it is. Pit bulls get a bad rap. But they can be really nice. Unfortunately, there's only one shelter around here that takes them, and they're full right now."

"Oh. So, um... you want a dog?"

The receptionist laughed. "I'd take all the dogs if I could. But I already have two at home."

"What am I supposed to do with him?" Bratty asked.

"You said he just showed up?"

"Yeah."

"But he looks healthy. Maybe he's not a stray. Maybe he's lost. Let's scan him and see if he has a chip."

Bratty took off the backpack. He let This Random Dog out. The receptionist scanned the dog with some scanner. Bratty shuddered at the thought of under-skin microchips, body scanners, registries of numbers embedded under the skin. The dystopia toward which they were all headed, dogs first.

"Yep," the receptionist said. "Let's look him up. I bet someone'll be glad to have this nice boy home for Christmas."

Bratty rubbed the nice boy's head. The receptionist looked him up in Big Brother's National Doggie Database, or whatever it was called. Bratty looked at the TV in the waiting room. It played an old western, one of his dad's favorites. *Shotgun Solstice*, starring Ricardo Merman. Bratty shivered.

"There he is," the receptionist said. "Looks like he lives less than a mile from here. It says his owner is Bradford Pierson. Should I—"

"Stop."

The receptionist froze.

Bratty froze.

He looked over his shoulder, down at the dog, then back up at the receptionist. This was the moment he wondered whether he had somehow accidentally ingested an entire sheet of acid.

"What?"

"You said— What was the name? Say it again. Please."

"Bradford... Pierson," she said slowly.

"Bradford Pierson."

"Yeah. What, do you know him?"

"I... *I'm* Bradford Pierson."

"Oh." She frowned. Like here was this crazy dude who'd forgotten his own dog. Here was this jerk, trying to abandon his dog. Right before Christmas.

"Yeah, that's... this is... it doesn't make sense."

"Sir—" Her tone, which had been jovial moments before, turned harsh. She looked at him with cold eyes.

"Wait, I'm *not* crazy, I swear," he said, even though he might be. "I'm not a jerk. I'm not trying to leave him here, I just really don't remember owning this dog. Or any dog. But if he was my dog, if I found a dog or something, I probably would have brought him here. Would you mind checking to see if maybe this dog has been here before?"

She scowled, but said, "Fine."

"I'm *not* crazy."

"Uh-huh." She typed something into her computer. "Oh. Yeah, he's been here. Last month. Rabies vaccine. Flea meds. Neutered. His records say he was a stray. *Bradford Pierson* brought him in here and then adopted him."

"Huh. What day?"

"What day?"

"Yeah."

"Let's see... dropped off November 28. Right after Thanksgiving. Picked up November 29—" The receptionist stopped mid-sentence. Her brow furrowed.

"What?"

"That doesn't make sense."

"What?"

"I was working both those days. And it says right here that *I* filled out the forms. I... But I don't remember."

"Maybe I'm forgettable."

The receptionist shook her head. "No. I mean, this was last month. A stray. A pit bull. I should remember."

"I wouldn't feel bad. I forget things all the time," Bratty said. "But I wouldn't forget my own dog."

They looked at each other, Bratty and the receptionist. This Random Dog flopped down on the floor between them.

This Random Dog wasn't some random dog. He was Bratty's dog, apparently.

"So weird," the receptionist said.

"Yeah."

They stared at each other for a moment longer.

Then Bratty said, "I guess me and my dog are gonna go."

He picked up the new-old pet and put it back in the backpack. Just like before, the dog did not resist. It seemed to like the backpack.

"Hey," the receptionist said as Bratty put the backpack on and turned toward the door. "The dog's name is Tux. Tux the Lux, it says here. And . . . you're not forgettable."

BRADFORD AND THE THERAPIST

HE WAS FORGETTABLE. Also forgetful. Disorganized. Unmotivated. Lazy. Gluttonous. Disrespectful. Delusional. Didn't he know that the good life didn't get handed out on a silver platter? You had to work hard. You had to play by the rules. You had to not simply skate by. A passing grade might as well be an F-minus-minus-minus, if it wasn't an A-plus.

Bratty didn't believe any of these things.

He didn't merely *not believe*. He was adamantly against them all. He planted his flag on the opposite hill, two middle fingers raised at the Pierson Estate.

But ideas seeped through.

And once the words got into his brain, "like, I can't just scoop them out," he told his therapist. "I can't just, like, stick an ice-cream scoop into my brain and scoop all those things out like they're chunks of cookie dough or whatever."

He had done this exact thing with chunks of chocolate chip cookie dough. He de-chunked an entire pint of ice cream. He left the cratered pint in the freezer, where his stepmom found it, then explained what it meant about his worth as a human.

But *she* didn't eat ice cream, and his dad didn't eat ice cream, so why was the ice cream in the freezer? Had it been placed there as a test?

He thought about this now, as he strolled along the dirty sidewalk on a frigid winter afternoon, dog strapped to his back, stomach empty. He had fed the dog, but he hadn't eaten, and the voice in his head said, *Maybe you don't deserve to eat, fatso.*

Maybe he should call his therapist.

He didn't call right away. He needed to ponder his new be-dogged state. His dogly status. His sanity, or lack thereof.

Okay, it was comforting that the receptionist also didn't remember the thing he clearly didn't remember. He wasn't alone in his delusion.

Though he was alone, except for this dog. Tux. Tuxasaurus Lux. Captain Tuxy. He imagined the names he might call the dog. Names he had called or did call the dog.

"Who are you, really?" he asked it. "Are you a test?"

The dog didn't answer.

He had been alone ever since his best friend, Tommy—officially Thomas Duluth Fischer—moved to LA, to pursue his music full-time. Around then was the last time Bratty had dinner at his dad's house. Their conversation, as reconstructed by his brain, went like this:

Dad:	*He did* WHAT NOW?
Bradford:	*LA. To pursue his music.*
Dad:	*But what about college?*
Bradford:	*He's taking a year off.*
Dad:	*That's the stupidest, most shortsighted thing a man could do. What about his résumé? What about internships? How will he get a good investment banking job now? What firm*

would even hire him? J. P. Morgan? Barrington Equity? He doesn't stand a chance! He's WASTING HIS FUTURE! (Blood vessels pop in his eyes.) (Steam shoots out of his ears.)

Helena: *You know all about wasting the future, don't you, Bradford?*

(Silence.)

(Helena Pierson pokes at the food on her plate, but she doesn't eat. She never eats.)

(Dad guzzles his glass of wine.)

Bradford: *But... he's really goo—*

Helena: *At wasting his family's money.*

Dad: *All that rap music, it all sounds the same to me.*

Helena: *I don't even know how they call it music.*

Dad: *Promise me, Bradford, promise me you'll never do something that idiotic.*

Bradford: *Of course. I would never.*

Except, he had, last week. A few credits shy of a degree. Tommy already three thousand miles from the Ivy League. Bratty at his state school, post-finals. He turned in his final essay on microeconomics and his professor said, *Mr. Pierson, are you coming to the career fair?* And he said, *Yes, of course*, even though he had no intention of going. But then he went. In his suit coat, tie, sweat stains blooming in his pits, flowering his back, sweat beading his forehead. He shook hands, but his hand was slick with sweat. His hand was a dead, wet fish, flopping from his wrist. His hand collected brochures and scanned QR codes. He could look forward to an exciting future in data processing, in-home nursing care, tax return preparation. He could climb the sales pyramid of gourmet kitchen cookware.

It wasn't a panic attack, he told his therapist, when he described what happened next. *But it also wasn't* not *a panic attack.*

It was more like . . . a general limpness. His legs turned noodle-ish. The floor came at him, fast. His arms didn't respond. He fell. His torso hit first. His impact shook the gymnasium floor. People gathered around him, their eyes rife with concern, but also pity and disgust. His breath came in heaving gusts. His pores gushed sweat. His heart pounded a thousand beats a minute, but no, he was fine he was fine, he insisted. He just needed to get out.

He got up.

He ran.

"But you know what's weird?" he told the dog, as if this whole thing wasn't extra weird. "If I'd adopted you when the vet said, then you were already there when I had the panic attack. You were already my dog. And if you were already my dog, when the professor said, 'Mr. Pierson, are you coming to the career fair?' I woulda said, 'I'd like to, sir, but I have to get home to my dog.' And then I wouldn't have had the panic attack. But that didn't happen, because you weren't there. So technically, it's your fault that I dropped out of school."

He looked over his shoulder at the dog. Tux. The Tuxinator. Dog-o-Tuxmatic. Tux the Dog-Brained, Keeper of the Realm.

The realm had changed since he left the vet. He hadn't gone home, because he hadn't solved the Dog + NO PETS equation. He had no destination. He wandered, and his legs carried him naturally downslope, past the string-lit bistros and festive downtown storefronts, the glistening displays of fake snow, the thirty-foot

Christmas tree, sponsored by the First Bank of Lake Orange, all lit up, all sparkle in the gloomy daylight of the shortest day of the year. All sparkle. And when he saw it—

No, when he saw the dog, against the sparkle backdrop, more luminous than every light on the corporate tree, he felt an overwhelming urge to break out of himself. To shed his skin. To slop off every fleshy layer beneath, until only he was left.

This urge manifested in an ungainly sprint to the river. He removed the dog from his backpack, wrapped the leash around his hand, and took off running. The dog galloped beside him, tongue out, gleeful. This was a fun game. This was freedom. To sprint through the cold mist, unshackled by any destination.

They ran over the highway, past the stadiums, through the park. They turned onto the riverside trail. The river was murky, brown, an archetype of chemical pollution. The trees were bare and sad. They ran, and everything was damp and dreary and gray, except this bright beautiful streak of dog, and the blood that pounded through Bratty's heart, so suddenly full.

He ran way too far, and then his legs were like, *Dude, no.*

He stopped. Something had just happened. He didn't understand what. But he felt it, in his heart, his bones, his shaking legs.

He sat down on a bench. The dog climbed up beside him.

"What do I do?" he asked it. "What do we do?"

They sat there in silence for a long while. Then Bratty took out his phone and called Tommy. Tommy didn't pick up. Tommy was probably still asleep, early afternoon, California time. Music happened at night.

He texted Tommy a photo of the dog, no explanation. Then he called his therapist. The phone rang three-four-five times.

At the sixth ring, she picked up. "Hello. Bradford."

"Hi. Yeah. It's me. I..."

"Are you okay?"

"I... there's... there's something wrong with me. There's something wrong...."

"Okay. Are you in a safe space? Are you safe right now—"

"It's—yes—I mean, I'm like, not in danger or whatever." He looked at Tux. The dog smiled. "It's just that... it's, I'm not sure how to describe it. It's complicated."

"Okay," his therapist said. "Do you want to talk about it? I know our next appointment isn't until the first week of January, but— *Hey, Lindsey! Rory! Quiet!* Mama's on the phone! Sorry about that—"

Children giggled in the background.

"It's cool."

"If you need, I could move some things around—"

"No, it's cool. I can wait."

"Are you sure? You called—"

"I know, I just... I'm having a weird day. Like, a really weird day. But it's fine. I'll be fine."

"Okay. If you're sure."

"I'm sure."

"I'm here, Bradford. If you need me."

"I know... Hey, have a good Christmas," Bratty said.

He hung up. Then he and the dog took a long walk home, away from the river, upslope, past the edges of gentrification, to the crap apartment that Bratty had paid for himself. He walked through the alley to the back side, loaded Tux into the backpack, and started up the fire escape ladder.

His legs revolted. His whole body unified in hatred of this ladder, this fire escape, this building and its unjust rental policies, as if any pet could make this slum worse. But the Bratty deep inside made him climb-climb-climb. Up to the third floor. Where a window opened and a man with an unruly salt-and-pepper beard stuck his head out.

The man stared at Bratty standing on the fire escape, sweaty, disheveled, with a pit bull on his back.

"Nice dog," the man said.

Bratty nodded.

"Too cold to be out here," the man said.

Bratty nodded again.

"Hey, you want a cigarette?" the man offered.

"No thanks," Bratty said, even though he kind of did.

The man lit a cigarette. He took a deep drag, then closed the window.

Bratty opened his own window. He hoisted the dog through. He climbed inside. He made himself a bowl of ramen. He poured more food and water for the dog. Then he sat down on the floor with his laptop and controller, the only valuable things he owned, put on his headphones, and lost himself in music.

THE THERAPIST AND HER FAILING MARRIAGE

MIRIAM SHIPLEY hung up the phone.

"Who was that?" Lindsey asked. "Was it Dad?"

"No—"

"Was it Santa Claus?" asked Rory.

"No. It was just one of my patients," Miriam said. *Bradford Pierson.*

But unless it was Dad or Santa, the kids didn't care. The only thing they cared about right then was cookies. It was late afternoon on the first day of winter break, and the kids had a brilliant idea. They would all eat cookies for dinner.

"But there might be too many for just today," Lindsey said. "We might have to eat cookies for dinner all week."

So now Miriam had one batch in the oven, another rolled out on the table, cut into reindeer shapes, a powdered-sugar and sprinkle delivery en route from the Value Valley, one kid who insisted on cracking every egg and shattering every eggshell into dozens of tiny shards, some of which inevitably got baked into the cookies, another kid who insisted on eating raw cookie dough, heedless of salmonella, and a dog that paced the kitchen and, when unwatched, would stick his paws on the counter and try to knock the mixing bowls onto the floor to make a mess he could then lick up, and throughout the cooking ordeal, she called and texted her husband a dozen plus times, but he didn't respond or pick up.

Miriam: *When are you coming home?*

Miriam: *It's almost dinnertime*

Miriam: *New Christmas tradition starts tonight. You can't miss it.*

He could miss it, apparently.

Miriam and her two kids and the dog, an old black-and-white border collie named Roxster, ate cookie dinner in front of the TV. They watched the holiday special for some cartoon the kids liked, about a weird squid-like creature that could travel through space and time. The creature had only three appendages, attached to a weird lump body/head with a big expressive eye. It wore a Santa hat. It slithered down a chimney and was greeted by three cartoon kids who fed it cookies. The cookies made it grow large enough to barf out Christmas trees and wrapped gifts, like bicycles and pinball machines, that gave children unreasonable expectations about what Santa might bring.

"I don't feel good," Rory said, nibbling his thousandth cookie.

On screen, the Santa-squid barfed out a pogo stick.

"You're fine," Miriam told him. "We're all fine."

We're great!

It's the holidays!

She texted her husband, Jack: *We ate without you.*

He came home about an hour later. He burst through the door, laptop bag slung over his shoulder, briefcase in hand. He was dressed in a suit and tie, but he had forgone the fedora he wore in his youth. He was too serious for hats.

"You missed dinner."

"Work," he said. He gave her a peck on the cheek, but there was no time to look her in the eye.

"We had cookies for dinner," she said, as he bustled past her. "It's a new holiday tradition."

"Mm-hmm."

He also brushed past the dog, who had come to greet him. Normally, the dog flopped down on the floor, belly exposed, paws in the air, to show what a complacent dog he was. But when the dog sniffed Jack, he recoiled. He looked up at him, eyes wary, and yelped.

Jack Shipley didn't notice. He set his laptop up on the kitchen table. He took his precious work papers out of his briefcase and sprawled them out, forming a paper wreath around his workspace.

"You're working," she said. "Now."

"Mm-hmm."

"It's Friday night."

"What?"

"It's Friday night."

"Mm-hmm."

She filled a plate with cookies. She slammed it down on the table in front of him. He didn't notice. She wanted to smack him across the face. To yell, *Jack! Jack! Snap out of it!*

Instead, she emptied the dishwasher. She clanked the plates together loudly. Jack sighed. She banged the pots against the pans. She slammed the cupboard doors. She ran the mini-vacuum, sucking up stray sprinkles and bits of dog-floof.

Jack huffed. He smacked his lips with displeasure. But he was too busy working to stop and complain about the noise.

She poured herself a glass of wine. She took a sip. She looked over at her husband. He looked so boringly workish. So unlike the man she'd married, the whiskey-sipping Sherlock with a five-o'clock shadow.

That Jack had disappeared.

That Jack would have tried to solve the mystery of his own disappearance. He would have sensed his wife's concomitant displeasure with this surrogate Jack, who only had one mode. Work-mode.

He was a terrible typist, for a man so committed to work. His index fingers plucked at the keyboard while the rest of his fingers hung uselessly. His grade-school typing produced an irregular crunching sound. His email pinged. Whenever he stopped typing, he tapped his fingernails on the table. He gnawed on his plastic pens. A bad example, for children.

Their children loped into the kitchen. Rory looked unusually pale. Lindsey prodded her father.

"Not now. I'm working, honey," Jack grunted without looking up. The partners needed him to get this deal wrapped up, he had explained, unapologetically, self-importantly, two months ago, when the Big Deal landed on his desk.

It was always one Big Deal or another, unless it was a Big Deadline or a Big Presentation or an Important Client. *Of course you're important, too,* he would tell Miriam, if she complained. *Why do you think I work so hard?*

There wasn't any retort to the I-do-it-for-you defense. She couldn't rebut his arguments that a person should get their work done, that they should do a good job, that they should honor their commitments. But at least Jack could have the decency not to commandeer the kitchen in the name of work.

"I don't feel good," Rory said, again. He was wearing a paper plate on his head, like a hat. He clutched his stomach.

"You probably just ate too many cookies," Miriam said. But Lindsey looked pasty, too. She had a sheen of sweat on her brow.

"I didn't get enough cookies," Lindsey said. "My stomach wasn't that hungry for cookies."

"Well maybe you shouldn't have snuck all that cookie dough," Miriam said, as her elder child lurched forward and vomited all over the floor.

And so began a two-day pukefest.

MIRIAM AND THE BARF-LOAF

THE THING TO COOK after a day spent cleaning puke was obviously meat loaf. The kids—who had mastered the art of vomiting on bedsheets, carpets, upholstered furniture, and into their own hair—wouldn't eat the meat loaf anyway. *Barf-loaf,* Lindsey called it. Miriam had never really liked it either. But Jack loved the stuff. Meat loaf was an archetypal main course of the idyllic American childhood, Jack's childhood, a leisurely era of bicycle rides and video games and Sunday family dinners. Meat loaf and mashed potatoes and corn on the cob. Gravy served in a fancy silver boat. Were there biscuits? *Yes, of course there were biscuits*: flakey, buttery, slathered with butter.

Miriam didn't cook these things. She cooked stir-fry with lean chicken breast, tofu tacos, lentil soup. Nutritious, non-artery-clogging foods. Jack claimed he didn't mind. But sometimes, when he thought she wasn't looking, he would feed his beans and broccoli to the dog.

Jack didn't ever cook, because of work. He didn't launder the clothes or pick up Hot Wheels off the stairs or scrape up half-eaten gummy worms mixed with espresso grounds mashed into the carpet, when the kids played "gardening." He woke up, went to work, came home, worked at home, and when he stopped to talk to her, he had nothing to say except *work-work-work-work*, peppered with depressing factoids he'd heard on the news.

But maybe she should be more understanding. This is what Miriam the Therapist told Miriam the Disgruntled Wife: *Of course you're annoyed. This isn't what you signed up for. But try to see the situation from your husband's point of view.*

Jack worked all day Saturday. He had to work on Sunday. His firm preferred him in the office. But he could work from home on Christmas Eve. He hadn't taken a whole weekend off work in months, and when he came home, the wife was (understandably) pissed. And then she served him a slab of seitan on whole wheat bread with a side of cooked spinach.

It was this effort to be more understanding that inspired the Surprise Meat Loaf Dinner. She baked two loafs, so he would have lunch leftovers to take to work. She added extra butter to the corn. She cooked mashed potatoes. She texted Jack twice, to make sure he'd be home for dinner. He assured her yes, he would.

At seven p.m., he called. "I'm so sorry. I won't be home in time for dinner."

"Oh."

"Yeah, I thought I'd make it, but you know, this big deal…"

"Right."

"Well, kiss the kids good night for me," Jack said, and then he hung up.

Miriam stifled her rage. *You don't* really *want to punch him in the face*, her inner therapist reminded her.

She kept the food in the oven, on warm. She fed saltine crackers to the kids. She read them stories and tucked them in to bed. She paced the kitchen, feeling resentful. She ate a sleeve of saltine crackers and poured a glass of wine. Then she heard Jack's car in the driveway.

The dog, Roxster, started to bark.

"Shhh! Roxster, quiet!"

She looked at the clock: 9:35.

BARK BARK BARK BARK BARK

Try to be understanding, she told herself. *Compassion. Have compassion.* She felt a sudden, inexplicable craving for a cigarette. Which was odd, because she had never smoked a cigarette in her life. Jack used to smoke, but she convinced him to quit before they got married. People shouldn't smoke. It was a filthy habit.

The car door slammed shut. *Compassion. He's tired. He's been working all day. Be calm. Be calm.*

BARK BARK BARK BARK BARK

Be calm.

Her jaw clenched. The dog wouldn't stop barking. It paddled its paws on the front door, as if running on a vertical treadmill.

"Roxster!" Miriam yelled. "What's gotten into you? Geez!" The dog glanced at her, the clueless human, then resumed its barking and paddling.

The front door opened. Roxster snarled. He leapt through the door and clobbered Jack.

"Hey!"

"Roxster!"

Roxster snapped. He sprayed Jack with foamy flecks of drool.

"Get him off! Get him off!" Jack yelled, trying to push the dog away. Miriam grabbed the dog's collar and yanked him back. She pinned him to the ground.

"Are you okay?" she asked Jack. Her gaze shifted from husband to dog, wary of both. She had never seen Roxster react like that before, with anyone.

"I'm fine," Jack replied. "What the hell's gotten into him?" He shook his head. He stepped past Miriam, into the living room. "It's been a long day. I'm gonna watch some news while you get dinner."

Miriam imagined, for a gleeful instant, a universe in which their strangely savage dog bit off Jack's typing fingers and swallowed them whole. Then how would he type?

Not a compassionate thought. *Think nice thoughts! Empathy!* the therapist voice chided.

Miriam went into the kitchen to assemble dinner. She added more butter to the mashed potatoes. She poured more wine for her, and a glass for Jack. She set the table. She kept an eye on the dog, who stood in the doorway, his eyes fixed on the dubious husband.

Jack reclined on the couch with his beloved television news. He watched it obsessively, in every moment not consumed by work. Miriam couldn't fathom why he didn't just read the newspaper on his telephone like a modern man. But no, Jack preferred to see it on TV.

Miriam hated the drone of television news. It made her want a cigarette.

It took Jack three and a half minutes to turn off the television and come into the kitchen after she told him that dinner was ready. Not that she was timing him.

"Finally," she said. "Here." She handed him the glass of wine.

"Did you hear about the stock market?" he asked.

Barf.

"What about it?" she asked, pretending to care.

"It was crazy today." He took a gulp of wine. "It's all over the news."

"Oh?"

"Yeah, this morning the Dow dropped to, like, lower than it's been in years, and then by this afternoon it was already way up again. Crazy, right?" Jack took another gulp of wine. "So what's for dinner?"

Jack cleared away every kernel of corn. He heaped buttery forkfuls of mashed potato down his throat so fast that she wondered how he didn't choke. Then, after he'd devoured everything else, he examined the meaty slab on his plate.

"Saving the best for last?" Miriam asked him.

"What? Oh, yeah."

"Well?"

"Yes?"

"Well?"

"It's meat loaf." Jack poked at the meat loaf with his fork.

"Aren't you excited? I got the recipe from your sister."

"My sister?" Jack laughed.

"What? What's so funny?"

"She's probably laughing at me right now. I'll have to think of a way to get her back for this."

"Wait, why? What are you talking about, Jack?"

Jack chuckled. He pushed away the dejected plate of meat loaf. "Miriam, I hate meat loaf."

"What? No! No, you don't hate meat loaf."

"I hate it."

"No, you love it. You told me. Sunday dinners. Potatoes. Gravy.

Meat loaf. It's your favorite. It's me who doesn't like it. That's why we never have it."

"Why did you make it if you don't like it?"

"I was trying to—to— But I've seen you eat it!" She couldn't remember the name of the restaurant, but she could see it in her mind: a younger Jack across the table, the white tablecloth, the polished gleam of his wineglass, his eyes, looking back at her in a way she had forgotten about until just then. The happy meat loaf on his plate.

"You must be remembering wrong," Jack replied. "I would never eat it. I hate it. I've hated it ever since I was a kid, when I ate it and then got the flu and threw it all up. After that, I could never eat it again without, you know..."

"Well..."

"Yes?"

"Well, maybe now it'll be different," she suggested, "if it's been that long. Maybe now you'll like it."

"What, you want me to *try it*?"

Obviously. She had placed a good deal of hope in her reconciliatory-meat-loaf plan.

"I made it just for you" was all she said.

Jack sighed. He sliced a bite of the meat loaf with his fork and directed it, cautiously, into his mouth. He gagged. He made an awful retching sound. He grabbed his napkin and spit the meat loaf into it.

"Ugh, it's terrible."

"You didn't even chew it!" she yelled. "How can you tell if you don't even chew it? You have to have at least two more bites." Which was exactly what she said, often, to her daughter, in a continually futile attempt to expose the girl to such exotic foods as mangoes and yogurt.

"I don't need to chew it," Jack said. "I can tell just from the taste that it's terrible."

"But I made it just for you!"

"I know, and that was nice, I guess. But that doesn't change the fact that it's terrible. If you don't believe me, why don't you try it?"

"Fine," she said. She stabbed a bite of meat loaf and shoved it into her mouth. It tasted disgusting. She gagged and spit the stuff back out onto her plate.

"Oh, god, that's horrible." She took a swig of wine to wash away the taste. "That's the worst thing I've ever tried to eat."

"See? I told you."

"Terrible. You were right," she admitted. "But I feel so bad. I was trying to do something nice, and all I've done is waste food."

As if on cue, Roxster strutted into the room and sat down politely in front of the table. He glanced, disapprovingly, at Jack. Miriam stood up and grabbed both of their plates. She scraped the meat loaf into the dog's bowl.

As the dog greedily slurped up the unwanted meat loaf, Miriam scooted over next to Jack and placed her hand casually on his shoulder. It felt strange, his shoulder. Touching him. She had forgotten how it felt, this nice, casual touching. Jack must have forgotten, too, because he shuddered slightly, when her hand first landed. But then he put his hand over hers, and together they watched the dog inhale meat loaf dinner, as if it was the best thing he had ever eaten in his life.

THE RABBIT

ON SUNDAY EVENING, Jack called from work. He had to stay late.

"Go ahead and eat without me," he said. "I might be very late."

"On a Sunday night."

"Well, yes."

Billable hours paid no deference to weekends and evenings.

The kids had finally stopped puking and graduated to cold pasta, plain, which they ate with their fingers. The dog paced by the front door. Outside, cold rain torpedoed hopes for a festive Christmas. Miriam felt anxious. She felt a wrongness, but she couldn't pinpoint why or what. Yes, Jack, obviously. But there was something else, something that bristled under her skin. She recalled the phone call from her client, Bradford. *There's something wrong with me,* he had said. *There's something wrong.* He had never called her before, not like that. His calls and texts had always been limited to scheduling issues. Once, he had texted a link to a song he'd told her about in their session. It was odd that he called, yet it hadn't alarmed her.

It should have alarmed her. But instead, she let the kids have cookies for dinner, and her atypical lenience lapped at the edges of this wrongness.

"But it's fine, right, Roxster?" she asked, as if the dog could understand. "It'll all be fine."

But they both kept pacing.

The clock clicked toward bedtime. The dog chewed the rug tassels. He chewed the running shoe that Jack didn't have time to wear. He clip-clopped back and forth across the kitchen. He tucked the children in to bed, then ran off to bark at the back door.

"What's wrong with him?" Lindsey asked. "He should be happy after all that butter I gave him."

"You gave him butter?"

"Maybe there's someone at the back door," said Rory, as Miriam kissed him good night. "Maybe Santa came early."

She checked the back door. There was no Santa. No sign of intruders. Only a rabbit, small and brown and soaked, huddled on the back patio, as the icy rain pattered down.

This was perfectly normal. Of course the dog would bark at a rabbit. There was no need to consider going back on her anxiety meds.

She brushed her teeth and climbed into an empty bed. Sometime after she had fallen asleep, Jack came home. He stumbled into their dark room, bumping into the dresser, creaking the floorboards with his careless feet. He peeled off his clothes and left them in a pile on the floor. He flopped onto the bed, shaking the mattress. He didn't bother with a peck on her cheek, a *hello I missed you.* He closed his eyes and was out.

And she was awake.

"Jack?"

Dead asleep.

She lay there, irritated at the man who had just woken her up and was now soundly asleep beside her.

"Jack!" she hissed. He snorted, but didn't wake.

She turned her back toward the detestable husband. He snored. He breathed through his mouth. He rolled over, taking the covers with him.

She lay there for what felt like hours, restless, resentful. She had just started to drift off when she heard the splat of little feet, coming down the hall. The bedroom door opened. Rory padded in. He walked around the bed, to Jack's side.

"Daddy," he whispered, "there's a spida. In my woom."

"There's a what in your what?" Jack mumbled.

"A spida."

"A spider," Miriam clarified.

"A spida." Rory nodded.

"That's okay, Rory," Jack said, his eyes still closed. "It won't hurt you. Go back to bed."

"But, Dad," Rory protested, "I might get bited."

"Okay, okay," Jack said. He yawned. And then, instead of getting up to deal with the spider, he batted at his wife. "Miriam? Miriam? Can you go take care of the spider? I've got a big day tomorrow."

"NO! You, Dad," Rory demanded. "*You* kill the spida."

"Miriam, can you handle this?" Jack poked at her.

"No, not Mom. DAD!"

"Jack—"

"Miriam—"

"I want Dad!"

"Jack, can you just—"

"Jesus!" Jack yelled. "I can never get any rest around here!"

Jack thrust himself out of bed. He picked up the boy and stomped down the hall.

He returned a few minutes later. He closed the door—not quite a slam—and hurled himself onto the bed.

"What took you so long?" she asked.

"I couldn't find it," Jack grumbled, as he commandeered all the covers.

"The spider?"

"I don't think there was a spider. If there was, it was gone."

"Well, thanks, for putting him back to bed," she said.

But she didn't feel thankful. She tugged the covers back toward her side of the bed.

"Yeah, well, now I'll be lucky to get five hours of sleep," Jack complained. He yanked the covers back.

"At least you got to sleep this weekend." She sat up. She grabbed a corner of blanket and tugged. "I spent all weekend cleaning up puke."

Jack sat up. He looked at her. "I was *working* this weekend. Or did you forget, because you were so busy having fun without me?"

"You work every weekend. You always have an excuse. 'Oh, I can't take care of the kids,' " she mocked, " 'I'm working. Oh, I can't do the dishes, I'm working. Oh, I can't clean up puke, I'm working. Oh, but Fred and Tom are going golfing, so, sure! I can take the afternoon off.' "

"So this is all because I went golfing," Jack protested. "It was one time. One time! Am I not allowed to do anything fun?"

"No, this has nothing to do with golfing. It's *you,* Jack. You expect me to do everything. Mrs. Pretty-Little-Housewife. Did you forget, Jack, that I have a job? Did you forget that I have appointments tomorrow? That I have to wake up in less than five hours too?"

"Well, it's not the same."

"Oh?"

"Your job isn't like, it isn't..."

"It isn't what?"

"Well, it's not like you can't still do your job if you don't get enough sleep. I mean, I have to read stuff and write stuff and stay sharp all the time. What you do, it's just like, like all you have to do is sit there."

"You jerk," she growled.

She yanked the covers back, hard, pulling them off her husband entirely. She could see his legs, bare and greenish in the dim light of the clock, which now read 1:19. He had such hairy legs. Such skinny, hairy legs. *Like goat legs*, she thought. She wanted to kick them right off the bed.

"What? What did I say?" Jack asked, densely.

"I *sit there*? Don't you even know what I do?"

"Sure, you're a, a—"

"I'm a therapist, Jack." She was yelling now, loud enough that Rory might hear if he was still awake. "It's a bit more complicated than just sitting there. You think people pay me just to sit there? Do you think I went to grad school so I could just sit there? Or did you forget I went to school, Jack? It's not like you pay any attention to anything that happens here."

"Because I have to work. I have to work, Miriam. All the time. Do you think I want it to be like this?"

"It sure seems like it."

"I don't have a choice." His voice was desperate. He believed this lie.

"You *always* have a choice. There are other jobs, Jack. Jobs that don't make you work a thousand hours a week."

"But I do it for you, Miriam," Jack said. "I work for us, for our kids. For their future."

"You work for you, Jack. It makes you feel important, doesn't it? *You* feel all big and important, working all the time, strutting around in your stupid suit. You're a prick, Jack. A selfish, pompous buffoon!"

Jack tossed his hairy goat legs over the side of the bed. He grabbed his pillow and trotted out of the room, banging the door shut behind him. Miriam finally had all the covers to herself. She stared at the empty side of the bed. She regretted what she had said, kind of, but she also felt like she hadn't gotten to say it all.

And, she said to herself, *and, I hate you!*

But she didn't say it out loud. She wanted to. She wanted to yell it. But there was another voice.

Zip it, sailor! the voice ordered. *Silent like a starfish!*

She tried to sleep, but she couldn't. She was wound up. Itchy. Hot. She could hear the dog in the hallway, pacing.

She got up and crept downstairs.

Silent like a starfish.

Jack was on the couch. He looked asleep. His hairy goat legs stuck out beneath the blanket. She resisted the urge to poke him.

"Jack," she whispered. "I... I think we should see a marriage counselor."

He didn't hear her, or he pretended not to. She pulled the blanket down over his legs and left him on the couch. She walked to the closet by the front door. She wanted to go out. She had to go out.

She was dressed in pajamas, but whatever. She put on a jacket. She slipped her bare feet into rain boots. She opened the door, silent, like a starfish, and stepped out.

It was damp and awful outside. The sky spit cold mist. The houses were dark, but their eaves glistened with Christmas lights. Miriam walked through the yard. She turned onto the sidewalk. She walked up the street, past Kate and Fred's house, their solar string-lights dim after days of gloom, past Holly and Tom's house with its looming inflatables, twinkling lights strung around every window. Inflatable Rudolph seemed to watch as she passed, its black nylon eyes impassive, and curious. What was she doing out here, in the middle of the night?

She didn't know.

And yet here she was, at the top of her sloping residential street, where it intersected a busier artery that flowed all the way downtown. It was empty now. Except for the rabbit.

The rabbit sat in the middle of the northbound lane. It was plump, white, with glossy eyes. Except for the slightest twitch of its nose, it was perfectly still.

It stayed perfectly still when the car coasted over the hill, headed north, at a highway speed. It stayed still as the car sped toward it.

"Hey! Rabbit!" Miriam called, as if it could understand her. "Get out of the road!"

The rabbit didn't move.

The car sped up. It was three blocks away, then two, then one. Its engine roared. Its tinted windows vibrated with irreverent bass. Its high beams glared at the rabbit.

The rabbit didn't move.

"Hey!" Miriam waved her hands. But the car didn't see, and the rabbit was a statue of a rabbit, stuck on the street.

She turned away and covered her ears, not wanting to see it, or to hear the sick crunch of bones. The car sped away. When she could no longer hear it, she turned back, expecting a smear of fur and guts.

But there, on the road, was the rabbit. Fully intact, nose twitching. Then, as she stared, the rabbit hopped up and ran across the road, toward her.

"Oh, *now* you move."

Not just toward her. At her. Head down, ears back, right at her.

She didn't wait for the next scene in *Attack of the Suburban Ghost Rabbit*. She ran, down the street, toward her house. She ran awkwardly, in her rain boots, more aware with each step how ridiculous it was to fear a tiny, furry, adorable bunny.

Her pace slowed. She glanced back over her shoulder. The rabbit was behind her, keeping pace, looking harmless.

It's just a rabbit, she told herself.

It was just a rabbit. It didn't have glowing eyes or excess teeth. But as she walked home, it followed behind her. It followed her down the driveway, across the yard. She had her keys in hand. She lunged for the door. She hastily opened it and pulled the storm door closed. Then she turned around and looked down at the rabbit on the stoop.

Something was wrong with them both.

FATTY BRATTY AND THE LEAP

"JUST COME FOR LUNCH," his dad had said. "It's Christmas."

Bratty didn't want to go for lunch. He had entirely forgotten Christmas. He had purchased zero presents with his zero dollars. He had already spent part of his rent money on the dog.

Tuxerson Max. Tux, the Dogliest. Tux of the Long and Lonely Tongue.

The dog ate like a horse. The dog needed bones and chew toys. The dog needed to go out, so out they went, down the fire escape, through the back alley, down the slum streets. The dog needed to run. Bratty didn't run before the dog, but now he couldn't not run. He couldn't disappoint the dog. He ran holes through the toes of his shoes, so now, because of the dog, he needed new shoes. He ordered them, and he'd gotten a delivery notification, but the shoes weren't there.

So when he got dressed for Christmas lunch, he only had the old shoes, full of holes, and his dress shirt had lost a button, and he knew that whatever he wore, whoever he was, it would never be good enough.

He had a 1996 Toyota hatchback that was not good enough to be parked in front of his parents' house. It had rusted wheel wells and a back door that wouldn't open. *It looks like a homeless person's car,* his dad had once said, repeating what Helena had once said.

He parked the car around the corner. He arrived giftless. He stood on the porch for a long while, wondering whether to ring the bell or flee. He could hear the television inside, the guitar-and-fiddle theme music for *Shotgun Solstice*. His dad never got tired of those old westerns. For a moment, he felt almost glad he'd come home.

The security system must have detected him, because the door opened.

"Bradford."

His father wore black slacks, a white shirt, a bland tie. His hair was gray along the temples. His face was etched with stress lines. He held a tumbler of scotch.

"Dad."

"Come in."

Bradford tracked mud into the foyer. Bradford was required to remove his shoes, but his socks also had holes. The socks had been white, once, but against the stark white of the carpets, they were dingy gray.

Christmas lunch was ham, potatoes au gratin, green bean casserole, a discussion of Bradford's career prospects.

"You've got all your grad school applications in?" his dad asked.

"Yeah." He had submitted zero grad school applications.

"If you don't get into a good MBA program, you could shoot for an internship and try again next year."

"Uh-huh."

"You should have gone to a better college," Helena, his

stepmom, said. She pretended to take a bite of potato. "Instead of settling for the state school. You might have more options now."

The conversation went on like this, twenty-some minutes of Dad's expectations for the banking-trading-lawyering future, his stepmom's condescending digs, him nodding along, trying to eat while avoiding the appearance of eating too much, wishing he was back in his crap apartment with The Random Dog, where they could celebrate Tuxmas Day in peace. Unpleasant, but tolerable, until his dad said, "If only you had done some real extracurriculars, like sports, or debate club. Instead of wasting all that time with Tommy."

And his stepmom said, "Tommy at least went to an Ivy League college. Before he dropped out."

Then his dad said, "That music stuff was always a pipe dream."

Then his stepmom said, "If you could even call it music."

Then something broke inside Bratty. Maybe it was already broken. But this felt like a severance. Like some part of him was done, gone, forever.

"That's it, I'm done," he said. He pushed away his plate, the food half eaten, and stood up.

"What do you mean? Lunch isn't over."

His stepmom looked at him with disdain. "You're missing a button on your shirt."

"I'm done," Bratty repeated. "I'm going."

He was going.

"But you haven't finished eating."

"Just let him go, Brian. If he doesn't want to be here with us."

"So what, would you just go back to that god-awful apartment?"

his dad asked. "You can't celebrate Christmas there. I mean, it's so— It's not festive."

His parents' house was festive white: white carpets, white marble, white walls, white furniture, only the sparsest hint of holiday color. A pair of gold Christmas trees decked the white-clothed table. A fake tree with white lights stood by the fireplace.

"Seriously, just let him go." Helena pushed her own plate away. "Now that he's ruined lunch."

"So you're going home? I'd thought we could watch *The Last Train to Topeka*—"

"He doesn't want to watch your stupid movie, Brian. Let him go."

"Bradford, are you—"

"I'm—"

He hadn't thought it through. He had no plan. Only a sense that he needed to get out. That something was wrong, in him, in the world, and he meant to make it right. "I don't know where. But I'm going." Bratty pushed back his chair. He walked away.

"After everything we've done—"

After everything they'd done.

He put on his ratty shoes. They spoke about him as if he'd left already.

"What a brat."

"What does he think he's doing? Ruining Christmas like this."

"Well, there's nothing we can do to stop him. If he wants to make poor choices—"

He didn't want to make poor choices.

He wanted to fling open the door, and leave it open, so the wind would blow wet leaves into his parents' foyer and it would be the worst thing that had ever happened to them. The Great Tragedy of Wet Leaves on Christmas. He wanted to skip through the vast yard, waving his arms, singing and hooting. So he did. And he knew, at that moment, where he was going.

LA.

He skipped and spun and when he reached the street he ran back to his car. He was going to LA. Screw Dad and Helena and business school and internships and Christmas lunches with the conversation topic of *Bradford Is a Fuckup.* If he was, he would at least go out in an impetuous blaze of bad decisions. He was moving to LA. To join Tommy. To make music.

Tommy wrote lyrics. He had a voice like liquid gold. He had a stage presence. But he also got distracted, lost, blitzed. He was a moth, lured by bright lights and heady bass drops. Bratty was background. He wrote the beats. He mixed and sampled. He wove Tommy's lyrics into songs. At least he had, until college and distance made it hard.

He texted Tommy: *I'm coming to LA*

Tommy: U r what?!!!!!
Bratty: I'm coming to LA.
Tommy: Dude!!!!!
Tommy: I've been working on something
Tommy: It's madness
Tommy: Magic
Tommy: IDFK what
Tommy: Can't wait to share
Bratty: Ditto. I'm coming.

Bratty climbed into his car and drove back to his apartment. When he got home, he packed. He didn't have boxes, but he also didn't have much stuff. He packed in suitcases, paper bags, garbage bags. He wrapped a bundle of clothes in his sheets. He carried loads down to his car until he'd filled it. He left the couch. He left a note for the landlord: *I'm leaving. Peace out. Apartment 309.*

He made one last trip upstairs, to retrieve the dog. When he got to his door, the adjacent door opened. Smoke wafted out. His beardy neighbor stepped into the hall, cigarette between his lips, a package in his hand. He gave the package to Bratty.

"It's addressed to you," he said. "Mailman left it on the stoop outside. I picked it up before someone could steal it."

The package, Bratty saw from the return address, contained his shoes.

"Thanks, yo."

"You movin' out?"

"Yeah."

The neighbor took a drag of his cigarette. "Yeah... sometimes you gotta just... hold your breath and leap into the water, you know?"

Bratty nodded. "Yeah."

"Fearless like flounder. Bold like a barracuda."

Bold, like a barracuda. "Yeah. Well. I'll catch you later, dude."

"No. No you won't," the neighbor said, as he shut the door.

Bratty went into his mostly empty apartment. He clipped the leash onto Tux.

"You ready?"

The dog looked ready.

"All right then. Bold like a barracuda, I guess."

They stepped out into the hall. They walked down the stairs, out the lobby. Cold drizzle fell outside. The streetlamps flickered on. It was dusk, on Christmas night, and back at the Pierson Estate, Bratty's dad sat stiffly on the white couch with his glass of Cognac and his eyes fixed on the screen and Bratty's stepmom said *I don't see how you can watch this same stupid western every year* and she turned the TV off. Bratty wasn't there, but he saw it, in his mind. This same scene unfolded year after year. They were in their big, warm house, with good liquor, the gas fireplace flickering, together, but their hearts were empty.

Bratty was cold, his socks damp, his fingers icy. He loaded the dog into the front seat of his car. He climbed in. He set sail for the future. Over the hills. Across the dark plains. He cut south, through flat and arid lands. Music jingled on the radio, then static, then music.

"Maybe someday," he said to the dog, as the red sun rose behind him in the east. "Maybe someday that'll be Tommy on the radio. Tommy and me."

FATTY BRATTY AND HIS BFF TOMMY

BOLD LIKE A BARRACUDA.

Daring like a dogfish shark, Tommy texted. *Swift like a seal. Certain as a seahorse.*

Bratty didn't know what his best friend meant, but it felt right.

The past faded behind him, but its magic lingered. He drove and drove, through the great empty middle of the country, a thousand miles from the coast, but his thoughts circled back to the sea, to an old movie he had watched like a hundred-plus times as a child. The movie was called *Peregrine.* It followed a disillusioned detective, played by Ricardo Merman, hired to solve the mystery of an heiress who'd mysteriously vanished at sea. Maybe she'd been murdered. Or maybe she'd never set sail. Her behavior was erratic, and no one knew why. Bratty didn't know why he liked the movie so much. But every time he rewatched, it felt transformational. The characters and their trajectories seemed to shift faster than the current. Which was unsettling, but also invigorating.

"We can do anything," Bratty told the dog, as they crossed the Arizona border, still very far from the sea. "You and me, Tux. We can make it."

And don't expect help when you fail, said the contrary voice in his head. The voice came from Helena, but it sounded like his own voice. Because he'd internalized her criticism, his therapist said.

He'd believed it. But the thing was, they'd never helped him. He'd bought this car himself, with money he made flipping burgers at the Buck-a-Bacon. He'd taken loans to pay for his state school. His dad wouldn't help pay, he'd claimed, because handouts wouldn't teach Bratty to be responsible. But the message embedded in this absence of help was that he, Bratty, was not worth betting on.

"We can make it," Bratty said again, but the words rang hollow.

Still, he stayed optimistic right up until he reached the outskirts of Las Vegas and his engine sputtered, then started to smoke.

He pulled over on the side of the freeway. Smoke gusted from under the hood. Cars zipped past him at a billion miles an hour. The dog looked over at him, eyes wide, his expression asking, *What the fuck do we do now, dude?*

The voice in Bratty's head said, *What did you expect would happen, Bradford? You really thought that your shit car could make it across the country?* Okay, in truth, he hadn't thought about it. He had ignored the 240,000-plus miles on his odometer, and the burnt-rubber smell, and the rattling of his rusted frame.

He didn't have cash to tow the car, fix the car, or rent a dog-friendly hotel while the car got repaired. He lacked the skills to identify the cause of his smoldering engine. His phone had 20 percent battery power.

"We can make it," he said, but the words now felt like an outright lie.

He leashed the dog, got out of the car, and walked several paces out into the desert, a safe distance, in case the car decided to explode. Frost crunched beneath his feet. The moon dangled low over glittering Vegas.

"Look," he told the dog, "if you see a scorpion, just run, okay? Don't try to fight it."

He called Tommy on the phone. The first two times, Tommy didn't pick up. The third time, Tommy answered, "Yo, hold on."

Music throbbed in the background. Bratty shivered. He wished for a smoke, a beer, a hot plate of chili cheese fries, a life raft so he and the dog could sail off into the desert darkness, bound for the oasis of casino lights. The dog pressed himself against Bratty's legs, sharing his warmth. The song played, stopped, restarted.

"Hey, sorry," Tommy said. "I'm in the zone. Where you at?"

"I'm in the desert. Near Vegas. My engine is smoking."

"Oh, damn." Tommy paused to consider. And he didn't say something callous like *just buy a plane ticket* or *just get a new car* or *ask your dad to wire some money*. He said, "Dude, I'm coming."

"Here?"

"You need an extraction, yo. Ping me your coordinates. I'm coming."

Four hours passed.

Tommy drove like a madman, not stopping, bass throbbing, one hand drumming the wheel while the other chain-smoked the spliffs that gave his golden voice its gritty edge. Driving east, he whipped past Bratty, made a U-turn in the middle of the highway, and screeched to a stop behind Bratty's dead car. He leapt out. His eyes were wide and wild. He flung his arms around Bratty.

He let go of his friend and looked at him. "Fuck yeah. Dude! You're here!" He hugged Bratty again.

"Vegas."

"Fuckin' Vegas. On a rescue mission. Yo, I'm like Captain Barksford. You know, the dog, in that episode where the baboon wanted to swim, so it jumped into the shark-infested waters, and it would have gotten torn up if the captain didn't save its ass. But it *did* learn to swim."

Bratty nodded. "So, I'm the baboon."

"Fuck yeah. Yo, I can't wait to show you what I've been doing. I... I can't even explain it. I've been like, like manic. Nonstop music. I been writing and writing and it's like, like even my dreams are music. Enough to make me wonder, like, is this a manic episode? Am I going crazy? But no, yo, I don't think it's that. It's..." He spoke at a rapid pace, then paused. He looked up at the sky, like something was up there, some answer beyond that random swirl of stars. "It's... something else. Like a shift in the current. You know?"

Bratty nodded. He didn't know what Tommy meant exactly, but he felt something. He had been there, alone, in Ohio, in his crap apartment, on track to get his degree. Now he was here, on the Nevada interstate, with his best friend and his dog. Something had shifted.

"Come on, dude," Tommy said. "Let's go home."

They loaded all of Bratty's stuff into Tommy's car. They abandoned Bratty's car. They drove, the dog on Bratty's lap, a straight shot to LA. They pulled up outside Tommy's apartment building just before dawn.

"Oh shit," Bratty said.

"What?"

"I forgot to ask about the dog. Are you allowed to have a dog?"

"Well... we've got a dog," Tommy said. "So yes!"

They unloaded. Ate breakfast. Slept through the day. When the sun went down, Bratty woke up. He was on a couch, the dog at his feet. Tommy sat on the floor, his notebook and laptop on the coffee table before him. He had a joint in one hand and a mic in the other.

"Bradford," he said, in a deep voice, into the mic. "Are you ready, Bradford? It's time to make some music."

THE ALBUM

THEY WROTE THE SONGS that became the Album in a frantic week. Tommy didn't sleep.

Bratty slept on the couch in random stretches, two hours in the afternoon, three hours predawn, the dog always at his feet. He dreamed the same dream every sleep: *The Dog, the Boat, the Inimitable Sea.* He sailed silver waves, him and the dog, who wore the captain's hat. The dog's identity changed. He was Tux in some dreams, the original Captain Barksford in others. He was the fox terrier companion to the detective in *Peregrine.* He was the dog Tommy had as a kid, or the dog Bratty wanted but never owned. Once, he was an Airedale named Barry, and his fur was matted with green goo. He was captain, which made Bratty first mate, or the boat itself, or the wind that blew it. Or maybe just a dude, out for a pleasure cruise. To what destination? No one knew, and it seemed beside the point, when he had the dog, the boat, and the sea. The sky above was milky with stars, or lucid yellow dawn, or the lavender shade of a lullaby.

There were no pirates in his dreams.

"But what if there were?" Tommy asked, as he paced, frenetic, notebook in hand. He had a joint between his lips, a cigarette behind his ear, a pen that leaked black ink all over his fingers.

"What if there was a giant squid?"

"How could there not be? Maybe *you're* the pirate."

"Do I look like a pirate?" Bratty said.

"You could. If you had an eye patch. Would you rather have an eye patch, or little flags sticking out of your ears?"

"Pirate flags?"

"Yar."

"What happens if I pluck them out?"

"They grow back. Like flags do."

"So I could be, like, a human flag factory."

"Aye, matey!"

"Bradford the Flag Factory."

Tommy wrote a rap about Bradford the Flag Factory. He scribbled it out.

He's a human machine
For all your flag needs
And all your flag dreams
That be blowing in the breeze
That be sailing the high seas
He's no skeeze
He's a man, a fatty, a friend
No matter what the skies portend
Yo I'm with him till the end—

"Okay that's dumb," Tommy said after he rapped.

"It's a start."

"But I can hear the melody in my head."

"So keep going."

He kept going. This kept going. The raps. The beats. The conversations in between. Tommy pacing, rolling joints, spitting rhymes, refining, tasting the words in his mouth, as they melted, or sizzled, or spiked new sounds or wordplay that made him weep, or shout *huzzah!* and leap from the couch, over the dog, and for a midair moment Bratty thought he might land wrong and snap his ankle, and in his mind he heard the scream, saw the pain, observed this other reality, plans foiled by a broken leg, him pushing stoned sullen Tommy around in a wheelchair, them fighting and failing to find music in the wake of this setback.

But it didn't happen like that.

Tommy landed flat on his feet. He stopped. He stared at Bratty. He had a look on his face like, *WTF, bro? What was that?* Like he too had glimpsed behind some curtain that was supposed to be opaque, according to everyone everywhere, but nope. It was flimsy. Fragile. Translucent. Thinner than the wing of a dragonfly.

Bratty didn't know what to say then. He was a man—or would be, later, when he grew into himself—who thought things through. Who deliberated and produced. That would come later.

Tommy busted up laughing. He fell over laughing. He lay on his back, laughing, while Mr. Tux the Lickersaurus slobbered all over his face, and then he sat up and said:

"Would you rather be a cat, or a dog?"

"Do I get to pick what kind?"

"Sure. I'd be a Maine coon."

"I'd be a wolf," Bratty said.

"That doesn't count."

"What, so I have to be domesticated? No, dude, I reject your hypothetical. I'm a wolf."

But yeah, he hadn't been a wolf before. Not until that moment, right then, in Tommy's LA apartment, at the magic hour of two a.m., his BFF sitting on the floor, the floor a sea of crumpled paper flotsam amid the jetsam of discarded rap lines, bags of stale chips, empty beer cans, dog toys. He had always felt like the dejected dog who got left outside in the yard, in the cold rain and hail, while the family inside drank congratulatory champagne to celebrate their success as humans. But in that moment, he saw the Bratty he could become—Wolf—and the figurative rain stopped and maybe he had no clue what would happen next, maybe it was a lifetime of ramen noodles and cheap apartments, maybe it was heartbreak. But right then, his heart was full and free.

Right then, he heard a click. A flutter. A *tap-tap-tap.*

"What was that?" Tommy asked.

Tux's ears perked up.

"It's probably nothing. Wind."

Tap-tap-tap.

"It's not nothing," Tommy said. "It's outside. There's something outside."

"I don't want to look outside," Bratty said. He felt suddenly afraid, and way too stoned.

"I'm opening the door."

"No."

"I'm gonna do it."

"Dude—"

Tap-tap-tap.

Tommy opened the door. He walked outside, into a bland apartment-scape courtyard. He laughed. "Ha! Bratty! Come out here! You gotta see this!"

Slowly, stoned-AF Bratty and his mystery dog crept outside, into the setting of an Alfred Hitchcock film.

In the courtyard, on the cement and grass, in the trees, on the roof, all around them, there were birds. Crows and ravens, plovers, pigeons, doves and terns, gulls and loons, what the fuck were all these birds? There were hundreds of them, all different kinds and colors. Though they all looked black, in the starless night, in the blue-lit television shadow of Tommy's apartment.

"Dark fucking birds," Bratty murmured.

Except that wasn't quite right, because they seemed jolly. With their funny stick legs, their silly beaks. Like this was some practical bird joke. And they kept popping in and out. Not flying. Popping. In empty space, a bird would appear. A bird would disappear. Another bird would pop up.

"Whack-A-Bird," Tommy said, and then he doubled over laughing. The birds popped in and out and Tommy laughed and laughed and could not stop laughing, until this fat goose popped up right in front of him and he laughed so hard he got the hiccups.

"Damn..." he said, in between hiccups. "I'm way too fucking stoned."

"We shouldn't have eaten all those gummies."

"Or maybe"—the goose popped out of existence—"it was exactly (hiccup) the right amount of gummies."

Then, in an instant, all the birds disappeared, except for one single blackbird, which stood on the windowsill, glass eyes gazing up at Tommy, then Bratty.

As they stared, transfixed by the animal, it turned and tapped the window with its beak.

Tap. Tap. Tap-tap-tap-tap.

And Bratty heard the beat. In his head. The beat to the song he would write that night. He knew how it felt. Full and free.

On the tenth night (or eleventh, or twelfth) (who was counting?) (they lost track), they had an album recorded on Bratty's laptop. They sat at the table, the dog spread on the floor beneath them. Tommy popped the top on a bottle of malt liquor. He poured two mugs.

"A toast. To us."

Bratty pressed Play.

They listened.

As they listened, the glee on Tommy's face faded. By the end, he wore an expression of concern, and resolve.

"It's not it," he said.

Bratty felt fairly certain that it *was* it, whatever it was. "Dude— No, dude."

"No, I mean... it's there," Tommy clarified. "The music is there. But the sound."

"Oh. Sure. But like, what do we do?"

They were just two dudes with a mic, recording inside their apartment.

"We need to record this. Like for real. In a studio."

"Yeah, me and all my millions of dollars," said Bratty.

"Hmm."

"You could call your dad. He'd probably help."

"Yo, he was *sooo* pissed when I moved out here. I can't give him the satisfaction."

"So pride wins out."

"Whatever, you could ask your dad," Tommy said.

"You know he hasn't given me a penny in, like, three years. You remember how he said he'd pay my tuition then changed his mind, but didn't tell me until after it was too late to get student loans."

"Yeah. Douchey McDoucherson."

"You don't have to be ashamed of your privilege. As long as you recognize it for what it is."

"Yeah. Still . . ." Tommy stroked his chin. He glanced out the window. Nothing was happening out there in the dark. But the wheels in Tommy's mind were turning, and after a silent minute he chugged his mug of malt liquor, banged it on the table, and said, "That's it!"

"What, you're gonna call him?"

"My dad?"

"Yeah."

"No. I'm calling the guy I met who knows the guy who owns the studio. And then I'm gonna sell my car."

If the older Mr. Pierson had a list of *All the Dumb-Ass Things My Kid and His Friend Have Done,* selling Tommy's car to pay recording studio fees, when you could just be a responsible adult and go to business school and forget music altogether (except if you found a way to exploit music, from the business end [*hello, concert ticket fees*]), would be at the top of that list. Until wayward Bradford found a way to top it, which he inevitably would.

But this wasn't a rational timeline.

Art didn't happen because of prudent choices. It happened because you had a dream or a vision or an itch and you scratched and scratched so hard that you tore your skin open and art poured out. It happened because, as Tommy explained it, with a sweep of his arms and an unfurling of hands: *Kablam! Your head explodes with art!* It happened because you had something to say, something to mourn or ponder or praise, and regular words didn't do it justice. It happened because there wasn't justice in the universe, but with a verse or a note or a brushstroke, the world could be remade into a better version of itself, with more color, more glitter, more bass line.

It happened that the guy who knew the guy who knew Tommy was awake in the middle of the night, and there was a cancelation, and tomorrow night was theirs if they wanted.

"It's ours, Bratty," Tommy said. "It's ours."

It happened that there was a used car dealership not far from the studio, that they paid in cash, that yes, they would take Tommy's car for less than it was probably worth.

He sold it.

Then they walked.

They walked and walked and walked, lugging Bratty's equipment in a camping wagon behind them. The dog walked with them. He had demanded to come, had followed Bratty out to the car, had ridden on his lap. He glanced back every block to smile at Bratty behind him.

They didn't bring any water. They didn't remember to charge their phones before they left. Bratty's phone died.

"Maybe you should call an Uber?" he said to Tommy, a mere hour into the trek.

"Yeah . . . I don't want to spend the money. But maybe, yeah . . ." He tried. His phone searched for a driver for several minutes, expending the last of his battery power, until it, too, died.

They walked. They walked and walked. The studio wasn't far, if you drove.

"Dude . . ." Tommy said.

"Yeah?"

"We live in LA."

Cars roared past them. Cars sped all around them. They were alone, on foot, in an ocean of cars.

Then, at last, they were at the door. Going in, setting up, recording, mixing, recording, remixing, and Bratty's hands were shaking.

Tommy's voice was liquid gold.

Then it was dawn, and they were outside, catching a ride from a guy who knew the guy who owned the studio, stumbling back into Tommy's apartment, wondering what came next.

"Should we listen?" Bratty asked.

"No," said Tommy. "I don't need to listen now. I know what it is."

"Yeah."

"Yeah. It's great."

"Yeah."

"So. Let's post a single."

"Yeah," Bratty agreed. "Except . . . you need a name."

"*We* need a name, you mean."

"No, *you*. You're the rapper. You're the front man. I'm just beats. I'm behind the curtain."

"Is that what you want?"

"Yeah."

They stared at each other for a long while. The dog shoved himself between them. Bratty felt woozy, dizzy, almost seasick. His mind heard the words before Tommy said them aloud.

"The name," Tommy said, "is Mr. Yay."

INTERLUDE

THE FISHERMAN

IMAGINE YOU are a fisherman.

Your whole life you have been a fisherman in the Aegean Sea, and your existence is picturesque, bountiful, perfect, until one summer there are less fish, and less the summer after that, less and less, and then a storm wrecks your boat and you can't afford to pay your crew and when you fix the boat, you've only got you. You and your boy.

Your boy is eager. Give him credit for that. He wants to fish. But he's got half the strength of a full-grown man, and ten times the mouth. He talks and talks and talks and talks and you try to be grateful, but this life is not serene. You can scarcely hear the sound of the waves because the boy talks. He talks loudly. He talks from the moment he wakes until the moment sleep whisks him away. Often, he talks in his sleep.

Today he is talking about dolphins. He tells you everything he knows about dolphins, and everything he doesn't, every detail, every type. There are *Sousa sahulensis* and *Tursiops truncatus*, the bottlenose. There are *Delphinus delphis* and *Grampus griseus*.

They are friendly, but also competition for the fishing boat. Will he see them? the boy wants to know. When will he see them? Is that shadow in the water a dolphin? What about—

You look up and for the first fraction of a second your mind thinks *dolphin* but it is bigger, much bigger. It is massive. It consumes the whole horizon. It is all you can see, and it is nothing like a dolphin.

It is a boat. An enormous boat. A battleship or a cruise ship, you can't tell which, and you don't have the chance to think about it, because you are airborne. Sideways. Your boat is flipping. Your boat is capsized. You are underwater. You are thinking, *What in the holy hell just happened?* and *Where is my boy?* and *Where did that boat come from?* because it wasn't there before.

You are upside down in the water, but you know what to do. You swim toward the light. You surface. Your boat sinks, but you are afloat.

On the deck of the massive ship, high above you, people shout and wave. *Are you okay?* they ask. *Where did you come from?*

Then, with a flash and fizzle, the ship is gone.

The water, once displaced by its bulk, becomes a whirlpool. It is spinning, crushing, sucking you under, and you are thrashing, flailing, grasping at nothing because there is nothing but water, and you can't see the light. You are drowning. You are dying. You are—

—on the deck of your boat.

Dad?

You are dry. You are alive.

Dad, do you think the dolphins will— Hey, are you listening? Dad? What's wrong?

You are not crazy, but still. What can you tell the boy?

You say nothing, for now. You know how crazy it will sound, if you say anything ever. You can scarcely believe what happened yourself. You hug your boy. You are alive and he is alive and over his shoulder you see a shadow in the water, dolphin-shaped.

FLASHBACK

MIRIAM + JACK

ON A WARM EVENING in October, ten years earlier, a man sat in his car at a red light. Led Zeppelin played on the radio. The man drummed his fingers on the steering wheel. He thought about what he would do when he got back to his apartment. The beers he would drink. The movie he would watch, until he fell asleep on the couch.

As he waited, a woman approached on a bicycle. The most beautiful woman he'd ever seen. This was what he said, when he told the story later.

He wanted her to slow down so he could see her better.

He wanted her to jump off the bike and into his car, and ride home with him, and ride him. And after, they would watch movies and drink beers and fall asleep together. Just like that, every night, for the rest of his life.

But it didn't happen like that. What happened was that as the woman coasted into the intersection, as she passed in front of his car, her beauty laid bare by his headlights, there was a loud crash. Another car slammed into the back of his car. His car lurched forward. It hit her. He heard a thump, her body against the hood. He heard the skitter and crunch of metal as her bike sailed through the intersection, beneath the wheels of another car.

He leapt out of his car. His heart pounded. This was the moment his life ended, or started, or inexorably changed.

She was lying on the ground. He ran to her.

"I'm sorry. Oh fuck, I'm sorry! Are you—"

She lifted her head. She looked down at her body. There was no blood. No twisted limbs. Nothing mangled, except the bike.

"Are you okay?"

She nodded. "I think so."

"I— Should we call an ambulance? Or I could drive you to the hospital, or—"

"No," the woman said. Slowly, she stood up. "No, I . . . I think I'm fine. I guess I'm good at falling. I just rolled off your hood."

"Oh. Good."

"Yeah."

They looked at each other.

There was a spark, he said, when he told this story.

And through the lens of memory, it became uncertain whether the spark had been figurative or tangible, blooming into a fire he could hold in his hands.

"I'm so sorry," the man said, again. "I— That car hit me. I—"

"I see," she said. "It wasn't your fault."

At this point, the driver of the other car had gotten out, was walking over, was saying things, but neither the man nor the woman noticed him. A bubble had formed around them, impervious to everything and everyone else.

"Are you really okay?" he asked. "No scrapes, bruises?"

"My bike. It's totaled."

"I can get you a new bike."

"You don't need to."

"I want to. I want—" He had never wanted anyone more in his life. "Can I give you a ride home?"

"A ride from a stranger?"

"I'm not that strange."

"Yes. You can give me a ride. But first, do you want to buy me a beer?"

"Yes." He would buy her a lifetime of beers. "What's your name?"

"Miriam. And you?"

"Jack."

The scene shifted. They were still inside the bubble, but the bubble was in a bar, surrounding a booth, two empty glasses, two full glasses, two pairs of feet that touched beneath the table.

We played footsie, she said later, when she told the story. It sounded trite, a joke. There was something magnetic between them. Their feet parts just came together first.

"What do you do, Jack?" she asked, then added, "I hate that question."

"It's a fair question."

"The better question is... who are you really, Jack?"

"I'm... What if I told you I was a detective?"

She laughed. "What kind?"

"Classic detective. Like in one of those 1940s crime novels. Or that movie *Peregrine*. I wear a suit and a fedora. I carry a gun. I smoke in my office. My clients are seedy, or dangerous, or sensual. Sometimes I get into shoot-outs."

"Sounds like fiction. You could just as easily be a cowboy. Or a circus performer. Or a professional rapper."

"Not for me. I'm just a detective."

"I can get down with that."

"But I've got a really boring alter ego."

"Oh?"

"I work at a coffee shop."

"That's not boring."

"It's kind of nice," Jack said. "I'm happy. And making good use of my college degree."

She laughed, and he laughed, but there was a fleck of resentment in his eyes.

"Actually," he said, "I'm thinking of going to law school."

"Oh? Sounds reasonable. And *lawyer* might make a better front than barista for your true detective self."

JANUARY

BRATTY AND HIS THERAPIST

Bradford: *Thanks for, you know, pushing this back a week. And switching to video call.*

Miriam: *It's no problem at all.*

Bradford: *I couldn't make it in person. I'm in LA.*

Miriam: *That's good. A change of scenery. How is LA?*

Bradford: *It's... I dunno. I'm at Tommy's. I haven't gone outside for, like, days.*

Miriam: *Oh. Are you—*

Bradford: *No, it's not like that. I mean, I'm not depressed. Or like, not more depressed than I was. I'm actually... It's weird. I feel like, good. Anyway, we were working really hard on this album. And then we finished it, and I just crashed.*

Miriam: *That's great that you're feeling good. And that you're getting back into making music.*

Bradford: *It feels like... like this is what I should have been doing all along. Like before, for like years, I wasn't me. I was someone else. But now, here in LA with Tommy, I... I feel like myself.*

Which . . . I mean, maybe doesn't mean anything. I probably shouldn't have just moved out here, right?

Miriam: *So you moved—*

Bradford: *Yeah, I dropped out of school. Don't judge.*

Miriam: *There's no judgment. You said, before you started to second-guess yourself, that you felt like yourself.*

Bradford: *Yeah.*

Miriam: *Maybe that's how you're supposed to feel. Like yourself. But you need to trust yourself in order to do that.*

Bradford: *Yeah, I know. I know in the past I felt . . . as trustworthy as a tentacle.*

Miriam: *Wait, what did you just say?*

Bradford: *That I didn't trust myself. You're right.*

Miriam: *No, that thing, about the tentacle.*

Bradford: *Oh, yeah, that's just a random thing my friend Tommy says, from some old TV show. It's nothing.*

Miriam: *It's . . . so, um, you made an album?*

Bradford: *Yeah. . . . It's a pipe dream. I know how it is. Almost no one makes it in the music biz. So we're probably just fucking around, wasting our time, but still—*

Miriam: *It's not a waste of time. It brings you joy, right?*

Bradford: *Yeah.*

Miriam: *If it brings you joy, it's never a waste of time.*

MIRIAM AND THE MARRIAGE COUNSELOR

MIRIAM SCHEDULED AN APPOINTMENT with a marriage counselor for four thirty p.m. on a Tuesday. Jack would meet her there, he promised. He would drive straight from work.

She left early for the appointment. She thought she knew where she was going, at least the general vicinity. And she had GPS to direct her.

But she got lost. GPS routed her onto a curvy two-lane road, flanked by older houses, churches, boarded-up storefronts, pawnshops, check-cashing shops, cell phone providers, restaurants that sold hook-fish and fried chicken, and interspersed between them there were weedy lots and small patches of forest that defied the city around them. The trees were spindly and bare. The world was damp and brown, all dead leaves and patches of mud, no snow. Not this winter. Just mist and frozen rain.

GPS didn't tell her to turn. It felt like the right direction. Marriage counseling. Her and Jack working together to resolve their problems—or, frankly, Jack's problem, namely his addiction to work.

Miriam turned on the radio. She flipped through stations. Boring. Boring. Boring. News. Heard this song before.

Then she felt an electric jolt through her finger.

"Ow!"

She yanked her hand back. She swerved, then pulled to a stop along the side of the road. She looked down at her hand. It looked fine. It didn't hurt, not any more than a static electricity shock. But the radio dial had shocked her. Which did not seem like something a plastic dial should do.

"Weird," she muttered, then pulled back onto the road.

The radio station played rap music. Miriam didn't really listen to rap—it was more her friend Kate's vibe—but she didn't want to touch the dial to change it. And there was something distinct about the sound of the rapper's voice. It made her think of root beer floats and summer afternoons at the pool, the way the water glistened in the sunlight, the way her body moved through it. *Lithe and limber like a lamprey.*

—and elastic, I'm elated
I been baited by this blond
she says DeLeón
she says Patrón
she says naked, walk the plank and
the whole sea is vodka
yo, I'm bout to be faded.
Faced. Blazed. Laid waste
Cuz the blond got friends
and the friends got taste
and I lick pussy till
my tongue falls outta my face. Yo,
I'm loved by babes
But shunned by moms?
No way. For sure, I drop the f-bomb

But fuck. What them moms gonna say
When I say moms, open your legs,
And I'll lick—

Wait, what? Could they say that on the radio? Didn't the radio censor cunnilingus-talk?

Was Miriam offended? She wasn't sure. She was a mom, and the last time Jack had—

Okay, she wasn't going to think about that. There was no sense in thinking about something Jack didn't have time to lick.

She couldn't even recall the last time he'd really kissed her. He had all the libido of a legal brief, and all the passion of a tax return.

Or maybe, it was just her.

She pulled her sleeve up over her hand so she could turn the radio off without the dial touching her skin. She drove in silence. At a red light, she glanced at her face in the rearview mirror, the emerging chin grooves, herald to flapping jowls, the bags beneath her eyes, the pinched lips of a woman who hadn't—

Who wasn't going to think about it.

She drove along for several miles farther than she should have gone, reliant on a GPS that refused to speak up, until she admitted that maybe she was lost. She had driven down this road before, she thought. But now it looked unfamiliar.

She pulled over and took out her phone to consult GPS. *No Service*, the phone told her. She drove a little farther, and then pulled over and checked again. *No Service.* Which made no sense here, in the middle of the city. She turned the car off and got out. She would have to figure it out the old-fashioned way, with maps and street signs.

She walked until she reached an intersection. The side street had no street sign, only an empty post where the sign had been. She looked around, for a gas station, a restaurant, some place with people who could tell her where exactly she was. She saw a café, breakfast until two p.m. and closed for the day, a row of empty storefronts, and one storefront with a sign that said PSYCHIC—MYSTIC—FORTUNE-TELLING in swirly orange letters above the door.

Miriam opened the door and stepped inside. The place had all the flourishes typical (Miriam imagined) of a fortune-telling shop: beaded curtains, plush velvet chairs, a pink fluorescent-lit sign that read PALMISTRY and a smaller one that read HYPNOSIS, a lava lamp, the heady smell of incense. Yet other items seemed incongruous: a framed poster of a kitten dangling from a tree branch; a red-and-blue plastic machine that Miriam recognized from her childhood as a snow-cone maker; various articles of Cincinnati Reds regalia—pennants, oversized foam hands, autographed baseballs displayed in clear plastic boxes. She felt suddenly uncomfortable, as if she had inadvertently wandered into a weird person's bedroom.

As she stood staring at the snow-cone maker, wondering whether it still worked, a young woman emerged from behind the beaded curtain. The woman had thin blond hair and hazy blue eyes. She wore a long boho skirt, a Cincinnati Reds T-shirt, and a fuzzy red beret. She flashed Miriam a toothy smile.

"Oh, you're here for the palm reading," the woman said, with a Kentucky twang. "Well, it'll be just a sec, I need to recharge."

"Actually," said Miriam, "I'm just a bit lost. I was hoping—"

"Yes, darlin', you are lost. That's as clear as a creek on a summer's day."

"So I was hoping you could tell me—"

"Sure, just have a seat now."

"I was hoping you could tell me what that street is called." Miriam gestured behind her. "There's no street sign, and—"

"Wait a second." The woman stepped closer to Miriam. She stared, squinty-eyed. "You're tellin' me you're *not* here for a palm reading?"

"Um, no. Yes. I mean, I don't need my palm read."

"Yep. You do. You are here to get your palm read. I know, I know, you're lost. And I can tell you the street now, if you like, but it would be better to wait until after, so you don't forget. Anyhow, you still have plenty of time before your appointment."

"Well, I, what—"

"So why don't ya have a seat, while I recharge. We can share a root beer. Always helps me recharge faster," the woman said. Which was weird because Miriam had just been thinking about root beer.

And now she was sitting on a purple velvet couch with a plastic Cincinnati Reds cup half full of diet root beer, across from a Kentucky psychic who called herself Destinia Amber Rose.

"But everyone calls me Rosy," the psychic said, taking a sip of root beer through a curly straw. "And you . . . you go by many names. Wife. Mom. And you work, too, I see."

"Yes," said Miriam. "I'm self-employed. I'm a therapist."

"Yes, yes," said Rosy. "Me too. For folks who don't realize they need one. But you know you need one, don't ya, darling."

"Well, yes, I—"

"Because of your family, causin' strife.... No, no strike that. It's your husband."

"Um, yeah, I guess so."

"Your relationship..." The psychic closed her eyes. Her head lolled to the side. "It's... strained. You are... angry. I can see it. You were on your way, just now, to see someone...."

"Wait, how do you know all this?" Miriam asked.

The psychic's eyes snapped open. They were ocean blue, with waves of foreboding.

"I'm psychic. Obviously. Now, lemme see your palm."

Miriam didn't believe in psychics. Marital problems were an easy guess. But she was there, and curious, so she held her hand open.

The psychic stared into it for several long minutes. She sucked root beer from her straw. Finally, she spoke.

"Your husband, he works all the time. You feel he don't appreciate you. You got somethin' growin' beneath your surface. Hatred. No, not quite. But almost. Gnawin' at you. Your marriage"—the psychic fell silent for a minute, staring at her palm with uncomfortable intensity—"it's... over."

This was not the answer Miriam expected. Psychics were supposed to offer vague predictions that might prove true for anyone. Psychics weren't *actually* psychic, in the rational scientific world. They were new-age therapists with more crystals and fewer advanced degrees. They were humans who needed paychecks and wouldn't imperil their credibility with doomsayer declarations of the end of a marriage.

Also, the psychic was just wrong. Sorry. But no, her marriage had to continue because she had promised herself she would never get divorced. She made the promise at age twelve, over Christmas. Miriam and her mother opened gifts wrapped in paper saved from the last Christmas. They strung tinsel and popcorn around a table-top tree. They ate leftover cookies salvaged from her mom's office party. Then Miriam's dad picked her up. His new wife waited in the car. Was it Vicki? Margie? Laurie? Ruby? Jennifer? Lynn? Miriam couldn't recall. The new wife gave Miriam a present: a stuffed dog wearing a ship captain's hat. Captain Barksford, the German shepherd version. Miriam rolled her eyes. Did the new wife think Miriam was five years old? She sulkily slipped the stuffed dog into a plastic bag and buried it in the garbage. But later, she imagined it buried forever in a landfill of rotting banana peels and smelly diapers, and it made her sad. That a person could casually carelessly throw something perfectly good in the trash. The way her dad had dumped her mom. She dug the plush Captain Barksford from the trash, carried it up to her part-time bedroom, buried her face in its fur, and cried. *No, I will never,* she told herself, and Captain Barksford. She would never subject her own children to partitioned Christmases. She would never toss out a thing that could be salvaged.

Even after the psychic declared the end of Miriam's marriage, she did not let go of Miriam's hand. She continued to stare, a curious expression on her face. Miriam felt an odd tingle in her hand, not unlike the radio-dial shock that had surprised her earlier, but more continuous and subtle. Her head felt swimmy.

The seas of life get choppy sometimes, but you must keep sailing, she thought, in a voice that didn't belong to her.

Then the voice shouted: *Abandon ship!*

And, at the same time, the psychic dropped Miriam's hand and jerked back, startled.

"No!" the psychic yelled. "No! It's not over!"

"It's . . . not?"

"It's— I need to look again." She snatched Miriam's hand and gazed into her palm.

"Wait, it is! Your marriage is over!"

"But you just said—"

"No, it's not. Or, wait . . ." She pulled Miriam's hand closer, right up to her eye. "No! Yes! No! It's, it's . . ."

"What? What!"

"I can't—unless . . ." She poked Miriam's palm with her pointer finger.

"Ow, what are you doing?" Miriam pulled her hand back.

"The consistency is right, at least. So . . ."

"So what? What do you mean?"

The psychic shook her head. "Nope. I think you'd better go. No charge, all right? Not for the root beer neither. You can even take the cup with you. Now go on, go on." She scooted Miriam toward the entrance.

"Okay, well whatever. I didn't believe you anyways," Miriam said as the psychic opened the door, pushed her out, and slammed the door behind her.

She heard the lock click. The lights in the store went out.

Miriam got back into her car. She still had no idea where she was going, but she drove back the way she had come until the road began to look more familiar and her GPS finally spoke up. *Make a U-turn,* it said.

At that point, she was already late.

She called Jack on the phone. "Hey, are you there already?" she said, when he picked up. "I'm running late."

"Well, actually... I'm still at work."

"You're at work?" It sounded like a question when she said it, but it felt like a battle cry, full of rage: *YOU'RE AT WORK!!!*

"There was a project that came up," Jack said. "I called the therapist and canceled."

"Oh. And were you planning on telling me?"

"I tried to call you, but your phone went straight to voicemail. I called twice."

"Oh." She pulled up behind a long line of cars waiting at a red light.

"I rescheduled for next week. Look, it's not like I want to be at work, but it's important."

"We're important, Jack. Us. You and me. Our marriage. At least, one of us thinks so."

"I think so, too. It's just that—"

The car behind her honked, but the light was still red. "Whatever, Jack. Whatever. You love work so much? You want to be with your darling work all the time? Why don't you get married to work instead?"

MIRIAM'S PARTY FRIENDS

MIRIAM STEPPED OUT into the chilly evening. Jack and the children were already outside. The children scoured the dormant grass for stray twigs. They ran past the yard, to where Ravenswood Drive dead-ended into forest, and hurled the twigs they'd gathered.

"Take that!" Rory yelled, at the trees.

Jack watched from the front porch. He looked anxious. He shifted back and forth, one foot to the other. This momentary lapse of work made him squirmy.

"You ready?" she asked. She locked the door.

Jack nodded. "Kids! Come on, we're going!"

They walked up Ravenswood Drive. Rory and Lindsey scurried ahead.

"We're rats!" Lindsey explained. She waved her tail and wiggled her whiskers. "We're winning the race! But really, I'm going to win. I'm a better rat than Rory." She sped past him, to prove her point.

Miriam and Jack walked past the quaint Craftsman cottages of Ravenswood Drive, past the broad front porches, where in the warmer months neighbors drank beers and watched the kids ride bikes. They walked past the house that belonged to their friends Kate and Fred Marino, whose two children had played with their two children their whole lives. They walked in silence, because Miriam had told Jack that she didn't want to talk about his work, or the news, and apparently there was nothing else to say, until he said:

"Stop."

"What?"

"Look." He pointed at Kate and Fred's yard. There was a bunny, fat and glossy-eyed. It might have been the one that had followed Miriam down the street last month. She had forgotten about that bunny, in all the holiday chaos. And that bunny had been alone. This one had a brood.

"That's . . . a lot of rabbits," she said. She tried to count, but there were too many. At least fifteen. Maybe twenty. All soft and fluffy and, in that quantity, somewhat menacing.

"Shouldn't they be, like, underground somewhere?" Jack asked.

"It's a mystery. Gosh, if you were a detective—"

"Come on. The kids are way ahead."

The kids had almost reached their destination—Holly and Tom Waters's house, at the top of the street on the opposite side. They waited for their parents to cross, like good little rats. Then they scurried across the lawn, up some front steps, and scratched on the door. The door opened.

"Grrrrrr!" A boy leapt out from behind the door. He ran past the two rat kids, to Jack. He growled and swiped his claws.

"Chad!" Holly yelled. "Chad, that's not how we answer the door."

"But, Mom, I'm a velociraptor!" Chad snarled, to demonstrate.

"Chad!" His mother shook her head, but she didn't stop the boy from circling Jack and snapping his fangs. "I'm so glad you could make it! Come in! I made cocktails!"

Miriam drank cocktails in the living room with Holly and Kate. The children ran twirling, shrieking laps through the house.

"They don't seem to ever get tired of this game," said Miriam, as the kids ran past.

"It's hypnotic," said Kate.

"It's exhausting," said Holly.

"Look at that string of drool on Rory's chin," said Miriam. Rory also had a drool-bib, soaked into his shirt.

"I just hope it doesn't turn out like last time," said Holly. The last happy hour, Chad had taken a spinning leap into the hutch. "We're lucky he didn't lose that tooth."

Miriam sipped her cocktail, hibiscus honey vodka with fresh pureed strawberry, garnished with a sprig of mint.

"This is amazing," she said.

"It evokes spring." Holly looked wistful. Outside, cold rain began to fall. "I've already had one, so you've got to catch up."

Miriam would have already had one, too, if she had Chad loose in her house.

Chad ran past, snarling and frothing, then mounted a velociraptor attack on the unsuspecting husbands. The men were in the kitchen, drinking beers and chopping vegetables.

Fred Marino and Tom Waters looked, from afar, like brothers. They both had sharp jaws and brown hair, chopped short. They were clean-shaven. They wore ball caps and striped shirts with collars, tucked into expensive jeans. They had the same laugh:

manly, confident. They had played football together in high school and studied business at the same university and drunk at the same frat house, where they probably spent their evenings playing beer pong and foosball and giving each other high fives and chest bumps. Miriam's husband, with his glasses and his corduroy jacket and his five-o'clock shadow, looked almost freaky next to these frat boys.

The velociraptor spit at him. Miriam didn't want to see what came next. She turned back to her girlfriends.

"Want to hear the neighborhood gossip?" Holly said. She looked thrilled. "You know that cop car parked in front of the Elliots' house last night?"

"Yeah." Kate frowned. "The flashing lights scared away the rabbits."

"Well, apparently," Holly continued, "the Elliot boy—what's his name?"

"Buster."

"Right, Buster. Little Buster got caught shoplifting at the Value Valley."

"Oh. That's— Poor kid," Kate said.

"Not really. He shouldn't have been shoplifting," said Holly.

"What'd he steal?" Miriam asked.

"Yeah, that's the crazy thing," Holly said. "Beef jerky. And not just one. Dozens. He filled his pockets, his sleeves. He even had them in his socks."

"Why would he steel beef jerky?"

"He seemed like such a... straitlaced kid."

"He was! But you never know how a person will turn out," Holly said. "Anyway, they let him off with a warning since he's still just a kid. But his mom is pretty freaked out about it. I saw—"

A loud crash sounded from the dining room, followed by crying.

"Chad!" Holly yelled. She practically jumped out of her seat. She looked alarmed, unusually so for someone whose kid was a maelstrom of crashes.

"It wasn't me, Mom!" Chad yelled back. "It wasn't my fault! It was Nicky, he knocked the chair over on Mabel."

Kate, mom to Nicky and Mabel, ran to the dining room to comfort and scold. Holly ran off to confirm that it really wasn't Chad's fault. Miriam got up to check on her own kids. She found Lindsey in the upstairs hall with a plastic castle full of ponies.

"Where's Rory?"

Lindsey pointed at Chad's bedroom. The door was closed. Miriam tried to open it, but it was locked.

"Rory?" She knocked. "Rory, are you in there?"

No answer.

She knocked again.

"Rory! Open the door!"

No answer. She tried the knob again.

"Hey, Rory—" She heard a click. The door opened. Rory stood in the middle of the bedroom, empty-handed. He looked disappointed to see her.

"Mom! You made me lose my toy!"

"What toy?"

"The dinosaw. It's Chad's. But he said I could play wif it. But now it's gone!"

Miriam stepped into the room. The air in the room was stale, almost musty. A layer of dust coated the dresser and headboard. There was a book on the bedside table, *Escape Intensityville,* also covered with dust. The bed was unmade, the blankets shoved into a mound at the corner. There was no sign of any dinosaur toy.

"I don't see any dino."

"It was here."

"Well... everything else okay?"

Rory pouted. "I like that dino."

"I'm sure you'll find it," she said. "I'll be downstairs if you need anything, okay?"

Rory nodded. She kissed his forehead and then headed back out into the hall. Then she heard a happy squeal, and Rory yelled, "Shut the door!"

When she turned back around, Rory had a Tyrannosaurus toy in his hand. He smiled at her. She smiled back, and shut the door, and only after, when she got back downstairs, did it register that Chad's bed had looked different—it was made, even though a moment earlier, it hadn't been.

"Good, you're back," Holly said. The worried expression hadn't faded from her face.

"You all right?" Miriam asked.

"No. I mean, yes. I'm fine. I'm just juggling a lot right now. Between work and— It's just been hard to keep it all together."

"Yeah, I feel that."

"Except you *are* keeping things together," Holly said. "Me, on the other hand—last week, Chad went over to a friend's house for a playdate, and I totally forgot to pick him up. It was like my mind had just blanked the whole thing out, like it didn't exist. Until the other mom texted me and was like, 'um, you were supposed to be here an hour ago.' Fuck, it was so embarrassing. But—promise you won't tell Kate."

"I won't. But I don't think Kate would judge."

"She might. She's . . ." Holly scooted close to Miriam. "Have you noticed anything different about her lately?"

"Um, no. She seems the same. Why?"

"Did you see that necklace she's wearing?"

"Oh, yeah." A wire-wrapped crystal hung on a strand of seed beads. "Is it new?"

"I think so. I never saw it before last week. Her kids are wearing them, too. She said the crystals would help align their chakras, or something."

"That doesn't sound . . . unlike Kate," Miriam said. "She's always been a little hippy-dippy."

"Right, but she never displayed it on her neck before. In crystal form."

In appearance, Kate, for as long as Miriam had known her, had looked like she belonged to the same sorority as Holly. They had manicured nails and long, blown-out hair. They wore blouses with jeans and heels, blush and lipstick, lengthening mascara. They had the same taste in handbags.

"True," Miriam said.

"And you know what else?"

"What?"

"The other morning," Holly said, "when I was out jogging, I saw her doing tai chi."

"Huh."

"Have you ever heard Kate say anything about tai chi?"

"I don't think so."

Kate walked back into the living room. Miriam and Holly scooched apart and reached conspiratorially for their cocktails.

"Everything okay?" Miriam asked.

"Yes," Kate said. "Just a temporary misalignment. But we did our deep-breathing exercise and imagined the pain floating away."

Miriam hadn't even finished her first cocktail when Jack's phone rang. She watched him take the phone out of his pocket, consider for a moment, and then return the phone to his pocket unanswered. But a few minutes later, his phone rang again. He answered it. She couldn't hear what he was saying from the other room, but she saw him nod agreeably.

A minute later, he sidled into the living room where Miriam sat with her friends.

"So," he said, sheepishly, "that was just Jessica on the phone."

"Who's Jessica?"

"Oh, she's just, um, one of the partners. Anyway, she's got this big case going to trial next week, and she needs more help with it, and one of the other associates came down with the flu, so..."

"So?"

"So I've got to go into work."

"What, now?"

"Uh, yeah. Just, um, for a few hours tonight. And tomorrow."

"It's Saturday night."

"Yeah, I know."

"You worked every night last week. And last weekend."

"I know but this is *important,* Miriam. Jessica's a partner and—"

Miriam stood up. She tossed back the rest of her cocktail. God she wanted a cigarette, so she could snuff it out on her husband's typing fingers.

"It's like..." She stared at him, seething. "It's like you're not even my husband anymore. You're just some stranger living in my house."

"That's not fair, Miriam."

"What's not fair is you getting called into work without any notice on a Saturday night. Is this what you want, Jack? You want to go into work?"

"I have to go. I said that I would, so I—I—" Jack stammered.

"So you're going. You made your choice. Okay, Jack. Fine. Go. But if that's what you're going to do, don't bother coming back."

"You mean, you mean back to... to Tom and Holly's house?"

Jack's skin looked sallow and bloodless. He was floundering. She could almost hate him now. Just a few steps further and a rip-tide of hate would wash over her, drag her away far, far out into the endless deep, where she could never swim back.

Holly held out her own half-full cocktail glass. Miriam took it. She drank it in a single gulp.

"You're a smart guy, Jack," she answered. "You figure it out."

MIRIAM AND THE FOX

JACK MUST HAVE COME HOME in the middle of the night, because there he was, in bed beside her, snoring, mouth open, a trickle of drool down his chin. It was seven a.m. on Sunday morning.

Miriam got out of bed and put on her jogging clothes. She laced up her sneakers. She didn't attempt to be quiet. But she made it out of the house without waking anyone, except the dog, who clearly wanted to run. He loped through the house behind her, whimpering, until she finally put on his leash.

When she stepped outside into the gloom, Roxster lunged. She tugged the leash back and fumbled with her keys, unaware, at first, why the dog was so excited. But when she finished locking the door, she turned and saw it.

A fox.

Roxster barked and scrambled, trying to break free of his leash.

"Roxster, stop. It's just a fox."

Except, something about the animal weirded her out.

It stood on her lawn, motionless, oddly unperturbed by the barking, frothing dog. It stared at her. Its black eyes felt like an inquisition.

Where did he go? the fox seemed to be asking. *Where?*

Miriam shook her head.

Where did he go?

No, it hadn't asked anything. It couldn't talk, obviously.

"Roxster, stop," she said. But Roxster didn't stop, and the fox didn't move. It stood there in the middle of the lawn, even as she walked past it with the dog, even as the dog's barks got more vicious. Its eyes stayed fixed on Miriam.

She tried to ignore it. She started jogging up the sidewalk. It was wretched running weather, misty and bleak. She ran past Kate and Fred's house, then past Holly and Tom's. Her friends, whose marriages were better than her own, who parented together, who went on date nights together, who woke up in the same bed on Sunday mornings. On most mornings, most weekends, when she woke up, Jack was already gone.

She felt starkly alone.

She didn't remember her own parents ever fighting before they divorced. She remembered them existing in their own separate orbits, rotating the house, their paths never crossing. Her dad on his leather recliner. Her mom in the kitchen mincing onions. Her dad and his microwaved beef burgundy in a white paper tray. Her mom on the floor doing crunches, bicycling her legs. They did not brush their teeth at the same time. Her mom went to bed early. Her dad stayed up late. Then he stayed out late. Then, months before their divorce, he changed.

He became, in her estimation as a child, suddenly more fun and available. He was always whistling, high-fiving, buying her treats. He took her out for ice cream, mini-golf, movies. Did she want popcorn or candy? He wouldn't make her choose. She could have both. He learned her favorite songs. He read her favorite books. He bought her favorite foods. He cultivated an image of himself—the engaged and delightful father—to support his narrative. *He* was there, being a good dad. It was *the wife* who wanted him gone.

Or so Miriam understood, until she got older and her mom explained. *You remember those weekend work retreats? You remember how he was when he came home? Soooo refreshed. Ha!*

The cycle repeated with his future wives. He got married. He got disinterested. And then a series of "mandatory weekend work retreats" left him refreshed and ready for divorce.

Miriam ran two miserable miles out and two back, and Roxster pulled the whole time. He barked at every animal he saw—every squirrel, every rabbit, every cat, inside or out. She hadn't realized just how many animals there were in suburbia, until Roxster took up the hobby of barking at *all of them*. He had never barked so much before. He had never been loud or anxious, until right around Christmas. Maybe he sensed the impending breakup of his pack. Maybe he needed doggie Prozac.

She walked the last stretch down Ravenswood Drive. She expected to find her husband already showered and dressed for work, in his tie and jacket despite there being no office dress code on Sundays. He would have snuck in a few minutes of television news, but neglected the dirty dishes, and the children, who would pounce the moment she opened the door.

Fuck, she wanted a cigarette.

She did not expect to find the fox still there in her yard. The same fox. In the same spot. It watched her as she approached.

Where did he go?

Roxster snarled.

"Hey! Get out of the yard!"

The fox didn't move. It just stared at her through the voids of its eyes. She walked closer, thinking that Roxster would scare it away. But it didn't run. Instead, it trotted toward her house, up the front steps, onto the porch, where it stood directly in between her and the front door.

"Hey! Fox! Get away!"

She led the dog halfway up the steps. Roxster snapped and barked. The fox wouldn't leave. It just stood, loitering, seemingly oblivious to the dog, its eyes still fixed on her.

Where? Where did he go?

Where was she going? She wasn't about to let Roxster catch the creature and try to eat it. That would be messy. And she didn't want to get too close. Atypical behavior might mean rabies, or prions, or some other scary new disease. So she ceded the front porch to the fox and walked around the back.

She knocked on the back door. The lights were on inside. She heard child voices.

"Hey! Someone let me in!"

She knocked again. No one came. She pounded.

At last, she heard the patter of kid-feet. Rory opened the door. Roxster bolted inside. He barked, viciously, as if there was an intruder. But it was just Jack.

He was in the kitchen, with Lindsey.

Bark-bark-bark-bark-bark!

"Roxster, shhh!"

"Mom!" Lindsey yelled. "We're making French toast!"

Bark-bark-bark-bark-bark!

Jack was at the counter in his bathrobe. He had a carton of

eggs, a stack of sliced bread, and a bag of salmon treats. He tossed a treat to the dog.

"That better make you shut up," he said. "Sheesh. What is wrong with him lately?"

"I thought you had to work," Miriam said.

"Oh, um, no," Jack said. "Or, well, I have to go in this afternoon for a few hours. But Jessica doesn't need me until then."

"Oh."

"You want French toast, right?" Jack said. "And coffee? If you want to take a shower first, it should be done by the time you get out." He smiled meekly.

"Okay," she replied. She did want a warm shower and French toast. She was also suspicious. "But first I need to check something."

"Sure," Jack said. "Just let me know when you're ready for me to fry it up."

Miriam walked into the living room. She pulled back the curtains so that she could see the front porch. The fox was still there, lurking by the door.

"Hey, Lindsey, c'mere!" she called. Lindsey came running. "Look out the window. What's out there?"

"A dog?"

"A fox. You can see it?"

So she wasn't crazy, in this instance.

"Of course I can see it," Lindsey said. "But it's kind of creepy. What's it doing?"

THE ENGAGED AND DELIGHTFUL FATHER COMES HOME FOR DINNER

MIRIAM STOOD AT THE STOVE, stirring a pot of spaghetti. Lindsey would eat spaghetti with tomato sauce, but only if the sauce had no tomato chunks. Rory would eat spaghetti only with butter and salt. Roxster would eat the whole pot of spaghetti if she let him. Miriam didn't care how Jack felt about spaghetti, because Jack wouldn't be home for dinner. Jack had work.

Except then, unexpectedly, Jack came home.

Roxster leapt up. He growled—a deep, menacing growl, like he'd just seen the poltergeist who would purloin his spaghetti dinner. He charged the door. When the door opened and Jack stepped through, he pounced.

"Stop! Stop!" Jack yelled. He fell back against the door. The dog mounted him. It snapped and barked. Miriam ran over and yanked the dog off. Jack stood up and brushed himself off. "Is he rabid or something? I swear, half the times I see him lately he just goes ballistic. What the hell's wrong with him?"

"He was fine until you came home," Miriam said.

The kids also pounced on their father.

"Dad! Dad! You're home!"

"Dad! Guess where we went? The park!"

"Dad! Guess what we're having for dinner? Spaghetti!"

"Dad, you smell funny." Rory pressed his face to Jack's leg. He scrunched up his nose.

"Rory, that's not a nice thing to say."

"But he *does* smell funny!"

"But it's not polite," Miriam said, as she took Jack's coat, so she could sniff to confirm.

Rory was right. The coat smelled funny. But Miriam couldn't place the scent. "We don't say things like that, even if they're true. Why don't you just give Dad a hug and tell him you're glad he's home."

Rory flung arms around Jack's legs. "I'm glad you're home!"

"Me too!" Lindsey joined the hug.

Miriam stood there with her arms crossed. She *should* hug him. But his surprise arrival made her uneasy.

"You're home early," she said. "What's up?"

"I got off at six today," said Jack. He didn't look at her.

"That is early. There must not have been traffic?"

"No," said Jack, his gaze fixed on the children. "Smooth sailing all the way."

"So you're eating dinner with us tonight?"

Most nights she just set out a plate of leftovers for Jack to microwave when he got home.

"Of course. Spaghetti sounds great. But have I got a few minutes to watch the news first?"

Miriam restrained herself. She didn't complain about the drone of TV news. She didn't drop spaghetti on the floor then scoop it up and serve the floor-pasta to Jack. She let both children sit next to their father, the shiny parent. They insisted. Dad and the two kids sat on one side of the table and Miriam sat on the other side, alone.

Lindsey ate her spaghetti one noodle at a time. She inspected every bite, for chunks. Rory was a speedy pasta-eating machine. He shoveled each oversized bite into his mouth before he'd swallowed the last one, which meant that sometimes the machine got overloaded and excess pasta slid out, onto the floor, where Roxster slurped it up.

"Did you hear about the senator from Georgia?" Jack asked, with his mouth full. He ate his pasta like Rory, as if from a trough.

"No," Miriam answered.

She didn't care about the senator from Georgia.

"Senator Johnston," Jack said. "It's all over the news."

She didn't care about the news.

"I haven't watched."

"He just got arrested. At the airport."

"Okay."

"At the security checkpoint."

"Uh-huh."

"TSA searched his briefcase and found a bunch of cocaine. A few bricks of it. Plus thirty thousand in cash. And..." Even though the kids weren't paying attention and wouldn't know what it was anyway, Jack spelled, "a D-I-L-D-O."

"Oh."

Jack hadn't said anything remotely related to S-E-X in months, only to now broach the sexy topic of the senator's dildo.

"Senator Johnston—isn't he the senator who said that women

shouldn't be allowed to work in stressful occupations like law and medicine, for their own good?"

"That's him."

"What a moron. Who tries to skate through airport security with a briefcase full of drugs and cash?"

"He claims he had no idea how any of it got in his briefcase, that someone must have planted it on him," Jack said. "But of course his fingerprints were all over everything, and—"

"Mom," Lindsey screeched. "There's a chunk!"

"Eat around it," Miriam replied.

"But, Mom, how many more bites?"

"Mom, can I have dessert?" Rory begged. He slid his finger across his empty plate to wipe up the butter residue.

"Ten bites, and no, Rory, you already had a piece of candy today, remember?"

"But ten, that's so many!"

"But, Mom, I want dessert!"

"How about six bites?"

"Pleeeeeeease?"

Time stopped. Miriam's jaw clenched. Her neck muscles tensed. Her existence was a hurricane of *I-wants* and *how-manys* and *why-can't-Is*, and at the center, in the windless eye, absolved through excessive work hours of having to ever refuse or enforce or otherwise interact with the two unreasonable creatures he had spawned, was Jack.

"Kids, chill out," Jack said. "Eat four more bites, and then you can both have dessert."

"Yay!"

"Then will you read us books, Dad?" Lindsey asked.

"I want the hundwed twucks book!"

"I want the Curious George books! Can I pick three?"

"Sure," said Jack. "We can read whatever you want."

"Don't you have to work tonight?" Miriam asked.

"Actually, um, no," Jack said. He poked at the noodles on his plate. "But hey, if you don't want to be on bedtime duty tonight, I can handle it. I'll hang out with the kids so you can relax."

"I thought you were helping out with that trial."

"Yeah, well, um, Jessica said she didn't need me to work late. So I came home."

While Jack read books to the kids, Miriam snuck outside. She got into her car. She drove, not quite certain where she was going until she pulled into the gas station parking lot. She sat in her car for a while, wondering why she had come.

But she knew exactly why.

She knew exactly what brand of cigarette she would buy.

"One pack of the Mt. Airy Spirits," she told the clerk.

She would only ever buy one pack, because smoking was a bad habit, especially for moms with impressionable kids. But she also had this sense, not grounded in reality, that she would finish this pack and come back for another.

She paid the clerk. She took a book of matches. She stepped back outside, then walked around the corner, where no one would see her.

She removed the plastic wrapping from her first ever pack of cigarettes. It reminded her of sea-foam, white sticks in a teal box, light in her hand. She pulled out one cigarette, flipped it over, and returned it to the box. The lucky cigarette. She would smoke it last. She knew this ritual, but she didn't know how or why. She knew how to hold it between her lips. She knew how to light it.

She struck the match. She lit the cigarette. She felt a surge of guilt. A guilt that never left. It just ebbed and flowed, like waves in the sea.

After the guilt came a nicotine rush. Damn that was delightful. She was alone, behaving irresponsibly, and no one else would ever know. She was alone, and she could let go. Her jaw could unclench. Her shoulders could relax. Her mind could soften.

Except it didn't. It kept tumbling back to the evening's earlier stress points. Roxster acting rabid. The kids arguing about dinner and dessert. Jack giving them exactly what they wanted. Jack coming home early from work. *Smooth sailing all the way,* he had said. *Jessica said she didn't need me to work late.*

He didn't look her in the eye.

There was a delay between her question and his answer, a fraction of a second too long.

HOLES IN THE WALL, AND THE HOT LAWYER

MIRIAM RAN INTO HOLLY in the morning, at the Value Valley.

"I'm sick of grocery shopping," Holly said. She had two cases of wine in her cart, a bottle of vodka, and a twelve pack of Blue Lagoon. "And cooking. Come over tonight. We'll order pizza."

When Miriam got home, she called Jack's cell to tell him the plan. His phone rang once and then went to voicemail. She didn't leave a message. Jack never checked it. She texted instead. She fed and walked the dog. She took a quick shower. She met with two patients. She picked the kids up from day care. By the time they got home, she still hadn't heard from Jack.

She texted again. He didn't reply. She called his office number. His secretary answered.

"Hi, Doreen, it's Miriam. Is Jack in?"

"Hi, Miriam. No, he's out all afternoon."

"Oh. Do you know where he went?"

"No, he didn't say. He just said he'd be out."

"Was it for that trial?"

"What trial?"

"He said—"

"Oh—oh, sorry, I forgot. He did mention something about that."

"Oh. Well, if he comes back, will you have him call me?"

He didn't. So they went to Holly and Tom's without him.

Tom and the kids left Miriam and Holly alone. Holly poured two glasses of wine, filled to the brim.

"This still just counts as one drink, right?" Holly said.

"Who's counting?"

"Well, it is after six. As long as I can wait until after six before I pour a drink... I swear, some days I'd start drinking with breakfast if I could get away with it. Did I tell you what Tom's planning for next weekend?"

"No, what?"

"Skydiving." Holly rolled her eyes and took a slurp of wine. "As if I don't have enough to worry about with Chad. Now I have to worry about Tom. I swear. Why would anyone want to jump out of a plane? On purpose?"

"Isn't it supposed to be pretty safe? I mean, lots of people do it. And they strap you to an instructor, right?"

"Well, yeah. But it doesn't make me worry less. I mean, I just keep picturing what could happen. Like, like—" Holly paused. Her eyes flickered, as if she could see the tragedy unfolding.

"Hey," Miriam said, "I know it's hard not to worry. But Tom'll be fine."

"I don't know what's got into him." Holly took a gulp from her now half-full glass of wine. "It's like he's having a midlife crisis or something."

"There are worse symptoms of midlife crisis than a little thrill-seeking."

"Speaking of thrill-seeking, did you see the mess in the hall?"

Holly led Miriam into the hallway. She pointed at the two large holes in the wall.

"This was yesterday," she said. "Chad's been unhappy about

the lack of snow this winter. Because he can't go sledding. So yesterday he got dressed up in his winter coat and boots and his snow pants and he rode his toboggan down the stairs."

"Geez."

"Those holes are from where the toboggan crashed through the wall."

"Is he okay?"

"Oh, he's fine. He's fine!" Holly said. But her mouth quivered, and a small tear welled up at the corner of her eye. "This is why I told him—why I told him *and* Tom—no skateboarding. I mean, can you even imagine Chad on a skateboard? Tom bought him one, you know. Last year, when I was on a business trip. But I made him get rid of it as soon as I found out. Chad was *so* pissed." Holly shook her head. She inhaled sharply. "Anyway, I swear these holes have gotten bigger since yesterday. I think Chad's been picking at the plaster. I just know I'm going to find a pile of plaster hidden in his sock drawer or something."

Holly finished her glass of wine. She poured herself another. Upstairs, three kids stampeded across the floor.

"So," Holly asked, "how's everything with Jack?"

"Things are... I don't know. Frustrating. He's been working less."

"That's good."

"And on Monday night he even did the dishes and put the kids to bed."

"As he should."

"Yeah, but... it's weird."

"What?"

"It's probably nothing," Miriam said. "But . . . I get the feeling he's lying about something."

"Oh?" Holly perked up. "Wait—the other night, before he left, I heard him mention some woman. What was her name . . . Jessica?"

"Yeah. She's a partner at his firm."

"Have you met her?"

"No."

"So you don't know how hot she is?"

Miriam hadn't thought about it, until right then. She had just assumed that work had zapped Jack's libido, that no romance could possibly exist in the mergers and acquisitions world of corporate law. But now this legal bombshell materialized in Miriam's mind. A senior partner, but still young and hot, in a tailored skirt-suit, stockings, silk shirt with the top buttons undone. She leaned against Jack's desk, then over it, so he could see. Then she was on top of it, skirt up, back arched, fingers dug into Jack's biceps, moaning and—

"Oh god," Miriam gasped. "What if he's having an affair?"

And it all fit. The late nights at work. The sexlessness of their marriage. The way Jack breezed past her. The strange scent on his coat. Roxster's reaction. The way he said the other woman's name—*Jessica*—as if he could taste her.

INTERLUDE

THE VP

IMAGINE YOU are *not* the VP of marketing for the multinational technology corporation Machsai Inc., headquartered in Tokyo, Japan.

Imagine you are nobody.

You are a mail clerk and you have been a mail clerk for a decade and you will never be anything other than a mail clerk.

This is not the life you wanted, but we don't always get what we want. Or so the song goes.

Once, you had aspiration. You worked hard to land a coveted job as a mail clerk for the Machsai corporation. The mail room was in the basement of a thirty-story building, but you would work your way up, you told yourself, to the very top floor.

You saw possibility, in the form of an interview. Supervisory mail clerk. One step up the ladder, but only the first of many. You studied. You conducted mock interviews in the bathroom mirror. You wore your very best suit, and on the morning of that interview you took the elevator down from your box-sized apartment, instead of the stairs, so you would not break a sweat.

You remember that moment, on the tenth floor of the apartment building in which you still reside, where you made that choice. Ten floors. No air-conditioning on a summer morning. Your brain made you press the call button. The right choice, your brain insisted, despite that odd flutter in your heart.

You remember the moment when the elevator sputtered, the power cut. You were plunged into darkness. You remember the panic when you reached into your bag for your phone and found it not there.

Yes, you had a good excuse, but your mistake bespoke an inattention antithetical to the Machsai corporate mission. A trivial mistake might cost a fortune.

And so.

One long decade. Young versions of Aspirational You arrived in the basement and climbed out of the basement, and you stayed put. You worked hard, but still, you could not find your way out.

Imagine one day you fall asleep at your desk, in the mail room where you will forever and always be a mail clerk. Until someone wakes you.

They're ready for you, the someone says.

You recognize him. He was a mail clerk seven years ago, but then he scrambled up, from title to ascending title, to become assistant to the VP of marketing.

You do not recognize the room in which you now find yourself. It is not the mail room. It has plush carpets, gold lamps, big windows with a Tokyo view, thirty stories down.

You recognize the name on the placard on the desk. The name belongs to you. And the title? VP, marketing.

Sir, you look ill. Are you all right? the assistant to the VP of marketing asks you.

You do not know how it happened. But frankly, you do not care. It happened. None of the details matter. You reply quickly. *Fine. I'm very well. You will handle the presentation today.*

Thank you, sir.

You guessed correctly.

You made a mistake once. You will not err again.

It will be a significant opportunity, you say, to your assistant. *I trust you will not let us down.*

FLASHBACK

MIRIAM + JACK

ON A CRISP NOVEMBER EVENING, nine years in the past, a man climbed out a window onto a third-story fire escape. He did not fear falling—at least, not from the fire escape. His fear was more amorphous than that.

He wore a corduroy jacket and a fedora. He lit a cigarette. He was a silhouette against the downtown skyline, and all around him the city clamored, a discord of sirens, engines, bottles breaking, dogs barking, bass. His face was hidden by shadow. A wisp of smoke coiled around him. *Who was this man?* He might have been the star of a 1940s noir. He might have packed heat. He might have loved a dangerous broad with bloodred lips, who would never love him in return.

He might have been a man who gazed across the rooftops, brooding. But his gaze was drawn to the scene inside: kitchen table, empty mug, pens and highlighters and sticky tabs, laptop, law books. He was a man who would make something of himself, who wouldn't languish in squalor, who wouldn't fade or fizzle. He had all the certitude of youth.

Inside, a young woman walked across a kitchen. She opened a window. She stuck her head out. Her hair was pulled back in a ponytail. Her eyes glittered. She was the most beautiful woman the man had ever seen, and she lived there, in that third-story apartment, with him.

"Jack," she said. "You almost ready?"

"Yeah."

"Are you taking that stuff on the table?"

"I think..." He thought. About what it meant, to tether himself, to fully commit, to leap, and be a different man when he landed. "I think I'll leave it here. It's just a weekend. I don't need to study this weekend."

He finished his cigarette. He went inside, grabbed his suitcase, wheeled it out to the hall, locked the door, called the elevator, opened and shut its rickety gate.

"What if we get stuck in here?" She had asked this question many times.

The elevator lurched and jangled. It was a thousand years old. A mystery of levers and gears.

"Who cares," he said. "As long as we're stuck here together."

He kissed her, biting her lip, pressing her up against the ancient wood. Maybe they should get stuck in the elevator. Maybe the life where they did would be a better one.

Instead, the elevator delivered them to a lobby, which led out to a street, where there was a car that they drove across the state to a house in a small town where Jack's parents still lived. The house was a ranch, brick, with a two-car garage and a giant inflatable turkey in the front lawn. The turkey wore a pilgrim's hat. It held a musket. It held, for the young couple who stood gazing up at it, a message of tragedy. The bird would invite itself to dinner, as the main course, and would facilitate its own destruction. The young couple would abandon their ideals, their aspirations, their wild selves, and plant an inflatable turkey in their suburban yard.

The small town was a nexus of cornfields and potato fields and strip malls and factories. It was called Kernville, and no one who hadn't grown up in or nearby had ever heard of it. There were only five giant, inflatable, light-up turkeys in the town of Kernville, Jack's mother said, proudly, as she rolled out a pie crust. But next year there would be far more. The Shipleys were trendsetters.

The Shipleys put up their Christmas tree before Thanksgiving. They served spiked eggnog in a crystal punch bowl. They ate eggs and bacon for breakfast. Every slice of toast and pancake and biscuit came pre-buttered.

The young man was anxious. He feared what all this butter meant about him, as a person.

The young woman was curious. She wanted to understand the young man and all that made him.

The parents were pushy, persistent, and unyielding. They had become the people they were and would never be anything else.

The father watched television news from his pleather recliner. When Jack introduced his girlfriend, the father said: "So, this is the girl? The one we've heard so much about?" He repeated this phrase three times over the weekend. He looked as if he wanted to pinch her cheeks, but he did not.

The mother set out bowls of mixed nuts and cheese balls and plates of bite-sized pigs in blankets for happy hour. She filled crystal goblets with spiked eggnog, which she assumed was wanted. She didn't ask first. Aunts and uncles and cousins all got spiked eggnog, as they filed into the Shipley house, bearing Crock-Pots and Jell-O molds and casseroles. Jack's sister got virgin eggnog, because she was pregnant with twins.

"So, Audrey," the mother said, "how long is it that you're taking off work again?"

"I don't know yet."

Four months, she had told Jack.

"You don't want to take too much time," the mother said. "You don't want them thinking you're not devoted to your job."

The father tried to sneak off to watch TV. He tried to read the news on his phone. The mother yanked him back.

"Richard! Put that away! It's family time! You're supposed to be getting to know Jack's girlfriend."

"I know, I know," he said. He took a drink. He turned to the young couple. "So, this is the girl, huh? The one we've heard so much about?"

She was, obviously, the *woman*. And Jack had told his parents as much about her as he told them about anything. Which was not much.

He didn't tell them much about law school, because they didn't care about the interesting parts. They only wanted to know the after-parts.

"So, Jack," his mother asked, "have you decided what you're going to do with that law degree?"

"Not yet. I mean, I just started school."

"You need a realistic plan. Nothing absurd or fanciful. Like that plan you had to be a detective. Did Jack ever tell you about this?" she asked Miriam. "He was *obsessed*."

"I was not obsessed."

"He was obsessed. He used to parade around the house with

his spyglass. He had this silly costume. Like Sherlock Holmes, except it was a plastic smock. For months he refused to take it off."

"I was just a kid. That's what kids do."

"That's not just what kids do. Audrey never did anything like that. She used to love the My Little Ponies, but she never believed that she was a pony."

"I was just pretending."

"Kids who are 'just pretending' do not purposefully let the dog escape so that their parents will hire them to track it down."

"Mom, I told you a thousand times, it was just pretend. I was five. I had a vivid imagination. Besides, I hated that dog. He used to eat my toys. He was mean."

The mother, of course, had pictures. She gathered the whole family around to flip through the photo album. There was five-year-old Jack dressed in a trench coat and fedora. Jack with a plastic detective smock and bubblegum cigar. Jack peering through his magnifying glass. Jack beside a crayon sign that read: JACK SHIPLEY, PRIVATE EYE.

At the end of embarrassing family photo hour, the mother circled back to her original question: "Jack, what are you going to do with your law degree?"

"I'm not sure."

"You have to have some idea."

"Well... I really like criminal law. I've been considering becoming a public defender."

"Oh, that's... well, your idealism is admirable." Jack's mother scoffed. "But it doesn't pay well, does it? Have you thought about how you'll support a family, on that sort of salary?"

"I imagine that if Jack had a family," Miriam said, "he wouldn't be the only one supporting it."

After happy hour, the young couple snuck out to the porch. It was dark, except for the white Christmas lights already strung around the railings and the orange glow of the inflatable turkey. Jack lit a cigarette.

"You really should stop smoking," Miriam said.

"I know."

"It's bad for your health."

"Lots of things are bad for your health."

"Like visiting your parents for Thanksgiving."

"Like that, yeah."

"But I liked seeing those pictures of you as a kid."

"I was not obsessed."

"Oh, of course not."

"I was just, you know, a regular kid. Pretending. Like kids do."

"You were adorable. With you little hat and your spyglass. You should ask your mom if she'll let you take some of those pictures. Or borrow them, so you could scan them. You don't have any pictures, at the apartment."

"Maybe I'm a man who needs to forget his dark and dangerous past."

"Uh-huh. The perils of Kernville."

"Maybe I'll just steal the pictures," Jack joked. "Then my mom can hire me to investigate the mystery of where they went."

FLASHBACK

BRATTY

HE WAS HUNGRY.

He was eight.

He was so-so-so-so-so hungry, like a black hole of hunger, and no matter what food he shoved inside that hole the hunger was still there.

Bradford Pierson stood in the pantry in the dark.

He did not dare to turn on the lights.

He was dull, she had said. Not daring. And so his hands felt around in the darkness, in search of some edible thing.

Last time, he stuck a box of capellini in his pocket. He had liked its heft, its shifting sound. He had imagined crackers, but heartier. Lembas bread. Instead, he got thin hard sticks, and he crunched them between his teeth and swallowed, but they didn't fill him up.

This time was because he was supposed to take out the trash. Collect the bags. Replace them. Stick them in the bins. Drag the bins to the curb. He did all the parts except the last part, which he forgot. And now the bins would sit in the garage all week and the garage would smell and the smell would seep into the house and how would she be able to eat, with that smell in the house? And why should he get to eat dinner, if she couldn't?

This time he did better. He filled his pockets. He crept out of the pantry, through the dark kitchen, down the dark stairs. His dad was still awake, watching *Deadhand Diego* on TV. He was supposed to do homework, but he couldn't focus when his stomach gnawed like this.

Bradford Pierson made it back to his bedroom. Safe, for now. He emptied his pockets onto the bed. He had a box of water crackers, a jar of stuffed green olives, a bottle of ketchup, a chocolate-flavored protein bar.

He ate the protein bar first, in two bites. He made ketchup-cracker sandwiches. He ate a handful of olives. He heard a knock on the window of his basement bedroom. He looked up and saw Tommy. Tommy waved. He pressed his face against the wet glass and ballooned his cheeks.

Bradford opened the window. Cold wind blew through. Stray droplets rained down from the half-bare trees. Their red-yellow leaves glistened like casino lights against the black October sky.

"Your shoes," Bradford whispered, through a mouthful of olives. The ground under Tommy's feet was soggy with rain and dead leaves.

"Oh, right." Tommy pulled off his muddy Spider-Man sneakers and put them on the windowsill. He slithered through. His socked feet made dirty prints on the white carpet. He tried to wipe them with his coat sleeve, but it just smeared the dirt. "Sorry," he said, too loudly.

"Quiet. They might hear you."

Tommy nodded. "Silent like a starfish."

"You want some?" Bradford asked. He gestured to the snacks. "The crackers are all right, if you add ketchup."

"No thanks. I ate."

"The olives are weird." They were stuffed with mushrooms and pimentos.

"My parents have the same weird stuff in their house. I wonder if that's, like, a thing that happens when you get old. You forget about all the normal foods and only eat weird stuff."

"My stepmom mostly just eats these shakes. But they're not even milkshakes. They're chalky." He ate another handful of olives. He chewed slowly, now that his hunger hurt less.

Tommy crab-walked across the carpet. The carpet was strikingly white, except for his footprints. The walls were white, and bare. The room smelled like ammonia.

"I didn't get dinner," Bradford told his friend.

"Why not?"

"I forgot to take out the trash."

"So they didn't feed you?" Tommy scowled. He looked at Bradford, at the cracker-ketchup sandwich in his friend's hand, at the oppressive white carpet and soulless white walls.

This was just another hungry Tuesday in his best friend's life.

This was a formative moment. The seed of rebellion sowed. The vow taken, in Tommy's heart, to reject this callous blandness, this injustice.

"She says I'm bad," Bradford said. He considered the possibility. "Tommy, do you think I'm bad?"

Tommy's scowl deepened. He shook his head. "No," he said. He had never sworn before, and he would never not swear after now. "No. Fuck that. Fuck her."

FEBRUARY

THE SHOT-SKI

MR. YAY WANTED FUN.

"Would you rather sweat beer," he asked Bratty, "or fart weed smoke?"

"Would I always fart smoke? Or could I control it?"

"Always."

"At least with beer sweat I could make myself cold so I didn't sweat."

"Unless you got nervous. Then you'd have beer pits."

"Either way, it'd be hard to keep a job."

"Unless you're a rapper," Tommy said. "Or his DJ."

Mr. Yay went shopping. He bought flower, vapes, edibles, tinctures. He bought a tapestry covered with glowing alien heads, and a black light to go with it. He bought a gold chain and a gold cap for his tooth. Not real gold, but who the fuck would find out? He bought a case of Fireball, a case of rum, and fifty pounds of dog food.

He spent the last of the car money on a really fucking huge speaker, and for a week or three or four, he and Bratty got faced and played a lot of video games and blasted themselves with bass.

Somewhere in the haze of those weeks, Bratty did productive things. Or, he threw darts in the dark. He didn't know what would stick. He made a website. He uploaded to every streaming music site. He sent tracks to studios and agents. He made a music video. The video was really just clips of Tux in a pirate hat and Tommy with an eye patch, smoking joints, two at a time. Tommy had drawn the eye patch in permanent marker.

"It makes me look hard," he said, as the eye patch faded to a blue-gray blob. "Like I got in a fight."

Tommy had never been in a fight.

Tommy didn't watch the music video, because Bratty didn't tell him that he'd made it, because Bratty didn't know what would happen to all those darts. He didn't want to think about it. He didn't want to imagine the broke future where they boarded a bus back to Ohio to live with Tommy's parents and Tommy's dad saw Bratty's dad at the country club and Tommy's dad said *It's too bad the music thing didn't work out* but what Bratty's dad heard was *Your kid is a fuckup*. He didn't want it to be true, just as much as he didn't want to go to business school. He didn't want to leave his dog behind because the bus said NO DOGS. He already loathed the bus for their anti-dog position.

So he didn't tell Tommy, and he didn't check to see if anyone had watched his silly video or listened to the songs. Instead, he got really high and went on runs with his dog and scavenged things that people had left with their trash. The dog scavenged chicken bones and street pizza. Bratty scavenged a dartboard, but there were no darts. Then he found a single ski, to which he and Tommy glued four shot glasses, to make a shot-ski.

"Now we just need to find two hotties to do the shot-ski with us," Tommy said.

Except they were out of rum, and they'd almost finished the Fireball.

"Maybe we need to find jobs," said Bratty.

Mr. Yay didn't want a job.

"It's boring. And look at this gold tooth. Like what, am I supposed to just go bag groceries with a tooth like this?"

Mr. Yay wanted to sleep until afternoon and stay up all night.

Mr. Yay wanted to dance.

Mr. Yay wanted to make music, and they did, him and Bratty, crafting and vibing through the late hours. But they didn't talk logistics.

"I'm big-picture," Mr. Yay said. "I'm like, all soul and poetry, like, fuckin' Jack Kerouac, or, uh, Lord Byron. But with better abs and a bigger dick."

He was all sex and smoke and swagger, as a rapper should be, as Mr. Yay. As Tommy, he was more reserved. But he had a prophetic glint in his eye, as if he could intuit what was coming.

The wind had already shifted.

"But we need money to pay rent." Bratty was practical. "What if we find something, I dunno, job-like? But not an actual job."

"What, like, we sell our plasma?"

"We could. But I was thinking more like, like..."

Three miles from the apartment, there was a strip of bars and restaurants and nightclubs, where a rapper with a gold tooth and a faded black eye might find something like a job. Tommy had met a dude who knew another dude who knew a chick who managed a nightclub that needed someone to hand out flyers. The pay was free entry, two free drinks, and twenty bucks for a stack of flyers. But they could earn an extra ten bucks if they walked the strip wearing a sandwich board.

Bratty assumed Tommy would be like, *No fuck that, how am I supposed to wear a sandwich board with a tooth like this?* But for some inexplicable reason, Tommy wanted to wear the sandwich board.

He liked it.

"It's jaunty," he said. "It's like a sail, and my body is the ship."

Tommy popped a gummy in his mouth and put on the pirate hat. They walked three miles in their sandwich boards to the strip. They drifted the sidewalk, handing out flyers. Tommy whistled a sea shanty. Bratty felt a sudden gust of wind, and he tried not to think about what it meant. He felt suddenly afraid. Anxiety, his therapist had named it. But this felt more raucous, like he was riding the crest of a wave about to break all around him, terrifying and awesome. The wind picked up. He peered down the street. His heart pounded. He saw two women, mid-twenties, brown hair, walking toward them. Yeah, they were hot. But like, background hot. In the foreground was the eyes. One of them, the shorter one, had these big, expressive eyes, and they were staring at Tommy. They squinted. Her head tilted. She said something to her taller friend. She pointed. The friend nodded. Her eyes lit up. She squealed, and the shorter friend squealed, and then they were both squealing and gushing and flitting up to Tommy.

"OH MY GOD!"

"It's him!"

"It's you!"

"Mr. Yay!"

"Is it really—"

Mr. Yay grinned. His fake gold tooth gleamed in the sunlight.

"Ahhhhhh!"

"I can't believe it!"

"I love you so much!"

"Holy fuck!"

"What are you doing here?"

"Are you playing this club?"

"Please say yes, I would fucking die!"

"Oh my god, can I have your autograph?"

"Ooh me too! Please?"

"Fuck yeah," said Mr. Yay. "Where do you want it?"

"Um... right here." The shorter woman lifted her shirt and pointed to her breast. "But sign on top of my bra. I don't want it to just wash off."

Mr. Yay reached into his pocket. He took out a permanent marker, as if he had known he would need it, and signed his name.

"So," he said, "you ladies wanna do a shot-ski?"

BRATTY AND HIS THERAPIST

Miriam: *Have you told them yet?*

Bradford: *I... I told them about the dog... or, that maybe I might get a dog. And my dad was like, "Now is not the time for a dog, son. What will you do with the dog when you get your internship? You'll be working too many hours. You won't have time, blah blah blah blah blah."*

Miriam: *I see. So you haven't told your parents you moved to LA?*

Bradford: *Well, um, like, I mean I know I* should *tell them. Like I totally will. But... okay, they'll probably kick me off the health insurance when they find out I quit school. So if I tell them, I'll never be able to tell you I told them, 'cause I won't be able to afford to see you anymore.*

Miriam: *Bradford, I— Don't worry about that, okay? We can figure it out, whether you have insurance or not.*

Bradford: *Dude—*

Miriam: *You've been seeing me for six years. I'm not just going to drop you.*

Bradford: *I, um... thanks.*

Miriam: *But you are going to have to tell them. You can't*

	keep a big secret like this from your family.
Bradford:	*Even if I hate them?*
Miriam:	*Do you hate them?*
Bradford:	*I... There was this time, after my mom, you know... but before my dad met Helena, when it was just me and him. I was like, what, six years old? And this one day, during recess, this other kid dared me to eat a cicada.*
Miriam:	*Did you eat it?*
Bradford:	*Yo, I ate, like, five of them. Like I was trying to prove what a badass I was by eating bugs or whatever. But then when I got home, I got sick. But I didn't make it to the toilet. I threw up all over the bathroom rug. Fucking gross-ass bug guts. And I wasn't about to clean that shit up. So I rolled the rug up and put it in the trash. I didn't tell my dad. I thought he was going to be pissed about the cicadas, so I just didn't say anything, and he didn't ask about the rug, and it was just, like, this big secret, eating away at me, for like, weeks. It felt like years. 'Cause, you know how time is when you're a kid. But then this one day, my dad comes home, and he's got a new rug. And he puts it in the bathroom, and he's looking at me like,* I know what you did. *And I just couldn't take it anymore and I told him everything.*
Miriam:	*How did he respond?*
Bradford:	*He... he hugged me. I dunno, maybe he said*

something too, but I don't remember that. I just remember him hugging me. And then it was like... it was the last time he ever hugged me. Because right after that, he met her. And ever since then, I've been Bratty-the-Fuckup.

Miriam: *But you're not. You know that.*

Bradford: *I... What I know is, there was this brief sliver of time when my dad was like... like himself. When he was who he was, and there was no, like, Gríma Wormtongue whispering snaky shit in his ear, and he wasn't trying to project someone else's perfect vision of who he should be. He was just him. Fuck. I remember him dancing. And he played music. Banjo, guitar, harmonica. Like, old-school country stuff. And then she comes along, and his dancing days are over. He'd never. Not unless you paid him, like, a million gold doubloons. It's like now he only cares about being a boring, rich-ass douche-nozzle.*

Miriam: *But that's his choice.*

Bradford: *It's lame. He's not happy.*

Miriam: *Plenty of people aren't.*

Bradford: *I don't understand.... I never understood. Why do they stay together? It's not like my stepmom's happy. She's always complaining about me and him and how much we both suck. She's miserable as fuck. And he's miserable. He could just leave her and go, like, ski the Alps or ride around on a yacht and do other rich-fuck stuff. But instead, they just stay there together in their boring house, and they never go anywhere or do anything except perpetuate this endless cycle of misery. And like, why? For what?*

WTF, DEER?

FOR THE SECOND NIGHT IN A ROW, Jack came home before dinner. Roxster met him at the door, teeth bared, but his barks were intermingled with sloppy licks. Jack fended off the dog with his briefcase. He set the briefcase on the floor. Roxster thwacked it with his tail, knocking it over. It landed with a hollow thud, as if it was almost empty.

"There's a deer on the lawn," Jack announced.

The kids came running. "Where? Where?"

The kids ran past Jack. They pressed their faces to the storm door.

"Mommy, can we go pet it?" Rory asked.

"Mommy," Lindsey exclaimed, "the deer is trying to break into the car!"

Miriam peered outside. The deer stood on three legs. The hoof of its fourth leg scraped at the passenger-side handle of Miriam's car.

"*What the f—fudge!* It's totally scratching up my car!"

"I'll take care of it," Jack said. He picked up his briefcase, a blunt weapon, and stepped outside. Miriam put on her boots and ran out after him.

"Hey! Deer!" Jack yelled. "Get away from there!" He shook his scary briefcase.

The deer wasn't threatened by this lawyer and his briefcase. It galloped around the car, then reared up on its hind legs and thrust its front legs against the driver's-side window. The window didn't break—this deer wasn't especially large—but the deer didn't relent. It stood on its hind legs and stamped its front legs against the glass again.

Miriam brushed past her ineffective husband. She ran toward the deer, waving her arms.

"Hey!" she yelled. "Get away from there! Get!"

The deer stayed put, front hooves pressed against the window. It stared at her with its big black eyes.

"What? What do you want?"

The deer stared.

Where did he go? it seemed to ask.

The deer wasn't making any sense. *Where did who go?* Besides, deer couldn't speak.

Where did he go?

Miriam opened the passenger-side door. She hopped in. She blasted the horn.

The startled deer leapt back and ran away.

There was a half-eaten container of french fries in the cup-holder. Deer bait. Maybe. If deer ate fries. She got out of the car. She inspected the damage. Scraped paint. A few small dents.

"What did it want?" Jack asked, as if that was the question that mattered.

They went back inside.

"Dad," Rory asked, "why is you weawing a hat?"

Jack wore his brown fedora, a hat he'd had for years but rarely wore to work.

"Why are you *not* wearing a hat," Jack replied, with a mischievous smile, "when children who aren't wearing hats are about... to get... tickled!"

Rory squealed. Jack scooped him up and tickled him.

"Dad! Eeeeee!"

"Rory, run!"

"Ahhhhhh!"

How nice. These delightful noises. Children screaming. Children laughing and playing with their real live home-for-dinner father. They loved him so much. Of course. He was the shiny parent. Dad played chase games and tickled and never had to make the little gremlins bathe or cook their dinners or take them to the doctor or scrape the boogers they'd smeared on their headboard or make them eat things they hated to eat, in the name of proper nutrition. And while she cooked dinner, Shiny Dad plopped down on the couch for his nightly news fix.

"But Dad, you have to chase!"

"Not now, Rory. I'm all tired out. I need to relax. I had a long day at work."

Miriam had a long day at work, and she needed a glass of wine and a cigarette, but instead she got the smoke alarm overreacting to a burnt shred of cheese, the dog overreacting to the smoke alarm, the two kids stomping into the kitchen to whine and complain.

"I'm huuuungwee." Rory tugged at her pant leg.

BEEP BEEP BEEP BEEP

"Dinner's almost ready."

"Mom, stop the beeping!"

BEEP BEEP BEEP BEEP

"I'm trying!" She turned on the fan, opened the window.

"But now it's cold!"

BEEP BE—

"Ewwww, are we having broccoli?"

"I want something else!"

"I haaaate broccoli!"

"I want waffles!"

"If he's having waffles, I want waffles too!"

"I want silence!" Miriam snapped. "And no one's having waffles!"

The children retreated to the living room, where they could squabble over who had the dinosaurs first or who got to play with the laser gun that neither of them wanted until the other one had it. Miriam snuck out to the back deck. She lit a cigarette. A dangerous, morally reprehensible, delicious cigarette.

If she ever got divorced—

If her life unraveled, if she couldn't weave the threads back together, if she found herself alone, overwhelmed, crushed by the weight of her failures, she would smoke cigarettes.

She would start with cigarettes, then add prescriptions. Adderall, Lexapro. Weed gummies to help her sleep through the night.

She knew this about herself. She could see the trajectory: Miriam Shipley, the sinking ship. Already she had sprung a leak, but it wasn't irreparable. Not yet. It was just her, on the back deck, smoking.

And fuck it. If she was honest with herself, she liked smoking. It reminded her of when she was a kid and would mix all the different sodas together or stick gummy worms in her peanut butter sandwich. She liked the head rush, the burn. She liked having a reason to step outside and shut the door behind her. From the back deck, she couldn't hear the drone of television news, or the demands of children. She couldn't be asked unanswerable questions, like: *Mommy, why does Dad smell weird?* He did smell weird. She had caught a trace of it when he stepped through the door. An earthy, milky smell that was both strange and familiar. A smell that made her want to smoke more cigarettes.

"Miriam!" Jack yelled, from inside. "Where are you?"

She stomped out her cigarette. She stuck the butt into the bottle she'd hidden in the bushes.

"Coming," she yelled. "I'm coming!"

"So we're having breakfast for dinner?" Jack asked, as she stepped inside.

"What?"

"The kids said we were having waffles."

"We're not having waffles."

"Darn. I don't know what you already cooked, but I was looking forward to waffles. Maybe you could—"

"We are not having waffles!"

"Oh. You don't have to get so mad."

"I'm not mad."

"Just because the kids and I want waffles. But what were you doing outside?"

"I—I was just—" Of course, she lied. "Checking for that deer. To make sure it didn't come back."

Miriam served baked potatoes and broccoli and chicken. Lindsey picked her broccoli apart into tiny buds and ate them one at a time. She peeled her chicken into slivers, like a string cheese.

She ate her baked potato, but only the parts that hadn't touched the parts that touched the skin.

Rory mashed his chicken and potato together into a patty. He asked for the maple syrup.

"It's a waffle," he explained.

"It's not a waffle," Miriam said. "You can't just mash your food together and call it a waffle."

"But I want waffle."

"But that's not what we're having."

Rory's face scrunched up. He started to cry.

"But, but waffle..."

He cried for a whole minute, and then she gave in.

"Fine," she said. She retrieved the maple syrup and poured it over the potato-chicken mound on Rory's plate. "There you go!"

Rory grinned and gobbled it up. Lindsey eyed her brother with revulsion. Jack bored them all with a recap of the evening's news.

"The stock market's been totally erratic," he said.

Yes. Oh, really? Nod, nod.

"Congress is holding up judicial nominations," he said.

Uh-huh. Uh-huh.

"Greece is opening its borders to thousands more refugees," he said.

Oh, good. Nod. Nod. Smile.

"A huge flock of endangered birds from a remote island in the Pacific mysteriously disappeared."

"Where did they go?" Lindsey asked.

"Nobody knows," said Jack. "Apparently the birds spend part

of the year somewhere in South America, and then the other part of the year on this island in the Pacific. But this year they left South America but never reached the island. They were just suddenly gone. They had trackers, and now they're untrackable."

"But why?"

Jack grinned. He had an investigative glint in his eyes. "Well, one theory is, the birds are still there, but their trackers got turned off. Like by an electromagnetic pulse, or ecoterrorists. I also read one article suggesting spontaneous combustion. But without a thorough inquiry, nobody will ever know why."

MIRIAM AND THE DETECTIVES

HOLLY SOAKED BLUEBERRIES and basil in vodka overnight. She strained the vodka, keeping a few berries for garnish. She mixed the vodka with blueberry juice and seltzer. She poured a glass for herself, just to taste. Then she heard a yowling noise outside. Then a thud. A scream. Crying. She ran outside. She found Chad sitting in the mud under the deck. He had a bloody gash across his cheek. Blood and tears and snot dripped down his face, onto the collar of his white shirt.

"Chad! What happened!"

Mournful Chad looked up at his mother. "The cat clawed my face," he sobbed.

He had only wanted the cat to come along when he leapt off the deck. He was going skydiving, like Dad. He had to have a partner who knew how to skydive, and the cat was the only one who knew. He had seen it leap off the deck before.

Holly cleaned and bandaged Chad's bloody cheek. She changed him out of his bloody, muddy clothes. Into nice, dark-colored clothes that wouldn't show stains. She chugged a second blueberry-basil cocktail. By the time Jack, Miriam, Kate, Fred, and all their kids arrived, she had already started her third.

"But I needed it," Holly said. "After all that." She poured a glass and handed it to Miriam. Miriam took a sip.

"Oh, that's delicious."

"Kate?"

"I think I'll pass tonight."

"What? It's Friday! Wait, are you... pregnant?"

"I'm on a kombucha cleanse," Kate said. She had a small cooler, from which she produced a bottle of cloudy greenish liquid. She poured some of the liquid into her cocktail glass.

"Is that kombucha? What is it?"

"It's a tea fermented by using a symbiotic colony of bacteria and yeast," said Kate. "I've been brewing it myself."

"That's... weird," Holly said. She shot a glance at Miriam. "Does it get you drunk?"

"Probably not."

"Darn. Ugh. Sorry, I'm just—" Holly took a gulp of cocktail. "I'm so on edge. That whole thing with Chad leaping off the deck with the cat..."

"It could have been so much worse."

But Chad was fine. Chad was upstairs, stampeding through the hall, yelling at the top of his lungs.

"I know. Obviously. I—" Holly took another drink. "The thing is, after it happened, I... I totally lost it. I locked myself in the bathroom and sobbed. Like, so hard that I started to hyperventilate."

"Oh, Holly—"

"I know." A tear blossomed in the corner of Holly's eye. She wiped it away. "It doesn't even make sense. I mean, Chad is fine."

"Chad is fine."

"It's me," Holly said. "My emotions have just gone haywire. Like on Monday, I told Chad to clean his dinosaurs up off the floor, and of course he didn't, and I nearly tripped on the triceratops, and then I just started bawling. I was, like, staring down at this stupid triceratops, crying my eyes out. I was so profoundly sad. Sadder than I've ever been in my life. And then the sadness just suddenly stopped, and I'm just standing there wondering what the heck I'd been crying about."

"I remember getting something like that after I had Mabel," Kate said. "Postpartum depression."

"Yeah, I got that too," Holly said. "But this was different. It was more intense. It was like... like the sadness swallowed me up and then spit me back out. I don't know how else to explain it. Do you think... Miriam, should I see someone? You think maybe I could be bipolar or something?"

"It's never a bad idea to see a therapist," Miriam said. "But what you're describing doesn't seem like a bipolar disorder. And I haven't seen anything that would make me think you have one."

"Well, that's good." Holly finished her cocktail. She poured another. "But then what's wrong with me? I mean, other than probably drinking too much."

From the living room, they could see the husbands cooking dinner. Miriam's husband wore a new fedora. He had declined beer and opted for a tumbler of whiskey, but from the way his nose and lips puckered up, it looked like he despised the stuff. Holly's husband wore a blue striped shirt tucked into an ironed pair of jeans. He was chiseled and tan, thanks to regular applications of his wife's sunless tanning lotion. Kate's husband wore his matching uniform of striped shirt tucked into pressed jeans. Except instead of his usual loafers, he wore Birkenstocks, with socks, and his usually short hair looked a bit shaggy.

"I guess there's also my husband," Holly said. "He's been

unbearable. Ever since he got back from skydiving, it's 'skydiving this' and 'skydiving that.' I swear, if I hear any more about it... And he's been all pouty that I won't go with him."

"At least he's fine," Miriam said.

"He's *obsessed.* And now he wants to try bungee jumping. And guess what he wants us to do for vacation this year? Zip-lining. I mean, he can. But the whole family? I told him, 'Tom, don't you dare even talk about zip-lining, or you know Chad is going to tie a rope from the roof to that tree there and try to slide down it. Is that what you want?' Really, I swear, I'm at the end of *my* rope. But enough about me." Holly turned to Miriam. "How are things with Mr. Casablanca over there?"

"Okay, I guess..." Miriam answered.

"Is that a new hat?" Holly asked.

"It is."

"He looks sharp. Which is..."

"What?"

"Well, I'd watch out, if my husband started dressing better," Holly said.

"It's sus," Kate agreed. "Not that my husband doesn't look very sharp in his socks and sandals."

"Ha! True."

"There's a woman in my yoga class," Kate said, "and her husband—well, they're divorced now—but she told me how before it happened, her husband started dressing nicer, using cologne, working out more. Because, you know, there was somebody he was trying to impress."

Miriam glanced over at her husband. He looked sharper,

happier, more relaxed. He had a smile on his face and a gleam in his eye.

"Jack has been acting kind of weird," said Miriam. "And he does smell different lately. I hadn't thought of cologne, but that's probably what it is. Jesus, he hasn't really worn cologne since back before we got married."

"Did you ask him about it?" Kate asked.

"No...."

"You should confront him," Holly said, too excitedly. She was on her fourth cocktail. "You should come right out and demand to know whether he's having an affair."

"Oh, no, you can't do it like that," said Kate. "What if he's not? Then you'll look totally jealous."

"That's a good point," said Holly. "If he thinks you don't trust him, well, that might *make* him cheat. If he isn't cheating already. No, you need to find out some other way."

"Didn't he mention some woman?" said Kate. "Jessica or something?"

"She's a partner in his firm," Miriam said. "He has been working for her a lot. He's supposed to work on some case for her tomorrow afternoon."

"But what if he's not really going to work?" said Holly.

"Totally sus," said Kate. "I mean, who works on Saturday afternoon?"

"Jack," said Miriam. "Jack is always working."

"Which makes it even more suspicious," Holly said drunkenly. "How do you know he's really going to work?

"You should follow him and find out."

"But you'll have to be careful he doesn't catch you."

"We can take my car," Holly said.

"Fred can watch all the kids," said Kate. "We'll tell them we're going shopping."

"Do you have binoculars? We'll need those."

"We should take walkie-talkies."

"And cameras."

"And we should wear some kind of disguise."

"Like wigs and hats."

"And glasses."

"So he doesn't recognize us."

Miriam chugged the rest of her cocktail, a salve to her friends' alarming enthusiasm.

Holly grinned. "We'll be like real detectives."

JACK AND THE BLOND

IT WAS THE CLOSEST any Shipley had ever come to fulfilling Jack's dream of being a real detective.

On Saturday afternoon, Miriam, Kate, and Holly met at Holly's house for their pretend shopping trip. Jack was still at home, so they waited for him to leave. They waited in Holly's car, slouched down so Jack wouldn't see them when he passed. Holly had purchased disguises—a baseball cap with a fake blond ponytail for Miriam, a red bobbed wig for Kate, and a blond beehive for herself. They swapped sunglasses and applied lipstick, bright red and bubblegum pink. They didn't exactly look inconspicuous. But they didn't look like Miriam, Kate, and Holly either.

Holly's husband, Tom, rapped on the window. "Hey! What are you ladies doing?"

Holly rolled down the window a crack.

"We're getting ready to go shopping!" she whispered loudly. "This is our pre-shopping ritual. And you're disturbing it."

"Oh, sorry." Tom shrugged. "Have a good time. And nice hair, babe."

"Do you think he believed you?" Miriam asked, after he left.

"Oh, totally," said Holly. "I mean, why wouldn't we get dressed up like this to go shopping?"

Miriam had just started to get a cramp in her leg when Kate, who had been watching through binoculars, squealed, "He's leaving!" Miriam peeked over the edge of her window. She saw Jack's car pull out of the driveway. He drove up the street. He was wearing his new fedora.

Miriam's father had been a serial philanderer. He liked dyed blonds with flower decals painted on their fingernails, women who did dance aerobics and read tabloid magazines and drank white zinfandel on ice. Woman whom he intuited were less likely to suspect him of philandering.

Miriam's mother had brown hair and never painted her nails. She was too observant, too empathic, too confrontational. Miriam blamed her, right after the divorce. She bought her father's narrative, because she wanted to believe that things could be fixed, if her mother chose to fix them. But after the second wife, then the third, the logic had worn off.

The cramp in Miriam's leg spread through her knee. Her hands felt clammy. Her stomach roiled. She could taste acid in the back of her throat, mingled with nicotine from the cigarette she'd snuck after breakfast. Jack's car passed them and turned right off Ravenswood Drive.

Holly peeled out of the driveway. Then she slammed on the breaks.

"Damn it!" she yelled. "Stupid deer!"

The deer stood in the middle of Ravenswood Drive. It stared at them, black-eyed and inquisitive.

Where is he?

Holly grunted. She edged the car closer to the deer.

"Holly, go!" Kate yelled. "He's getting away!"

Holly revved the engine. The deer blinked. Then it sprung to life and bounded away. But the car didn't move, and Holly sat staring at where the deer had been.

"Holly! Holly, go!"

"He's getting away!"

A tear rolled down her cheek.

Then she snapped back. She put her foot on the gas. The car made a whinnying noise, like a horse.

"Hurry!" Kate yelled. "He's getting away!"

Holly drove, but not fast. She turned the corner and continued down the main street at a moderate pace, as Jack's car got farther ahead. They would have lost him, but he stopped at a red light. They stopped behind him, three cars back. Holly unscrewed the cap on a silver travel mug. She took a long drink.

"Thirsty?" Miriam asked.

"Just a little afternoon pick-me-up," Holly replied.

The light turned green. The car rolled forward.

"Wait, what's in the mug?"

"Oh, just a tangerine juice with rum, and a squirt of lime."

"What?!" Kate yelled from the back seat. "You're *literally* drinking and driving?"

"You shouldn't drink and drive. What if you crash?"

"I drive better when I've had a little something to drink," Holly said. "That's what Tom says. He says otherwise my driving is choppy."

To demonstrate, Holly sped up. She glided through the next light as it turned from yellow to red. There was only one car in between them and Jack now. Miriam could see the back of Jack's head, the curve of his neck. She had buried her face in that neck. She had laced her hands around that neck when they kissed. She had shaved the scraggly hairs on the back of his neck between haircuts, but at some point she had stopped. She couldn't remember when. Someone else must shave them now. Maybe the other woman. She shuddered at the thought. Holly must have noticed, because she handed Miriam her travel mug of pick-me-up rum. Miriam took a sip, but it didn't help. She needed a cigarette to go with it. She needed this to not be happening.

Holly adjusted her blond beehive and zipped through another yellow light. She kept a safe tailing distance behind Jack. Until Jack made a right turn, pulled up to the curb, and stopped.

Holly turned and drove past him. She pulled into a parking spot halfway down the block.

"Did he see us?"

"I don't think so," Kate said. She looked out the back window with her binoculars. "He's getting out of his car."

"Keep low," Holly said. "And don't turn around. It'll look suspicious. Here, pretend you're fixing your lipstick and watch him through the mirror." Holly handed Miriam a tube of poppy red. She applied the lipstick. She adjusted her wig. She watched the mirror for Jack. She saw him close his car door. He wore a brown suit coat and dark jeans. He straightened his fedora and nodded at his reflection in the car window.

"He's coming this way," said Kate. She stashed the binoculars in her purse and slid down in her seat.

"Just try to act normal," Holly said. She took another swig from her travel mug and fluffed her beehive.

Jack walked toward their car. But then he turned and crossed the street—skipping—and headed toward the coffee shop on the other side.

"Oh my god, is he skipping?" Holly said.

"He's skipping," Kate replied, nodding.

"This isn't good," Holly said.

The coffee shop was called the Brew Nest. From the outside, it looked like the coffee shop near Jack and Miriam's first apartment, a cozy place with worn rattan chairs and an overflowing shelf of books and board games, and a covered porch in the back, strung with colored lights, where she would read and Jack would study, their legs touching beneath the table.

"What's he doing?" Holly asked.

"I can't tell," said Kate. She watched through the binoculars. "It looks like he's talking to someone."

"Let me see," Holly instructed. Kate handed over the binoculars. "He's definitely talking to someone. It's a woman... She... Oh, shoot, I lost them."

They passed the binoculars around, but for thirty or so minutes, they saw no sign of Jack. They debated whether one of them, Kate or Holly, should go into the coffee shop to investigate, but they decided against it.

Then Jack reappeared outside the coffee shop with the woman. Miriam wanted to look away, but instead she stared. The woman was young, with thick blond hair pulled into a ponytail. She had perky breasts and a trim waist and big beamy eyes. She was lovely. She smiled, adoringly it seemed, at Jack. Jack smiled back.

"Look at her," said Holly. She prodded her beehive self-consciously.

"She's so young," said Kate.

Jack said something that made the woman laugh. She reached

out and touched his arm casually. Her fingernails were painted a deep reddish brown, the color of a squashed bug.

Miriam couldn't watch anymore.

"Can we go?" she said.

"But what if they—"

"I don't want to see it. Please, let's just go."

Jack wore a big, cackling grin. He said something clever. The pretty blond laughed.

"Wait," said Holly. "We need to get a picture. For, you know, court."

"It's not going to help her in court, if they're just standing there like that," said Kate. "You've got to get a picture of them kissing."

"I don't want to see. Please. Let's go."

But she didn't need to argue, because Jack and the woman said goodbye, without kissing, and Holly quickly turned on the car and drove away before he could catch them.

LOVE NOTES

MIRIAM WOKE UP COLD. All the covers were piled on Jack's side of the bed, but Jack wasn't there. She put on her robe and her slippers and went downstairs. She found a note on the kitchen counter.

Went in to work early.
Love, Jack

Naturally.

She scooped her husband's note off the counter and dropped it in the trash. She woke up the children. She made breakfast. Strawberries and English muffin for Lindsey, who licked each strawberry like a lollipop and who would still have half a muffin left when they got to school. Banana and Cheerios for Rory, who had embarked on a culinary beige phase, to the exclusion of all non-beige foods.

After making breakfast, she brushed her teeth. Jack's toothbrush was still damp.

No stale morning breath for his *hard* day at "work."

No, no, no, she would not torture herself. She would not. She just needed a cigarette. She needed to get laid, but Jack spent all his energy on "work." There was no libido left for her.

She would not do this. Unless she found real proof. Like

lipstick on his collar. Thong panties crumpled in his coat pocket. Love notes in his desk drawers. *XOXO. Can't wait for tonight, Big Man!* Miriam had once found a note just like that in her father's desk drawer. The loopy handwriting didn't belong to her father's wife, whichever wife that was at the time.

That wife had been perky and tan and blond, like the woman she saw with her husband and unlike Miriam, with her sallow February complexion, her deepening wrinkles, her brown hair threaded with early gray. She examined the fine lines spidering out from the corners of her eyes, the fret lines on her forehead, the gooseskin of her neck. She untied the belt on her terry cloth robe. She looked down at her pendulous breasts, her stretch marks, her puckered belly, her gnarled veins. Her legs were a canvas for the blue-purple marker scribbles of children. Her children had made these veins pop, as they grew inside her womb, as they changed her.

She hadn't looked like this when she met Jack.

She had looked like the most beautiful woman he had ever seen. He was effusive.

Now he was terse. He signed his short note with a simple closing: *Love, Jack.* Simple enough to write out of reflex. Because over the years, fervor became fondness. Adulation settled into habit. Affections were shed to shorten the routine. *I love you* became *Have a good day* became *Don't forget to stop at the post office.* Bedtime sex became a good-night kiss, soon forgotten, sporadically at first, then more and more, until it wasn't there anymore to forget.

She almost wished Jack had made this easier. He could have just made his cheating blatant, instead of pretending it was "work."

She got the kids ready and delivered them to school, Rory to his preschool class and Lindsey to kindergarten. Then she canceled her first appointment and spent the rest of the morning doing things she knew she shouldn't be doing. But Jack had forced her to this point.

She smoked a cigarette on the back deck. Then she rifled through her husband's things.

In his drawers she found folded shirts, balled-up socks, pairs of jeans that Jack never got to wear because he couldn't wear jeans to work, because jeans had a negative correlation with billable hours. She searched the pockets of his suit pants, finding nothing. She sniffed the crotch of each pair for clues. They smelled like laundry and crayons. Like Jack, though not quite.

She smoked another cigarette and then searched his desk. He rarely used the desk, because he liked to work at the kitchen table, to visibly remind her that work took priority. She checked the drawers in his bedside table. She examined his jackets and sweaters for stray blond hairs. She looked beneath the bed, aware, as she slid her hand between the mattress and the box spring, of just how ridiculous and pitiful she was.

Jack would never hide paper love notes under his mattress. He would send them via text, or through a messaging app, like a regular modern male.

This didn't stop her from also searching the coat that Jack had tossed over a dining room chair, so that she could hang it up for him. And there, in one of the pockets, she found a matchbook. The matchbook cover was printed with the words *Mossy Glen Inn and Spa,* above a picture of a heart-shaped tree. Most of the matches had been used.

She had never been to the *Mossy Glen Inn and Spa.* But the

matchbook design made it seem like a place where a person (not her) might get laid. And Jack had opportunities. He'd done an "overnight deposition" last month, and two nights of "witness interviews" the month before.

Miriam called the telephone number listed on the matchbook.

"Good morning, Mossy Glen Inn and Spa. How can I help you?"

"Um, my husband may have stayed there not too long ago, and, um... he thinks he might have left his phone charger there."

"That happens all the time. I'll check to see if we've got it. Do you know when he stayed here?"

"I don't remember exactly."

"What's your husband's name?"

"Jack Shipley."

"Let's see...." The receptionist clicked on his keyboard. "It doesn't look like we've got a record of him staying here."

"Oh, well, thanks."

Miriam hung up the phone. Maybe Jack had used a fake name. Maybe she should just call Jack and confront him directly, instead of searching his pockets.

She called his cell phone, uncertain whether she would confront him or continue to pretend that everything was okay. The call went straight to voicemail. She called his work number. His secretary answered the phone.

"Good morning, Rufus Mather."

"Hi, Doreen, this is Miriam."

"Miriam...?"

"Jack's wife. Is Jack in?

"Oh, hi, *Miriam.* Um, no, he's not. He's... Oh, wait, uh, yes. He's here. But he's in a meeting."

"Do you know when he'll be done?"

"Um, noon-ish? Should I let him know you called?"

"That's all right, I'll just call back later."

As soon as she hung up the phone, the doorbell rang.

"Flower delivery, for a... Mrs. Miriam Shipley," a delivery man said as she opened the door. He handed her a large bouquet of red and pink roses, already in a vase. There was a tiny envelope taped to the vase. Miriam opened it. She read the card inside.

To my wife, the most beautiful woman I've ever met. For you, I would set my hair on fire. I would leap off a bridge. I would eat these roses, thorns and all. I would leave everything I've worked for behind.

CONSPIRACY!

WHILE JACK DID WHATEVER or whoever it was that Jack was doing, Miriam got to take the children to the grocery store. She got to listen to them complain while she stuffed their limp feet into shoes and scooted them out the door. They complained through most of the drive, until they decided that at the store, they would ride the germy car-cart and pick sugary breakfast cereals. Lindsey liked chocolate rice crisps. She ate the crisps one at a time, as their crisp turned to sludge. Rory liked puffy sugar-coated corn, blandly sweet and beige.

Miriam parked. Rory squirmed out of his seat belt and launched himself into the front seat. He liked to climb out the driver's-side door so he could honk the horn on his way. He banged the steering wheel. He left little dirty footprints on the seat.

Lindsey waited for her seat belt to unbuckle itself. She disembarked from the passenger vehicle like an astronaut taking her first steps on the pavement-gray surface of the moon.

"Mom, make her hurry!" Rory whined. "If she takes too long, all the car-carts will be gone!"

Near the Value Valley entrance stood a woman holding a neon-green hand-printed sign. The sign said, simply: CONSPIRACY! There was a circle drawn around CONSPIRACY! with lines coming out of it, like a child's drawing of the sun.

The Conspiracy! woman wore a black sweatshirt with the pink logo of a pharmaceutical company. She grinned at Miriam as she approached the entrance. Her teeth were white and perfect. Miriam glanced back at the woman after they passed her. The other side of the woman's sign had a different message: WHERE ARE MY CHICKENS?

The first car-cart—a red-and-yellow plastic two-seater with a shopping basket on the back end—was incurably sticky. Even after several antibacterial wipes, it still had a tacky film.

Rory complained: "But I want car-cart!"

And I want a cigarette and a good fuck, she thought. *But that isn't happening.*

Miriam silently retrieved the next car-cart in the corral. She wiped it down.

"I'm driving!" Rory scrambled into the car-cart.

"You drove last time!" Lindsey shoved her brother out of the way.

The Conspiracy! woman stared at them. She swiveled her sign, back, forth, back, forth. She smiled, with either pity or condescension. Her teeth were absurdly white.

Miriam wheeled the cumbersome car-cart through the aisles while her children bickered in the front seat. They bargained for four cereals, two with pictures of cartoon animals on the box and two that claimed to be natural and enriched. She steered the car-cart into the bakery section. As she selected bread, she noticed the Conspiracy! woman hovering near a table of sugary baked goods in clear plastic packaging. She also had a car-cart, but no children bickering in its front seat.

"Can we get cupcakes?" Rory asked.

"I want cupcakes!"

Miriam let the kids pick a box of yellow cupcakes with white cream frosting. *Enriched,* claimed the label on its packaging.

"It's not really 'enriched,' " the Conspiracy! woman said, approaching as Miriam put the cupcakes in her cart. "Who knows what it is, really. It could be anything."

"Uh-huh." Miriam nodded. She wasn't in the mood to engage with crazy.

"I saw how you looked at me outside," the Conspiracy! woman said. "I get it. You think I'm crazy as a clown fish."

"I, um—" Miriam wanted to leave, but the other woman's car-cart had created a traffic jam.

"But I'll tell you this. Things are disappearing. No one's talking about it, but oh, they should be. They should be! You've got something, and then, *poof!* Just like that, it's gone."

An image of Jack flashed through Miriam's mind. Jack, with a smile on his face. Jack with his eyes fixed on her. His hands. His lips. The shape of his body in the darkness of their bedroom, as he pulled her on top of him.

A cry rippled through her. "I—" She looked at the woman, but her mind saw Jack. She stuttered. "I—I'm sure—things don't just disappear—I mean, for no reason—"

"I don't know the reason. But I know it's happening. You can feel it. Like a crackle in the air. Right before the lightning strikes."

The Conspiracy! woman put a package of cupcakes in her own car-cart, then turned and walked away. Miriam saw her again at the checkout counter, one line over. Her car-cart was full of groceries. She paid with a credit card. She slid the card into a billfold in a leather purse.

Miriam followed the Conspiracy! woman into the parking lot. The woman opened the trunk of a glossy, new Rolls-Royce. She loaded her groceries and her neon-green sign into the car. Then she patted the car gently, got in, and drove away.

Jack's car was in the driveway when they got home. Rory wormed out of his seat belt. He dove over the back seat. He swam through the grocery bags in search of treasure. Miriam pried the cupcakes from his hands and carried him inside, as he kicked and squirmed. She returned for the groceries, and for the elder child, who sat still buckled in the back seat.

"Lindsey, come on, hurry it up," she said, for the billionth time.

Jack was inside on the couch, watching the news. He turned it off and helped her carry the groceries into the kitchen.

"You're home from work early." It was only six.

"Um, yeah..." Jack replied, suspiciously.

"But you're probably working from home tonight?"

"A bit, yeah... Did you, um, get the flowers I sent?"

The flowers were on the kitchen table right in front of him, looking lovely and suspicious.

"Yes. Thanks. But what's the occasion?"

"No occasion. Do I need an occasion?"

She didn't know what to say, so she snuck out onto the back deck to smoke a cigarette, while Jack the Suspicious put away groceries, for probably the first time in his tenure as Dad. He put everything away in the wrong spots. But, as she fixed the disorder he'd brought to the fridge, Miriam told herself it was the thought that counted. Unless the thought centered on concealing your infidelity.

They ate dinner as a family. Rory sucked down his chicken and potato, but he wouldn't touch his corn until he received his cupcake. He scooped a hole in the middle of the cupcake and filled it with corn paste.

"Gross." Lindsey sculpted a corn-caterpillar on her plate and then ate it one kernel-leg at a time.

Jack told them all about the news. "There's a city in Texas that has officially declared that it's seceding from the US."

"Uh-huh."

"They had to send in the National Guard."

"Oh?"

"There's been a series of bizarre bank robberies."

"Uh-huh."

"The robbers are all dressed like police. Except, S-E-X-Y police. With short shorts and thigh-high boots."

Okay, maybe that bit was interesting.

"There've been several sightings of a ship off the coast of Greece that doesn't really exist."

Miriam shivered. "How can there be sightings of something that doesn't exist?"

"I don't know. But it couldn't have been the ship people claimed because *that* ship was at a port in Italy. And the people who saw it near Greece claimed it appeared and then vanished right in front of them. So logically," Jack the Sleuth deduced, "either the sightings are fabricated, or hallucinated. Or the ship does exist, but for some reason its existence is being covered up. But the question is *why*. . . ."

After they put the kids to bed, Miriam snuck out to smoke another cigarette. She lit her cigarette and crept around the side of the house, to the kitchen window where she could spy on Jack. He opened his laptop. As it booted up, he walked over to the liquor cabinet, reached for the bottle of whiskey, and took a swig, straight from the bottle. His face puckered in disgust. He tucked the bottle back into the cabinet and took a package of mints out of his pocket and popped one into his mouth. Then he sat down at his laptop and began to type.

Miriam smoked a second cigarette. When she finished it, she sprayed herself with the bottle of perfume she kept hidden in the bushes and went inside, to the kitchen. As she approached, Jack lowered the screen on his laptop so that she couldn't see it.

"You smell nice," he said.

Not nice enough to get laid that night.

"Busy with work?" Miriam asked.

"Oh yes, very busy," he replied, suspiciously.

THE OTHER WOMAN

THE NEXT MORNING, Miriam woke early in an empty bed. Jack had left another note: *Had to work early again. I'll be home for dinner. Love, Jack.* She folded the note and tucked it into her purse. She woke the children, dressed them, fed them, and delivered them to school. She met with a patient by video call. Then her second appointment canceled, so instead she met Holly and Kate for their morning coffee break.

"The flowers are totally suspicious," Kate said, after Miriam described the delivery. "He's trying to cover something up."

"Or make amends," said Holly. She took a flask from her purse, unscrewed the cap, and poured some into her coffee cup. "Oh my gosh, Kate! Your hair! I just noticed it looks different."

"Thanks," Kate said. "I'm going all natural. No more dye. And I've given up using products." Her dyed-blond hair had a greasy sheen. Natural browns and grays sprouted at the roots.

"What do you mean *all* products? What about shampoo?"

"Shampoo strips away the natural beneficial bacteria," Kate said. "You don't see cats and dogs using shampoo, do you?"

"Um..."

"But it takes a few bad hair days to restore the bacterial balance."

“Okay, no thanks.” Holly took a sip of coffee. She frowned, then added another splash of liquor. “It’s just for flavor.”

“So I’m thinking I should just confront Jack,” Miriam said. “If he is cheating, I’d rather know.”

“Do it,” Holly said.

“I don’t know,” said Kate. “If he’s not—”

“If he is—”

“If he’s not, you’ll look sneaky and jealous.”

“I am sneaky and jealous.”

“But he doesn’t need to *know* how sneaky and jealous you are. I still think you need to get proof before you say something.”

“But if he isn’t cheating, there won’t be any proof of cheating,” Miriam said. “And I’ll never know for sure if I don’t confront him.”

“Still, it might be worth poking around some more,” Kate said. “Have you even checked his text messages?”

“Well, no . . .”

“What about that Jessica woman?” Holly said. “The ‘partner.’ Why don’t we try and track her down?”

“I don’t know,” Miriam said. “I mean, I don’t want to make things weird for him at work.”

She did kind of want to make things weird for him at work.

“We can look her up on the firm’s website,” Kate said, barreling ahead.

Holly found the firm’s website on her phone. “There’s only one Jessica.” She held her phone where they could see. Jessica Scriber, senior partner. The website had a brief biography of the woman, but no picture.

"That settles it," Holly said. "We need to do a reconnaissance mission."

"Uh, what exactly do you mean by *reconnaissance*?" Miriam asked.

"We'll go to Jack's office and scope her out."

"But they'll recognize me."

"You can wait in the car. Kate and I will go in."

"Don't you have to go back to work?"

"My schedule is flexible," said Kate.

"And I'll call in sick," said Holly.

"But what if Jack's there? What if he sees you?"

"We'll wear our disguises."

Miriam wore her baseball cap with fake blond ponytail, bright red lipstick, a pair of fake glasses. She waited alone in Holly's car, at a parking meter outside Jack's office building, while her friends did reconnaissance inside. She thought about what the Conspiracy! woman had said: Things were disappearing. Things were *poof!* There was a crackle in the air, a faint scent of something burning, an even fainter scent of the faraway sea.

She shivered, as a man walked by who might have been Jack. But he wasn't Jack. All these men who passed on the sidewalk, in their suits, their ties, their polished shoes, they might have been Jack. But they weren't. Jack might have been someone else. He might have turned his back and flashed his middle fingers at Work. He might have loved her so hard she didn't have to wonder.

The building's revolving door turned. Holly and Kate burst out.

Holly's beehive hung lopsided. Kate's red bob was unmistakably a wig. They ran giggling toward the car.

"What happened?" Miriam asked, as they climbed in.

"This old guy totally hit on Kate in the elevator," said Holly.

Kate laughed. "He asked me to go out dancing with him. He must have liked my wig."

"No, I mean, with Jessica?" Miriam clarified.

"Oh, she wasn't there," Holly said. "But you know, there's this new restaurant just around the corner that I've been wanting to try. It's supposed to be fabulous. Let's go out for lunch."

The restaurant had white tablecloths and a prix fixe menu. They took off their wigs and glasses for lunch.

"The wigs are all just plastic fibers," Kate said. "You don't want to wear them more than necessary. You don't want the plastic to accumulate in your body."

Holly rolled her eyes. "The only thing I want in my body right now is this cocktail."

Miriam scanned the restaurant for Jack. Jack and a pretty blond. Jack with his hand on a pencil-skirted butt. Miriam had never worn a pencil skirt. Maybe that was her problem.

She didn't see Jack, or the pretty blond. But there was an older woman who sat alone at a table by the window, with a bowl of soup and a stack of papers. She wore a black skirt-suit, pantyhose, and low black heels. She had gray hair, chopped short. She looked familiar, though Miriam didn't know from where, until the woman turned and looked straight at her.

This woman looked like a lawyer.

She stood up. She walked toward Miriam.

"Mrs. Shipley? Miriam—did I get that right?"

"Um, yes."

"I thought I recognized you. I don't know if you remember me from the holiday party. I'm a partner at Rufus Mather. Jessica Scriber."

Miriam sat up straight in her chair. Kate squeezed her hand. Holly took a gulp of cocktail.

Jessica.

Her eyes were old and sad. Her lips were pinched. Her hands shook slightly.

"Oh, that's right. Jessica. I'm terrible with names. It's nice to see you."

"You too, dear. You know we really do miss Jack. You and Jack have two kids, right? How are they doing?"

"Oh, they're good."

"That's so good to hear.... I never had a family. I was always too busy working, I suppose.... Anyway, please do tell Jack I said hello. And tell him we all hope things are going well for him."

INTERLUDE

THE LONG-DISTANCE RUNNER

IMAGINE YOU are a long-distance runner.

You run marathons and ultra-marathons and once you ran for Mozambique's Olympic running team. You run for medals, but also for joy. Because you can. Because you love the rhythm of your body on the trail, the wind and sun on your face, the meditation. Running is prayer.

Run, far enough, fast enough, and maybe you will catch God.

Imagine you are running along a trail. Around you, there is no one. It is just you and the blue sky and the baobab trees. You and the trail, and your feet, and your legs, which have served your life so well.

You and the music from your earbuds, the songs curated to pace your run. Until, quite suddenly, the song cuts out and a different song plays instead. A song you have never heard before.

You like this new song and would have added it to your playlist if you'd heard it before, but you have not, and this distracts you. And this distraction is why you do not see the rock on the trail.

Your foot catches. Your ankle twists. You hear a snap. You feel a bolt of pain. The worst pain you have felt in your entire life. Pain like death. You scream, and no one hears you. You scream, and you are alone, and you might die alone, out on that trail, miles from anywhere, with your broken leg.

It is not dying that scares you.

What scares you is that you might not run again.

You scream, and the pain shoots up, around, an arrow through your heart, and you pray, *Please God mercy, let me do what I am born to do*. You scream and—

—then the pain is gone.

Your earbuds play the first song, the one you knew.

You don't know how, but you are running.

You imagined it, you tell yourself. The broken leg. The new song. None of it happened. It wasn't real. You will tell yourself it wasn't real, again and again, until the lie becomes true.

FLASHBACK

MIRIAM + JACK

THE MAN SHOULD send flowers. Roses. Overpriced bouquets with sonnets the man had written himself. The man should serenade. Under her window, on a starlit night. The man should offer heart and soul and cunnilingus, if he wanted his proposal to be met with acceptance.

A gift might also help. Like a puppy.

"What about a goat?" the man asked.

"Where would I keep the goat?"

"A flock of chickens?"

"For my mom. For me, a puppy."

"Noted."

And then the man should drop to his knees. He should gaze up, in adoration, as joyful tears of love streamed from his eyes.

"That last part is a little much."

"What? Why?"

"Well, for starters, I don't think I can produce love-tears. And even if I could, I don't think they would stream. Leak maybe. But not stream."

"You could squirt yourself in the eye with some lemon juice. That might create the same effect."

"Fantastic. That's the thing to do, right before I propose. Squirt lemon juice in my eye. But you know what?"

"What?"

"I'd squirt lemon juice in my eyes for you."

Jack jumped up. He ran to the fridge. He grabbed a lemon-shaped squeeze bottle.

"No!" Miriam snatched the bottle from his hand.

Jack dropped to his knees. He begged. "Please, oh most beautiful goddess, holder of my heart, tormentor of my loins. Please let me squirt this juice in my eyes for you!"

He would blind himself, if he could sear his brain with the sight of her beauty. This was true.

Also true: His eye had begun to wander.

It wasn't hips or lips or breasts, but the lush leather seats in the conference room of Rufus Mather LLP, the firm's box seats at the stadium, the white tablecloth luncheons, the black-tie fundraiser galas. The view, from the twenty-third-floor office, at sunset, when all the city lights sparkled on and the river gleamed silver, studded with the diamond crests of summer waves. He gazed down with the dreamy eyes of an intern. He took a riverboat cruise with the other interns. He shook hands with judges, executives, senators, jockeying with the other interns for position. Not all of them would win a corner office. Not all of them would strive the hardest, and none of them had to strive over the summer.

The internship was just a taste.

The man came home at exactly five p.m. "In just a few years, if I make partner, we could have a beach vacation house."

The man slept in late on Saturday. "Of course we'd hire a housekeeper. And a nanny, for the kids."

The man took a lazy bike ride on a Sunday afternoon. "But wouldn't it be swell to spend sunny afternoons cruising around the river on our boat?"

The woman, alone, was practical. "You know it won't be like this, if you take a job at this firm. You know they wine you and dine you now, but later, it'll be nothing but work."

He nodded, shrugged. *Of course* he knew how it worked. He wasn't a dolt.

Still, he'd gotten a taste.

But he had paid attention. His wandering gaze circled, always, back to her.

He was a fledgling corporate lawyer, not a poet. Still, he wrote a poem and left it on the kitchen counter:

My lady love,
My love for you swells like a tsunami
It sweeps away my heart.
The way I love you shakes me like an earthquake
It breaks my soul apart.
My love for you is like a flooding river,
a lightning strike, a hurricane, a gale.
Compared to it
All other things in life doth pale.

She laughed at the word *doth*. At the thought of Jack penning this verse. At her good fortune, to be loved like this.

She had, at that moment, in that lazy golden summer, the two things her heart wanted most. She had Jack, and she had time.

She made herself an omelet and a cup of coffee and she sat

and read her novel, until someone knocked on the door.

Flower delivery.

An armful of red roses, with a note, from Jack:

To my beautiful Miriam: Compared to
you, these roses smell like poo.

He was a terrible poet. She laughed, and found a vase for the roses, but before she'd cut the stems, there was another knock on her door.

Another delivery of roses.

Another note.

For you, dearest Miriam, I would sleep every night on
a bed of thorns. I would suffer un-scratchable itches.
I would let myself be stung by a thousand bees.

Which was prophetic, because the next flower delivery came with a stowaway bee. It shot out from the bouquet, right at her face. Miriam swatted it away. She ran into the bathroom and slammed the door shut.

She sat there, wondering what to do, until there was another knock on the door. She made a break. She flung open the door. The bee buzzed past her head, out into the hallway.

"Oh good," she said to an armful of flowers.

The roses kept coming. She ran out of vases. She ran out of items to substitute for vases. The bathtub was filled with roses. The apartment reeked of roses. She went out onto the fire escape with her book and a glass of iced tea.

Jack appeared on the sidewalk below. He had a boom box, black, the size of a briefcase. He held it up over his head.

"I can't sing!" he yelled.

She laughed.

He lip-synched to a playlist of the cheesiest love songs. He danced. He was a terrible dancer. But it didn't matter.

He blew kisses. He bowed. He tipped his hat. For a moment, he disappeared.

Poof!

Then there was a knock on the door. A scratch. A whimper.

She opened the door, to Roxster.

He wasn't yet called Roxster. He was still a puppy, a fluffy black-and-white border collie. He had a red ribbon tied around his neck. He sniffed her. He licked her shin. She bent down and stroked his head. A glint of something caught her eye. She untied the red ribbon. A ring slid off. It clunked on the floor. It had a dazzling chunk of diamond. She picked it up and slid it onto her finger.

Jack watched from the elevator window. Happy love-tears leaked from his eyes. He pulled open the elevator gate and stepped out. He dropped down onto his knees.

"Miriam..."

He took her hand. He didn't need to say anything else.

FLASHBACK

BRATTY

HE WAS SILENT as a starfish.

He was placid as a peregrine.

He was not supposed to watch TV. Was not supposed to sit on the couch. Was not supposed to eat snacks before dinner. Was not supposed to wear socks in the house if those socks had been inside his shoes. Was not supposed to exist.

When you were silent, when you were placid, you heard things like: *We're still paying for your mistake,* which in the context of *Look at this stain on Bradford's shirt! Now we have to throw it out* meant that he, Bradford, was the mistake.

He wasn't stupid, despite what she said. He made deductions. He strategized. He decided not to ask his dad, because his dad was compromised.

Instead, he asked Tommy to ask his mom. Tommy's mom trafficked in gossip. She also baked chocolate chip cookies, and those cookies made their way to Brad's house, where he hid them in his closet.

He ate one now, out in the open, on the white couch. Crumbs fell on the white rug. He would vacuum them up, because he didn't have a dog to lick them up, because dogs were filthy creatures.

Not that it would make a difference, his stepmom said. *Living with Bradford is just like living with a dog, except he's less obedient and talks back.*

He knew in his heart he was more wolf than dog, but he stayed silent.

He turned on the TV. He rested his feet on the coffee table. His socks were dirty. His ears were attuned to the garage door sound. He would hear the door open, would hear her car pull in, her door slam shut. If he hadn't run by then, she would catch him, in the living room, existing.

He kept the TV volume low to be safe. He put on a movie. *Peregrine,* starring Ricardo Merman as Detective Eddie Tides. *I don't know how you can watch that dumb movie again and again,* Helena said, every time she caught him. He had watched the movie at least a hundred times. He'd memorized the lines. He imagined how it would feel to sleuth, to solve, to unravel the mystery. To board the old catamaran and set sail, like the detective did at the end, toward the shining future. To put these years, in this house, with its white rugs and white walls and white sofa that existed not for sitting but as a symbol, all behind him, until they faded into the background of his life. They would matter less and less, until one day they didn't matter at all.

He didn't care what Helena said, because she was a misery storm, a deluge, a gale that would blow past him. One day, she wouldn't matter.

Today, she didn't matter.

She didn't catch him. The movie ended. He heard a noise. A

knock. He startled. But it was just Tommy at the door.

"Hey, dude." Tommy brought fresh cookies, still warm. "Whatcha watchin'?"

"*Peregrine.* It's over though."

Tommy flipped through the channels until he landed on his favorite TV show, about a globe-traversing boat with a dog captain and a crew of animals. The episode on TV was a season seven rerun, from the five-episode stretch where the SS *Deliverance* got lost at sea. Captain Barksford had steered them south to avoid a hurricane, but the hurricane shifted course and caught them. It destroyed the boat's navigation and communication and electrical systems. The navigator—a turtle that season—had to chart a course by the stars. The giraffe fell overboard twice. The lion, fatigued from a diet of cold raw fish, menaced the crew. The first mate got scurvy. (A violent disease downplayed for the youthful audience.) These were not happy times aboard the SS *Deliverance*. But somehow, the sorrow and struggle seemed like background. In the foreground, stark against the flat sky and gray sea, was camaraderie, ingenuity, perseverance. Growth. The lion could have killed and eaten the giraffe, but he saved the giraffe instead. The giraffe could have let her fear of water drive her off the show, but in season eight, she learned to swim.

"I love this episode," Tommy said. "Would you rather be stuck in the body of the giraffe, or the lion? Just for this episode."

"The lion. I'd rather be hungry than almost drown."

"Me too." Tommy reached for another cookie. A chocolate chip crumbled off and fell to the floor. He picked it up, but it left behind a small brown stain. "Oh. Sorry—"

"It's okay," Bradford said.

"We could get the bleach. Or—"

"Leave it."

"I'm sorry. I don't want you to get in trouble."

"It doesn't matter what I do. I still get in trouble."

"That's lame."

"You know, someday... someday I'm gonna cover this whole place in mud. All over the carpets, the walls, all the furniture. Dirt and mud everywhere."

Tommy laughed. "I hope I get to watch."

"Yeah... yeah me too."

"Oh, hey, so, um, Brad?"

"Yeah?"

"There's something I gotta tell you."

"What?"

"You remember how you asked me to ask my mom about your mom and dad, and, well—?"

"Yeah."

"She told me," Tommy said. "She told me not to tell you. But she said your mom was— She said your mom didn't exactly fit in at the country club. Which is stupid, because why does it matter if you fit in at the country club or not? Unless you're my mom and that's all that matters. But she said your parents weren't married."

"I knew that."

"And that they didn't plan to have you. You just happened."

Bradford considered this. On the television, Captain Barksford took the wheel. His first mate gazed out over the churning sea. The scene reminded Bradford of something, but he wasn't sure what. It felt both familiar and completely new.

One day, the clouds would lift and the waves would be smooth and blue and none of this would matter. But not yet. Today, Bradford was still stuck in the storm. "So . . . I guess I was . . . a mistake."

"No," Tommy said. "No, that's not what it means. You exist. That means you're supposed to exist. No, I think it's more like . . . like a miracle."

MARCH

THE PARTY CRUISE

MR. YAY WANTED a bottle of rum from the duty-free shop.

He wanted to run down the moving walkway.

He wanted a hot flight attendant in a short skirt who would initiate him into the Mile High Club.

"I'm only a little high right now," he said, as they meandered through the concourse. "Not a whole mile. Or eight miles. Fuck, that's an awesome song. Dude, what if someday, someone made a movie about us?"

Mr. Yay was elated.

He wore his sunglasses in the airport, and the pirate hat, because it wouldn't fit in his carry-on. He and Bratty had matching shirts, yellow, printed with an image of Tux in the same hat, plus eye patch, tongue out. A string of rainbow drool dripped from his jowls and puddled into a name: MR. YAY.

As Mr. Yay passed, heads turned. Kids pointed. People stared, perplexed, because he reminded them of something they had seen before, though they didn't know when or what. There was an unmistakable spark of recognition in their eyes.

Just a spark.

Every blaze started with a spark.

Mr. Yay had four lighters, a coffee can packed with flower, a package of 25 mg gummies, and now a bottle of rum. The pockets of his baggy jeans were stuffed with airplane bottles of rum. His jeans were excessively baggy, enough jean to make the sail of a boat.

"Would you rather live on a boat, forever and ever," he asked, "or never see the sea again?"

"Depends," Bratty said. "Have we already taken the cruise?"

"No. You gotta answer now, before the cruise."

"Then I'm on the boat forever."

Captain Barksford—the first through tenth Captain Barksfords—lived and died aboard the SS *Deliverance*. Their bodies were buried at sea. The eleventh Captain Barksford was still alive when the show ended. He moved to a Manhattan penthouse. He did the celebrity talk show circuit. But he still dined on fresh fish. Bratty recalled the article he'd read last year—"A Captain's Life, After the Series Finale." He recalled the pain of wanting a dog and not having a dog.

He missed his dog.

"On second thought . . . are dogs allowed on the boat?"

"The fuck kind of boat would it be, if you couldn't take your dog?"

"Uh, a party cruise?"

"Point."

"Yeah, that's the only problem with this cruise."

"Maybe next year, I'll headline," Tommy said. "And as a headliner, I'll make demands. Dogs for everyone. Packs of dogs just roaming the deck, swimming in the pools, dancing at the shows. Fuckin' glorious."

They sat down at the gate. Twenty minutes till boarding. Bratty scrolled on his phone. He had emails from venues in LA, Santa Barbara, Santa Cruz, San Francisco. He had a hundred-some comments on the last pic he'd posted to Mr. Yay's UniTab page, plus a dozen DMs. Everyone wanted more dog. He opened the app for Boogie Boat. Four nights of music aboard the *Vibe Siren*, the grooviest vessel on the high seas. Tickets sold out. He stared at the lineup.

Tommy stared at the lineup.

"Holy ship," he murmured. "This is sick as fuck."

It was sick as fuck.

There, in tiny font, on the lineup undercard, was *Mr. Yay*.

"Dude, that's you," Bratty said.

"It's us."

"It's you."

"I still can't believe it."

"Yeah. Me neither."

"Yo, we're playing an actual festival."

It had happened like this: The Mr. Yay official email account got an email from the Boogie Boat official email account that said something like *Dear Mr. Yay, we would love you to play this year's Boogie Boat, are you interested in joining the lineup?* And Tommy was like WTF and Bratty was like WTF and for several hours they pretended it wasn't real. It couldn't be real. The shot-ski, that was real. The shots of Fireball were real. The dog on the couch was real, despite Bratty's initial suspicion that he was not. But then real money got wired and real airline tickets got sent and now they were about to board.

"But I miss my dog," Bratty said.

Tux, the Very Good Dog. Tuxmaster 3000. Pirate Tux, Pillager of Chicken.

Tux loved chicken. If Bratty ever got rich—like penthouse-and-celebrity-talk-show-circuit rich—he would hire a personal chef just to cook chicken for the dog, but with different sauces and seasonings, to expand the dog's palate.

Like Captain Barksford, Tommy had said in comparison and then explained how once, in season twelve, Captain Barksford ate a deep-fried-chicken-and-banana sandwich. And in season fifteen, he ate ghost pepper–marinated chicken, then retched for three hours. Not a good idea.

It was time to board.

"All aboard!" Tommy yelled. People turned to look at the weird pirate. Some looked away or rolled their eyes. In other eyes, there were sparks.

Tommy slipped airline bottles of rum to the flight attendants, and the pretty sisters in the row behind him, and the dude in the adjacent seat, because he liked the dude's hat.

Bratty was subdued, in the shadow of his best friend's largesse. Bratty was the steady beat, the anchor, the North Star. He slept the whole flight, LA to Miami, while Tommy made friends and emptied his pockets. Bratty dreamed of the dog, his dog, in otherworldly scenarios. His dog on a spaceship with a bunch of cats. His dog on a beach, covered in green goo. His dog in a desert at night, as a hole tore open in the space behind him and blackened hands reached out of it. His dream dog was a ghost, and he woke with a sense that his real dog existed, as his dog, only here and now: that only the precise sequence of facts and events that comprised the tapestry of this life would result in the best-friend-trio of Tommy plus Bratty plus Tux.

In the great glittering world, their union was unique.

The plane descended. There were the lights of Miami. There was the vast sea. There was an excited hum aboard the plane. Something had happened. Was happening. Who could say what it was?

Bratty didn't know. But he felt it. A shiver. A vibe. A dream-like swell that washed over everything. The captain turned on the lights. The plane touched down. Someone cheered, and the cheer spread through the cabin, a palpable, nonsensical excitement. It was just a regular cross-country flight, no weather, no delays, no turbulence.

"Tommy?" Bratty asked. The fasten seat belt light turned off. People stood up. They reached for their carry-ons. "Do you feel that?" He wasn't even sure what he was asking.

Tommy's eyes were glazed. He stared at the seatback, as if he could see through it, beyond it, to some distant place.

For a minute he didn't answer. Then he shook his head, and his eyes came into focus. "Holy ship." He laughed. "That was fun. Yo, this cruise is gonna be soooo fun."

"Yeah." Bratty smiled. That strange, shivery feeling abruptly faded. In its wake, he felt giddy.

They deplaned. They took a shuttle. They stopped to grab a drink with a guy Tommy had met on the plane, then again to pick up an unwanted pair of used water skis, which they could transform into water-shot-skis. Tommy had packed his glue gun.

They boarded the *Vibe Siren.* They had separate cabins on the starboard side, where all the musicians stayed. Bratty kept his head down, his sunglasses on. He didn't want to gawk at all the stars.

But holy-fucking-festival.

He gazed out the round window of his private cabin. The ocean view was surreal.

He ran laps around the upper deck. He was not quite Fatty Bratty anymore. He'd lost two notches from his belt. But he still felt flabby and awkward and not at all famous. He missed his dog.

Tux the Speedy Sprinter. Doggie McJoggerson. *Run, Tux, Run.*

He partied.

Maybe too hard that first night. Too many piña coladas in coconut cups. Too many shots from the water-shot-ski. Bratty danced on after his brain stopped recording. In the morning, he woke up on a lounge chair, poolside, beneath a blue sky tufted with white lace clouds. He ordered eggs and hash browns to his lounge chair. Coffee and mimosa. He drifted back to sleep. Tommy found him.

"Dude. I'm nervous."

"You're Tommy-Fucking-Fischer," Bratty said. "You're Mr. Yay. You don't get nervous."

Bratty was scared as shit.

"Okay, yeah, but this is like . . . it's not just local. This is a real festival. With real famous artists."

"You're famous."

"Just because that one music video—"

"It's not just that. It's—" Bratty couldn't articulate what it was. But in the pool, a woman on an inflatable raft drifted past, and when she saw Tommy, her eyes lit up.

"All I'm saying is, what if no one comes?"

"I don't think that'll happen," Bratty said, even though he'd had the same anxious vision of Tommy rapping for a crowd of no one.

"There are three overlapping sets. They're all gonna be fire."

"You'll be fire."

"*We'll* be fire."

A waiter brought Tommy a quart of orange juice and a bottle of champagne.

"Double-fisting?"

He drank straight from the bottle.

"What kind of rapper would I even be if I didn't drink breakfast champagne?"

They drank less the second day. Bratty went to bed in his own cabin that night. He could hear Tommy in the cabin next door, with a girl, then two or three. He fell asleep to the sounds of laughter, the throb of bass, the whir of the motor that propelled the *Vibe Siren* through the Party Sea.

On the third day, Mr. Yay was scheduled for an eight p.m. set on the Cabana Stage, the smallest stage, belowdecks. Tommy and Bratty waited in a tiny windowless room, which was supposed to be the green room someone had said, though it was painted blue. Bratty paced. Tommy lay on the floor and stared up at the ceiling, at the shadows of laser light. He took deep breaths. He might have been meditating, or zoning, or asleep. Bratty couldn't tell. Tommy was mostly always on, intensely present. But at odd moments he sometimes slipped away, to somewhere else.

The set before theirs ended. Bratty set up. He went backstage. His heart pounded. He could hear people out there. A crowd. He didn't speculate how big. But the room wasn't empty at least.

"Hey, you're up!"

The lights turned down. Bratty approached the DJ booth. He looked out at the dance floor. It was already packed. People poured through the doors. The hallway beyond was thick with people.

Somewhere, in that dense mass, a voice cried out: "We want Mr. Yay!"

BRATTY AND HIS THERAPIST

Bradford: *Okay, so see this little rubber duck toy here?*

Miriam: *Yeah.*

Bradford: *Let's say that's me. And this shot-ski, this is the timeline. Right here, this first shot glass, that's where we are now. March.*

Miriam: *Okay.*

Bradford: *And the next glass is April, then May, and then, oh, there's graduation! And the duck—me—I'm just going to keep moving forward along the shot-ski. Time just keeps slipping, right? And then I'm here. At graduation. And maybe my parents will try to show up, but security won't let them through because they don't have tickets and my dad will call me up like,* Bradford, what's going on? *but I won't answer the phone, because I never answer when he calls. I gotta steel myself for that shit. But he'll figure it out before I call him back, so then I won't ever have to tell him I dropped out.*

Miriam: *That's . . . a plan.*

Bradford: *The path of least resistance.*

Miriam: *Do you think it'll be worse, if you wait longer to tell him?*

Bradford: *Honestly . . . no. I'll be a disappointment no matter what. Even if I'd finished school—and maybe someday I will, but like, on my own terms—but even if I had, they'd be like,* You really should have gotten better grades, Bradford, *or* Too bad you didn't go to a decent school, Bradford. *They'd never be proud.*

Miriam: *But you know they're not right. You know you're not a disappointment.*

Bradford: *Yeah, yeah, I know, I got self-worth and shit. But like, I know, but I don't* really *know. All the things they said, their disappointment, their rejection, their cruelty, it's like a seed that took root, and sprouted and grew into this nasty tree. And I managed to cut it down—thanks, Doc—but the roots are still there. And sometimes little shooters blossom up from the stump, and I can hear her voice in my head, reminding me what a fuckup I am. But it's not even her voice anymore. It's my voice. (Pause.) Sometimes I wish . . . I could be more like Tommy. Not that I want to* be *him. I don't. But he doesn't have those fucked-up roots. He's totally rooted in himself. He's, like, one thousand percent pure Tommy, all the time. He's always been that way. But especially now—like with his rapping.*

Miriam: *Yeah, you told me about that. It's great.*

Bradford: *When he's onstage, he's just like, so fucking bright. He's like, Mr. Yay, but weirder and wilder. He's magnetic. He's— Wait, what is it?*

Miriam: *Sorry. You said* Mr. Yay, *and I... It's nothing...*

Bradford: *That's Tommy. Mr. Yay.*

Miriam: *Mr. Yay...*

Bradford: *Mr. Yay. But the rapper. I guess, so technically it's both of us. But he's the rapper. I just make the beats. He's just starting out, so you probably haven't heard of Mr. Yay, unless you're like, really deep in the rap scene, so— Doc, are you okay?*

Miriam: *I'm fine. It's just... when you said* Mr. Yay, *I don't know what came over me.*

THE MOLAR AND THE GREEN BEAN

JACK SAT at the kitchen table with his laptop. He plucked at the keys with his index fingers. He leaned back in his chair. He had a white mug with the Rufus Mather logo. He picked up the mug, took a sip, read whatever he had just written. He nodded in approval.

It was nine thirty on Wednesday night. Time for work.

Except was it work?

Miriam tried to stay casual, as she snuck a glance at his screen. But she couldn't see clearly, and when she moved closer, whatever had been there was replaced by the Rufus Mather home page. *Insight and Dedication: The Rufus Mather Way. Be a Part of the Rufus Mather Family. Abandon Your Own Family for the Rufus Mather Family. Our Loyalty to Billable Hours Gives You the Freedom to Work Yourself to Death.*

Miriam pretended not to be spying. She opened the cabinet and pretended to look for something inside. Jack pretended not to be waiting for her to leave. But she could feel him waiting. He shifted impatiently. He wanted her gone.

When she stepped away, Jack resumed typing with his single digits. It was a mystery how he'd gotten this far along in life without ever learning to properly type.

She felt an overwhelming urge to annoy him. To expel him. To poke holes in his I-have-to-work story, which seemed implausible now, after what that partner had said. *We all hope things are going well for him.* But Miriam hadn't confirmed. She should have asked: *What do you mean?* But instead she'd nodded and said *I sure will* and now she was here, playing spy.

She opened the cupboard door, then slammed it shut. She emptied the dishwasher. She banged dishes and silverware. She ran the garbage disposal. She coughed and sighed. She interrupted him.

"Whatcha drinking?"

"Oh, just some coffee."

"At this time of night?"

"I've got to keep alert. For work."

"I didn't see you make coffee."

"It's leftover."

"Right."

She stomped out of the room, then doubled back to the doorway. She listened to him type. She wasn't going to get a good look at his computer. She needed a ruse.

"Jack!" She improvised. "Jack! There's a spider!"

"What?"

"A spider!"

"What?"

"A spider. In the bathroom." She walked back into the kitchen. "Can you get it? Please? It was huge and gross."

"Okay." Jack grunted. He left the room. She ran over to check his computer. He had locked the screen.

"I don't see any spider!"

"Keep looking. It was right there in the tub."

She tried to guess his password, without success. She picked up his mug and took a sip. She tasted a trace of coffee, but mostly it was whiskey.

The next day, Jack went to work early (he said) and Miriam spent two hours constructing a giant papier-mâché tooth for the elementary school pageant. The tooth had leg- and armholes, and a hole on top where her daughter's head would stick out. Lindsey had been cast in the role of Molar in the kindergarten play on dental hygiene. *You don't HAVE to make a costume*, the teacher had said, which translated to *You must make a costume, or else be judged.*

Rory had taken advantage of the situation. The day before, after she had sketched out the costume and gathered the newspaper and cut it in strips for papier-mâché and was busy multitasking dog-puke cleanup and packing lunches and burning dinner, Rory struck. He could, at such an opportune moment, extract a promise that undistracted Mom would never make. Such as a custom tooth costume, so that he, too, could come dressed as a tooth to the elementary school pageant.

"Can I wear the toof costume now?" Rory asked, when she picked him up from preschool.

"What, now? In the car?"

"Can I wear the toof costume to school?" Rory asked, when he got home and put the costume on.

"Can I wear the toof to bed?" he asked, as they filed into the school auditorium. His costume was too wide. His arms stuck straight out of it, like the arms of a stick-figure human in a child's drawing.

She found empty seats for herself and Rory-the-Tooth. Lindsey was backstage. Jack didn't deserve a seat, because he wasn't coming. Not that she'd reminded him.

Right after she sat down, she spotted Holly. Holly waved. She hurried over and sat down next to Miriam.

"This better be the show of the century." Holly unscrewed the cap from a travel mug and took a large gulp. "Want some?"

"Um, no thanks."

"Yeah, it's not very good. It's just Fizz Wizard Limeonade and vodka. I was running late. I swear, what it took to make that damn costume."

"Yep."

Rory-the-Tooth squirmed in his chair.

"After those misadventures in sewing, I needed something," Holly said.

The auditorium lights dimmed. The audience hushed. The stage lights came on. A gaggle of kindergartener-sized teeth marched across the stage and formed a half circle, the shape of a mouth. Lindsey, the molar, stood at the edge of the circle. Once all the teeth had arranged themselves in their proper places, three more kindergarteners, dressed as a toothbrush, dental floss, and a dentist, trotted onto the stage. The music started. The children sang a song about brushing and flossing, and cavities and plaque. When they got to the part about cavities and plaque, two fearsome-looking kindergarteners dressed all in black ran onto the stage and growled at the teeth.

"Next time, I want to be the cavity," Rory whispered.

The song ended, and all the kindergarteners held hands and bowed. The audience clapped and cheered. Lindsey scanned the audience for Mom. Miriam waved. Lindsey's face lit up. She smiled and waved. But not at Miriam. Miriam turned and scanned the crowd behind her.

There, standing in the far back of the auditorium, was Jack.

After the kindergarteners finished, first- and second-graders dressed as assorted fruits and vegetables walked onto the stage. They sang a song about eating fruits and vegetables. The children rotated to center stage, and each took a turn identifying their produce self. The number of children exceeded the number of good-old-American fruits and vegetables, so the roster included unusual varieties, like the dragon fruit, the durian, the lychee, and the seaweed. Most of the children wore papier-mâché costumes that only slightly resembled their designated fruit or vegetable. At least a third of the kids looked like potatoes.

Halfway through the song, Rory pointed and said, loudly, "That's Chad! Look, Mom, it's Chad! He's a worm!"

"A worm isn't a vegetable," Miriam whispered. "But shhhhh."

"But why can't I be a worm?"

Chad shuffled to center stage. He wore a green felt tube that was supposed to make him look like a green bean, but he looked more like a stubby snake. He yelled, "Green bean!" He attempted a leap-kick-twirl. It didn't work the same, with his legs and arms bound inside the bean pod. He landed awkwardly. His foot slipped. He stumbled forward to the edge of the stage, and for a second Miriam thought he would fall, headfirst, onto the linoleum below.

But then he found his balance. He stood up tall. He yelled again: "Green! Bean!"

The audience let out a collective sigh of relief. Casualty averted. Except Holly made a different sound. A muffled whimper. And when Miriam turned and looked at her, she had tears streaming down her cheeks.

Holly didn't want to talk about it.

She dried her eyes, chugged her vodka-limeonade, and by the end of the show she seemed perfectly fine.

"I'm fine! Really. I'm just tired. I stayed up till two a.m. sewing that damned green bean, and frankly, it looks like a fat green cock. That's what I thought when I saw it. My seven-year-old looks like a green penis. And someone took his picture looking like that, and the picture is going to end up on the internet and follow him around for the rest of his life—" Holly stopped. She gulped, as if stifling a sob. "Anyway, we need to get home. I'll see you over the weekend."

She left. Miriam collected Lindsey and walked the kids out to the parking lot. She kept her head down. She meant to drive straight home and pretend like she hadn't seen Jack, because wasn't Jack pretending he was supposed to be at work?

"Dad!"

He wasn't at work. He was standing in front of her car, unavoidable.

The kids charged him. They wrapped their arms around his legs. Their tooth costumes crunched and scraped as they jostled for position.

"Dad! Dad!"

"Did you see me? On the stage?"

"Dad! I's got a costume!"

"Did you hear me sing?"

"I'm a toof! I'm a sharp toof!"

Jack patted the kids' papier-mâché shoulders. "Yes, I heard you sing, Lindsey. And Rory you are very sharp. You both make great teeth. You know, I had something planned . . . but you're both such nice clean teeth, I just don't know. . . ."

"What is it, Dad?"

"What?"

"Well, I don't know . . ." Jack said, coyly.

"Dad!"

"Well, okay . . . I was thinking my little teeth might like . . . ice cream!"

"Hurrah!"

Miriam felt a twinge of resentment, that she had to spend hours slogging through papier-mâché while Jack got to swoop in with ice cream. She stood, feeling grumpy, as the children pranced around their magical ice cream–wielding father. She hardly noticed when Jack laced his hand around hers and kissed her softly on the cheek.

Jack drove them to the ice-cream parlor. Miriam fumed in the front seat. She should be glad that Jack was present. But Jack didn't have a crick in his neck from hours of crafting. Jack hadn't delivered kids to school or picked them up after. Jack hadn't force-fed them carrots (Lindsey: thirty minutes for a single baby carrot!) (Rory: dipped in mayo) and bathed them and brushed their hair. Jack just got to swoop in at the end, to feed them ice cream for dinner.

Jack was lying to her.

"I'm having mint chocolate chip!" Lindsey said.

"I'm having plain!" said Rory.

She was mad, and she didn't notice Jack's hand sneak across the center console and land on her thigh. She didn't notice the woman standing on the corner outside the Diggity Hot-Doggery, waving her CONSPIRACY! sign. She didn't notice at first when the song came on the radio, the dial changed by a hand other than hers to KISS 95 FM.

"Turn it up!" the kids yelled. Dad complied. Heavy bass blared from the speakers. The windows vibrated. Electronic sounds bubbled up from the bass line, weird and wobbly, but also pleasantly melodic. Sounds reminiscent of a voyage across a sparkling sea, far far away from the maddening Land of Jack.

But also: Something about the song sent a shiver down her spine.

It was not unpleasant. But it felt like a switch flipped inside her head. Whereas moments before, she had been confined by her fury and detached from the world around her, she now felt acutely attuned to the sensation of her body in this seat in this car on the road, speeding through space-time; the heat imprint of her husband's hand on her leg; the creatures in the back seat, in their tooth costumes, bobbing and swinging their legs to the beat. They both seemed to recognize the song.

Damn, yo, this boy's crazy
That's what they say
When they see me getting wasted
Drinkin' like a fish

Like I can't even taste it
So fuckin' high, I'm—

"Whoa, whoa, whoa!" Jack flipped off the radio.

"—flyin' like a spaceship!" Rory finished the line.

"Hey!" Lindsey growled. "Turn it back on!"

"No," Jack said, firmly. "That's— It's inappropriate language for kids."

"But you swear, Dad. I heard you. And Mom too."

"Well, yes, but—but not on the radio."

"But I *love* that song!" Lindsey protested.

Jack doubled down. "No. Those lyrics are inappropriate."

"But *DAD*!" Lindsey moaned. "*Everyone* knows that song. All the kids. It's—"

"I don't care who it is," Jack said, "or what the other kids are doing. Come on, Miriam, back me up here."

"The song..." she started. But she couldn't find words to follow. Her senses felt inundated, against a backdrop of fury. She agreed with Jack, in principle, about appropriate kid songs on the radio. But she didn't understand why he'd reacted so fervently, calling attention to the swears he wanted to shield the children from. She also relished his sudden decline, in the kids' eyes, from purveyor of ice cream to withholder of music.

And she had wanted to listen to that song.

They drove in silence, until Jack turned the radio back on, to Channel News.

"Boring!"

"Dad!"

"Kids, shhh! Do you want ice cream or not?"

—the former Georgia Senator Roland Johnston has declined a plea deal and faces trial next month on charges of drug trafficking and money laundering.

Former Senator Johnston maintains that he is innocent of all charges, despite the overwhelming evidence against him. Johnston's wife has been outspoken in his defense. In an interview given with CNN yesterday, she insisted that the man she married would never become involved in illicit activity of any kind.

In other news, law enforcement is still unable to confirm the identity of the Snail's Lake Shooter, captured over a month ago. The shooter has no ID, no fingerprints on record, no credit cards or any other records of any kind. The name he initially gave to police belonged to a child who died in a Snail's Lake boating accident twenty years ago. The shooter is charged with—

Miriam flipped the radio off.

"Hey!" Jack said. "I was listening!"

"But the kids don't need to hear that stuff," Miriam said. "It's not appropriate. They'd be better off listening to that song."

"Does that mean we can listen to the song?" Lindsey asked.

"No."

They drove on in silence. Miriam stared out the window. They drove past tidy houses with green lawns and early clusters of daffodils. Houses where spouses cooked dinner together, or argued, or ignored each other, or set the children in front of the television and snuck up to the bedroom for an evening romp. Houses where kids drew dinosaur pictures, or spilt milk on the floor, or officiated the wedding ceremony of their two favorite stuffed animals, or hid in the closet while their dad got angry-drunk. They drove past cars full of families on their way out to dinner, or to the grocery store, or to drop children off at overnight day care en route to work. They all continued along a trajectory that was seemingly determined, but at any moment might unravel. Determined as a dolphin. Unsettled as an urchin. They were all flopping around in the strange soup of life, feigning autonomy, until the currents shifted. Like that TV episode Miriam recalled from her childhood, about a boat called the SS *Deliverance* that left port on a windless blue-sky day, but then a sudden wind steered it off course, and it crashed on an island in the South Pacific, and the turtle-navigator who had meant to journey on to India decided to leave the show and stay there, on the island, for the rest of his sunbaked days.

THE ZOO

ON FRIDAY MORNING, Jack left the house before dawn. He left a note on the counter.

Went in to work early. Love, Jack.

Miriam fed, washed, and dressed the kids. She took them to school. She only had two appointments that day, both later in the afternoon. She took Roxster for a run. On Kate and Fred's front lawn, between the patches of frost on the grass and blooming snowdrops, were about fifty rabbits. Roxster lunged. She jerked him back. Some of the rabbits scattered, but others just sat and stared at the stupid dog.

On the way back, she saw Holly unloading groceries. Holly waved.

"I think Kate has a rabbit problem," Miriam said, as she jogged up.

"She *says* it's not a problem," Holly said. She looked pale. Her hands shook slightly.

"Two or three rabbits is not a problem. That's like—"

"Fifty-four. She counted. She's been feeding them."

"Where did they come from?"

"I think they came about the natural way."

"That's, um, fast."

"There is a reason for the stereotype. She's also been feeding racoons."

"Seriously?"

"Seriously. But also, seriously... there's something I've got to tell you."

"What?"

Holly sighed. "This morning, on my way back from the Value Valley, I saw Jack. I think. I didn't get out and talk to him. But I swear it was him."

"Where?"

"In his car. But it looked like he was asleep."

"He was sleeping in his car? You're sure it was him?"

"Almost positive. I know his car. And he had on that fedora. I almost pulled over and knocked on the window. But I didn't want him to know I'd seen him."

"Where was his car?"

"Not far. Near that coffee shop where we followed him. He was parked on the opposite side of the street. He's probably still there. And I'd go with you, if you wanted to investigate. But I've got to wait here for the window people to show up." She gestured to her front window, which was covered with cardboard and duct tape.

"What happened?"

"It was... a golfing accident."

Miriam ran home. She called Jack's cell, but he didn't answer. She skipped the shower. She hopped in the car and drove to the coffee shop where Jack had met the perky blond. There, parked right where Holly had said, was Jack's car.

If Jack had been asleep, he wasn't now. His window was open.

His car was on. White tufts of carbon monoxide drifted from his exhaust pipe. His radio played jazz—the jazz interlude between the 10:00 and 11:00 news. It was 10:59. Jack tossed something out his window. Then he rolled up the window and drove away.

She didn't have time to see what he had tossed. She pulled out after him. He didn't seem to notice. She followed him through three right turns, back down Rosewood Boulevard, through a U-turn and two yellow lights. Then he pulled up in front of Toddlin' Tots Enrichment Center. Rory's preschool.

Jack parked. He got out. He went inside. He came back out with Rory. He buckled Rory into the back seat and drove off. Miriam followed him through more yellow lights. But she knew where he was going. He was going to get Lindsey. He pulled into the Pleasant View Elementary parking lot. He and Rory went into the school. They came back out with Lindsey.

He was stealing the children.

She had a horrifying vision. Jack driving off to where she could never find them. Jack subjecting the kids to a life of musty motel beds with stiff rayon quilts, microwavable gas station breakfast sandwiches, endless games of slug bug, an unfillable void where Mom had been. Herself, alone.

She peeled out and sped after them. For several miles, she followed them through the city. She told herself, again and again, that the vision was false. Jack would never. He would never. She knew him. She knew Jack.

She had. Except the Jack she knew was gone. He had disappeared inside the Dark Work Tunnel, and she couldn't see what happened there. She didn't know what parts of Jack got chipped away. Or what other parts grew, foreign and grotesque in that lightless grind of billable hours. And now he had emerged, changed, but in what way?

He drove toward downtown. She could see the kids through the back windshield, heads bobbing, arms waving, as if they were dancing. They looked excited.

Jack took a sharp right turn, away from downtown. He drove through several residential blocks. Then he turned into the zoo parking lot.

Miriam slowed down and turned in after him. Jack parked. She parked, far enough away that he wouldn't spot her if he wasn't looking. Then Jack got the children out of the car and took them to the zoo.

She didn't follow them in. Instead, she walked over to his car.

She tried the door. He'd locked it, and she hadn't brought the spare key. She peered inside. His suit hung in a plastic dry-cleaning bag in the back seat. Empty coffee cups collected on the passenger-side floor. And there was a novel on the seat. *A Dashing Death.* From the cover, it looked like a detective novel.

TOM AND FRED TURN THIRTY-EIGHT

TOM AND FRED TURN 38!!!

PARTY AT TOM'S HOUSE

632 RAVENSWOOD DRIVE

SATURDAY MARCH 19

7:00 UNTIL LATE LATE LATE

YES, THERE WILL BE JELL-O SHOTS!

YES, THERE WILL BE BEER PONG!

LEAVE THE KIDDIES AT HOME FOR THIS ONE.

7:00 P.M.

JACK WORE a brown velvet blazer, his fedora, and a T-shirt with a picture of Tom Selleck in a Hawaiian shirt.

"I thought I might bring my flask," he said, as they got ready.

"You know there'll be booze there?"

"Sure, but it's a nice flask, right?" He took the flask from his pocket to show her, then filled it with whiskey. She knew it was nice. She'd bought it for him for their first dating anniversary, back when a flask seemed like a practical gift.

"You're drinking tonight," she said. Her tone was accusatory.

"I hadn't planned to play any beer pong."

"But you're drinking."

"Yes."

"So you're not going to work tomorrow?"

"Tomorrow's Saturday."

"That never stopped you before."

She hadn't confronted him about work, or the blond. Maybe she should. But she wanted him to volunteer the truth. And she feared the Jack that truth would reveal.

They walked up the street in silence to Holly and Tom's house. They let themselves in. Miriam found Holly slicing limes in the kitchen.

"Try a Jell-O shot," Holly said. On the counter was a tray of plastic Jell-O shot cups in neon orange and pink.

"What's better, orange or pink?"

"Hard to say." Holly squeezed a wedge of lime into her cocktail. She took a sip. "I had one of each, and I liked them both."

8:00 P.M.

Tom and Fred had a lot of friends who looked just like Tom and Fred, except that Fred's hair had started to get long.

"They're college friends," Holly said.

"And work friends," said Kate.

"And friends from golf."

The work and college and golf friends of Tom and Fred had all gotten their hair done at the same salon. They all wore the same shirt in different colors. They all drank pint glasses of beer and worked in finance and had pretty wives with names like Holly and Kate. The friends and wives multiplied until a line formed behind the keg and an audience formed around the game of beer pong.

"Damn, did you see that shot!"

"Drink up, drink up!"

Holly muddled limes and mint in a glass. She poured in rum and seltzer and handed the glass to Miriam.

"I can make you one, too," she offered Kate, "unless you're still not drinking."

"I finished the kombucha cleanse. But I brought my own vodka." Kate took a tall bottle of vodka out of her purse. "It's organic goji berry."

Holly gave Miriam a look that said: *What the hell are goji berries?*

"I've got some cranberry spritzer in the fridge that you can mix it with," Holly said. "But you don't want these limes. These limes are covered in pesticides."

9:00 P.M.

A man in a teal shirt gave Jack a hearty handshake. His teal shirt had white vertical stripes and a collar. It was tucked neatly into his expensive jeans. It looked just like Tom's olive shirt, but in teal.

"I'm Brent," the man said. He shook Miriam's hand. "And this is my wife, Katie." Miriam immediately forgot both of their names.

"I'm Jack, and this is my wife, Miriam."

"So how do you know Tom?"

"We're neighbors. You?"

"Tom and I pledged together. Phi Beta Kappa."

"So you knew Tom back in his wild and crazy days?"

"Sure. Except, I don't think those days are over."

Tom stood at the beer pong table. A guy wearing a navy shirt that looked just like Tom's olive shirt, except navy, stood opposite him. The guy knocked a Ping-Pong ball into a red plastic cup filled to the brim with beer.

"Chug, chug, chug, chug!"

Tom chugged. He wiped the foam from his mouth with the back of his hand. He beat his chest like a gorilla. He scooped up the Ping-Pong ball and tossed it back to his navy-shirted opponent.

"Say, dude," the teal-shirted guy said to Jack, "you look kind of familiar. Do you work in the Vermster building, downtown?"

"Nope."

"Oh. Thought I might have seen you in the elevator. That's where I work. I'm in finance. Oh wait, I know! I know where I've seen you. At that co—"

"At Tom's birthday party last year," Jack interrupted. "That must have been it. And you know, watching beer pong really makes me want to drink a beer. Come on, Miriam, let's go get a beer."

Fred poured them beers from the keg. Miriam almost didn't recognize him. He'd lost his shirt. His smooth, bare chest was partially covered by a long, furry vest. His feet were also bare.

"Neighbors!" Fred looked shiny, radiant almost. Miriam had never realized he was so tanned.

"Happy birthday!"

"Thank you."

"Your, um, shirt—"

"It was time for the shirt to go."

"That's a nice necklace though," Miriam said. A hefty crystal wrapped in wire hung around Fred's neck.

"Thank you, truly. I'm blessed. I'm blessed to have you and all these wonderful people here to celebrate with me." Fred reached out and hugged them both at once. He smelled salty and earthy, like a grove of redwoods caressed by sea breeze. "You guys are amazing. It has been an amazing thirty-eight years. And this year just blows them all away. Have you guys tried hot yoga?"

"No."

"You've got to try hot yoga. I have a class tomorrow morning at seven if you want to join."

"I think we might still be drunk tomorrow at seven a.m."

"That doesn't matter. Just take a shot of raw apple cider vinegar mixed with local wildflower honey. The yoga will do the rest."

Fred poured himself a beer from the keg. He beamed. He looked like a strapping woodland god—the God of Fermenting and Outdoor Fornication. His hair had grown out to almost woodland-god length. It was golden-brown, glossy and soft as a baby rabbit on his head.

"Fred, your hair looks amazing," Miriam said.

"It does," Jack agreed.

"It's so glossy. Can I touch it?"

Fred nodded. "Please." She stroked his hair. Jack also touched it.

"Wow. How did you get it so soft?"

"I'll tell you," Fred whispered. "The secret is, I never wash it."

10:00 P.M.

Holly mixed fresh tangerine juice and rum in a cocktail shaker.

"The thing about rafting," she said, "is they just let anyone do it. All you need is the raft. They don't even make you wear a life vest!" Holly poured the drink. She added lime and grenadine. The grenadine swirled and sank to the bottom, like candy lava. She garnished with a maraschino cherry and a slice of tangerine.

"It's river rafting, right?" Miriam asked. "Who owns the river?"

"No one. You can just toss your raft in the river and jump on." Holly gulped her cocktail. "And what if there are rapids? How would you even know?"

"Aren't there supposed to be rapids? I mean, isn't that the point of rafting?"

"Maybe. But how big are the rapids? You tell me." Holly took another drink. "What if they're huge? What if they knock over your raft? And you drown? Or get your head bashed on the rocks. It's not like there are lifeguards all along the river." Holly waved her hands as she spoke. Her drink splashed over the sides of her glass.

"But they'll be wearing life vests, right?"

"Oh, sure, Tom *swears* they'll wear life vests. Just like he swears he always wears his helmet when he rides his bike. But you know what?"

"What?"

"He stashes it."

"His helmet?"

"Yep. Tom leaves the house with his helmet on, and then when he turns the corner, he takes it off and stashes it under a bush."

"No, really?"

"I swear. I saw him do it."

"Maybe you could get some sort of lock, for the life vest. To like, lock it onto him."

"You think they make those?"

"It's worth looking into. Like a chastity belt. But for a life vest."

"Sure." Holly finished her drink. Her eyes blurred, as if she was about to cry. "That'd be great. For rafting. But what about the next thing?"

In the other room, Tom and Fred circled each other. A crowd gathered around them. The crowd began to chant.

"Bump, bump, bump! Bump, bump, bump!"

"Happy thirty-eighth birthday, Fred," yelled Tom.

"Happy thirty-eighth birthday, Tom," yelled Fred.

Tom and Fred shook hands. They backed away from each other. They stood, roughly ten feet apart, shoulders back, chests puffed out. Their eyes locked. Then, at the same moment, they ran at each other. They collided. Their chests bumped together. The crowd stomped and clapped and chugged beer.

"Bump! Bump! Bump!"

Tom and Fred stepped apart and circled each other again. Fred growled. Tom snorted. Tom had unbuttoned his olive shirt. Fred had removed his vest. Their bare chests were oiled and tanned.

"They've been doing bench presses in Fred's basement to get ready for this," Holly whispered.

"They went to the tanning salon," Kate added.

"Are they oiled up?"

"Of course."

"They claim the bumping sounds better when they're oiled."

Tom and Fred pounded their chests and ran at each other again, like rams during mating season. Their chests smacked together. They repeated the ritual thirty-six more times, for a birthday total of thirty-eight.

11:00 P.M.

Miriam spotted Jack across the party with a pretty blond. For a moment she thought it might be the same woman she had seen him with outside that coffee shop, but this woman was older. Still hot though. Jack leaned in. He said something. He had an ardent gleam in his eyes. The blond's lips were full and moist, coated in shimmering pink gloss. She nodded. She gazed at Jack with wistful eyes. Jack took a sip of whiskey from his flask. He offered the flask to the blond. She shook her head, *no thanks*. Jack said something else. She pouted sympathetically. She batted her eyelashes like a cartoon baby deer.

Miriam pushed her way through the crowd toward Jack and the blond. Beer sloshed over the side of her glass and dripped down her hand. The whole floor was sticky with beer. She shoved past the beer pong table and stepped between Jack and the blond.

"This is Miriam," he said.

"Nice to meet you." The blond offered her hand. She didn't look nearly as pretty or threatening up close. She wasn't even a true blond. Her brown roots peeked through.

"Miriam, this is, um..."

"Ashley."

"Right, Ashley."

"Well, darn," Ashley said. "It looks like I need a refill. Gotta go!" She hurried away.

Later, Miriam overheard her mention Jack, with a giggle, to another woman: "Stay away from that one. Such a downer. If I wanted to hear about Syria and the stock market, I'd be talking to my own husband. Come on, let's go get some Jell-O shots...."

12:00 A.M.

Holly had a glass half full of tangerine and rum. She filled it up to the top with beer.

"Are you mixing beer with your cocktail?" Kate asked.

Holly looked down at her glass. She looked surprised. She started to laugh.

"It's a, a beer-tail." She giggled.

"Are you going to drink it?"

"Waste not, want not! That's what my mother always said. But she had a touch of bulimia. She used to eat whole boxes of cookies and then barf them back up, so..."

Kate looked disturbed. Holly laughed. She pantomime-barfed. The combo of fake barf and laughter gave her hiccups.

"Waste not, want not! (Hiccup!)" Holly took a sip.

"How is it?"

"Not bad," Holly said. "Like, (hiccup) citrus beer. You wanna try it?"

Miriam and Kate shook their heads. "No thanks."

"Your loss (hiccup). Waste not, want not."

Holly looked lovingly at her beer-tail. She chugged it down, every drop.

1:00 A.M.

Holly stumbled out of the kitchen. She pushed through the crowd, toward the beer pong table. Tom was crouched beneath it

"You!" Holly yelled. "Birthday boy!"

"I can't find the Ping-Pong ball," Tom said.

"Stand up, birthday boy," Holly slurred. "Lesh play some beer pong."

Tom crawled out from under the table. "But I can't find the Ping-Pong ball."

"Isn't there another ball?"

"No."

"What about a glof ball."

"A golf ball?"

"That's what I said. A GOLF ball." Holly wavered from side to side, as if her living room floor was the deck of a sailing ship.

"We can't play beer pong with a golf ball."

"Why not? You let Chad go golfing in the house!"

"That's not what happened."

"So play me." Holly picked up a Ping-Pong paddle. She slapped it against the table.

"Holly—"

"What, are you afraid, Tom? Are you afraid I might beat you at beer pong? Is big stwong Tom-tom afwaid?"

"No, it's—"

"You're not afraid to jump out of an airplane. You're not afraid to jump off a bridge. You're not afraid to go white-water rafting. Oh no, *not at all*. You're not afraid to make your wife *a widow*, are you, Tom? And you're not afraid to take Chad along with you." Holly picked up the other paddle. She threw it at him. "But losing to me in beer pong scares you? Well, you better face up to your fears, birthday boy!"

Holly stomped out of the room. Tom stood at the beer pong table, clutching his paddle, looking confused. Everyone else stood still, waiting to see what Holly would do next.

A moment later, Holly wobbled back into the room. She had a golf ball in her hand. She dropped the golf ball on the table and served it to Tom. Tom hit it back. Holly swung and missed. The golf ball rolled onto the floor. She bent down and picked it up.

"Now drink!" she ordered.

"That's not how the game works," Tom protested. "You don't use the paddle. And—"

"It's how this game works now, birthday boy!"

Holly handed a cup of beer to Tom and picked up one of her own. She gave him a sloppy toast. They both drank.

Holly tossed her empty cup onto the floor. She picked up the golf ball. Tom was still drinking. But Holly served the ball anyway, as hard as she could. The ball smacked Tom in the eye. He screamed. He staggered backward, spilling beer all over his shirt.

"My eye! Damn it, Holly, my eye!"

"See!" Holly laughed. "See! Now who's the beer pong!"

2:00 A.M.

"Tom and Fred are both wearing eye patches," Miriam told Kate. They were outside, alone on the deck. The March air was mild, foretelling of early summer. The moon was a giant egg in the sky. The grass glistened with dew.

"Wait, is Fred all right?" Kate asked.

"He's wearing the eye patch out of solidarity."

"Is Tom all right?"

"He's got a black eye. I really don't know what point the eye patch serves."

"Is Holly all right?"

"Like, now?" Miriam said. "Or in a larger sense?"

Kate stared at the moon. "Her spirit is in turmoil. She needs to realign her energies."

"Right...."

Kate fondled the crystal around her neck. "Don't you ever want to just get closer to the earth?"

"Uh... sure?"

"I can feel the pull of it. The earth power. It's so powerful. It's like... I just want to feel the grass on my skin. I want to feel the moonlight, all over my body."

Kate pulled off her shirt. She was braless. She walked across the deck, down the stairs, into the grass. She kicked off her shoes and shimmied out of her jeans. She walked out into the middle of the yard. She lay down in the grass, naked, and stared up at the big egg moon.

Any moment now, a thousand baby stars would hatch.

Miriam left her there. She crept along the side of the house, where the moonlight couldn't touch her. She lit a cigarette. She watched the smoke curl slowly skyward. She heard a noise. A rustle. A racoon crept out of the bushes. It gazed at her with its obsidian eyes.

Where? it asked. *Where did he go?* But she couldn't answer, and the racoon turned and scurried away.

She lit another cigarette from the tip of her last one. She heard another rustle from the bushes. She walked toward the noise, expecting another elusive animal. But instead, she saw a man-shape. She saw the burning red cherry of his cigarette.

The man stepped out from behind the bushes, into the moonlight. He took a drag from his cigarette. He smiled at her.

"Hello, Miriam."

"Hello, Jack."

ROXSTER AND THE DEER

THEY DIDN'T TALK about the smoking habit they had both secretly taken up. Or Jack's work. Or the blond. They didn't talk at all on Sunday. Jack slept late, then he hopped in his car and drove off.

"To work!" he claimed.

Miriam had a terrible hangover, and then she had to clean up glitter slime that had seeped between the couch cushions, and then she had to get slime out of Lindsey's hair. It had congealed into a sticky tangle, which had to be cut out, which made Lindsey cry, which made Rory cry because he wanted a haircut, too. They both got haircuts.

"But where did the slime come from?" She hadn't bought it. She knew better than to let glitter slime inside the house.

"We got it at the—"

"Shhh! We're not supposed to tell her!"

"Oh, um—"

"It's okay. Dad got it for you, didn't he?"

"Um, maybe?"

It was just like Jack to set a slime-trap then conveniently flee. She didn't want to talk to him. Even when he got back from wherever he'd been they avoided each other. They snuck out separately to smoke. Jack languished with his precious cable news. Miriam put on her headphones. She listened to a podcast called *Dr. Sex*.

The host, Dr. Sex, had a guest who had left her adulterous husband and discovered a passion for burlesque.

Guest: *The whole time we were together, it was always about his orgasms. Not that I didn't orgasm, now and then. But every time it happened he'd say something like,* I sure gave it to you good. *As if even my orgasm was about him.*

Dr. Sex: *When you had one.*

Guest: *Right, right. When I didn't? Not his fault. Just another failure of my body.*

Dr. Sex: *And the adultery?*

Guest: *Oh, absolutely my fault. I shouldn't have gotten old.*

Dr. Sex: *Okay, but you're not old.*

Guest: *I mean, in the not-new-to-him sense. Though I am the oldest burlesque dancer in my troupe.*

Dr. Sex: *So what finally made you trade your husband for burlesque?*

Guest: *I guess... I just got tired of pretending. I'd been pretending for years, long before his first affair. I was unhappy, but I told myself it was fine. I was sexually unfulfilled, but that was just my fate, as a hetero woman.*

Dr. Sex: *Right.*

Guest: *Then... I don't know what came over me. I just left. It was right before Christmas. The winter solstice. I packed a bag and booked a hotel and left. And that night, my friend calls me up and*

> *says, "Hey you wanna go to this burlesque show" and I was like "Okay, why not?" I'd never seen one before. And when I went, I—I loved it. The liberation of it. The freedom. The body positivity. It felt like a dam had burst inside me or something. And right then I knew, this was what I was going to do. Burlesque. This was me. The true me. And fuck pretending.*

Miriam pretended not to see Jack pour whiskey in his coffee mug. She pretended not to notice him toggle screens when she walked past. She didn't confront him about the glitter slime, the zoo trip, the early morning car nap. She feared what she would do, when she stopped pretending.

She invented a resurgent headache as an excuse to put herself to bed early, without him. She feigned sleep when he came to bed. She lay in the dark, eyes open, thoughts tumbling, words reverberating in her tired brain: *Me. The true me. Fuck pretending.*

He wasn't there when she woke up. He left a note on the counter. *Went to work early*. Of course. *Hope you are feeling better. Love, Jack.*

She did not feel better. She woke, fed, and clothed the children and delivered them to school. She came home and screamed into her pillow. She googled the burlesque dancer. What was this troupe? Could she join it? Could she strip off her clothes and find the real her?

Instead, she threw in a load of laundry, ran the dishes, and fed the dog.

"Would you like to go for a run, Roxy? Would you?"

Roxster wagged his tail. He pawed at the door. She put on his leash and took him outside. They ran up the street, on the opposite side as Kate and Fred's house, to avoid the rabbits. Roxster pulled her along. He couldn't pull like he used to. He had gotten old. He usually lost his steam after a few blocks, and she would have to drag him along.

But he was a big dog, and strong, and he still had steam left when they ran past the pair of deer in Holly and Tom's front yard. The jingle of his collar spooked them. The deer ran up the street, toward the intersection. Roxster bolted after them. Miriam tried to hold him back. But he pulled with all his weight, and she didn't see the raised square of sidewalk. Her foot caught. She tripped. She fell hard. She hit the cement, first her knees and then her hands.

"Ahhhh!"

The leash slipped away.

Roxster slipped away.

He chased the deer. Up the street. Into the intersection. She didn't see it happen. Her palms burned. Her knees throbbed. She didn't see, but she heard.

A thud.

A howl.

A crunch.

Bones beneath tires.

She picked herself up. She half ran, half limped toward the intersection. The deer had fled. The car was gone. The driver had left the scene. The scene was Roxster, limp, in the road.

"Ahhhhhh! Fuck!"

Another car sped toward him. It swerved around. She ran into the street.

"Fuck, fuck, fuck, fuck, fuck. Please be okay. Please."

She had to at least get him out of the street.

She picked him up. She could barely carry him. Her knees wobbled. Pain shot through her back. Her hands bled into his fur. She lugged him to the corner. She set him down in the neighbor's grass.

"Fuck."

She crouched down and checked for a pulse. She felt his heartbeat. He opened his eyes and whimpered. Okay, he wasn't dead. Not yet. But she couldn't see his insides. One of his back legs was mangled. Nothing could walk on a leg like that.

She started to cry.

"Fuck…"

She needed to get him to the vet. She doubted she could pick him up again, even to put him in the car. She needed help. She needed Jack.

Fuck Jack.

She fucking needed him and loved him and hated him and his dog had just been hit by a car and might die and where the fuck was Jack?

She called him on his cell phone. He didn't pick up.

She called his office. The secretary answered.

"Doreen, it's Miriam." Her voice quivered. "I need to talk to Jack."

"Um, Jack's not in right now."

"Where is he?"

"I don't…"

"Look, I need to talk to Jack. Now. Tell him to call me."

She hung up the phone. She sat down and pressed her head to the dog's head and thought, *Please please please don't die.*

She didn't want this ending.

She called Jack's office again.

"Doreen, have you found Jack?"

"Uh, no..."

"Please, find him right away. Whatever he's doing, just find him, interrupt him. Tell him to call me *now.*"

She called the vet. No one picked up. They weren't open yet. She left a message. Her face felt hot and sticky. She stroked the dog's head. Here lies Roxster. She remembered him as a puppy, outside her apartment door, a ring tied around his neck.

She called Jack's office. Even though she knew he wasn't there.

"Have you found him?"

"Uh..."

"Jack. Have you found him?"

"No, I—"

"Where is he?"

"I'm not certain, but—"

"Did he even come in today? Does he even still work there? Damn it, I need him. Now!"

"Um, is this... an emergency?"

"Yes, it's a goddamn emergency!"

"Miriam, I, uh, I wasn't supposed to say anything, but..."

"But what? What?"

"I don't have any idea where Jack is. Jack hasn't worked here for months."

SPRING EQUINOX - BRIDGE

MATH

IMAGINE YOU are an astrophysicist.

Imagine that your name is Robert Kai. That you are renowned. That there are three moons in orbit around a distant planet, each named after you. Kai-1. Kai-2. Kai-3. On these moons, there may be life.

This is a cocktail-party fact. A triviality, here on Earth. What matters, here and now, is the hydroponic lettuce you are growing in your basement. Your vinyl collection. Your corgi. His name is Samwise, and he sleeps on your bed. He sits on your lap, at the window, as you gaze through your personal telescope at the elusive stars. The telescope was a birthday gift from your parents. You were ten. An infinitesimal fraction of the age of those billion-year-old stars.

The stars are just orbs of fiery gas, or sky volcanoes, or disco balls adrift in empty space, or math.

It's all math.

Math is the only thing that always makes sense.

Imagine that it is thirty-ish years in the past and you are the boy Robert Kai and you have just turned ten. You are home. You are safe. Your mom is safe and your dad is safe and you just ate pizza and cake and now you are outside, in the yard, setting up your telescope, staring up at the night sky, and then at something much closer. Something moving fast. So fast you don't even see it. It's only a streak of flame. And then it hits. And everything explodes. The ground shakes. The air burns. Wood and shingles and bricks rain down. There is smoke and dust and screaming. You are screaming. Your mom is screaming, and your dad is screaming, and they converge around you. They squeeze you between them like a boy sandwich. Their faces are covered in ash and blood, and they hold you and weep, and you do not yet fully comprehend how lucky and unlucky you are.

The meteor destroyed your house and everything inside it.

But because it is your birthday, because you got that telescope, *you* were not inside it. You were outside, contemplating the odds that your telescope would reveal extraterrestrial spacecraft or eldritch horrors or vast planetary cities teeming with alien life. Your parents were outside, watching you, their marvel. Their creation.

If the meteor fell on any day other than your birthday, you and your mom and your dad would all be dead; instead you spend seven months living in a hotel while your house gets rebuilt. Your new house is better than your old one. The odds that a meteor will hit your house now are exactly the same as they were before the first meteor hit, even though it doesn't feel that way. You feel safe.

You feel, throughout your life, unsettled by the disconnect between perception and math. You want certainty. You want answers. You go to college. You apply for a PhD. You must make a choice: physics or astrophysics. You graduate. You are offered a high-paying job for a nanotech corporation, but you choose academia instead. You buy a house in Raleigh. You adopt a dog. There are so many to choose from. Can you explain why you picked the corgi?

Math can explain.

Or, math could explain, if you knew every variable. If you plugged them in to the correct equation. All the numbers would add up to corgi, or pit bull, or retriever, or mutt. A slight variation could produce a different dog, or a cat, or an astrophysicist with a bearded dragon.

But this math made you and your corgi. You go together to the Green Creek Observatory. You evaluate the data collected by the telescope array. You fall asleep to the background hum of a distant star. You and Samwise Corgi watch the desert sunrise, and then you attempt to unravel the mismatch in measured rates of universal expansion. Dark energy is math, which means that you can understand it, theoretically. Sometimes, in the vacant hours of a star-studded night, you almost feel like you do understand it. The numbers flicker in the corner of your eye. The equation is almost tangible. A thing you can hold, in defiance of all that empty space.

You are almost there, when Samwise Corgi barks. At nothing. There is nothing, and yet there is something. You can feel it. But what, or how, or why, you don't know. It is faint as a bristle, soft as a breeze. It is nothing and everything and when you turn back to the numbers they make no sense.

What? What the hell?

Samwise barks again.

The numbers howl.

The numbers that had shown a rate of cosmic expansion of 73.3 kilometers per second per megaparsec now say 67.1 then 58.9 then 52.7 then 49.8. They are falling, falling, falling and nothing has ever made less sense in your life than this math.

No, no, no, this is impossible....

You check and recheck, and the numbers return to their prior normal rate, but you are still bothered. For days you haunt the banks of supercomputers. You pace and mutter. You calculate and recalculate. You make frantic phone calls to the math-wraiths of other telescope arrays. Some of them noticed something odd, but no one else recorded this exact data. *It must be an error,* they say.

But it wasn't. You have the record. Math doesn't lie.

Still, you check and recheck and recheck, and you try to reenvision the universe. The grand equation. You forget to eat. Your sleep is broken by phantom math. Your dog eventually insists: Time to go home. And there is nothing now to do but let it settle in your mind, and hope that big brain of yours can make sense of the nonsensical. Brains are great for that. They gather random data, stray numbers, strange events, and weave a story to explain, or to comfort.

There is nothing now for you to do but let go. To *hang low like a hermit crab,* like they used to say on that old kids' TV show you loved so much. To listen to your dog, get into your car, and drive and drive.

THE LAST ADVENTURE OF THE OTHER MR. YAY

NO ONE TOLD HIM they had booked the dog.

"It was supposed to be a surprise," his agent said. "Just act surprised."

"I don't act. I'm a terrible actor."

"Ricky, you are one of the greatest performers in the history of children's television. I think you can act just fine."

He couldn't. Not anymore. Not after *Peregrine.* Even if the choice was: act versus walk the plank. Even if bound and dangled above the snapping jaws of a great white. He had staked his career, his life, on total authenticity. Decades ago, he had looked at his washed-out, broke-ass self in the mirror and said *Yep that's a weird dude, that's me* and leaned in. All in. And, improbably, his gamble paid out.

Now, he was moderately rich, but you wouldn't know from the look of him. He wore a plain black turtleneck and black Converse with holes in the toes. His signature patchwork pants had gotten an upgrade. The multicolored squares, tattered and faded through his sailing days, were crisp and bright. He had a long, unruly beard, all gray. His face looked younger than his seventy-eight years, despite half a lifetime of sea and sun. He lived comfortably in a Blue Ridge cabin. The surrounding forest teemed with bears and rabbits and wild turkeys and deer. The sky was infinitely vast. Sometimes he hiked to the summit of his little mountain and he gazed up and out at the world and he felt the ground beneath him rock and sway, like on the boat. The SS *Deliverance.*

He never wore makeup on the boat, except black eyeliner to block the glare. But here, backstage, on the set of *The Whimsy Hour,* he sat still and let the makeup artist blot and brush and smear.

"I remember you from before the show," the makeup artist said. She was older, close to his age. "*The Treacherous Ten. Shotgun Solstice. Connie at the Crossroads.* My brother loved westerns. Oh, *The Lucky and Unlucky,* that was his favorite."

"Mine too," he said. But he hadn't loved it. He always played the heavy, the guy who started fights, the guy who shot first, no questions asked. He always felt confined, despite those open ranges and big skies.

The makeup artist brushed de-frizzer through his hair and beard. She stepped back. "Very handsome. You look twenty years younger."

And inauthentic.

The Real Ricardo Merman cared less for appearances and more for sailing smoothly through life, which required accepting things he couldn't easily change. Like preshow makeup.

Like the cancer that decided it was time to cancel the show.

No chemo at sea.

Do you want to live, Mr. Merman?

He did, intensely.

He felt better now. Maybe almost strong, years after the last round of chemo. The tumor had shrunk.

It's basically gone. You see? Congratulations.

He had named the tumor *Boris* so that he would hate it less. He didn't want to hate what he couldn't change. He couldn't hate it if it had a name. If it was part of him.

Boris wasn't gone. *Boris* had just gone into hibernation, for months or years or decades. The future was elusive. Like water in his hands.

In the vibrant present, someone pinned a mic to his shirt. He did a sound check. He drank a glass of lemon water. He paced. His hands got clammy. His heart rate suggested nerves. He shouldn't be nervous, after more than five decades on film and TV. And yet he felt unsettled, as if his body sensed what was coming.

"You ready, Mr. Merman?"

"Ready as a rockfish."

Ricardo Merman walked out onto the stage. A jam band played his entrance tune, a jazzy rendition of the opening credits for *The Adventures of Mr. Yay*, one of the most popular children's television shows of all time.

Ricardo Merman meant to replicate the other talk show entrances he had watched on TV, but an urge seized him. He twirled. He shimmied. He danced up to the host and offered a bow, then a handshake, then a hug.

"Mr. Ricardo Merman." The host hugged him back. The host was forty years his junior. The host, as a child, had watched *The Adventures of Mr. Yay* on TV, and it inspired him to become a dolphin trainer, a career goal his parents insisted was impractical. So he went into television. "Such a pleasure to have you here on *The Whimsy Hour*."

"It's a blessing to be here."

"I heard you're a landlubber now."

"My heart will always be at sea."

"Ladies and gentlemen, please welcome our first guest today, Mr. Ricardo Merman. Most of you know him as Mr. Yay, from the long-running children's television show *The Adventures of Mr. Yay.*"

The host described the adventures. The ports and islands and cities and volcanos visited by the SS *Deliverance* and its crew. The revolving crew of animals, led by the enigmatic first mate Mr. Yay and the illustrious Captain Barksford. The exotic foods they tasted. The storms they survived. Their devotion to fun and adventure, sincerity, perseverance.

They played clips from the show. The lobster boil where the jaguar decided to become a vegetarian. The Galápagos shipwreck. The episode where the giraffe learned to swim. Ricardo Merman's heart thrummed faster, and he didn't know why. But what a wild blur. What a life.

"But before you became Mr. Yay," the host said, "you had worked in film. You did *Canyon of Arrows, Outlaw Forever, With Love, Deadhand Diego,* to name a few. And then you made this drastic shift. What inspired you? Was there an event? Can you pinpoint the precise moment when you decided, *Yes, I'm done with westerns. I'm making this show. I'm Mr. Yay*?"

Ricardo Merman stroked his beard. This gave the appearance of reflection. But he recalled the moment vividly.

He had been such a weird kid, everyone said, as if it was a bad thing. He collected odd pets: a spider, a squirrel, a blind dog, a two-legged rat. He studied philosophy and theater in college. He moved to LA and auditioned for movies. He got a job at a seafood processing plant. In his spare hours, he labored with his sewing machine. He made a pair of wide-legged patchwork pants, like a quilt for his legs. He had a dream where he danced across the deck of a ship, all the colors of his pants flowing around him, and he talked to children and told them how they could grow up to be them, just them, because there was nobody better.

But he felt awkward in his weird skin.

He landed a breakout role as the villain in *Sundown Saddle*. For a decade, he played bandits and robbers and hard, treacherous men. He made himself feel hard and treacherous. He smoked two packs a day. He guzzled whiskey. He collected black eyes. He told himself this was the self he should be. His agent, his costars, his fans all agreed.

Until the market shifted, and the studios stopped filming westerns, and he ran out of money, and he played his last ever role, a different sort of role: Detective Eddie Tides in *Peregrine*.

The movie became a cult classic decades later. But at release, *Peregrine* bombed.

The next week, he had several tragedies or opportunities arise: an eviction notice, a job offer as a stuntman, a dead car battery, acceptance into a master's program in theater, an unexpected visit from an old friend who had just started working for PBS television.

He had options. It was a blessing. Not every washed-up actor got so lucky.

He lost his wallet, and for three days he ate nothing but canned tuna while he waited for his replacement cards to arrive. On day three, he felt weak from the pressure of indecision. He wished he could go back to *Peregrine*, to the moment in between *then* and *now*, when now still might have become something different. He stared at himself in the mirror. He crossed one eye. He imagined the long long long beard he might grow, all crusty with sand and salt brine. He had safe, smart, steady choices. Job and school. He also had this fucking crazy dream.

He stared at himself in the mirror, and for a long while he felt very afraid. He felt the tide-pull of safer options. He heard the words of every adult, every critic, every director ever inside his brain. *Follow the script.* All that wisdom, it had to be right.

Right?

He stared into his crossing-uncrossing eyes. Then, right then, he had a choice. The fact that every moment was imbued with choice was overshadowed by the reality that this moment was the only one that mattered. To stay or to leap. The script or the dream.

He was very afraid, because what did a weird sailor-tailor-philosopher-actor with a bad smoking-drinking habit and a pair of handsewn quilt pants have to offer the chock-full world?

He almost turned away.

But then, in his mirror eye, he saw a spark that he imagined was a dolphin, breaching the waves. *Daring as a dolphin,* he whispered to himself. And the rest of the story became the history of *The Adventures of Mr. Yay*.

"I can see it," he told the host. "That moment. It's a moment, I think, that everyone faces. You can choose to be the scripted version of yourself, to play the role that everyone expects of you. Like I did in my early career. And, I suppose, that can be a good choice. Easier, at least, for some of us. Or you can take a leap of faith in yourself. You can embrace the most *you* version of you. Even if, like me, you're a freak. That was how it happened. That was how *The Adventures of Mr. Yay* came to be."

The host asked about the evolution of the show, his favorite episodes, his life after it ended. Did he miss it?

"Of course."

"And what about the crew?"

"Yes."

"And the captain?"

"A very good dog. Every one of them."

"Did you have a favorite?"

"Maybe the husky we lost in Singapore. But honestly . . . it's impossible to choose."

"What if I was to tell you that we brought another very good guest here to the show today?"

"I would say . . . wow. That would be great."

He couldn't feign surprise. But his smile was genuine when the eleventh and final Captain Barksford trotted out onto the stage. The dog saw him and ran to meet him. He ran to meet his captain. They embraced. Captain Barksford licked his scruffy cheek. Ricardo Merman picked up the dog and spun him around. He was so immensely happy for this moment in this life.

The last moment before things got truly weird.

The audience clapped and the host thanked him for coming on the show and promised he could visit more with Captain Barksford backstage. He went backstage. He was jittery and anxious and delighted. And caught off guard, by the man he nearly ran into outside his dressing room.

The man had a badge on a lanyard, but Ricardo Merman

couldn't see what the badge said. The words blurred, somehow, when he looked at them.

The man had shoulder-length hair, lustrous, the mane of a lion tamer. He was strapping. He wore a skintight jean jumpsuit, with an embroidered patch that said SVEN BRAWNSON.

As the man walked past, Ricardo Merman heard the golden jingle of a bell. He couldn't see or hear where it came from. Maybe from inside him. Maybe from everywhere all around him. The sound was like raindrops on the hull of the SS *Deliverance*, but also like the underwater echo of a dolphin.

Everything blurred.

Ricardo Merman's head felt swimmy. His eyes were full of water. He blinked, trying to wring them out. He crossed and uncrossed them. He spun around. The man in the jean jumpsuit was gone. Instead, there was a swirling hole in the empty hallway. And through the hole, he saw a different man. A man with a trim beard, a flannel shirt, and khakis. A man in a dim and lonely house, a house that made him sad. A man whose skin looked younger, but his eyes looked tired and washed out. A man who was him.

He didn't know how he knew what to do.

But he knew exactly.

He wasn't afraid. He'd spent the past forty years of his life not being afraid.

"You don't have to be afraid," he said to the man, himself. He reached out his hand, into the swirling hole. Tiny silver fish swarmed all around him.

"You can be you," he said. He could hear the crash of waves, the cry of seagulls, the rush of whirling wind.

"Take my hand," he said, to himself.

Ricardo Merman nodded. His hands reached out. He clasped them together. There was a bright flash of light, a blinding supernova of light, so fast that no one else saw it.

Then all of it—the light, the swirling hole, Ricardo Merman—was gone.

CONFESSION

DON'T DIE *please please please don't die please*

A mantra.

A prayer.

A song.

Miriam held the dog in her arms and the dog was the dog but he was also everything the dog meant, all the years of her life that the dog had spanned, all the love that had bloomed and eroded.

Everything had a beginning and an end, and now The End bled all over her jogging clothes. The End couldn't stand up. The End couldn't keep his eyes open. She couldn't carry him any farther. She called and called for help. Finally, Fred picked up.

Fred appeared before her, shirtless. He wore flowy pants and a wire-wrapped crystal and a patchwork vest that looked like he'd sewn it himself.

He picked up the dog.

"I can drive, if you want. I can come with. Tell me what you need."

"I just need—"

She needed the dog to not die.

She needed Jack, but Jack had receded to the back of her mind. He was almost not there.

Fred carried the dog down the street. He loaded the dog into her car. He wrapped the dog in a blanket and took off his crystal and strung it around the dog's neck, for protection. A robust version of the dog would have chewed through the cord and possibly maybe swallowed the crystal whole, but this broken version lay still.

"I like to believe that there's magic in the world," Fred said.

"Is there?"

"Some days, I think I can feel it. All the vibrations of the universe. I hope. But how would we ever know for sure?"

She climbed into the car. She drove to the vet but they weren't open and the sign said they wouldn't open until noon—NEW HOURS 12:00–5:00, MONDAY THROUGH FRIDAY, which in the maelstrom of this emergency seemed ridiculous—so she called another vet and then another and another until someone picked up and said *come in*. She drove downtown. The dog's breath was labored and raspy. She double-parked outside the Happy Paws Veterinary Clinic. She got out, ran to the door, yelled: "Please! My dog! Help!"

Please don't die please please don't die

The receptionist ran out, then in, then back out with a vet and a stretcher. They loaded Roxster. They carried him inside.

Miriam parked. She went into the waiting room. She waited. She called Jack and texted Jack and waited for an interminable time, and while she waited her heart broke.

Did it always happen like this, in every universe?

She waited, waited, waited, and then two things happened at once: Jack burst through the door, and all the animals went mad.

There were four dogs in the waiting room—a retriever, a corgi, a husky, and a Chihuahua—plus two cats in carriers and a guinea pig. The moment Jack showed up, the retriever howled. The corgi started barking. The husky bolted across the room. The Chihuahua scrambled free from its owner's arms. The cats meowled. The guinea pig scratched at its cage.

"Miriam! Miriam! Where is he? Where's Roxster?"

She stared at Jack, coldly. "He's with the vet."

"Is he—"

"He's alive. For now."

"Is he—are you—what happened?"

The retriever howled and howled and howled. The corgi barked its little head off. The husky ran furious laps around the room and the cats were both meowing and hissing, and in the back rooms of the vet's office other animals joined in, with barks and whimpers, hisses, thumps, thuds, attempts to run or claw their way out, and the humans that belonged to these animals tried to soothe or quiet or yelled or stood speechless, staring, and the Chihuahua scurried over chairs and tables with a wild look in its eyes, and on the street outside a dog ran past, leash streaming behind it, owners chasing after, and inside, the barks and meows and cries got louder and an escaped potbellied pig galloped down the hall, and pets and humans ran frenzied through the office and Miriam found that she couldn't move, couldn't speak, was fixed at the hurricane center of the turmoil that swirled around her and again, her heart broke.

It is broken.

It never broke.

It was the same heart and also a different heart and she didn't understand what was happening. None of them did.

"What's going on?" Jack said. "Tell me—"

"I can't—"

The barks and meows and sprinting scratching madness

intensified. The husky leapt up and spun circles on the counter until the computer crashed to the floor. The potbellied pig pounded its hooves on the glass door. The Chihuahua fell onto its back, legs up, like an overturned beetle.

"Miriam—"

"You tell me!" The words came out at last. "You were supposed to be at work!"

"I was at work."

"Don't lie."

"I was—"

"Stop lying! I called, Jack. I called your office and they told me. You don't work there anymore! You haven't worked there for months! Where do you go? What do you do? Are you having an affair? Who *are you*, Jack?"

"I—"

"Who the fuck are you?"

She was screaming. Tears poured down her face. Her clothes were still damp with blood. Animals barked and howled and ran past and around her. Jack's eyes crumpled up, like he might cry, and fuck that, fuck him. He didn't get to cry right now.

"Miriam, I'm—"

"Are you having an affair?"

"What? No," he said.

"But I found this matchbook in your pocket. For this romantic spa—"

"Oh, that—that was just, someone just gave it to me. When I needed a light. I never went there."

"And I saw you. With this blond—"

"You 'saw' me?"

"I...I followed you. And you went to this coffee shop, and you were outside flirting with this blond."

"Oh." His cheeks flushed.

"She was so pretty and young and the way you looked at her—"

"I'm not having an affair. I swear."

"Who is she?"

"She's..."

"WHO IS SHE?"

The thrashing potbellied pig got carried away by its owner. The husky circled around and over the counter.

"She's, well, technically...my boss."

"Your boss? She's like, twenty, Jack! Are you going to stand here and lie to my face?"

"No, no, I mean...at my, um, at my new job."

"Your new job."

A cat hissed. An escaped parrot flapped across the room.

"Yeah, so..." Jack rocked anxiously. "I quit the firm. I couldn't take it. I hated it. I hated me for being stuck there, and you hated me and—"

"I never said I hated you."

"But you did. You do. I could see it on your face, and I just couldn't take it, so I quit. I thought, I wanted to make you happy—"

"By lying?"

"I didn't mean to lie, I just— I didn't say, and then I was afraid and I kept not saying and then—"

"You said you were going to work! Where did you even go? *WHO ARE YOU?*"

He looked at her. He had Jack's eyes, Jack's face, Jack's voice, Jack's body, but this man, she didn't know him. The Jack she married had disappeared, somewhere beneath the mountain of endless work, and the Jack who emerged on the other side was a different man altogether.

"I... I've been working at that coffee shop. Part-time. Just the morning shift. But really..." he said, with a straight face, "I'm a detective."

"You're—what?"

Laughter tore through her.

Not because it was funny.

"I'm serious. I'm a detective."

"No."

"Yes."

"No."

"Yes. Well. Kind of. Except I don't have much work yet, which is why I'm at the coffee shop. And I'm writing a detective novel. To set the mood."

APRIL

PALMISTRY

MIRIAM GOT into her car and drove. She didn't know where she was going until she was almost there. Everything looked different than it had in January, when the bare tree branches dead-ended in a gloomy sky. But then she saw the storefront, PSYCHIC—MYSTIC—FORTUNE-TELLING painted in orange letters above the front door. A piece of cardboard hung loosely beneath it, as if someone had tried and failed to cover the sign.

She parked on the street out front. She tried the door, but it was locked. The palmistry sign in the window glowed fluorescent pink, but the blinds were pulled shut. She knocked. She heard a noise from inside. She knocked again. No one answered.

Miriam walked around the side of the building. On the ground beneath a window, there was a dead bird. She stepped over it and looked in the window. The psychic was inside, at the front window, peering out.

Miriam ran back around to the front door. She banged loudly. "I know you're in there!"

"Go away!" the psychic yelled. "We don't want any!"

"But I need your help! I need you to tell me—"

"I can't tell you shit! I ain't no psychic!"

"But you knew things, things about me and my marriage and—"

"No more!" Rosy clarified. "I ain't a psychic no more. Go away!"

Miriam sighed. She sat down on the front stoop. She didn't know why she was here. She shouldn't have come. The psychic wasn't psychic, because psychics weren't real. She was just a different brand of therapist. Which Miriam needed, at this moment.

Behind her, the lock clicked. The door opened. Rosy the Psychic stuck her head out. She glared at Miriam. "I told you, I ain't psychic."

"I know. I'm sorry. I'll leave."

"Why are you here?"

"I... I guess, I'm adrift. And last time I was here—"

"You were here?"

"You said my marriage was over. Then you said it wasn't. You gave me root beer."

"Hmm." Rosy opened the door a crack wider. She crinkled her nose. "You. I remember you. Well, fine then. You can come in, if that's what you want."

She didn't know what she wanted. She wanted someone to tell her it would all be okay. She wanted it to be okay.

She followed the psychic inside. The shop had a musty, sour smell. The counter was piled with takeout containers and fortune-cookie wrappers. Tumbleweeds of cat fur covered the floor. Dust had settled over everything. The psychic herself looked pale and gaunt. Her blond hair was greasy and tangled. She wore the same boho skirt and Cincinnati Reds T-shirt she'd worn the day that

Miriam met her, but both looked unwashed. Her eyes were unfathomably blue.

She stared at Miriam. "You've been shipwrecked."

"I... yes. It feels like that."

"You want to know what the sign means. That's why you're here."

"What sign?"

"Your dog getting hit by that car."

"Wait, how did you know—"

"It's ambivalent. As a sign, it could go either way."

There was a loud thud against the window glass.

"What was that?"

"Bird." The psychic shook her head. "They've been flying at the windows for months. Stupid birds. That's why I put up the blinds. But it don't do no good."

"You think it's dead?"

"Likely. Or it will be soon. My cat comes and gets 'em when they're down. Not fair sport. But hey, the world's hardly fair. You want some root beer?"

"Um, sure. Yes."

Miriam followed Rosy into a storage room, cluttered with boxes and life-sized cardboard cutouts of baseball players and rocks and crystals and mirrors in different shapes and sizes, and an ancient refrigerator plastered with Cincinnati Reds magnets. The psychic opened the refrigerator door. Several magnets fell off. Miriam picked them up. She tried to stick them back on, but they wouldn't stick.

"Don't bother." Rosy handed her a can of diet root beer and a plastic twisty straw.

"How did you know about my dog?" Miriam asked

"I didn't."

"But you said—"

"I *said*. But I didn't know. The words just popped out."

"Is that what happened when you read my palm?"

"Not sure. What did your palm say?"

"It said—you said, last time I was here, that my marriage was over. Then you said it wasn't. You kept going back and forth. I need to know what you meant. What did you see?"

Rosy shook her head. "I don't know. I don't remember."

"Could you read my palm again?"

"You know, I used to think I was psychic," the psychic said. "Everyone always thought I had the sight, growin' up. My mama would tell me, 'Destinia Amber Rose, you have the sight!' Though that ain't how it works. I don't see. Stuff just shoots outta my mouth, like it done today. And then after I say it, I can kinda see it. Or at least I could. But ever since you came around the first time, it's all been confused."

"What do you mean?"

"It's like, I say one thing, then I say the opposite thing, and I can see them both. Like a broken compass. But that can't be right. Makes me wonder if I'd just imagined I had the sight all along. So I'm done reading palms. Now why don't you finish that root beer and go. How'd you even get in? We're closed. The sign says closed."

There wasn't any such sign. "You let me in."

"And now we're closed."

"Please, I just—"

"Ugh. There! I just had a vision. You're gonna just keep on pestering me unless I read your palm."

"No, I'll leave," Miriam said. "I'm sorry I bothered you."

"Fine. I'll read it." The psychic grabbed Miriam's hand. She held it up close to her face. She traced the palm lines with her finger. "Huh. That's odd."

"What?"

"There's something here. From your recent past. A severance. Or a union. Or a conversion. I can't quite tell. . . . Did you convert recently?"

"Like, to a new religion? No."

"No. No, that's not it. It's something else."

"But what about my future? I know what happened in my past. What do you see about my future?"

"The future is never certain. No one knows what will happen."

"So you can't tell me what it says about my future?"

"I didn't say that. I just said the future wasn't certain. But there is *something*."

"What is it?"

"Hard to say, exactly. I see . . . a huge crowd. Yes. Lots of people, all together. And they're . . . they're upset. Or, no, happy? Maybe? They're chanting something. And there are bright lights. Flashing lights. I see smoke. And . . . and animals? It's very chaotic. But you're there. You're right in the middle of it. And so is Jack."

MISTRUST

THE KIDS HELD a memorial service for the leg in the backyard.

The kids each drew a picture of their beloved Roxster. Rory's Roxster looked, ironically, like a six-legged spider, with eyes in the middle of its body and sharp, spidery fangs. Lindsey sang a funeral song, to the tune of "The Farmer in the Dell."

"Oh Roxster was a dog, oh Roxster was a dog, hi-ho the derry oh, Roxster was a dog."

Rory joined in the second verse. "Oh Roxster had a leg, oh Roxster had a leg, hi-ho the derry oh, Roxster had a leg—"

The service was interrupted by whimpering and scratching from inside.

"Kids, hold on—"

"But, Mom, you can't let him out. What if he sees it? How would *you* feel if it was *your* leg?"

She wouldn't feel great about the kids singing songs about it, but *her* leg, if she ever lost it, would get properly disposed of, not buried in the backyard.

Roxster's leg—now a mangled mass of fur and bone sealed in several ziplock layers and stored in the freezer for two weeks, until the kids had sufficiently processed the tragedy and devised a plan to honor the leg—would be buried three feet deep, inside a plastic cooler, to prevent the dog from ever digging it up.

"Maybe he wants to see." Maybe the accident had also caused Roxster's incontinence, though the vet couldn't say for sure. She opened the back door. The old dog limped out. "Maybe he wants to be near his leg, one last time."

Lindsey nodded. Rory wrapped his arms around the dog. The song resumed.

"—hi-ho the derry oh, Roxster had a leg. They had to cut it off, they had to cut it off, hi-ho the derry oh, they had to cut it off."

Miriam sang along, as instructed.

Jack sang along, too. She side-eyed him from across the yard. She blamed him. Even though her logical brain could dissociate Jack from the crash that had taken Roxster's back leg and cost them more than five grand in veterinary bills, even though he was far from the scene of the crash, and would have been, irrespective of "work," she blamed him. His deceit had perpetuated the chain of events that led to the untimely demise of Roxster's leg.

Except, *deceit* didn't quite describe it.

In truth, Miriam didn't know anymore who Jack was.

"It was a sturdy leg, it was a sturdy leg, hi-ho the derry oh, it was a sturdy leg. But now it's in a bag, but now it's in a bag, hi-ho the derry oh, now it's in a bag."

With that unsentimental line, the song concluded. Jack dropped the bag in the cooler. He duct-taped the cooler shut and stuck it in the hole. He shoveled dirt.

"We're done," Lindsey said. "We're going inside."

"You don't want to watch Dad—"

"No. We're going to watch on the tablet until the food part of the ceremony."

The kids went inside. The dog limped after them, then

immediately peed on the kitchen floor. Miriam mopped up then led the dog back outside. He flopped down in a patch of sun. She sat down beside him. She watched her husband shovel.

"You could help, you know." He stopped for a moment. He wiped sweat from his brow.

"I know. But I'm not going to."

"You're still mad at me."

"*Mad* is an understatement. It's more like . . . I don't even know what to think about you."

"Miriam—"

"Don't."

"Miriam, I can explain. If you would just talk to me—"

"You did explain. But it doesn't make any sense."

"But you hated my job. You hated me working so much. You hated me."

She eyed him dubiously. "I don't know you."

"You do. It's me. I always wanted to be a detective—"

"But you were always too practical."

"Or scared."

"What's your favorite food, Jack?"

"I don't know, steak? Does whiskey count?"

"You don't even like whiskey."

"I do!"

"I've seen you drink it. It disgusts you. And you don't like meat loaf either, do you?"

"Are you cross-examining me?"

"Answer the question."

"No. I hate it."

"But that's the thing. I thought you loved it. I thought it was your absolute favorite ever. But I was wrong. What else did I get wrong about you, Jack?"

After he'd finished burying the leg, Jack went inside and made a memorial brunch, with French toast and coffee and bacon. Roxster loved bacon. They ate together as a family. Miriam tried to act normal and chipper, for the sake of the children. Jack drowned his French toast in maple syrup. An unnatural amount. Had he always eaten this much syrup with breakfast?

She didn't know.

She didn't know him. Except that sometimes he acted like quintessential Jack. Like when he busted out the newspaper, spread it before her, and insisted that she read along, while he read aloud.

"Listen to this."

"I don't want to."

"But it's fascinating. The news is fascinating."

"The news is always just news. There's an upper threshold on how interesting it can possibly be."

"But listen," Jack said, forging ahead. "Something strange is happening." He began to read:

The Unusual Alliance of Roger and Dale

On the night of December 21, Roger Harmon put on his nicest suit and caught a cab downtown, to the Hotel Roma, to attend the Ohio Entrepreneurs Gala.

Roger Harmon would receive an award that night, a lifetime achievement award for his contribution to small business. His business, Harmon's Hamburgers, had served some of the best burgers in the city for more than twenty years.

On that same evening, Dale Golding, an investor in nearly a dozen start-up businesses and the owner of the Lightning Taco food truck chain, had been invited to the Entrepreneurs Gala to give the keynote address.

Roger Harmon and Dale Golding met for the first time at the Entrepreneurs Gala. They sat at the same table. Sitting next to each other, they looked almost like brothers. They both had the same brown hair, cut short, graying around the temples, the same glittering brown eyes. They both ordered the salmon, with a glass of red wine. They talked about their businesses, their families. Roger Harmon was widowed, with a nineteen-year-old daughter whom he brought as his guest to the gala. Dale Golding was divorced. He had invited his girlfriend to come as his guest to the gala, but she had been feeling ill.

"That's too bad," Roger Harmon had remarked. "My girlfriend is feeling ill too."

The next day, Roger Harmon met his girlfriend, Elaine,

for dinner. She didn't seem well. She looked pale and sweaty, nervous. Her fingers twitched. She hardly ate. Roger drove her home. He walked her to the door and kissed her good night. He called the next morning, but she didn't answer. He sent her flowers. He ordered chicken soup and brought it to her house, but no one was there.

The day after that, Roger Harmon spotted Elaine downtown, with another man's arm around her waist. That man was Dale Golding. Roger approached the couple. He felt betrayed. He had only been dating Elaine for a few months, but he already had strong feelings for her. He wanted to confront her, but he never got the chance. Elaine saw him, and when she did, she took off. She ran down the street and disappeared around the corner before either Roger or Dale could stop her. Roger–

"You can stop reading," Miriam said.

"But it's not over."

"It's making me uneasy."

"Why is it making you uneasy?" Jack tapped the newspaper. "Don't you want to know what happens?"

"No. How is this even news? And this is in the newspaper? I don't get it."

"If you let me finish reading—"

"No."

"Miriam—"

"Just tell me what happened."

"Well, it turns out she's been dating both the guys at the same time. For months. Neither of them had any idea. They both thought they were the only one. But when she ran off, neither of them could find her. They both got worried, and they started searching for her together, and they became friends."

"And that's news?"

"It's... well, it's an unusual story," Jack said, flustered.

"Did they find her?"

"They just found her. Or, I should say, a certain detective helped them find her." Jack beamed. "But she was totally disoriented."

"Oh, how nice for him. Then what happened?"

"I don't know. We just found her."

"So why was she disoriented?"

"That part's unclear."

"But the real mystery," Miriam said, as she glared at Jack, "is how someone could live a totally separate life like that."

Jack fell asleep on the couch in the early afternoon. Miriam passed through the living room with heavy feet. She made the floorboards creak. She did not dissuade the kids from dumping a bucket of blocks on the wooden floor, right beside their sleeping father. It didn't wake him up.

Who was this man, indulging in a midday couch nap? He had Jack's long eyelashes, Jack's sharp jawline, Jack's hairy goat legs.

She didn't trust those legs.

The next morning, Jack slept in. She woke up, got the kids ready, dropped them off at school, and came home, with plans to take a jog. She stretched her hamstrings by the front door. Roxster limped over, a mournful look on his old face. Then Jack appeared, in shorts and running shoes.

"Are you going for a run?" he asked.

"You tell me, Sherlock."

"I think I'll come with you."

"You're going to run?"

"Well, yeah."

"Who are you and what have you done with my husband?"

She had never seen him run. Maybe a sprint once or twice, but not for a workout. She didn't think he could do it.

"We really ought to quit smoking," Jack said, as they jogged up Ravenswood Drive.

"Obviously."

Jack panted. Miriam picked up the pace. Halfway up the street, they saw Kate and Fred outside on their front lawn, barefoot, their legs spread apart, their arms pointed out. They stepped forward, slowly. Their arms sliced through the air. They moved in unison.

"All right, detective," Miriam said. "What are they doing? Are you suspicious?"

"Um..."

"It's tai chi."

"Oh. Since when?"

"Sounds like a mystery for our resident detective to solve.

When and why did the neighbors start acting weird?"

The tai chi wasn't particularly weird. Kate had always had a crystals-and-auras streak. But Fred had seemed like a typical frat boy turned investment banker. And now they were both barefoot, arms raised, fingers curled into claws, mouths open wide, in a fearsome tyrannosaur pose, while little bunnies frolicked on the grass all around them.

Jack had no answers. Only questions: "When did this start? How did Fred get so tan? What's with the bunnies?"

"You only noticed them just now?"

"I was... preoccupied."

"Your powers of observation are remarkable. They'll serve you well in your new career as Inspector Clouseau."

Jack completed the jog, then collapsed on the couch. He sat there all morning, chugging coffee, pecking at his keyboard, while Miriam worked a real job that paid in actual cash, and not just in childhood hopes and dreams. She had several appointments, and then a lunch break, which meant a protein bar plus grocery shopping. She slipped on her shoes and headed for the door.

"Where are you going?"

"Value Valley."

"I'll come with."

"You never come."

"But today I will." Jack put on his flip-flops and his fedora.

"That hat sure does make you a real gumshoe," Miriam said. "Especially with the sandals."

"Hey, I like these flip-flops!"

"Says the alien impostor who hijacked my husband's body."

They drove to the Value Valley. The Conspiracy! woman

paced in front of the entrance with her CONSPIRACY! sign. They walked past her, into the store. They filled a cart with fruits and vegetables and fluffy puffs of rice with pastel marshmallow spaceships and crunchy snacks in shades of yellow and beige and yogurt that came in tube form. The Conspiracy! woman was still there when they wheeled their cart out to the parking lot.

"I had five chickens," she muttered as they passed. "I had five chickens. I had five chickens. Five, five, five, five."

Jack looked puzzled. "What's up with her?"

"Gosh, it's a mystery!"

He didn't help unload the groceries at home. He stood in the kitchen, awkwardly, watching, like maybe he wanted to help but he didn't know how.

"What are you making for dinner?" he asked.

"I'm making your favorite. Meat loaf."

Jack got the hint. For dinner, he cooked pasta with tomato sauce.

"I don't want this sauce," Rory said. "I want it plain, wif butter."

"It has chunks," said Lindsey.

"You both need to expand your palates," Miriam said, as if either kid knew what that meant. But it didn't matter. She could already see how this experiment would end.

"I don't want red sauce."

"I don't want chunks."

"I'm not eating it."

"Me neither."

"Zip it, sailor!" Miriam said. "Silent like a starfish!"

After dinner and bedtime, they drank wine on the porch. The

night was warm. The sky was hazy with stars. The air smelled like spring. They hadn't sat like this together in months or years, or maybe ever.

The Jack she didn't know lit a cigarette.

"I don't blame you for hating me," he said. "I'd hate me too, for the times I wasn't there."

"I don't... hate you, exactly. You got a light?"

Jack sparked his lighter. He lit her cigarette. "Still, I wouldn't blame you if you did hate me. I get it. I should have realized sooner how terrible the job was. I should never have taken the job. Hell, I should never have gone to law school in the first place."

She didn't want to hear it. She wanted to sit and enjoy her wine and cigarette in peace. "Zip it, sailor! Silent like a starfish!"

"Why did you say that?"

"Because I don't want to talk about what you should and shouldn't have done. It was a long day. I just want to relax."

"No, I mean, that specifically. 'Silent like a starfish.' You said it at dinner too."

"Oh. It just popped into my head. It's a line from the *Mr. Yay* show."

"The what show?"

"*Mr. Yay.*"

Jack gave her a blank stare. "What's that?"

"Are you serious?

"Yeah."

"You don't remember that TV show? *The Adventures of Mr. Yay*?"

"Nope," said Jack. "Never heard of it."

"Mr. Yay used to say that. 'Zip it, sailor! Silent like a starfish.' Like in a situation where you might want to say something, but it would be better if you didn't. Like, 'This soup is disgusting,' or 'Gee, you're really hideous looking.' "

"Or, 'Honey, I hate you.' "

"Right. But wait, you seriously don't remember that show?"

"No."

"You've never heard of *The Adventures of Mr. Yay*?"

"No."

"Do you have, like, amnesia, or—"

"Nope."

"How is that even possible?" Miriam said, increasingly suspicious. "You did watch TV as a kid, right?"

"Sure."

"Then you must have seen him. He was everywhere. His show ran for, like, twenty-some seasons."

"Huh."

"You had to have seen him. He was a weird guy. He had this real long, thick beard, like, down to the middle of his chest. And he wore these flowing pants that looked like quilts for his legs."

"Not ringing any bells," Jack replied.

"And he rode around on this boat with all these animals, trying out exotic foods from different cultures. The captain was a dog."

"The man wasn't captain?"

"No. It was Captain Barksford. Mr. Yay was the first mate. Though of course he had to translate Captain Barksford's orders."

"That sounds like a ridiculous show."

"You really don't remember it?"

"Nope."

"Maybe if you saw a picture, you'd remember."

Jack pulled out his phone and searched for Mr. Yay. "This says Mr. Yay is a rap artist."

"Yeah, that's not the same Mr. Yay."

"But look, right there he's got a dog. Maybe he was a rapper *and* a TV star."

"No, I don't think so. Let me see."

Jack handed her his phone. Miriam scrolled through pictures of a young, beardless man with silky hair. She had heard about this rapper. He was one of her patients' best friends. In the pictures, the rapper was on a stage with a microphone in hand, or dressed in a teal tracksuit, or holding a ski with shot glasses glued to it (a *shot-ski*, Jack called it), a joint tucked behind his ear, an enormous bedazzled dollar sign around his neck, an unfamiliar dog with a pirate's hat at his side.

She scrolled and scrolled. But none of the pictures showed a long-bearded sailor wearing leg quilts.

SPIDER-MAN

IF A RESOURCEFUL CHILD stacked one lawn chair atop two other lawn chairs, said child could climb onto the roof of the garage.

While inside, the adults got drunk.

"But where's Tom?" Miriam asked.

"He'll be here," Holly said. "He said he had an errand to run."

"An errand. How nice that you trust him."

"I don't. I mean, I trust him to be Tom. I don't trust him not to give me a heart attack. Just watch him come home with, like, a backyard trampoline or some other dangerous thing we don't need."

Holly mixed a pitcher of tequila with strawberry lemonade, triple sec, and lime. She filled five glasses, chugged one, then refilled.

"That was fast," Miriam said.

"It's preemptive," said Holly.

"You better eat something," said Kate. "Drinking on an empty stomach is—"

"Highly efficient."

"I was going to say, bad for your microbiome."

"My micro-what-what?"

"Here. Have a cookie." Kate handed Holly a misshapen lump, speckled with black seeds.

"This is a cookie?"

"They're chia-applesauce cookies. All organic. Fred baked them himself."

"They're sugar-free," Fred added. "I substituted with stevia."

"Uh..." Holly eyed the cookie with disgust.

"Try it!"

"Um, you know, I think I better check on the kids!"

Holly and Miriam both slipped away to the living room window. They peered out at the children in the backyard. Nothing appeared amiss. There was no indication that lawn chairs had gotten stacked three high. The stack had been taken down, to dispel suspicion, while Spider-Man changed into his Spider-suit.

"They're so cute," Miriam said, meaning her own children and less so the urchins spawned by her friends.

"Mostly. Sometimes. But then they grow up into Toms and Jacks and Freds. And that's if you're lucky. If—" Holly stopped.

"If what?"

"If—" Holly's voice wavered. Her eyes teared up.

"Are you okay?"

"No. Yes, I— It's just allergies. God, my allergies are terrible this year. Come on, let's go drink."

They rejoined Kate, Fred, and Jack in the kitchen. Jack was already on his second cookie, which he washed down with a swig of whiskey from his flask. He grimaced.

"Good, you're back," Kate said. "Now you can try the cookies." She held out the plate.

They each took one. Holly shoved the whole cookie into her mouth, then chased it with half a margarita.

Kate nibbled at the spongy corner. "You can really taste the health, can't you!"

"Um, sure. I guess that's the taste."

"I also blessed them," Kate said.

"You blessed them?"

"With an invocation. For good energies to flow to all who eat them."

Holly stared, squint-eyed, at the friend who had once looked like her sorority sister but now wore a circlet of flowers atop her unwashed hair. The friend launched into a monologue on the processed-food industrial complex.

She's crazy, Holly mouthed, when only Miriam could see.

Miriam wondered how and when her friend had gotten so crunchy. There was a photo on Holly and Tom's fridge of the six of them from the summer before. They had taken a group trip to Hocking Hills. They'd spent a long weekend drinking wine and hiking and eating regular foods that came from cans and bags and boxes. Kate used flavored creamer in her coffee and styling products in her hair, which she washed every day. In the picture, she'd blown it out. She'd dyed it blond. She wore mascara and fingernail polish. She stood beside Fred, in his striped shirt and dock shoes, identical to Tom's. They all looked normal, and happy, except for her and Jack, who had been made to stop his weekend working while he posed for the picture.

Present-day Jack seemed much happier. He wore his fedora inside, and flip-flops, and the leisurely expression of someone who had napped through the afternoon. Fred had also shifted markedly, less in demeanor than in appearance. Fred wore hemp pants and a flowy shirt, embroidered around the collar. He radiated good health. Holly still seemed the same as she always had, but she looked stressed. She had split knuckles and dark hollows under her eyes. She'd let her fingernail paint peel away. She was twitchy.

Extra twitchy when they heard the rumble outside.

"What's that?"

Holly chugged the rest of her margarita. The rumble turned to a growl. Right outside. In the driveway.

What Tom brought home was, statistically, far more dangerous than a backyard zip line.

Holly's phone rang. She looked at the screen.

Ring—ring—ring—

The screen said: *Tom.*

"Are you going to answer that?"

Ring—ring—

"Hello?"

"Holly!" Tom yelled, loud enough against the rumbling background that they all heard. "Come outside! Come and see!"

Holly hung up. Her eye twitched. She poured another margarita.

"Are you—"

"Should we—"

Holly took a gulp, then turned and headed for the door. They followed her out, onto the porch, down the steps, into the yard. Tom was in the driveway, straddling his new motorcycle.

He beamed. "Isn't it great!"

"What the hell is that?!" Holly yelled.

"It's a motorcycle—"

"Ahhh! I know what it *is*, Tom. But why is it ***here***? Oh, god, tell me you didn't buy it!"

"I bought it!" he exclaimed, still somehow oblivious to his wife's mounting anger.

"Why?! What the fuck were you thinking?"

"I always wanted a motorcycle. And I thought—"

"Goddamn it, Tom, turn it off!"

Tom stroked the motorcycle. *I know, I'm fabulous,* it purred.

"You want to try it out?" he asked.

"What?"

"I thought we could ride together, and—"

"Are you *crazy,* Tom? *Really?*" Holly screamed. "You really thought you should just go out and buy a motorcycle? Do you have any idea how dangerous they are? What were you even thinking?"

"I just—"

"Turn it off, for fuck's sake!"

Tom turned it off. "I always wanted one—"

"What were you thinking? What!"

"Don't let the tide pass you by," Tom said. He had a wistful gleam in his eyes. "You gotta, you gotta just grab the bull shark by the snout and ride it out to sea!"

Holly's fingers curled into a fist. She made a noise that was part groan, part growl. "You asshole!" she yelled. "I'll bull-shark your snout!"

Then she punched him in the nose.

The kids—four of them, at least—had wandered from the back-yard to watch. When Holly punched her husband, Rory let out an excited yelp. Lindsey recoiled. The two Marino children clutched their crystals.

The fifth child, the most resourceful, the most adventurous, clad in his Spider-Man costume, had restacked the lawn chairs into a tower in the backyard. He had scuttled up, onto the roof of the garage. He had several spools of ribbon, which was really spider webbing. He'd planned, he told his mother later, in the ambulance, to shoot the webbing around the chimney and swing up from the garage to the roof of the house. But when he tossed the spool of ribbon at the chimney, it didn't adhere. It rolled off and fell to the ground. And without the webbing, he couldn't swing down. So he tried to descend the tower of lawn chairs.

He stepped off the roof, careful but confident, and too far to one side. The tower collapsed beneath him. He fell, arms out, onto the pavement below.

He screamed. "AHHHHHHH!"

Out front, as Tom bled all over his new motorcycle and Holly wound up to punch him again, everyone turned toward the screaming.

"AHHHHH! AHH! AHHHHHH!"

The kids and Fred and Kate and Jack all ran, but Holly froze.

Miriam looked at her friend, at the panic on her friend's face. "Holly?"

"No. . . ." Holly shook her head. "No, no, no, no, no, NOOOOOOOOOOO!"

Tom went to her. His one hand pinched his bleeding nose. His other reached for his wife. She slapped him away.

"It's Chad!" Jack called, from the backyard. They all already knew. Of course it was Chad.

"AH! AH! AHHHHH!"

"He's— He'll be okay!" Jack yelled. "I think he broke his arms."

Holly should have run to him. She should have been relieved. But she stood there, stuck, in the spectral shadow of unfathomable horror, and from her mouth came a deafening, primal scream.

A MYSTERY WORTH SOLVING

JACK-THE-DETECTIVE was out of work. He'd only had a few paid gigs. His website was still under construction. His three weekly shifts at the coffee shop had paid enough, so far, to cover a fraction of Roxster's vet bill. His primary occupation was leisure, with an unpaid-novelist side hustle.

He wrote in the evening, at the kitchen table, after the kids went to bed. He pecked the keys with his two typing fingers. He leaned back in his chair and stroked his scratchy chin. He wore his hat, to boost the detective vibes. His dark eyes glittered beneath it.

"What's a good name for a bar that a detective would drink at?" he asked.

"I don't know, how about Smitty's? Didn't we used to go to a bar called Smitty's? I'm terrible at coming up with names."

When Miriam was six, she got a cat. She named it Brownie, because it was brown. She took its picture to show-and-tell. *That's a stupid name,* another kid had said. She got so mad. She wanted to yell and punch that stupid boy in his stupid face. But she didn't. She told herself: *You are a sailboat in a calm sea. The words are waves rolling off you. Silent like a starfish.*

She'd heard these words on TV, on *The Adventures of Mr. Yay,* and she had, right then, an overpowering urge to see the show, to watch the weird sailor gaze through his telescope at the mysterious lands beyond the sea while the soundtrack of waves looped in the background. She sat down next to Jack, not so close as to delude him into believing she was there because of him, but close enough that she could see him type *S-M-I-T-T-Y-'-S* with his two plucky fingers.

She opened a browser window on her phone and typed *Mr. Yay*. The young rapper appeared. He had a smooth, playful look, like a sea otter pup. She scrolled through picture after picture, the rapper smiling back from every page. He posed shirtless. He basked on a California beach with a horde of gorgeous women in string bikinis. He double-fisted forties of malt liquor. He showed off the serpent tattoo that twisted up his arm. Beneath the stage lights, his face glistened with pearls and diamonds of sweat.

Okay, this rapper fellow was very enticing, albeit too young and wild for a suburban mom who needed to resolve things with her workaholic freeloading mystery husband; but he wasn't *the* Mr. Yay. Not the one she remembered.

She tried a search for *Mr. Yay* and *children's television*. The internet produced more pictures of Mr. Yay the rapper. She tried *The Adventures of Mr. Yay*. The internet showed a clip of Mr. Yay on a party boat cruise. She scrolled and scrolled but saw no trace of the Mr. Yay of her youth.

She sighed. "This doesn't make sense."

Jack sighed. "What?"

"Oh, I'm sorry, am I interrupting you?"

"Kind of. But you also add to the vibe. From the corner of my eye, you're like, the femme fatale."

"Can I pour you a glass of whiskey?" she said, in a seductive voice. "Mr. Shipley?"

"Would you mind?"

"I was joking. And also, you hate whiskey. Does the vibe matter that much?"

"Actually, yes."

"Why don't you have some wine instead?"

"I *guess* that'll do. If it's red. But what doesn't make sense?"

"You remember that kids' television star Mr. Yay?"

"The one I don't remember?"

"Yeah. Well, the internet doesn't remember him either," Miriam said.

"Huh."

"When I search, I just get photos of the rapper."

"Makes sense to me. I mean, I heard about that rapper on NPR, and I've never heard of the other guy."

"But the other guy, the television star, he's way more famous. Like a thousand times more famous."

"Why don't you try, 'Where is Mr. Yay?' " Jack suggested.

"What?"

"You're looking for *your* Mr. Yay, right?"

"Right."

"So type in, 'Where is Mr. Yay?' "

Miriam asked the internet: *Where is Mr. Yay?*

The internet answered:

Mr. Yay in Las Vegas.

Mr. Yay Gets Slap on Wrist After Night of Drunken Revelry.

Mr. Yay Plays Renegade Beach Party.

Mr. Yay Does Not Exist.

"Wait, what is this?" She clicked on the last answer.

"What?"

" 'The Mr. Yay Conspiracy,' " she read.

"Conspiracy?" Jack asked, adjusting his fedora.

The article was on an obviously unhinged site, the Conspiracy Chaser Blog, right beneath an article on the alleged werewolf conspiracy of the Nixon administration.

Do you remember Mr. Yay? Not the foul-mouthed rapper with the fake gold teeth and the heavy bass drops who materialized from a mysterious cloud of pot smoke and shot-skied his way to stardom. The other one. The iconic children's television star who sailed the world with his animal crew, who introduced you to hummus and kimchi and sashimi, who taught you to embrace your inner freak, to be kind and free, to set sail for the destination your heart would take you. That Mr. Yay.

You remember him, right?

You're not alone.

I remember that Mr. Yay, too. So do several other people here at Conspiracy Chasers. I remember watching that Mr. Yay on TV nearly every afternoon for three years of my life. But that Mr. Yay is gone.

Seriously. As I write this, there is no trace of Mr. Yay anywhere on the internet, other than right here in this article. Search for yourself. It's as if the show never existed. Now why do you think this is?

The disappearance of Mr. Yay is one more seemingly minor step taken by the moneyed fascists on their road to geo-political domination. Mr. Yay preached open-mindedness and acceptance of all cultures. Mr. Yay stood for adventure, exploration, and self-sufficiency. Mr. Yay encouraged us to think for ourselves, to not let our lives pass us by, to seize the bull sharks by their grubbing greedy noses and toss them out to sea. Of course the fascists wanted him gone, so much so that they erased him from existence.

The Mr. Yay of your youth has since been replaced by a rapper Mr. Yay, preaching a message that seems the same on its surface. But he's obviously blazed, and so are his listeners. And maybe that's the point. If everyone is drunk and high enough, they won't notice the tech bros siphoning away their money or the legislators chipping away at their civil rights. The real uncertainty here is whether this new Mr. Yay is just your typical rapper, or is himself a witting accomplice to the elimination of his namesake.

"So that guy's crazy," said Jack, who'd read the article over her shoulder.

"You think?"

"I think the 'fascists' have more effective means to achieve geopolitical domination than ridding the internet of every trace of a kooky children's television star."

"But it's strange that there would be no trace of him on the internet. I mean, *everything* is on the internet."

"So maybe he was called something else," Jack suggested. "And you're just misremembering."

"Along with a bunch of other people? I don't think so."

"It can happen. You know, the Mandela effect? People misremember all the time."

"I am not misremembering. I watched hundreds of episodes of that show. His name was Mr. Yay."

She resumed scouring the internet for traces of Mr. Yay. She found links to the Conspiracy Chaser Blog and articles debunking the Conspiracy Chaser Blog. She found a third, unrelated Mr. Yay who worked as a clown in Buffalo, New York, and a Japanese karaoke bar called Mr. Yay. She scrolled through picture after handsome picture of Mr. Yay the rapper.

She thought Jack had resumed his detective-noveling, but then he grabbed her arm and exclaimed, epiphanically, "Everything is on the internet!"

"That is . . . what I said."

"But everything!" He looked at her, wild-eyed, very un-detective-like.

"That is how the internet works."

"But he should be there... unless... this could be, gosh, who knows? Is it the fascists? Or something more nefarious, or a natural event, or a mass hallucination? And no one's even looking into it except that conspiracy blogger site! But they're not real detectives. And a case of this magnitude needs—"

Jack was interrupted by two kids in paper-plate masks. They stormed into the kitchen.

"Mom!"

"Mom! Dad!"

"Come see!"

Lindsey had a lion mask with a pink-and-purple mane. Rory had a dinosaur or alligator mask, scribbled green, with two reptilian slits for eyes.

"There's deer in the yard!" Lindsey said.

"They're fizzing," Rory said.

"That's nice," said Miriam, dismissively.

"But *Mom*, there's lots of deer. And they're all fizzy. You have to see."

Miriam and Jack followed their children into the living room. They looked out the window at a deer-covered lawn. There were at least a dozen deer, and two dozen black, glassy eyes, all fixed on the house.

"That's unnerving," Miriam said.

"What are they doing?" Jack asked.

"Maybe they're having a party," said Lindsey.

"No." Rory shook his head. "It can't be a party wif no cake."

Jack banged the glass. The deer didn't flinch. Miriam opened the front door and stepped outside. Her family followed. She should have been afraid. They could charge. They could invade her house. Jack had a fireplace poker. But for whatever reason, they didn't scare her.

She stared at the deer. The deer stared back.

"Well? What do you want?"

"Mom, can we invite them inside?"

"Uh—"

"No."

"I'm talking to you! Deer!" Miriam yelled. "What do you want?"

One deer, a young buck, lowered himself down to a sitting position. His legs splayed on the grass, as unnatural as a dog who captained a ship. Deer didn't really *sit*, did they? Didn't they sleep with all four hooves on the ground?

Miriam walked down the steps, into the herd. A deer bent beside her and chomped a mouthful of grass from the lawn. It chewed slowly. Its eyes stayed fixed on her.

She could almost hear its voice in her head.

Sorry about your dog.

Sorry.

Its eyes were char-black, and smooth as sea glass.

Where is he?

Where is Mr. Yay?

"He's disappeared completely from the internet," Jack said, and for a moment Miriam thought he'd heard the deer too before she realized his mind was still back in the prior conversation. His hand reached out to pet the deer.

"Don't pet it. You don't know what it's got."

Jack paused in the motion. "But there's still a trace . . ." he said. "And there's still *him*. Or the guy who played him. What was his name?"

"I don't remember."

"You know who I bet would remember? That guy who works at the video store."

"There's still a video store?"

"Yeah, down on Auburn."

The deer pushed its head at Jack's hand. It wanted him to pet it.

"Jack—"

"It's fine." He scratched behind its ear, like it was a cat, and not infested with prions.

"How does a video store even stay in business?"

"Nostalgia."

"So what, you can rent VHS?"

"You can. But the owner, he knows everything about TV and film," said Jack. "Maybe the studio just pulled the show. This guy would know."

"Why would they just pull the show?"

"Maybe so they can bring it back in a big way. With lots of merchandise. Come on, let's go ask him!"

"Like, now?"

"You want to know, right?"

Five minutes later, Miriam was in the car, kids with snacks buckled in the back seat. Deer idled in the driveway, blocking them in. Jack tried to clear a path, first with a broom, and then with Rory's Space Sorcerer™ sword, which had flashing lights and made bleeping swooshing sounds. The sword was magical, apparently, to deer. Jack managed to lure several out of the driveway. Then he hopped in the car, and they started up the street.

They drove past Kate and Fred's house. A yellow bulldozer sat in their front yard, on a mound of dirt. The grass was all gone.

Near Holly and Tom's house, they reached an impasse. Dozens of deer had gathered in the middle of Ravenswood Drive. Some stood and stared off with their placid black eyes. Others sat with hooves folded under them. The car rolled toward them, and they didn't budge.

Jack reached over and honked the horn.

Miriam rolled her window down. "Get off the road!"

"They've been there all afternoon," Holly yelled. She walked down the porch steps, across the lawn in their direction. Chad followed behind her. Casts covered both his arms, from the shoulders all the way down. Holly wore dark sunglasses and the blond beehive wig from their Jack-stalking days. She had a plate of pizza, cut into bites. She stabbed a piece and shoved it into Chad's mouth. "It's maddening. And *of course* Tom just used it to justify his motorcycle ride. He drove it on the sidewalk to get around them. Meanwhile, *Spider-Man* here has to be spoon-fed because his hands are useless."

The casts covered Chad's thumbs and knuckles. Only the tips of his fingers stuck out.

"Mom said my hands were like ham hocks," Chad said, proudly.

"How... is everything?" Miriam asked.

"Oh, it's great!" Chad replied. "I got to ride in an ambulance!"

"It is absolutely awful," Holly said. She stabbed another bite of pizza and thrust it at Chad's mouth. Chad snatched it off the fork with his teeth. "Six weeks of this. He can't do anything himself."

"What's with the wig?" Miriam asked.

"I like it," Holly said. She walked closer toward the car, and Miriam caught a whiff of lemony vodka. "I like it better than my real hair. So I figured, what the hell! Tom can jump out of planes. Tom can ride a motorcycle. I might as well wear a wig, if that's what I want!"

"You should. That's great," Jack said. He tapped his fedora. "Though I prefer a good hat myself."

"The thing is," Holly said, "the wig gets too hot if you've still got hair. So I had to shave all the hair off!"

Holly yanked the wig off. Underneath, her head was completely bald.

BRATTY AND HIS THERAPIST

Miriam: *Can I ask you a question?*

Bradford: *What?*

Miriam: *I know, it's odd, but—if you wouldn't mind saying, your best friend—*

Bradford: *Tommy?*

Miriam: *The rapper.*

Bradford: *Yeah, that's Tommy.*

Miriam: *And he's called Mr. Yay.*

Bradford: *Yup.*

Miriam: *Why?*

Bradford: *Like, what do you mean?*

Miriam: *Why is he called that? Or how did he pick that name?*

Bradford: *I dunno. It just came out of his mouth.*

Miriam: *And you never asked why?*

Bradford: *Why would I ask?*

Miriam: *Because... never mind—*

Bradford: *What was weird about it was like, I heard the name in my head before he said it.*

Miriam: *Oh?*

Bradford: *Yeah. I heard* Mr. Yay *and then he said "Mr. Yay," and I was, like,* huh. *But I was also probably high. And we were up all night. So you know, it's hard to say what really happened.*

Miriam: *That's... yeah. So... how are things?*

Bradford: *I want to say... Okay, it's, like...* spectacular? *Unbelievably awesomely* fucking *spectacular. But fuck, I don't want to jinx it. Aaaand... I'm still dodging my dad's phone calls. He thinks I've got an internship lined up at the First Bank of Lake Orange.*

Miriam: *Why would he think that?*

Bradford: *Um, well, like, Tommy thought it would be funny to mess around with Photoshop, and he posted all these pics of himself on UniTab in like, obviously photoshopped situations. Like there's Tommy walking his pet tyrannosaur. Shit like that. But he made one where it's me and him photoshopped into business suits, standing in front of this bank, looking douchey. It's so obviously fake. But somehow my dad saw Tommy's post and he just, like, assumed I had a job there.*

Miriam: *And you didn't correct him.*

Bradford: *Fuck no. I mean, I should. But like, whatever, he's off my back for a while.*

Miriam: *I know you think he'll disapprove of what you're doing—*

Bradford: *That's an understatement*

Miriam: *But maybe if he understands he'll come around. Or, at least, you'll know you gave him the chance to come around.*

Bradford: *Yeah, okay, I see your point.*

Miriam: *For what it's worth, if you were my kid, I'd be proud.*

Bradford: *I... Thanks.*

Miriam: *It takes guts to leave the path your parents set out for you, to follow your own dreams. And to accomplish so much—*

Bradford: *It's Tommy who accomplished everything. I'm just, you know, like, support.*

Miriam: *You're selling yourself short. You told me, last time we talked, that you were a team.*

Bradford: *Okay. You're right, yo. It's just... like, I can't believe I'm there.*

Miriam: *How so?*

Bradford: *Well like, with Tommy, I can see it. I could always imagine him rapping or playing music or throwing festivals or, like, making magic. He's magic. I mean, I know there's no such thing as magic. But if there were... Tommy's different. He's special. And I'm just, like, a regular dude.*

Miriam: *You and Tommy have been friends for most of your lives. He wouldn't be who he is if not for you.*

Bradford: *He'd still be special. But also, like, when I said, "I can't believe I'm there," I meant that it's... dreamlike. It's like, I can see and hear everything that's happening around me, but something's off. Something's different. And I don't know what it is, or why. I can't put my finger on it. And every time I try— You ever, like, trip out and start seeing cat tails in the corner of your eye?*

Miriam: *No.*

Bradford: *It's a thing. It's like, there's the tail, in your peripheral vision. But if you turn to look, there's no cat. It's like that. But... bigger. Or, more important. I don't know. I'm rambling, sorry. I shouldn't have eaten that edible before our call. But, Doc, I'm weak.*

Miriam: *You're fine.*

Bradford: *I'm... happier than I've ever been. But also freaked out. At the same time. And I know, maybe that's just what it's always like, when your life changes drastically. When you're, you know, doing what Tommy—what me and Tommy are doing. Like how could I not be freaked out? But it's also more than just that. It's surreal. I can feel it. In my gut, in my bones. You know what I mean? You know, don't you?*

MASTER OF ASS

WHERE WAS MR. YAY?

Mr. Yay was poolside. His lounge chair looked like a giant clamshell. He had a copy of *Rolling Stone* open on his lap, but he wasn't reading. He watched bikinis drift past.

This wasn't real life.

Fatty Bratty had, beneath the soft pudge of his receding belly, the faintest chisel of a six-pack. He had a spliff and a breakfast beer and a feeling in his gut, in his bones, that he'd stumbled into some alternate reality, or dosed the red and blue pills at the same time. The effect was a lucid dream. But his legs were tethered to Earth. A small green lizard darted past, over his toes, under his lounge chair, and away.

The hotel pool had an infestation of lizards.

"I'll fucking kill them if they try to get rid of the lizards," Tommy said. "I'll trash the room. I'll destroy them on the internet."

Six or seven lizards basked on Tommy's clamshell. They were happy, together, in this moment.

"Does it feel weird?" Bratty asked.

"What?"

"You know. This."

Tommy was, paradoxically, clairvoyant and obtuse. He seemed to perceive some anomaly, to understand to a greater degree than

Bratty ever would. But when pressed, he'd say something extraneous, like: "Would you rather have pegs for legs, or hooks for hands?"

The article on the open pages of his magazine had a picture of a peg-legged man, a victim of the corporatization of the American prison system, according to *Rolling Stone*. The for-profit prison had neglected to treat his injured leg, until it turned gangrenous and they had to chop it off, and then neglected to provide him with a proper prosthetic.

"Definitely pegs for legs," Bratty said.

"For sure. What the hell would you do with hooks for hands?"

Mr. Yay turned the page. The next article was about fraternity hazing, and the young men it had killed. The article after was about banned books and fascism and the systematic repression of ideas. Mr. Yay closed the magazine and tossed it on the ground outside his clamshell. The magazine had the audacity to flip open, on landing, to the picture of the peg-legged man.

"What the hell." Tommy glowered at the magazine. "I thought *Rolling Stone* was supposed to be rock and roll."

"And rap. I mean, they're interviewing you—"

"But the rest of this—this is dark as fuck."

"But that's the world."

"Yeah, well. It doesn't have to be. It could be fuckin' glorious."

Tommy swung his feet out of the clamshell. He kicked the magazine out of his sight. That sort of task would have been nearly impossible with peg legs. He got up and wandered over to the pool. There were four shell-shaped pools connected by moats, with an island in the middle. The island had a tiki bar and real palm trees that looked like fake palm trees, and other live tropical plants with plastic-looking leaves.

Tommy waded to the bar. He ordered a piña colada in a pineapple husk.

Where was Mr. Yay?

Mr. Yay was minus two days from his sold-out show at a Las Vegas nightclub.

Mr. Yay was minus four days from his interview with *Rolling Stone*.

Mr. Yay was on the diving board. He dove into the water. With hooks for hands or pegs for legs, he might never resurface. But he did, victorious, because this dream was the best dream he or Bratty ever had.

Bratty reclined in his clamshell lounger. He gazed up at the sky. It looked artificially blue, like the fake skies inside Vegas hotels, where daylight perpetually reigned.

Maybe this sky was fake, too. No way to know. He closed his eyes. He listened to pool sounds, the clink of ice in a cocktail shaker, the pages of a discarded magazine fluttering in the fake sea breeze. He heard a *clop-clop* like peg legs on a pool deck.

Land-ho!

His clamshell floated along beneath the fake sky. Was he dreaming?

"Yo, yo." Tommy shook him. "Wake up, dude."

Bratty opened his eyes. "How long have I been asleep?"

"I dunno, a while? I don't have a fuckin' watch."

But then a waiter arrived with two large orders of french fries and two Dr. Fizz sodas.

"It must be fry-o-clock," Bratty said.

"Fry-o-clock. Would you rather be always greasy and salty, like you're a french fry, or always wet and sticky like a soda?"

"My clothes too or just my skin?"

"Both."

"And I could never wash it off?"

"Nope. Never."

"I think I'll go greasy."

"Yep. More aerodynamic. Plus, you know, you could never get laid if you were always sticky. At least if you were greasy you might meet some greasy babe and then you could be greasy together."

After fry-o-clock came beer-o-clock, then cocktail hour. Then Mr. Yay and Fatty Bratty put on their favorite T-shirts and hats, did some dabs, and went to the club.

The hotel club, Titan's Kingdom, was an underwater dreamscape of neon lights and luminescent fish. Black-lit jellyfish floated beneath a glass-bottomed dance floor. Mermaid acrobats with shimmering tails glided overhead. Lights projected waves and corals and seaweed. Lasers made schools of fish and sharks and dancing octopi. Bartenders in gowns of rippling scales poured drinks into seashell cocktail glasses.

"Would you rather eat nothing but fish for the rest of your life," Bratty asked, "or have big googly fish eyes?"

"Would I only have fish eyes, or would I get to keep my regular eyes too?"

"Only fish eyes."

"I'll go with fish eyes. That'd be sick." Tommy ordered two mai tais. As they waited, women drifted toward him. They had short skirts, glittered eyelids, face jewels, glossy lips, keen eyes. They knew him. Or they were drawn to him. Mr. Yay, a bright light in the subaqueous darkness. Mr. Yay, the magnetic. He ordered two more mai tais. Four more. A round of beers.

"Would you rather have the head of a squid," he asked, "or the body of a walrus?"

"The head of a squid, for sure," Bratty said.

"The head of a squid," all the ladies agreed.

They got a booth, and more rounds of drinks, and drunk Tommy wanted everyone's life story. He wanted to know how they had gotten here, to this club, in this Vegas, in this moment in their lives. He wanted to know how they'd gotten so gorgeous, because fuck, all this beauty overwhelmed him.

"It's like, the world is so heartbreakingly beautiful." He gazed upon the dance floor. His eyes had a contemplative gleam. "If you think about it. The improbability of it. The improbability that you would exist, and also be so hot. And all of this." He waved his arms. "Vegas. This club. This music. How there can be all this music, all this beauty, and so many people don't see it? Or they don't think it matters. Or they're too busy fighting or fretting or working, and it's like, what the fuck are we really here for?"

"To party?"

"Yeah."

"And to love and make art and shit."

"To make the world better. More beautiful."

"I think about my dad," Tommy said. "He's a good guy. A good dad. But yo, his priorities. They're screwed. Like when I was a kid, he bought this boat. This nice-ass shiny speedboat. I helped him pick it out. And he was like, 'Tommy, we'll spend all summer out on the river, fishing and swimming and sailing around. It'll be glorious,' he said. But you know how many times he took me out on that boat?"

"How many?"

"Like, a dozen. Over, I don't know, ten years. Maybe once a year we'd go out on the boat. And the rest of the time it just sat around and grew moss. And every summer he'd say this was the summer we'd go boating, but we never did. He was always too busy working. Weekends, evenings, like nothing else existed in the universe except hedge funds and stock markets and all that financial shit. Like the boat was just some fever dream. And my dad was just a vessel for constant work. And yeah, sometimes he'd have these brief moments where he wasn't working, and he'd look around all bleary-eyed and shit, like he'd just woken up. And then work would come and knock him the fuck out again."

"That's... sad."

"Yeah it's fucking sad. What's sad is that he's, like, a model of success. He's what we're supposed to be. That's supposed to be happiness. He doesn't even know how miserable he is. He wanted me to follow in his footsteps. And I started to. But then I was like, no. Fuck business school. Fuck it."

"So you dropped out?" one of the hotties asked.

Mr. Yay busted out:

Cause I'm a rebel, like Luke Skywalker
Smokin' weed that looks like
A green Chewbacca
'Cause that bud's so hairy, got me scary stoned
The kind of weed that you nervous to smoke alone, yo...

He took a drink of mai tai. "Yeah I dropped out. Fuck college. Not the learning part. Like, learning is great. Books are great. If

I'd majored in English or psychology, instead of going to business school like my dad wanted... But see it's like this: You go to college—"

"You pay a fuck load of money to go to college," Bratty added.

"Right. A *fuck ton* of money. And you work hard, and you graduate, and then what? You go get your MBA or whatever the fuck. Then you get a job. And you work and you work, and then what? For what?"

"But everyone has to work," said one of the hotties. "At least if you go to college, you can get a better job."

"That is the story. But the whole premise of the story is false. It's like the lie the whole system tells itself to keep itself alive. It doesn't have to be like this. It could be better. It doesn't have to be about work. It doesn't have to be about money," Mr. Yay said, and then a silvery merman whisked away his empty glass, and he ordered another round for the whole table.

It didn't have to be about money, but, Bratty knew, money was also an undeniable facet of this timeline, and Tommy had never gone without it. His privilege allowed for idealism. He could afford it.

"I'm tired," Bratty said. And drunk. And he missed his dog. "I'm gonna head up to the room."

"Bratty, stay and party."

"I'm good. Plus, the dog—"

The hotties squealed. "Aww, the dog!"

"OMG, is it Tux? I saw him on KlipSwatch!"

"I want to see pictures!"

Tommy had pictures. Bratty slipped out of the booth. He glided out of the club, through the casino. He caught the elevator. He floated up, twenty-three stories. He drifted through an aquatic hallway, the plush carpet soft as sand beneath his feet, the walls rippling with blue waves of projected light. Ocean sounds burbled in the background. The door to their suite was a mirage of marine life. He swiped his key. He swam through.

His dog ran to greet him.

Tuxy Luxy. Tuxander the Great. Tux of the Hotel Tower.

"Hey, boy!"

Bratty took the dog out to pee. He scratched the dog, fed him, played tug-of-war. They sat together on the couch. Beyond the window was a blaze of hotel lights, casinos and strip clubs and spotlights, rainbow fountains, neon cowboys, illuminated billboards, and that massive sphere, an oasis of blinding luminescence. The Strip was a blur of headlights and taillights, and the lights arched out through city and suburb toward the distant highways and out into the dark nothingness of the empty desert until at last they reached LA, or Ohio, where Bratty's dad and Tommy's dad worked late into the evening, safe inside their big sad houses, where all their money meant nothing.

Neither of them had a dog.

"But I have you," Bratty told Tux. "And you have me."

Woof.

"But where did you come from?"

He could accept the reality of the dog. The dog's unexplained presence in his apartment. The dog food and the dog accessories and the veterinary records. They all said this was his dog. And so it was. But he wasn't fucking crazy.

"Would you tell me? If you knew?"

Woof.

He stood up. Pressed his hand against the glass. He half expected to phase through, as if the glass was porous, water.

"But it's mostly empty space. This window. You. Me. We're mostly just empty space. Which is fucked up, if you think about it. How something that's basically nothing can matter so much."

Between the couch and window was a table. On that table was a pad of hotel paper. On the paper were lyrics, scribbled by Tommy in the fringes of the Vegas night, when the sky smoldered red around the edges.

Yo, this rap is for those
Who been sayin' I can't
Who been sayin' go back
With empty hands because
Rappin' ain't a plan
That I should grow up
Get a job
Be a man
That the point of life is to raise fake stacks
But I don't buy that
See, I gotta be me
Gotta follow my dream
And cash don't matter
If I'm my own man
Gotta master fuckin' plan
Gonna make more tracks,
Gonna sip Cognac
With my bro Bratty and the dog

Yo, we a wolf pack
You wanna do blackjack
Well I don't fold
You wanna hit me
I'll hit back
And I'm all in
When it comes to rap, cuz see
I'mma be the master of that
I'mma be the master of rap

Bratty could hear the rap in his head. He opened his laptop. He started making beats. He played with sounds and rhythms and the dog lounged beside him, head on his lap, and, yeah, he ate a gummy and raided the minibar and wondered what-in-the-holy-fuck was this all? His reflection was a phantom in the glass, a pair of eyes staring down at the specter of Vegas, where the gods had squatted over the desert and expelled a bazillion precious jewels, diamonds and glittering rubies and sapphires and gold and shit. It was awe-fucking-inspiring. It was strange as hell.

He got lost in the music.

At some point, hours later, the door clicked open. Tommy stumbled through.

"Dude, you... You missed—"

"Don't tell me."

"Starts with an F-O-U-R—"

"But listen." Bratty played a clip of beats.

"That's sick." Tommy grinned. His smile had the straight, pearly gleam of substantial orthodontic investments. And those whitening strips. He denied it, but Bratty had seen evidence in the bathroom trash.

"It's for this." Bratty handed him the paper with his lyrics. "Try it." He fired up the beats.

Tommy cleared his throat. He grabbed a bottle of tequila from the minibar. He took a swig. He rapped.

Yeah they say I'm crass
'Cause I cuss, and I fuck
With a joint in my hand
But it ain't about that
It ain't about the lines
Or the booze
Or the bitches so fine
And yeah that slaps
But that's not why I rap
why I'm bad, like Capone to crime
why I bootleg rhymes
why I rap like the Flash
'Cause I spit real fast
But I ain't too fast
When I hit that grass
When I tap that ass
When I grab that ass and grind
When I play that track
That makes 'em dance
Makes the whole crowd shake their ass
Until they're outta her mind

'Cause I'm

I'mma be the master of that

I'mma be the master of ass

"So?" Tommy took another shot of tequila. He had a voice like smooth custard.

"It was great. Except, it needs a 'yo.' Like, 'I'mma be the master of that, yo.' "

" 'I'mma be the master of that, yo. I'mma be the master of ass.' Like that?"

"Yeah. Just like that."

"What should we call it?"

" 'Master of Rap'?"

" 'Master of Ass'?"

" 'AssMaster'?"

Bratty and Tommy burst out laughing. Then there was a knock on the door.

"What the fuck?"

"Who's there, yo?"

"Guest services."

"Oh, fuck, that's right," Tommy said. "I ordered a nightcap."

He opened the door. On the other side, a man in a tuxedo suit presented a bottle of champagne on a silver tray.

"Good morning, Mr. Fischer."

"Actually," Tommy said, "you can call me 'AssMaster.' " Bratty guffawed.

"As you wish, Mr.—"

"AssMaster."

"Mr. AssMaster. If there is anything else I can bring you

gentleman, please dial 'eight' on your phone for special guest services."

"Anything?"

"Anything at all, sir."

"What about some curly fries?" Tommy asked. "Can you bring us some curly fries?"

"Yes, sir."

"What about a cat?"

"What kind of cat would you like, sir?"

"Oh, I don't know. I just wanted to know if you could bring me a cat, if I wanted a cat."

"Yes, please let me know if that is what you would like."

"Sick. What about a zebra? Or a donkey?"

"Yes, sir. Would you like a zebra, sir, or a donkey, or both?"

"Oh, neither. But we could have one if we wanted?"

"Yes, sir."

"Ooh, what about—" Tommy stopped. He looked at Bratty, then down, at the dog by Bratty's feet. The dog was its regular dog self, eager-eyed, tongue out, tail wagging, and then it flickered. The whole dog flickered. It grew brighter, more vibrant, more real than the room around it. Then it faded, from dull to diaphanous. Its eyes were gossamer. Its tail was a glimmer. Bratty could see straight through its stocky form, as if it was the ghost of a dog, a shadow, a dream. There was a sound, barely audible, but the shadow dog's ears perked. It sounded like a zipper. Like wind in a void. Like the whistle of a tune once known but now forgotten. So faint that you wondered if you'd ever heard it, or just imagined it. The sound seemed to come from inside this pellucid dog, but maybe Bratty's brain produced it.

Then it stopped. The dog solidified. The dog was regular dog, but his ears stayed perked.

"About what, sir?" the man in the tuxedo asked. His face was impassive. He hadn't seen it. He hadn't heard anything beyond the animal requests of the stoned drunk rapper.

"About... you know, I think... we're good," Tommy said.

"Would you still like the curly fries, sir?"

"I... yes. Sure. Thank you."

He tipped the man a twenty. He closed the door. He looked at Bratty, then the dog, then Bratty.

"You saw that?" Bratty asked.

"Yeah." Tommy nodded. "Fuck."

"What was it?"

"I don't fuckin' know. Is he okay?"

They both crouched down beside the dog. They scratched and petted and hugged the dog. The dog felt solid. He seemed unperturbed.

"I think he's fine."

"Are you?"

"Am I?'

"Yeah. Your arms were like..."

"Like what?" Bratty asked.

"Translucent."

"Me? My arms?" His arms seemed fine. He hadn't noticed anything.

"For a second," Tommy said. "But I don't know. I ate a couple gummies. Could just be my brain, tripping out."

But his eyes said it wasn't. His eyes reflected the twinkle of unreality that Bratty felt, in his gut, in his bones, in his soul.

Interlude

FLASHBACK

BRATTY

BRATTY WAS SEVENTEEN when he started watching *The Adventures of Mr. Yay.* Yeah, he'd seen it as a kid, with Tommy. But he hadn't really *seen* it. He hadn't understood, until he began to understand who he wasn't.

It was the twinkle of unreality that enthralled him. The uniformity of the waves. The still-brilliant colors of clothes tattered by months of salt and sea. The wisdom imparted by a captain who chased his own tail, around and around, for fun. *A shark can't turn away from the sea,* the captain declared, and his first mate translated. They stood at the prow. The dog's tongue flapped in the ocean breeze. He spoke, each line on the screen displayed with the same stock footage.

But let us all be who we would be.

The octopus, the clown fish, the stingray, every creature of this silly realm.

It's okay to get lost, if it lets you find your true self.

He watched it even though, okay, he was too old, or whatever.

You're too old, Bradford.

When will you get serious, Bradford?

Life's too short to waste on a stupid TV show.

You have to focus on the future.

Okay okay okay okay *he heard them.* He did his homework.

But when it was done, he got high and watched *The Adventures of Mr. Yay.*

Captain Barksford and the giraffe and the kangaroo and the leopard and all the other animals didn't give two shits about whether Bradford Pierson III had taken the requisite arbitrary number of SAT practice tests that would, good old Dad assured, reward him with a successful and fulfilling life. Mr. Yay would *oops!* toss the study guide overboard. The SAT wasn't learning. Learning was learning enough Thai to not accidentally order fried bugs from a Bangkok street vendor. Learning was learning how to navigate from Eritrea to Istanbul, with culinary and cultural excursions to Athens and Damascus. Learning was learning how to tie a tourniquet in case of a shark attack, and yeah, the chimpanzee lost his hand, but he kept his life.

Learning was learning not to get so high that you zoned out and didn't notice when the garage door opened and the car rolled in and your stepmom got out, until she was right there, in the center field of your vision, irate.

"Bradford Pierson!"

"Uh...what?"

Learning was learning not to sound so obviously stoned.

"What? You're asking me what? I can't even. This is just... I am at my wit's end with your disrespect. God, this is giving me a migraine, just thinking about it. You're giving me a migraine. I can't even deal with you."

And then she left, and impalpable time passed before he understood what he'd done. If he ever understood.

It was that the neighbors had seen him in the backyard, and no, they hadn't smelled it. The houses were too big and too far apart to smell anything but money in between them. And no, they hadn't *seen* him smoke anything because, in fact, he hadn't. He had learned better than to smoke in full view of the neighbors. In fact, he had gone out to the yard to locate the dog shit that Helena Pierson claimed to have spotted in the yard, a gift from someone else's dog, who would not have trespassed and befouled the lawn if Bratty was a better human being, and so he better go clean it up, and gosh he sure did look suspicious, outside, with his headphones and his baggy pants.

It was the attention he failed to pay when he placed the order for Chinese food delivery. Helena Pierson had clearly loudly glaringly articulated her distaste for greasy salty delicious things, at some earlier juncture. If he was any sort of son, he would know what she liked and didn't like and endeavor to accommodate her. But the lo mein had too much salt and the egg rolls were too greasy and one bite, her stomach was wrecked, her night was ruined, her health was indelibly imperiled.

It was the beer he had *stolen* from the fridge, and yeah, okay, guilty as charged. A whole six-pack. He hadn't really thought of it as *stealing* when he took the beer from his own fridge. It was more like a rescue. But the Rescue Beer came with the red-letter *D*, for *Delinquent*, eternally.

It was his audacity to exist.

"You know what you've done, Bradford." His dad tried to sound impartial and judicious. "Some things can't be undone."

He didn't know, but he had learned to pretend.

"A squid can't take back its ink."

"See, that's just the sort of nonsense that—"

"I was just quoting from this show, I mean—"

"And it's totally disrespectful. Interrupting me like that. Joking, when you should be taking things seriously. Helena is very sensitive. She's a very sensitive soul."

"I know."

"You clearly don't. And that's why we've decided—"

She decided. It was decided, and any attempt by him to alter this decision was further evidence of his inherent delinquency. He packed his bags. Only the essentials:

(1) appropriate clothes and shoes

(2) toiletries

(3) SAT study materials

No headphones, no speakers, no turntables, none of those weird little toys and collectibles he insisted on keeping. He still had his Captain Barksford lunch box Tommy had given him for his tenth birthday. What sort of young man would keep a thing like that?

"But it's our last summer," Tommy said, when he found out. "It's the summer before our senior year. They can't send you away."

"I don't think you understand *can't*."

"I understand *fuck them.*"

"They can do whatever they want."

"Why should some people get to do whatever they want, and other people can't? It's fucked."

"I'm a kid. I have no legal rights."

"You're seventeen. And that's not my fucking point. My point is, it's not fair. It's not right. You don't deserve this."

"I did call her a turd-gurgling leech raptor."

"Okay, but that was *after* they said they were sending you away. And it's true. You spoke truth to power. You should be rewarded."

Tommy rewarded him with new headphones, delivered the day he arrived at the Franklin Academy for Truant Youth. Fatty Camp, the kids called it, for the fat joints they snuck and the pounds they lost from laps and push-ups and flavorless food.

Power rewarded him by cleaning out his bedroom during his summer away.

"You should thank her," his dad said. "Helena worked very hard cleaning out your room for you. It was very generous of her to take time from her busy schedule to get rid of all that junk."

His records. His action figures and comic books and trading cards. His old Captain Barksford lunch box. Just like that, it was all gone.

FLASHBACK

MIRIAM + JACK

A WOMAN WAS IN LOVE, and that was enough, right?

Love was all you needed, said songs and cinema. Love swelled large enough to fill your heart, your soul, your belly, your every waking thought.

Like a balloon, except it was filled with oxytocin.

A woman was in love, except at night, when she slept, her brain forgot. Her brain forged a strange vacancy in the bed beside her. Her brain conjured a ringing phone, a husband who wouldn't pick up, a choppy sea between them. Her dream gave her a carton of eggs. She cracked three in a bowl. She cracked a fourth, but instead of white and yolk, out came a little foot. It looked, at first, like a tiny human foot, the foot of a doll, or a pixie. Then it became the foot of a chick. The chick soaked in the bowl of egg. It shook bits of shell from its feathers. Then it hopped out, onto the table. It ran to the window. It leapt. She awaited the *thud-crunch* of chicken smacking glass, but instead it sailed through, as if the window was porous. Then, outside, it took flight. It was a black bird-shape in a neon sky. It was a dream a woman forgot, by the time it mattered. She thought, in the dream and on waking: *Where are my chickens?* But she forgot that, too. She had other suspicions to ponder.

But regardless, regardless, no matter how it turned out, love was enough. And she was smitten. She was a newlywed. She was Mrs. Miriam Shipley and she still shivered with glee to see her name in print. To hear it. *The Shipleys. Mister. Missus.* Plus a fine young dog. And what else?

She loved their house. *Their* house. A two-story Craftsman at the cul-de-sac end of Ravenswood Drive. She loved the big trees and cottage gardens and gas lamps of her 1930s suburb. She loved the neighborliness, the block parties, the stop-and-chats. She loved the density of plant and animal life, the birds nested in the leafy branches, the rabbits and foxes. She even loved the bees that burrowed holes in the wooden porch furniture, the deer who devoured her hostas, the brazen squirrels who plucked every ripe tomato from her garden plants, ate a single bite, then tossed the rest aside.

She loved all this because she loved Jack, so much that it felt like a neutron bomb, a mushroom cloud of love to envelop everything around her.

It was June. Hot and steamy. The air was sickeningly floral. A brood of cicadas had hatched. They abandoned their crunchy exoskeletons on streets and sidewalks, bushes and branches. She went for a run, *crunch crunch crunch* along the sidewalk, and wondered whether and how her life might change.

Maybe she would have to run less and swim more. Maybe she would take an extra year to finish grad school. Maybe she would paint the bedroom blue or yellow. Maybe she would buy a jogging stroller.

Maybe she should call Jack right then. But no, that was her swollen heart talking louder than reason. Jack was busy at work. Jack was a junior associate at Rufus Mather LLP and if he worked hard, he could climb, up and up to the partnership pinnacle. She shouldn't call him on a hunch.

She jogged to the drugstore and bought a four-pack of pregnancy tests. She jogged home. On the way, she passed by her neighbor Holly. Holly and Tom Waters had just bought the house at the top of Ravenswood Drive. Holly squatted in her garden, with a shovel and bucket. She pulled weeds. She wore a large sun hat. She had a huge pregnant belly, like she'd swallowed a watermelon whole.

"Garden looks nice," Miriam said.

"It's getting there." Holly stood up. She wiped sweat from her forehead. "Those damn deer have been eating my hostas again. The birds keep pooping on the steps. The weeds are relentless. And every time I bend down to pull one, I feel like I'm going to tip over. And look at my feet! They're so swollen I can't wear shoes. Pregnancy is torture."

"How much longer have you got?"

"Two weeks, three days. If he's on time."

"Fingers crossed."

"He better be on time. I'm so frickin' miserable. And all I want is a nice cold beer, but I'm not allowed to have one."

Miriam took the test as soon as she got home. The box had a drawing of a fat, dimpled baby with a curlicue of hair. The instructions said that a straight line meant *not pregnant* and a curlicue meant *pregnant*. The instructions said it would take two minutes, but it only took a few seconds before the curlicue appeared. She took a second test, just to be sure. She wanted to call Jack right then, to squeal into the phone, *Jack! Jack Jack Jack Jack, we're having a baby!!!* But also, she wanted the revelation to be special and perfect. She wanted to see the look on his face. To feel his arms, his hands, his lips. Their hearts, beating together.

She skipped class and spent the day idly surfing the internet, browsing for baby clothes, baby accessories, tips for healthy happy pregnant mothers. She went grocery shopping. She cooked Jack's favorite dinner foods: corn on the cob, buttermilk biscuits. Meat loaf. She set the table. She lit candles. She poured a glass of wine, for Jack. None for her. He was supposed to be home at seven. She'd timed everything perfectly.

At 6:55, he called. "Hey babe, I've got to work late tonight."

"Oh. How late?"

"*Late* late. Like, midnight, if I'm lucky. I'll try not to wake you."

"Okay... but just tonight, right? You'll be home for dinner tomorrow?"

"Yeah, I think so."

She turned off the oven. She blew out the candles. She hid the meat loaf in the back of the fridge, where Jack wouldn't stumble across it. She ordered a pizza and spent the night with the internet and the TV.

The next night, she tried again. She got him to confirm first.

"Seven, right?"

"Yeah, yeah, I'll be home."

"You're sure?"

"I'm sure."

She lit the candles, poured the wine, reheated the meat loaf. She put on music and lipstick. Then Jack called.

"So..."

"Yes?"

"I know I said I'd be home at seven, but something came up."

"Oh."

"We've been working on closing this big deal, and one of the partners has a sick kid, and so, well—"

"You're coming home late."

"Yes."

"As late as last night?"

"Yes. I'm sorry, babe. This should all be over by tomorrow. I wish I could come home. I really miss you."

The meat loaf went back in the fridge. She made a box of macaroni and cheese for herself. She ate it right out of the pan.

Tomorrow. Tomorrow would be better.

But then tomorrow came, and at least he called before she'd reheated the meat loaf again.

"I'm sorry. We closed that big deal, but one of the partners needs me to write a speech for his presentation at the bar association tomorrow. I just found out about it this afternoon."

"So..."

"So... I have to stay late again."

"Look, Jack, I really need to tell you—"

"Oh, shoot, my secretary just told me I've got a call. Can it wait?"

"Uh, sure. Sure, Jack."

"Thanks for being so understanding, babe."

She hung up. She moved the meat loaf to the front of the fridge, where Jack could find and reheat it himself. She ate a bag of potato chips, dipped in nacho cheese. She took another pregnancy test and left it out on the counter with a note, in case the test wasn't obvious enough.

Jack, we're having a baby. There's leftover meat loaf, corn, and biscuits in the fridge.

Later, she ate the biscuits. Then she climbed into an empty bed and fell asleep.

She woke up in Jack's arms. Sunlight streamed through the blinds. The clock read 9:17. Jack ran his hand across her hair, down her chest, around her belly.

"You're home."

"I'm home."

"Don't you have work?"

"I called in sick."

"Oh, good. But, will that be okay? I don't want you to get in trouble at work."

"They'll never know I wasn't actually sick," Jack said. "And besides, it doesn't matter. The only things that matter today are here in this bed."

THE SENATOR

IMAGINE YOU are a senator.

Imagine power.

Imagine temptation.

You can make things happen. People will pay money for you to make things happen. People will pay money to you, if you let it happen, but *oh you never would.*

Never ever never ever never ever.

As a senator, you are adept at doublespeak and deflection.

Let's be honest, Senator. For once.

It's not that you never would. Take a bribe. Smuggle drugs. Snort coke and pound the rent boy in the ass with the rubber cock you bought because—let's be honest, Senator—yours doesn't work anymore.

It's that you haven't. You took one glimpse at that lubed-up slope and saw just how far you might fall. And it has taken Every. Bit. Of. Your. Willpower. To stay on top.

Oh, poor senator.

You tried, I'll admit, but sometimes the Real You has to bust out.

You just didn't expect it to happen with the TSA, with a briefcase full of cash you never got to spend, cocaine you never got to snort. The sight of that dildo makes you weep.

You would never, you tell your wife, the cops, your lawyer.

Look, Mr. Senator, I'm on your side. But you need to tell me the truth. Or how can I defend you?

You would never. That is the truth, as far as you can admit to yourself. You didn't. You don't know where those drugs came from. You've no idea how that dildo got into your luggage. You must have been framed. Someone planted these things. Someone swapped your luggage. Even TSA is complicit. This is a conspiracy, to ruin you.

But gosh. What *is* true and what *feels* true don't always align. You know that better than anyone.

MAY

THE NOTE

EVER SINCE the trip to the video rental store, where the owner had confirmed that he too remembered a show that didn't seem to exist, starring an actor who'd also starred in the cult classic detective flick *Peregrine,* which Jack had seen no less than a dozen times, Jack had gone full-throttle sleuth, determined to solve the Case of the Missing Mr. Yay.

"Look at this," Jack said, stopping her as she passed through the kitchen.

He looked excited. He swiveled his laptop around on the table to show her. On the screen was a photo of a middle-aged Asian man in a cheap suit.

"What am I looking at?"

"Kenji Okiayo. Who, according to the lawsuit he filed, *was* the VP of marketing for the Machsai corporation, right up until a few months ago, when he materialized in the middle of a busy street."

"What do you mean 'materialized'?"

"I mean *materialized.* Like appeared out of thin air. Lucky for him he didn't get hit by a bus. But otherwise, he's not so lucky, because now he's unemployed."

"I thought you said—"

"Yep. He *was* marketing VP, he says. And he remembers details that he couldn't possibly know unless that was true. But Machsai says he hasn't worked there for years. There's also speculation that he was a test subject for some secretive Machsai experiment, or that he was replaced by a robot version of himself."

"That's absurd. But why are you telling me this?"

"Because it's all related! Don't you see? Kenji Okiayo, Mr. Yay, that boat in the Mediterranean that appeared and then disappeared, that Olympic marathon runner who broke her leg, but then it wasn't broken! I haven't fit all the pieces together yet, but I'm beginning to see how they fit."

"How all the conspiracies fit? I mean, except for Mr. Yay."

"Don't you see how—"

"No," she said, because the way Jack described it made it all seem insane. Because she couldn't even handle her own mystery husband. Maybe Jack should solve that riddle first, before looping in every random internet conspiracy. Miriam turned to leave.

"Wait, where are you going? You look nice."

"I'm going out," Miriam said.

"Oh."

"Holly texted. She wanted to meet out somewhere. I thought—"

"You should. You should go out."

"You got this? The kids need baths and dinner and—"

"Yep. No problem."

Jack unloaded the dishwasher. He scrubbed the pans. He bathed the kids. When she finished getting ready, he was in the kitchen, in his fedora and flip-flops, preemptively tweezering the tomato chunklets from Lindsey's sauce, while Lindsey and her brother played hopscotch with the three-legged dog, who just wanted to lie on the squares.

"That's generous of you."

"This is how she likes it, right?" Jack said.

Who was *this* Jack? This Jack who did dishes and washed children. This Jack who dropped the fork, walked toward her, brushed his hand across her cheek, down her neck, around her back. She shuddered. She pulled away.

"Oh—I'm sorry, I—" He let her go. He looked hurt.

"It's fine. I didn't mean— I just—" It had happened reflexively. He touched her. Her body reacted. Her body affirmed her suspicion. More than a month had passed since Jack confessed, and he still felt like a stranger.

It was then, as they stood in the kitchen, in the awkward shadow of their failing marriage, that Miriam recalled a moment in this kitchen, seven years earlier, when she wrote a note: *Jack, we're having a baby. There's leftover meat loaf, corn, and biscuits in the fridge.* And then she recalled another moment, the next morning, when she found the note and stuck it in a box in her closet, to save, to remember.

"No, I should have asked. I know you're still upset. I—"

"Hold on," she said. "I'll be right back."

She left her sorry husband in the kitchen and went upstairs. She dug the box of sentimental items from the back of her closet. She sifted through holiday cards and child-scribbles until she found the note. Then she stuck it in her pocket and went back downstairs to confront her husband.

"Jack!"

"What?"

"Do you like meat loaf?"

"What? Why?"

"Just answer. Do you like meat loaf?"

"No. I hate it. I told you."

"When?"

"December? Right before Christmas. You made it. I thought it was, like, revenge or something. Because you had to know. I mean, I'm sure I told you before then—"

"No."

"It's not like a secret," Jack said, with a dismissive shrug.

"No. You didn't tell me. My husband didn't tell me. Because *my husband* loves meat loaf."

"What? No, I just said—"

"He loves it. It's his favorite." She stepped closer, glaring at him. "Which means YOU are NOT my husband."

"Miriam—"

"My husband loves meat loaf. My husband didn't grow up in some cultural twilight zone where regular TV shows just don't exist. My husband would at least tell me before making a unilateral decision to just quit his job! But you—you're just—you're wandering around in flip-flops, playing detective! You're an impostor!"

"Miriam, this is crazy talk—"

"I am not crazy!"

"I'm not saying you're crazy. And you're right, I should have told you about the job, and I'm sorry. But I'm still your husband—"

"But you don't like meat loaf."

"What does meat loaf have to do with anything?"

"I have proof! From the night I told you I was pregnant with Lindsey. Do you remember that, Jack?"

"Of course I remember."

"Look!" She pulled the note from her pocket. She held it out for Jack to see. *Jack, we're having a baby. There's leftover meat loaf, corn, and biscuits in the fridge.* "You see? You remember this note?"

"I remember . . . but—"

"It's right there. Meat loaf. I made it for you. Because I wanted it to be special. And there's the proof—you're not Jack!"

She stormed out of the house without saying goodbye to Not-Jack and then realized when she got outside that she hadn't called an Uber, and then she had to wait and hope that the kids wouldn't wander into the front yard and see Mom smoking.

They didn't, and the car came and drove her downtown, past the first apartment of Miriam and Jack, to Smitty's Bar. The bar had no windows. Green paint peeled from its recessed door. A faded wooden sign over the front door said SMITTY'S BAR, ALCOHOL SERVED HERE. She went inside.

The original Smitty had died decades ago, but his bar retained his namesake and the same dingy feel that had made it unremarkable long ago, in the golden era of American alcoholism. Middling oil paintings of wildlife scenes hung on the wood-paneled walls. The gleaming eyes of a taxidermy buck gazed down at the bar with bemused concern. The wobbly tables were pocked with ancient cigarette burns. Some still had ashtrays. The floors and booths were sticky with a century of spilt drinks. The jukebox only played songs that no one remembered by musicians that no one had heard of.

Once upon a courtship, Miriam and Jack drank at Smitty's

Bar. This place had meant something. Even Not-Jack remembered it. But then they moved and got older and had kids, and the sticky booths and wood-paneled walls of Smitty's Bar sank down into the deep recesses of Miriam's mind, only to bubble up again, unexpectedly, when Holly had said she wanted to meet someplace discreet.

Holly sat alone at a booth in the back. She wore bubblegum-pink lipstick and her blond beehive wig. She had a half-empty glass, and another totally empty glass, and an empty shot glass, and she knew, they both knew, when Holly looked up, with bloodshot eyes, and flashed a smile, practiced, to hide the quiver of her lip, the clench of her jaw, that Holly had a problem.

Miriam stopped at the bar. She ordered a beer.

"Get me another!" Holly called.

Right.

Miriam sat down across from her friend.

"Did I ever tell you how Tom and I met?" Holly had dark circles under her eyes. Lipstick on her teeth. Dry, cracked lips.

"I don't think so."

"I was in college. I went on a ski trip to Colorado, me and three girlfriends. On the first morning, we were waiting for the chairlift and this handsome guy skis up behind me. Tom. I must have said something to my friends. I don't know. Or maybe they saw me checking him out. But when the chairlift came, they all squeezed on and left me behind, so I had to take the next seat. Next to Tom.

"So I'm riding up the lift with Tom, and I have no clue what we talked about. I've tried to remember, but it's just a big blank. But I do remember the feeling. I remember looking down on the slope below, all white and snowy, and the tops of the evergreen trees, and the way our breath made little clouds in the air. And I remember the way his eyes looked. The way they looked at me, as if, as if..." A tear slipped from Holly's eye. "You know?"

Miriam nodded. "Yeah."

"Like you're the only thing that matters in the universe." Holly drank. "Fuck."

"Yeah."

"Did Jack ever look at you like that?"

"Yes."

"Does he still?"

"I... I don't know." Miriam tried to picture how Jack looked at her now, but she couldn't conjure his eyes. She could only see the back of his head, or his blurry side-face. She had avoided his eyes, for more than a month now, because she didn't trust him. He was Not-Jack.

"Tom doesn't. He... I mean, that's just a thing that happens, right? The love part wears off, or it turns into something else, and what you're left with... Anyway, I remember when we got to the top of the lift, Tom asked if I wanted to ski with him. He said he knew the best slope. And I was like, hell yes, he's hot, so I followed him. I followed him right past the black diamond, to this unmarked slope on the other side of the mountain."

"Maybe not the best idea."

"It was dumb as fuck. Like I don't even know this guy and I go backcountry skiing with him. He could have been a total creep or a rapist or something."

"There could have been an avalanche."

"Yep. So dumb. And it was terrifying. I mean, we had to ski around trees and cliffs, and it was so steep. But it was also exhilarating. I never felt as alive as I did that day, skiing down that unmarked slope, the mountains all around me, the sky this crazy shade of blue, and this guy. Tom. The way he looked at me, when we stopped to catch our breath. The way his eyes lingered on me…" Holly gazed into her beer glass, as if it was a snow globe, where tiny Tom and tiny Holly skied a sparkling mountain through a blizzard of plastic snow, forever and ever. She laughed. "You know, I would never, ever, in a million years go skiing again."

"Why? What happened?"

"Nothing happened. It's just me, I guess. Once, I could ski, and now…"

Holly finished the last of her drink. She slid the glass across the table, leaving a trail of condensation. Someone had carved a heart on the table, around two sets of initials. *K. M. + A. H.* Miriam traced the initials with her finger. *K. M.* and *A. H.* Did they still love each other? Or did they falter and fail?

"Now you're… more responsible."

"I'm not."

"Skiing is dangerous."

"Drinking is dangerous. And I can't stop."

"Do you need help? We could look into rehab, or—"

"It's not—" Holly bit her lip. "I did stop. Last week. Four days. Not a drop."

"So you can stop."

"Oh, sure. Physically, it was fine. Except for the sleep-deprivation part… The thing is, I knew what I was getting into when I married Tom. And it wasn't that I thought I could change him. His daring, his lust for adventure, his thrill-seeking—that's what I liked about him. But now, good god. It's like, over-the-top. The skydiving. The motorcycle. I can't. I just can't. And the more he leans in, the more I freak out. I mean, I get the shakes every time I have to drive the car."

"Oh, Holly—"

"I can't walk down the stairs without imagining myself falling. And with Chad—with Chad it's even worse. I keep having these dreams where he's . . . he's . . . Fuck." Holly closed her eyes. "I can see it now. The blood. The ambulance lights. His eyes, just . . . all the light gone out of them."

"That's terrible."

"I know it's just a dream. I know. I know, but I can't tune it out. I can't stop it. I can't sleep. I keep waking up to check on him. Like I have to see him in his bed, asleep, before . . . But even then, it's not always enough."

"It understandable though," Miriam said. "After what just happened. I mean, he broke both his arms, so—"

"But it was happening *before* that."

"Oh."

"For months now. And I tried to ignore the dreams. Because they don't mean anything. They're just dreams. But . . ."

"Maybe . . . they're not."

"Don't say that. That's what Kate said. And she was like, 'Here, just do a chakra cleanse and then your dreams will heal.' But they don't mean anything. They can't. They can't."

"I'm not saying that they're prophetic. But . . . I don't know. There's something off. I can't explain exactly. But . . ."

Miriam could feel it. She could see it in the deer that lingered in the road, their black eyes beckoning; in Roxster's eyes, a glint of suspicion, when Jack approached; in Jack, who was her husband but wasn't.

She needed a cigarette.

"Whatever it is," Holly said, "that's why I keep drinking. I know, I know it's too much. But it's the only way to sleep. The only way I can tune it out. Especially if I black out—"

"You black out?"

"I know, it's bad. But hey, it's sleep."

"Holly—"

"You know what I did, last time I blacked out?"

"What?"

"This." Holly removed her wig, revealing her buzz cut beneath. "I don't remember shaving it off. I just blacked out. And the next morning my hair was all gone."

They had another round and talked about their kids and gossiped about the neighbors, and then Holly got a text from Tom. He'd come to pick her up.

"You want a ride home?" asked Holly.

"I . . . I think I'll stay." She wasn't ready to face Not-Jack. "But Holly—"

"Yeah?"

"Be careful, okay? And if you need help—"

"I know." Holly hugged her. "You too. If you need someone to kick your husband's ass—"

"I'll call you."

Then Holly left, and Miriam was alone in a mostly empty bar, ordering another drink, gazing up at the glass eyes of the stuffed buck. The buck had been there on that wall long before Mr. Yay existed, if he ever existed, and the buck would be there when the world crumbled. The TV behind the bar played news, on silent, but the screen showed riots. Riots in LA. Riots in Atlanta. Or was it a concert? The bartender lit a cigarette. Miriam asked for a light. She took her drink and her smoke back to the table. Once, drunk Jack Shipley had proposed to brand his love for her by burning his palm with the lit tip of his cigarette. For her, he would burn his flesh. For her, he'd burn anything. She'd talked him out if it, because people shouldn't burn themselves for love. But would he still, now that he wasn't Jack anymore?

She took a drag. She let the ash fall on the sticky table. The door opened and a man walked into the bar. He wore a fedora. He walked straight toward her.

"Where are the kids?"

"Babysitter."

"How did you know where I was?"

"I know you."

"You didn't ask Holly?"

"I know you."

"I don't know you. Why are you here?"

"I had to see you. I had to show you."

"What?"

Jack reached into his pocket. He pulled out a note. He put it on the table where they both could see it:

Jack, we're having a baby. There's leftover pot roast, corn, and biscuits in the fridge.

"What is this?"

It was written in her handwriting.

"I saved it."

"I don't understand."

"This is the note you left. When you told me you were pregnant with Lindsey. You made pot roast. My favorite. I remember sticking it in the microwave. I was so fucking giddy. And I saved the note. I put it in a box in my closet and saved it."

"No..."

"I did."

Miriam reached into her own pocket. She pulled out the note. She put it on the table next to Not-Jack's note. The two were nearly identical. The same paper, torn the same around the edges. The same grease stain near the bottom, from the butter on her finger when she wrote it. The same words and letters, scrawled identically, except for *pot roast* and *meat loaf.*

"What is this?" Her head spun. "This is just... Okay. I... I need a minute."

She stood up. She walked past Jack, through the door, outside. From the street she could see, several blocks down, the building where she and Jack used to live. She felt dizzy, jittery, bewildered. A deer galloped down the street. It shouldn't be here. Not downtown. It was off and she was off and she didn't know what to think or do about any of this.

She went back into the bar. Jack had ordered another round. Whiskey for him, even though he hated it. A cigarette dangled from his lips. He leaned over the table with his pocketknife. He was carving something into the wood.

"Miriam."

"Jack."

"I *fucking* love you. I'm sorry. I messed it all up. But I'd do anything. Anything."

He looked up at her, and his eyes looked like Jack's eyes, like she hadn't seen in an eternity. He set the knife down beside the two identical notes. He had carved their initials in the table. *J. S. + M. S.*, encased in a heart.

HAMMOCK JACK

MIRIAM WAS DRIVING HOME from a client appointment when she saw the sign at a red light, taped to a telephone pole. It looked like a lost pet sign, except instead of a photograph of a dog or a cat, it had a drawing of a man and a dog on a boat. The man had leg quilts. The dog wore a captain's hat. HAVE YOU SEEN MR. YAY?

She pulled over to the curb. She got out of her car. She examined the sign. The waves, the boat, and the smiling sun looked like the handiwork of a child. There was an oblong scribble with eyes and teeth in the water, and beneath that was a phone number and email address, J.ShipleyPrivateEye@unimail.com.

Miriam saw more signs on the drive home, stuck to phone poles and windshields. On her kitchen table she found a stack of HAVE YOU SEEN MR. YAY? signs.

"Have *you* seen Mr. Yay, Mom?" Lindsey asked.

"I have."

"There's a form to fill out. And Dad may want to interview you."

"Oh?"

"But look at the boat I drew!"

"That's a great boat."

"I dwew the cwocodile shaak." Rory pointed to the sharp-toothed scribble.

"The crocodile shark?"

"It's a cwocodile and a shaak."

"We're helping Dad solve the mystery of the missing Mr. Yay."

"Fantastic. Where is your dad?"

Dad aka Jack aka Not-Jack was on the back deck with power tools that white-collar Jack had never shown any capacity to use. But maybe now that he was underemployed, Not-Jack could devote a few of his many leisure hours to long-neglected home repairs.

"What are you doing?" she asked him.

"I'm hanging a hammock."

"A hammock?"

He screwed a heavy-duty hook into a freshly drilled hole.

"Who are you, and why are you hanging a hammock?"

"Have you ever relaxed in a hammock?"

"Um... I don't know, maybe?"

"You'll understand when you try it."

"Will I? Where did you get the money for the hammock? I thought we'd agreed not to buy things that aren't necessary."

"It *is* necessary. And I traded it for the bench."

She hadn't noticed that the wooden bench that used to be on their deck was gone. "The one that used to be right here?"

"You hated that bench. It was uncomfortable. It had bees."

"Right."

"Which is I guess why they wanted it. They wanted the bees. Which I don't understand. But it also supports my theory."

"Your theory of what?"

Jack stood up. He hung the hammock. He took a sip of

lemonade. He looked at her, and his eyes had that fiery shine, that I'll-burn-myself-for-you luster. She wanted to look away, but she was caught in his gaze.

"You know you're the most beautiful woman I've ever seen."

"Don't say that."

"It's true."

"Jack—"

"My theory about what's happening."

"What is happening?"

"I don't know for sure yet. I'm still investigating. But I theorize something larger is at play here. Some sort of . . . transdimensional altercation."

"What, are Kate and Fred and their crystals rubbing off on you?"

"Well actually, Kate and Fred are probably a part of it too! And maybe even their crystals, somehow—"

"Right."

"I know how it sounds. But you saw the notes. Meat loaf versus pot roast."

"The notes—it could just be a fluke. Maybe I was tired, and I messed up the first note and wrote the wrong thing and—"

"They have the same grease stain. God, I love that look you get, when you know something but don't want to admit it."

"That's a look?"

"Your lips scrunch up. Your eyes get squinty. You know something larger is going on. Listen to this." Jack pulled out his phone. "From today's *Los Angeles Tribune*. 'Americans Quitting Jobs in Record Numbers.' " He read the article:

> More Americans quit their jobs last month than any previous month on record. The walkouts spanned the employment spectrum, from the highest-paid lawyers and newscasters to minimum-wage clerks and burger flippers. There seems to be no apparent explanation for this sudden shift in employment patterns. "We've never seen anything like it," said Francis McBride, a sociologist at Princeton University and expert in employment statistics. "A huge number of people are suddenly changing careers or exiting the workforce altogether."
>
> This sudden shift has left employers scrambling. Glen Huckster, general manager at the Laguna Beach Value Valley, said that his store lost six employees just last week. "We're struggling to fill their shifts," said Huckster. "No one wants to work overtime. And we're still trying to backfill the positions vacated by employees who'd left in the weeks before."

"Who could blame them?" Miriam said. "I wouldn't want to work at the Value Valley either. But what does that have to do with anything?"

"It's part of a larger pattern."

"A pattern of late-stage capitalism?"

"No. Well, yes, that, but also no." Jack tugged at the hammock, testing its weight. "You remember that partner from my old firm I was working with—Jessica Scriber?"

"Yeah." Jessica Scriber, prime suspect in the saga of *Is My Husband Cheating?* At least until Miriam ran into the older woman at a fancy downtown restaurant, dining alone.

"She died."

"Oh. That's . . . That sucks. What happened?"

"She worked herself to death."

"Okay that's awful."

"No, I mean, she literally worked herself to death. Listen." Jack pulled up another article on his phone. He read:

> Jessica Scriber, a senior partner at the law firm of Rufus Mather LLP, had always worked hard. In a business known for long hours, Ms. Scriber's colleagues hardly noticed when she started coming to work early and leaving late. They didn't think anything of seeing her in the office over the weekend. Working weekends, in big-firm life, is par for the course. Ms. Scriber's devotion to her job hardly seemed unusual, until one Monday last month when her secretary arrived at work and found Ms. Scriber asleep in her office chair. She had been in the office, at work, for more than 60 hours straight.
>
> Billing records indicate an uptick in Ms. Scriber's work at the start of the year. Over several months, her hours climbed from an initial average of 60 hours per week–not uncommon for the legal profession–to more than 120 hours per week. The week before she died, Ms. Scriber had billed 127 hours.

On the morning of April 29, Ms. Scriber's associate found her unconscious on her office floor. By the time paramedics arrived, she was already deceased. Her official cause of death was cardiac arrest. The prescription drugs Ritalin and Adderall, both stimulants, were found in her desk drawer. She also had blisters on her fingers from excessive typing.

"That's awful," Miriam said again.

"You see? People are, well, they're reacting."

"To what?"

"*That* I don't know. But look, I knew this woman. And yeah, she worked a lot, like everyone at the firm. But she was also, well, she had other interests. She read books. She played the violin. She liked to travel and hike. I can't imagine her just abandoning everything for work. One hundred and twenty-seven hours in a week? It's inhuman."

"But that's what happened."

"But it wouldn't just happen," Jack said, sitting back on the hammock. "Not without some cause or event. Maybe the same kind of event that would result in you and I both having saved that same note."

Miriam looked at her husband. Her not-husband. She understood his point, but the fact that *he* had made it made her want to reject it, reflexively.

"You don't like meat loaf."

"I hate it."

"Where did you come from?"

"Where did *you* come from? My wife would never smoke cigarettes."

"The dog doesn't trust you."

"*I* don't trust me. I hadn't planned to just quit my job, and then—I... I feel reckless."

"Unmoored."

"Like I could just—"

"Walk the plank. Dive off the edge. Never mind what's in the water below."

"Exactly like that."

"But instead you're here, playing detective."

"I'm detecting sarcasm."

"And resentment."

"It's deserved," Jack said. "But what if there are other things? Like the meat loaf. Like Mr. Yay. Things that one or the other of us doesn't remember. Or things we remember differently. We need to investigate. You need to tell me everything you remember. Will you?"

"I, um—"

"You don't trust me either. I know. But I'm here. I'm Jack, as far as I know, and I'm the one here now. And those are my kids in there. And you're... you're the only woman I've ever loved. So please. Sit with me. Tell me what you remember."

Those eyes again.

He motioned for her to join him on the hammock. She wanted to punch him, to tear off his skin to find the Jack or Not-Jack inside, to climb on top of him and strip off her clothes and let herself be touched, in a way that he hadn't touched her, and she hadn't let him, for so, so long. She wanted a cigarette. Tears welled in her eyes and a sob shuddered through her chest and her heart pounded like it had the first time Jack had ever touched her. He reached out his hand.

“Miriam—”

“Okay.” She nodded. “Okay.”

She sank into the hammock beside him. Gravity squished them together. His lemonade breath grazed her neck. His hand rested on her shoulder. A hot tear rolled down her cheek. Jack wiped it away.

“It’s okay,” he said.

“What if it’s not?”

“It will be. We have each other.”

“Even if you’re not Jack?”

“Even if. We have the kids. We have this hammock.”

She closed her eyes. The hammock rocked in the warm breeze. She felt the thrum of Jack’s heart, the warmth of his skin, his lips as he kissed her forehead, her eyelids, the tip of her nose.

“You go first,” she said. “Tell me everything you remember.”

MUD PIT

THEY FOUND, after hours in the hammock and more hours at the kitchen table, all the photographs and relics of their lives spread out around them, that they remembered the exact same things, except for meat loaf and Mr. Yay, which led Jack to deduce that Mr. Yay—a farther-reaching phenomenon than meat loaf—was at the center of all of this, whatever all of this was. He was the linchpin.

He kept Jack up all night. And the next night. And the third night, with bass. It shook the windows and rattled the floorboards.

"Jack!"

"What?"

"Jack! Turn it down!"

"But I need inspiration!"

"What you need is headphones!"

He needed inspiration to solve the Mystery of the Missing Mr. Yay. That the tunes of Mr. Yay the Rapper might provide clues was the excuse. But the next morning Miriam found Jack passed out on the couch with an empty bottle of Hennessy.

"This is inspirational."

"What?" He rubbed his eyes. "Oh, god, it's so bright out. Make it stop."

The dog eyed him warily.

The kids had given him permanent-marker tattoos. He had a

skull and crossbones on his forehead, but it looked like a deformed roach. On his right forearm, in big block letters, were the words THUG LIFE.

"Dad! Did you find him?"

"What? Who?"

"Mr. Yay!"

"We put up all the posters."

"But Mom printed more."

"No. Well, yes, I found something, but—"

"Tell us outside," Miriam said. "Come on, get up. The kids want to ride their scooters."

The kids already had their helmets on—green with yellow stegosaurus spines for Rory and purple glitter for Lindsey. Jack groaned, but he got up. He poured coffee. He put on his sunglasses and hat. He followed his family outside.

"So what did you find?" Miriam asked, as they trailed the kids up Ravenswood Drive.

"I've got a name. Ricardo Merman."

"Wait, I thought you already knew that, from what that guy at the video rental store said."

"Well, yes, but now I've got maybe fifty or sixty emails to confirm."

"Already? Wow."

"Most of them aren't helpful. Just people reminiscing about watching Mr. Yay, or quoting Mr. Yay, or complaining about how so-and-so doesn't remember Mr. Yay when they should."

"Huh. So there are lots of other people who remember—"

"And people who don't," Jack said. "And there were at least five or six people who said that his name was Ricardo Merman. So we can confirm that was definitely his name. Even if it's not his given name."

"Does *he* exist? Ricardo Merman?"

"He did. All his old films are still around—*The Treacherous Ten, Shotgun Solstice, Connie at the Crossroads.* And *Peregrine,* of course. But whether he's still around, I don't know. I haven't found him. He has no internet presence. He—"

Rory interrupted with an excited "Dad! Dad!"

He and Lindsey had turned around. They rolled downhill.

"Dad!" Lindsey called. "Can we play in the mud?"

"Can we, Dad?"

"The mud?"

Halfway up the hill, where Kate and Fred had once kept a weed-free lawn, doused to chemical perfection, mowed to a perfect golf-course buzz cut, there was a field of mud, teeming with rabbits. Kate and Fred's kids, Nicky and Mabel, loped across the yard bearing fistfuls of mud. They were both filthy and entirely naked.

"I want a mud bunny!" Lindsey cried.

"Um..." Jack glanced at Miriam. "This is... unprecedented."

"Hey, don't look at me," she said. "The kids clearly asked you."

Jack shrugged and looked at his eldest. "No."

"But Dad, Nicky and Mabel said we could!"

"But the mud is... the mud is dirty. Do you want to be bathed? Do you want to have your hair washed?"

The children balked at the prospect of hair washing. This was enough to deter them. They turned around and scootered off. Mabel and Nicky watched from behind a mud fortress. As Miriam and Jack approached, Nicky slithered out.

"Hey there," Miriam said. "Nice, um, mud pit. What happened to your clothes?"

"I'm a snake," Nicky said. "Snakes don't wear clothes."

"Mom said we should free ourselves from clothes," Mabel said, as she crafted a mud ball.

"So your parents know what you're doing out here?"

"Yeah. We wanted to play video games, but they made us come out here and play."

"In the mud?"

"It wasn't mud until Mom got out the hose. Before that, it was just dirt."

"You see?" Jack said, excitedly, as they moved on from Kate and Fred's, following their own kids up the street. His excitement had apparently helped him shake the hangover. "That's exactly what I mean! Something larger is at work!"

"Something that . . . makes people muddy?"

"It's a, um, an intensification. And somehow, someway, it connects to Mr. Yay."

"Hmm. That sounds real scientific."

"But back to Mr. Yay," Jack said, "or Ricardo Merman. I haven't found him. Yet. But I did hear back from the network that supposedly played the show."

"What was it, PBS?"

"That's what everyone who reached out to me seems to think. So I reached out to the network, and I got ahold of some woman with access to all the archives of old shows. Like, pre-streaming stuff."

"Because it's obviously not streaming anywhere now."

"Right. And I asked her if she remembered *The Adventures of Mr. Yay*, and she was like, 'Yeah, that was such a great show.' And she agreed to see if she could get me copies of the recordings. But guess what?"

"She couldn't find them?"

"She couldn't find them," said Jack. "So I asked if she could check for anything else related to Mr. Yay in the network's archives, but it was the same."

"No record."

"Nope. The network has no record of having ever produced *The Adventures of Mr. Yay.*"

The scootering kids led them to the park, and then to the coffee shop, then back down Ravenswood Drive, where Kate and Fred had joined their children in the mud. But at least they weren't naked. Fred was shirtless, but he wore loose hemp pants. Kate wore a muddy bikini and a crystal around her neck. A wreath of flowers sat atop her unwashed hair. They both looked leaner and bronzer than Miriam remembered.

"Whatcha guys doing with your yard?" Miriam asked.

Kate crouched down and stroked the head of a baby rabbit with her muddy fingers. "We're building a wildlife refuge."

"All native flowers and grasses," Fred added.

"The bunnies and racoons and all the critters will finally have a nice home."

Wasn't that, Miriam thought, what the woods were for?

But she just nodded and said, "That's great!"

"We'll never have to mow again," Fred said. "Everything will grow freely, in its natural state."

Jack looked at Miriam. His look said: *You see? Look at them now? You remember how they were?* She remembered Fred as identical to Tom. The same striped shirt, the same ironed jeans, the same short haircut. She remembered Kate with a push-up bra, dyed hair, nails lacquered pink.

"Hey, I've got a question for you," Jack said to his neighbors. "Do you remember a television show called *The Adventures of Mr. Yay*?"

"Oh, yeah," Fred said. "I watched that all the time. Why?"

"I'm just... doing an investigation."

"Does this have something to do with those flyers?" Kate asked. "I was wondering about those. Who is Mr. Yay?"

"Mom, he's that rapper," Mabel said. "Is he missing?"

"Not that Mr. Yay," Jack said. "The other one. From the television show."

"Yeah, I've never heard of that," Kate said.

"Are you serious?" said Fred. "How have you never heard of it?"

Kate shrugged. "I don't know."

"It was everywhere when we were growing up."

"And now," Miriam said, "it's nowhere."

THE CASE OF THE MISSING CHICKENS

IT WAS A CONSPIRACY, according to the blogs and the Reddit threads.

It was *Kate smoked too much weed in college,* according to Fred, who had smoked at least as much. But he could still remember.

It was *just my clueless husband,* according to Jack's mom, who Miriam called from the car, on her way to the *Psychic—Mystic—Fortune-Telling* shop.

"Oh, Miriam! What are you up to?"

"I'm going to, um... the grocery store? But I was just wondering, do you have a meat loaf recipe you could send? I wanted to make it for Jack, because, you know—"

"It's his favorite!" Jack's mom confirmed.

Ding-ding-ding-ding-ding!

"Can I ask you something else?"

"Sure."

"Do you remember a TV show called *The Adventures of Mr. Yay*?"

"Of course. Jack used to watch that show all the time—"

In the background, Jack's dad interjected. "What did Jack used to watch?"

"Shhh, I'm on the phone! Ugh, my husband, I swear—"

"Actually, could you ask him if he remembers?"

"Yes, I'll ask."

She put the phone down, but Miriam overheard a muffled conversation morph into an argument, increasingly louder, that ended with Jack's mom exclaiming, "I swear, you are clueless!" And then to Miriam: "My husband is absolutely clueless. How could he not remember? It's like he's been living on another planet!"

And maybe he was. Because, as axiomatic as death and taxes, it was undeniable just how much we didn't know. Human knowledge, all of it, at best, was the iceberg tip of an unfathomable fount of knowledge. For every fact humans found were ten more facts we hadn't, and a hundred more we'd never know, which made detective work not so dissimilar from fortune-telling. There was science, and then there was the science we hadn't figured out yet, the science that got labeled mystic or magic or faith. But magic also offered refuge, and a sparkly narrative for understanding discordant events that science couldn't piece together. Which maybe explained why Miriam was headed back, again, that afternoon, to the *Psychic—Mystic—Fortune-Telling* shop.

The door was locked but she could hear music from inside, sloshing ocean waves overlaid with synthesizers. She knocked. She peered through the open window. The place looked cleaner than when she had last seen it, no more trash, everything dusted and tidy.

Miriam knocked again, but Rosy the psychic didn't answer, so she walked around to the back of the shop. Behind the building there was a patch of lumpy dirt. It was lined with rows of tiny crosses crafted from bits of twig and twine, like a miniature graveyard.

"Birds."

Miriam turned around. Rosy the psychic stood behind her, dressed in a Reds' jersey and cutoff shorts. Her lips were painted red. Her nails sparkled. She had amber rings on her fingers, a can of cream soda, and a big wad of bubble gum. She seemed to have recovered from her earlier malaise.

"Birds?"

"They were," Rosy said. "Now they're dead."

"Oh."

"They kept flyin' into my window. I let 'em pile up for a while, then I decided to bury them. But I ran out of twine."

"I see."

"Do you?"

"Not really," Miriam said. "Mostly I'm just confused."

"We're all confused. Lord, you wouldn't believe how confused. Why, this woman called me the other day to get her fortune told and—"

"Wait," Miriam said. "Should you maybe not tell me this? I mean, isn't it confidential, or—"

"This ain't like therapy. There are no rules. Not in that sense. Besides, I'm just trying to give you all the puzzle pieces."

"Oh."

"You see?"

"Nope. But okay."

"So this woman called me," the psychic went on. "A real fancy type. Said she was the wife of some senator from Georgia. Like they ain't got psychics in Georgia. Anyway, the senator's wife said her husband got sent to jail—"

"I think I heard this story."

"Yep. Mr. Senator got caught by TSA with a briefcase full of cash and cocaine, and somethin' else, too. Starts with a 'dill,' ends with a 'doe,' if you catch my drift. And his wife, she swore on her grandmother's grave that it wasn't his. She said he'd been framed. Said he was as good as a goldfish, sober as a stingray. Except then she'd started to wonder... so she called me to ask if he'd really done it."

"Had he?"

"That depends," Rosy said.

"What do you mean, it depends?"

"That's what she asked me. And I said, 'I wish I could help you, ma'am, but I read the future, not the past.' Besides, what am I supposed to do over the phone? You ever hear of a telephone psychic? That's a... Wait, wait a minute..." Rosy cocked her head, listening.

"What is it?"

"Shhhh! Listen."

Miriam listened. She heard the flap of tires on asphalt, the warble of a distant siren, the metal rods of a wind chime. The cream soda in Rosy's can fizzled. She blew a bubble. It popped. Then there was a sudden thump, as a sparrow crashed into the window.

"Did you—"

The sparrow fell dead on the ground. Rosy shook her head. "I tried coverin' up the window. But they just kept flyin' into it anyway. Now where was I?"

"The senator's wife—"

"No, not her. There was another woman who came to see me.

Elaine. That was her name. Elaine, who'd been dating two fellas at the same time. Roger and Dale, she said. And I said, 'Good for you.' " Rosy chuckled. "But then she said it wasn't like I thought. She said she had memories of being with both of 'em, separately, at the same time. Which is impossible."

"Right."

"Or maybe not," Rosy said. "Love is the ship that keeps you from sinking. Why not have two ships?"

"Can I ask you a question?"

"You may."

"Do you ever do hypnosis?" Miriam asked. "Because I've got this friend who—she's having trouble. And I wondered—"

"Sure, bring her on by. Whenever works."

"Can I ask you another question?"

"It depends."

"Did you ever watch a TV show, *The Adventures of Mr. Yay*?"

The psychic didn't answer. Her eyes flashed. She looked up at the sky, blue and radiant, not a cloud in sight. "You better go," she said. "You hear that? That sound in the distance? That's thunder. A storm is coming."

Which seemed absurd. The weather app said sun, no precipitation. The radar was spotless. But then a starling smacked into the window, and the psychic yelped, then ran inside and locked the door behind her.

Time to go.

Miriam stopped at the grocery on her way home.

She texted Jack: *I'm making your favorite, meat loaf! Need anything else?*

She filled her cart with useful, healthy things, plus a six-pack of Campette candy bars and a copy of *Hollywood Dreams*, a celebrity pulp magazine that she knew she shouldn't waste money on, especially when the checkout clerk gave her an exaggerated wink and said, "A fellow collector of the magazines."

"Um—"

The clerk stroked the magazine, dreamy-eyed. "I just finished a celebrity decoupage of my living room walls. I'm about to do the bathroom. It'll be entirely swimsuit." She flipped through the magazine pages, seemingly on the hunt for swimsuit cutouts.

"Oh... okay... that's, um—"

"Say 'That's great,' " said the clerk, who, Miriam noticed, had a group portrait tattoo on her arm of what appeared to be assorted television celebrities.

"That's... great?"

"Say it like you mean it!"

"That's great!"

Except it wasn't. It was weird. She shuddered, and shoved the magazine she now really didn't want to the bottom of her grocery bag, hidden beneath bananas and eggs. But the clerk reached into the bag and pulled it back up to the top.

Miriam pushed it back down and hurried for the door. Outside, it had turned suddenly dark. The clouds roiled. The wind blustered. The sky rumbled with thunder. The rain started as soon as she reached her car. She loaded the groceries into the hatch. The first fat drops gave way to a torrent.

When she climbed into the driver's seat, she was soaked. Rain gushed from the sky. She drove slowly, through ponds and eddies. She turned out of the parking lot. There was a *KA-BOOM*, and the flash of lightning striking a nearby tree. She could hardly see the road. She hit a puddle. Oily water sprayed out from under her tires. Then she saw the woman. She slammed on the brakes.

"Oh my god! Fuck!"

She didn't hear a thump.

The woman was still there. Still standing.

Miriam waved. She unrolled her window. "Hey!" she yelled. "Hey! I'm sorry! Do you need a ride?"

The woman ran over to the driver's side. She stuck her head through the open window, dripping water all over Miriam's lap. Her hair looked like a wet rat. But her face was familiar. Miriam had seen her at the grocery before, patrolling the entrance with her CONSPIRACY! sign.

"Do you, um, need a ride? You shouldn't be out there in the storm."

"Sure. Thanks," the woman said, in a perfectly ordinary, non-crazy voice. She walked around to the passenger door and climbed in. She bucked her seat belt and spread her soggy CONSPIRACY! sign across her lap.

"What were you doing out there in the rain?" Miriam asked

This woman had a car. A Rolls-Royce. Miriam had seen her drive it.

"It was such a lovely day. I thought I'd walk."

"It was nice. But—"

"Yes. Things . . . changed rather quickly. Anyway, thank you. What's your name?"

"Miriam."

"I'm Coral Cove. And I know what you're thinking. *Crazy Coral Cove.* But look, my parents were insufferable hippies. And I'm not crazy. But go ahead, ask me about the sign."

"What's up with the sign?"

"It's . . . It means that . . ." The Conspiracy! woman folded the sign in half. She rolled down her window. She tossed the sign out, onto the road, where the rain could devour it.

"Why did you just throw it out?"

"I was beginning to forget," Coral said.

"Forget?"

"The chickens. I remembered them perfectly. But now they're getting hazy. I'm starting to forget. I'm starting to wonder . . . I thought it was all just a big conspiracy. But . . . I don't know, maybe it's time to move on."

"That's what your sign said, right? 'Where are my chickens?' What does that mean?"

"I had five chickens," Coral said. "I had a henhouse in my backyard. I fed them every day. I collected their eggs. I . . . I loved those chickens. I never had kids, and my husband's allergic to cats and dogs. So those chickens, they were my babies. And then they were just gone. Henhouse and all. Like they never even existed. My husband said I was crazy, but—"

"You're not."

"That's kind of you to say. Though I might be. I don't even know. All I know is that I remember those chickens."

"Do you remember *Mr. Yay*?"

"What, that old TV show?"

"Yeah."

"Of course I remember," Coral Cove said. "How could anyone forget a show like that?"

HARMONY ANIMAL

THE FRONT YARD was still all mud and rabbits, but a hand-painted sign foretold wildflowers and native grasses. In the backyard, Mabel's sixth birthday party had already started. Lindsey carried her present, a set of colored pencils crafted from recycled wood and natural plant dyes.

"No plastics," Kate had said, when Miriam asked about birthday gifts. "Obviously."

Kate had invited an unreasonable number of kids, like thirty or forty of them. The backyard was chaos and screaming. Kate arranged trays of olives and falafels and dolmades on a picnic table. She looked gleeful, in her beige tunic, her bare feet, a wreath of brilliant pink peonies atop her unwashed hair. She waved. Miriam maneuvered toward her, through a game of duck, duck, goose, past the renegade kinder-artists busy transforming the lawn furniture with non-washable plant-dyed finger-paints.

"Uh, this is... ambitious." Miriam said. "You know that paint is non-washable?"

"I know. It's so invigorating!" Kate exclaimed. "To be surrounded by all these bright, young creative souls."

"Right..."

One of the artists cut a safety-scissor hole in a chair cushion and tore out a wad of foam stuffing.

"We invited Mabel's whole class," Kate said. "But to be fair, we also invited Nicky's whole class. And then of course all the neighborhood kids, the cousins, Mabel's soccer team. And no one listens when you say no plastics. All the grandparents sent plastic. But just wait till you see what we got her!"

Miriam mingled. She found Holly, who had a bottle of champagne and an extra glass on hand, just for Miriam, produced magically upon her arrival, as if Holly had a secret booze compartment in her shoe, the female James Bond of getting the neighbors drunk. The man beside her clapped. He wore a woven poncho—even though it was hot-pants weather outside—with a name tag that said GONZAGO.

"Gonzago here was just explaining how the earth is entering its rebirth cycle," Holly said, drunkenly.

"It's the earth's rebirthday!"

"Is that why we're drinking champagne?" Miriam asked.

"The change is already upon us," Gonzago said. "If you close your eyes and listen, you can hear it."

He closed his eyes and listened. All Miriam could hear was shrieking kids.

Holly took a swig from the champagne bottle. "So, Gonzago," she said. "How do you know Kate and Fred?"

"Know... in the biblical sense?"

"Um..."

"*Oh, right,* you mean, how did I meet them? Fred and I used to work together at the bank. But then I quit my job at the bank and sold my house, and I was camping in the park, but apparently the park closes at nine p.m. So now I'm living here."

"Here, as in, this house?" Miriam asked. "With Kate and Fred?"

"Oh, not inside the house," Gonzago said. "I've been camping in their backyard. I'd much rather sleep outside."

"Awww." Holly pinched Gonzago's scruffy cheek. She topped off his glass. "Sleeping outdoors. Isn't he cute?"

Then it was time for the piñata. The piñata looked like a three-legged bear with tusks. It was maroon, colored with a dye that Kate had extracted herself, from beets. It was also huge, the size of an armchair. It took the collective strength of both Fred and Tom to hoist it over the tree branch.

The several dozen children took turns batting. The piñata was impervious. Fred and Tom stepped in with their muscley man-arms, but they couldn't dent it. Fred eventually hacked the piñata open with an axe. Out spilt the loot, thirty-some pounds of carob chips, honey sticks, organic licorices, and fair-trade chocolate-coated goji berries. The several dozen children scrambled. They shoved, snatched, pinched, cried. Kate tried to intervene. She directed crying children to the falafel and dolmades spread, where they cried harder.

"I don't know why they're upset," Kate said. A line of ants exited her peony circlet and marched across her forehead. "Children love dolmades!"

"Children love corn syrup," Holly said.

"At least you cracked the piñata," Miriam said. "Rory looked like he was about to lose it. And Chad—"

"Shush!" Holly shoved her. Champagne sloshed from their glasses.

"What?"

"We're not talking about Chad. We're drinking. That's it!"

"Okay..."

"But that piñata—"

"The kids and I made it ourselves," said Kate.

"Did you make it out of cement?" said Holly.

"It was sturdy, wasn't it? We wanted to make it especially strong, to represent Mabel's inner strength."

Kate seemed to have missed the irony of the piñata's ultimate destruction.

"What animal was it supposed to be?" Miriam asked.

"It was an amalgamation of the animals that Mabel felt vibrated on her same frequency. Her harmony animals. There are at least four. Though there may be more."

But which one of them had three legs?

"That's . . . great."

"It's weird," Holly said. Her filter was gone. In its wake was drunken impudence. But Kate didn't seem to notice or care. She flung an arm around each of them.

"So now that you're both here together," Kate said, "I've got news!"

"Don't tell me you're in a throuple," said Holly.

"Well, um, that's not exactly news."

"What's the news?"

"Fred quit his job at the bank, and . . ." Kate paused. She grinned. Her whole body seemed to vibrate at some strange level. An ant emerged from her peony crown, dashed across her brow, and leapt into space.

"And what? Tell us!"

"We're opening a yoga and meditation studio! Really, it's a whole-person wellness studio. We'll have other classes there, too. You know, composting, home-brewing, spiritual cleansing, crystals. We bought the building just up the street, by the ice-cream parlor. We wanted to stay in the neighborhood so we could reduce our car dependence. And we can ride our bikes there. Though Fred's planning to get a unicycle. Won't that be great! I'm so excited!"

Kate gushed. Several more ants abandoned ship. Holly tossed back the rest of her champagne.

"That's great," Miriam said. "Good for you."

"It's nuts," said Holly. "Here's to nuts." She raised her empty glass.

"I'm becoming the me I was always meant to be," said Kate.

"So you said Fred quit the bank," said Miriam. "Did you—"

"Oh no. I wish." Kate worked in the marketing department of a pharmaceutical company. "But we couldn't get the loan for the wellness studio unless one of us kept our job. And we decided that I was more convincing than Fred." A steady stream of ants marched through her hair. "Fred looks like *such* a hippie."

Then it was time for presents. Mabel unwrapped plastic toys, plastic dolls, plastic art supplies, gummy candies made with red dye number 40, bubble guns that blasted toxic bubbles, stuffies that leeched toxic chemicals, etcetera, all of which Kate plucked from her hands and handed off to Fred, to deposit in a box in a quarantined section of the yard, which the absorbent children were prohibited from entering. Then, at last, came the big gift, the best gift. Kate and Fred brought it out together. A pet goat.

Mabel squealed. "My harmony animal!"

The goat was white, with a red ribbon around its neck. It had soft curls and dopey eyes. Mabel hugged it.

"Isn't it—"

Then it wasn't.

It wasn't there.

Mabel's arms held empty space.

She screamed. Kate gasped. Holly dropped her champagne glass. Some kids giggled and other kids cried. Lindsey ducked and covered. Rory patted himself down, confirming his physicality. Jack pulled out his phone and started recording, and was recording when, a moment later, the goat fizzed back into existence.

For a moment, the goat was half there, a goat-shaped shimmer, and Miriam feared the birthday girl's arms might get stuck inside it. It might suck her in. It might be a black-hole ruminant, consumer of planets, hollow-horned tear in the fabric of space-time.

But Fred yanked Mabel back, before the goat materialized, though not soon enough to stop its head from bonking her in the face. Blood spurted out of her nose. The goat looked confused. Gonzago looked vindicated by this turn of events. Holly stumbled out of the yard, leaving Chad behind. Miriam clutched Jack's arm.

It was weird. Touching his arm like this.

"It's okay," he said. "It's a clue." He smelled like a dark alley on a moonless night. "Sometimes a thing's gotta disappear so you can see what's really there."

SKATEBOARD

THE VIDEO of the disappearing-reappearing goat got posted on the internet, and all the crazies came out. Detective Jack Shipley's email was deluged with conspiracy claims, cultist propositions, invitations to attend Deepfake Boot Camp or enlist in the Freedom from Physics Militia or donate his blood to the cause of Molecular Stability Enhancement Pants, which after crowdfunding would be sold for $1,299.99 per pair, and would guarantee protection from spontaneous subatomic degradation. Also, thousands of emails about the missing Mr. Yay.

"Did you know there was a cartoon spin-off?" Jack said, as he skimmed through his emails. He sat on the deck, next to the hammock, laptop open, mystery-solving note cards with lots of question marks spread out around him.

"I did," Miriam said, from the hammock. "But I only watched it a few times. It wasn't comparable."

"The premise was the same. Except all the characters were animals."

"And Captain Barksford was a Chihuahua. Which, sorry, just seemed wrong. No offense to Chihuahuas."

"Did you know Mr. Yay released an album?" Jack asked.

"Wait, like—"

"The OG. Not the rapper."

"Huh. What kind of music?"

"Wait, make that two albums," Jack said. "One was... experimental synth-pop? And the other was a holiday album."

"Oh, I remember that!" Miriam could picture Mr. Yay in his Santa hat, Captain Barksford with his nose painted Rudolph-red, an antler tied to his head, the giraffe and the lion and the tortoise dressed in red and green stripes, the boat-sleigh on a frozen sea, the artificial snow drifting down.

"Or, hey, did you know that Mr. Yay was an extraterrestrial sleeper agent, and that his show was a plot by George Soros to brainwash kids into embracing socialism through advanced subliminal imaging technologies?"

"I always suspected...."

"Apparently the Captain Barksford plushies all had hidden cameras, per one Bezercher76821."

"He sounds like an expert."

"Oh, wait..." Jack stared at his computer, reading.

"What?"

"This guy..." He paused, as he read through the message. "This guy says he thinks he knows what happened to Mr. Yay."

"Isn't that what they all say?"

"Yes, but *this guy* is an astrophysicist. He has a PhD. And his name is *SherLok Ohms*."

"Okay, but that's a fake name, right?"

"Obviously. But he says he wants to meet. In person. He says he'll come to me. What should I—"

Jack didn't finish, because two kids ran into the backyard, up onto the deck, breathless, arms flapping, ranting about some special race that Mom and Dad had to come see.

"How about later?" Miriam said. "Mom and Dad are busy." The hammock swayed in the late-spring breeze.

"But it's happening now!" Lindsey said. "They're about to race!"

"Come and see!"

"Who's about to race?"

"Chad's dad and Mabel's dad."

"Oh... how are they—"

"Come on!"

"Miriam?" Jack stood up. "Should we—"

"The hammock doesn't want me to get up," Miriam said.

But she took Jack's hand and let him pull her out of it. They followed the kids around the house, out to the sidewalk. Tom and Fred stood at the top of the street. They both had skateboards. Tom hopped on his skateboard, rolled a few feet, then stopped. He picked the skateboard up and rejoined Fred. He pointed toward the end of the street. Fred nodded.

"Oh, this is not good," Miriam said. "You don't think they're really going to—"

"No," said Jack. "No, that would be crazy."

"Did you even know that they could skateboard?"

"I had no idea."

"Maybe we should—" *try to stop them,* Miriam thought. But it was already too late.

Tom and Fred exchanged a fist bump. They jumped on their skateboards. They pushed off.

They went slow at first. They rolled past one house, then the next, at a speed so moderate that Miriam questioned her own reaction. Tom and Fred were fine. They were grown boys. They would both be fine.

Then they started to pick up speed.

"Hey!" Miriam yelled. "Hey, slow down!"

They couldn't hear her, or didn't want to. Where were their wives? Mabel, Nicky, and Chad watched from the front-yard mud pit. But Kate wasn't with them. And Holly—

They rolled faster down the street. The street got steeper as they went. Then, about a third of the way down, Fred panicked. He leapt off his skateboard. His skateboard crashed into the curb. He stumbled, but didn't fall. He was fine.

Tom kept going. The slope got steeper. His board rolled faster. He neared the midpoint. He had a wild look on his face. The look of a man running at a tornado.

Chad ran down to the sidewalk to cheer. "Go, Dad! Faster! Faster!"

Tom went faster. He reached the halfway mark. He held his arms out for balance. He didn't try to slow or slalom. He rolled straight, down the hill, faster, faster, faster.

He zipped past Chad, then Fred and Kate's, where tiny seedlings had begun to sprout in the mud. Faster and faster. And then, far behind him, at the starting line of this one-man race, his front door opened and Holly ran out, arms waving, yelling at the top of her lungs.

"Tom! Stop! Stop!"

She tore down the street after him, screaming, crying. But he didn't stop. He couldn't stop. He couldn't hear her, over the sound of his wheels on the asphalt, the wind whipping past him, the lusty roar of adrenaline coursing through his blood. He was pure speed. Faster and faster he went.

Miriam could see his face clearly now, the fanatical glint in his eye, the spit string that trailed from the corner of his mouth, the speed-force grit of his teeth. He neared the bottom of the hill, where the street dead-ended. The finish line.

He'd won, and he grinned, and raised his arms to the sky, victorious. But he didn't know how to slow down. He thrust his leg out, an ungraceful attempt to catch the road with his foot, but it didn't slow him. It just put him off-balance. He tried to swerve into a driveway, but instead his skateboard slammed into the curb. And stopped. And Tom kept going. He flew, his arms spread wide before him. A one-man rocket ship. Until he crashed, and with a sickening crack, his bones broke against the earth, and he screamed, a single scream. He fell alarmingly silent, and there were only soft sounds, the birds in the trees, the wind, the distant wail of his wife, who had just witnessed a warped rendition of her most terrible, most persistent dream.

BRATTY AND HIS THERAPIST

Miriam:	*How are you? Where are you?*
Bradford:	*Laundromat.*
Miriam:	*Laundromat?*
Bradford:	*The apartment is packed. With like, ten billion boxes of T-shirts. There's no place to sit. So I'm here. I'm good.*
Miriam:	*Good.*
Bradford:	*I'm great. I…*
Miriam:	*You look healthy.*
Bradford:	*Blame the dog. Tux. Tuxerciser Maximus. He makes me run. But also, I remember how you said one time that you run, how it clears your head. And I was like, whatever, running is for suckers. But I know now. I needed it. I needed to, like, clear it all out, so that… how do I explain it?*
Miriam:	*Take your time.*
Bradford:	*It's like… Imagine you were always afraid. Imagine everything you did, you wondered, how did I mess it up? What did I do wrong?*
Miriam:	*That's how you felt.*
Bradford:	*Because… Imagine this fear, it's all centered on yourself. Sure, there are people in your life,*

jerks who will say jerky things and make you feel bad. Bullies. Abusers. But you can see them for who they are. You can see through them. You know how fucked up and fake they are, and they don't matter in the end. All that matters is you. So your fear, it all comes back to you. You are afraid of you. Of what you'll do or won't do. Of whether you'll mess up because you dropped out of college, or because you studied business when you should have studied science, or because you went to school when you should have been a plumber or explored the Arctic or whatever the shit you were meant to do. You do the opposite. You got one shot at love, and you fuck it up. You are worthless. Inherently. This is how it feels, no matter what you tell yourself. No matter how many mantras you say or self-help books you read or therapists you see. No offense. No matter how much weed you smoke, or how many degrees you earn, or how much money you make. There's a big gaping hole inside you. And in that hole is fear.

Miriam: *That is... That sounds—*

Bradford: *I know.*

Miriam: *Awful.*

Bradford: *That is how it is. I don't know why. But it is. But then imagine... imagine, in a blink, the fear is just... gone. Imagine you hear music. You close your eyes. You listen. You really listen.*

	You can feel it. The vibration. In your bones. And then you open your eyes, and the fear is gone. The hole, that's still there, but it doesn't scare you. It's filled with music. All around you, there's music. And you know, you can step into yourself. Whoever you are. You'll be fine. I...
Miriam:	*I'm proud of you, Bradford. I don't know what happened, but—*
Bradford:	*It's happening still. You can feel it, can't you? You can hear it? If you close your eyes—*
Miriam:	*I... It's weird. It's been weird.*
Bradford:	*Fuckin' A. Hey, you know I'm coming back there. Next month. We've got a show. We're going on tour.*
Miriam:	*That's amazing.*
Bradford:	*I'm gonna go see my dad. He still has no idea. I'm gonna tell him then. And whatever he says... fuck it. I will not be afraid.*

THE PARTY BUS

HE TALKED to his therapist in the laundromat because the apartment was filled with boxes, crammed, literally impassable. There was no floor space or counter space or room in the tub, no space for dogs, to the point that Tux had to drive around with Tommy in Tommy's brand-new car while Tommy tried to friend himself out of the ridiculous problem he'd haphazardly caused, by ordering a billion fucking T-shirts.

The T-shirts had a picture of Tux with a strand of neon-swirl drool that melted into neon-swirl letters that spelled out MR. YAY. Tux had a gold chain like a proper rap dog, and an eye patch like a proper pirate, and if you looked real close at the eye patch you could see the shadow of a boat. The SS *Deliverance*.

Bratty had designed the T-shirt because how the fuck else did a rapper make bank in the streaming era?

Bratty had said: *We need merch.*

And Tommy had said: *We need bong rips.*

And Bratty had smoked a blunt and designed a T-shirt, and then Tommy did that thing that Tommy always did: He went all in. One night, while Bratty was asleep on the couch, Tux curled at his feet, dreaming stoned dreams of the deep sea, Tommy had ordered five hundred bazillion T-shirts, and then he'd made a purchase link on the website so anyone could just come along and order a T-shirt, and then he'd got sucked up into The Legend of Zelda and totally forgot about both.

Until some delivery dudes had shown up at the apartment, confused as fuck, with a semitruck packed with boxes of T-shirts.

"Uh... is this... uh, the abode of Mr. AssMaster?"

"It's not... *not* the abode."

"Could you just sign on the line right there?"

Bratty signed.

"So where do you want all the boxes? You got a warehouse or something?"

"Uh... Tommy! Hey, Tommy!"

Tommy was just as confused. "I'm not Tommy. I'm Link."

"Link AssMaster?"

"Oh... oh fuck... are you... did I... ?"

He had, and it took him and Bratty and the delivery guys over an hour to load all the boxes into the apartment, and that had put an end to Tommy's Legend of Zelda ambitions. He couldn't sit on the couch, or reach the TV.

They could, at least, still open the fridge, where all the beer was stored. They could slink to the bathroom, or huddle by the doorway.

"But do you want the good news, or the bad news?" Tommy asked, after they'd sat down on the stoop outside after unloading everything. They had to smoke outside so they wouldn't skunk up the T-shirts.

"That's not the bad news?" Bratty motioned to the boxes.

"Um... no. The bad news is that, unless we want to piss off our fans, we've gotta unpack those boxes, pack up new boxes, address them all, and mail out like, um, seven thousand or so T-shirts."

"Oh."

"Before we go on tour."

"What the fuck..."

"I know."

"Dude."

"I know. But the good news is you just paid off your student loans. And then some."

"If we can mail seven thousand shirts."

"It might be closer to eight thousand."

"Dude, we leave in, like, three days."

Now it was more like two days, and while Tommy was out, working magic, Bratty was supposed to clear a path to the closet so they could both pack.

There were so fucking many boxes.

If there was an earthquake, even a little one, those towers of boxes could tumble down and pin Bratty beneath. They could crush him. He could die. *If only he wasn't such a fuckup,* his Dad would say, and his stepmom would nod and smirk and say, *At least the world is better off* and he wouldn't be able to punch that bitch, because he would be dead.

No.

He would not be afraid.

He would not fear these boxes.

When he talked to his therapist, he'd made it sound like he'd thrown off the yoke of fear. Like he'd heard courage as music, and in an instant was changed.

But it hadn't happened like that. It happened like the ebb and flow of the tide. It receded slow, and always with music. But sometimes in silence, the fear rolled back.

He stood in the apartment doorway thinking, *How the hell do I Tetris these boxes?* He heard a rumble. He shivered, and glanced back, at the sky. Hazy blue. Not a wisp of rain cloud. No thunder.

His gaze turned back inside to the apartment, and this was the WTF *how-many-gummies-did-I-eat* moment. The moment when fear seized him by the brain and smacked him around. Because what he saw—what his eyes saw—was not really happening.

There.

But it was. Clear as the LA sky.

He stood in the doorway of his apartment, but it wasn't *his* apartment. It looked how it had when he'd first arrived. Tommy's couch. Tommy's old TV. No giant speaker. Beer cans on the floor. Pizza box on the counter. No dog.

No dog.

No Bratty. No Bratty shoes on the floor. No Bratty hoodie slung over the chairback. No laptop, no controller, no music.

That was the fucking thing. No music. It was silent. Until Tommy came down the hall, stood there for a minute with this look on his face, this wrecked look, and his head drooped, and this sound came out of him. Like a sob. Except way worse.

Tommy turned into the kitchen, pulled a baggie from his pocket, white powder inside. He poured it onto the counter, cut a line, did a bump. Closed his eyes. And then he heaved, and another sob poured out of him—

—and—

Bratty knew.

He knew. He, Bratty, wasn't there. Not just not there in the apartment. He was *gone* gone. Whatever else this fucked-up scene meant, it meant no Fatty Bratty.

He touched his hands to his chest and yep, he was solid. His heart thumped *not-dead, not-dead, not-dead.* But this Tommy couldn't see him.

And for a minute or two or five, Bratty lurked there in the doorway and watched, as Tommy sobbed, cut another line, cracked open a beer, sobbed, lit a cigarette, and when the smoke drifted Bratty saw shadows behind it, ghosty outlines, rectangular, brown. Boxes. Boxes made of haze and dream. Boxes that Tommy didn't see, until there was a noise outside, a faint whistle, birdsong. His brow furrowed. His hand reached for a box but grasped empty space. He tried again. A tear rolled down his cheek. He shook his head. Then he turned. He looked straight at Bratty.

He saw Bratty.

His eyes lit up, and what the fuck? Bratty didn't know what to say. He didn't know what any of this meant. He only knew that Tommy was his best friend. Tommy was always and would always be his best friend. His brother. His soul spirit in debauchery and music and fun.

"Bratty..."

Words bubbled out of Bratty's mouth. "We're making it stronger," he said. But he didn't know why.

Tommy nodded. "You're really you."

Bratty gave a thumbs-up. "It's the music—"

And then the whole scene fizzed.

It was *boxes-boxes-boxes,* no Tommy anywhere.

Then Tommy, filled with bubbles. Tommy translucent. Tiny silvery bits of bubbles. Everything effervescent.

"Bratty!" Tommy yelled, but the sound came from somewhere else. "Bratty—"

"Tommy—the music—"

Then the sound cut out. Tommy was gone. The bubbles or whatever the fuck they were: gone. The warped scenery reforged as an apartment filled with boxes. Bratty heard music. "Gin and Juice." His ringtone. He pulled his phone from his pocket. The screen said *AssMaster.*

He answered. "Yo."

"Bratty, we found..." Tommy trailed off.

"What?"

"I... dude, I just had a totally weird-ass feeling. Are you okay?"

"I..."

Okay, he'd just seen some fucked-up shit. But Tommy was there, in LA. He was in LA. They were connected by sound waves and satellites, living the same rap-star dream. In the background, Tux barked. In the background, music played on the car stereo. There was the flick of a lighter. Tommy blew smoke into the phone. A wave washed over Bratty, like nothing he'd ever felt before. Call it peace. Call it power. It swept the last grains of fear away, and in its wake was grit and spunk and music. "I'm good. I'm great. What did you find?"

"We got a warehouse."

"Dope."

"And a big-ass truck. It'll be there in ten. You gotta go out and show 'em where to park."

"I'm on it."

"And we got, like, maybe a hundred people who said they'd come and help package up the shirts."

"How'd you manage that?"

"Free shirts," Tommy said. "And, we're throwing a warehouse party."

The warehouse party started a day before the tour, fifteen hours before the party bus would pull up outside their apartment, twenty-four hours before the first show in Santa Barbara. They backed a big-ass truck up to the loading dock, unloaded boxes, set up a stage. Some dude Tommy knew showed up with lasers, and some other dude brought in a few kegs and then a full bar, and more people showed up in a van that looked like a shark, with black lights, neon strips, more lasers, plus DJs and rappers to play opening sets, and then a crowd. More than a hundred. They all had pens and clipboards and copies of order lists. And as the music started up, they formed an assembly line, Bratty and Tommy and their hundred-plus friends. They sorted T-shirts, wrote addresses, added postage, took shots from the shot-ski, and by two a.m. everything was labeled and packed, and the headliner, Mr. Yay, came on.

They played until the sun came up. The party wound down. The truck drove off. Some friends of Tommy's had volunteered to handle mailing. Bratty hitched a ride in the shark van back to their apartment. He melted into the back seat. Sun streamed through the windows. LA blurred by, all concrete and hills and highways, so fucking beautiful, every bit of it.

And when he got home, the tour bus—the party bus—was already waiting.

Interlude

FLASHBACK

BRATTY

A WEEK BEFORE, his dad had said, *Bradford, you should come for Thanksgiving. It would mean a lot.* Except it didn't. When he showed up, at eleven a.m., just like they'd told him to, they weren't there.

Their car wasn't in the driveway. Their door was locked. He'd had a key once, but they'd changed the locks for no reason he could think of.

He called his dad. Dad didn't answer. He had made a green bean casserole, warm when he'd left his apartment, but the temperature was falling fast. It was gray, gloomy, almost winter. He didn't have enough gas in his tank to keep warm in an idle car. He didn't want to leave either. He wanted Thanksgiving.

He waited on the stoop, huddled over his cooling casserole. His toes froze. His nose dripped. He reached the moment of *fuck it, I'm out,* stood up to leave, and then their car pulled into the driveway.

"Bradford. You're early," his stepmom said. Surprise, surprise, she didn't seem happy to see him. "You were supposed to come at two p.m."

This was a lie.

This was gaslighting. But gaslighting only happened when things were dim, and you couldn't quite see. You'd second-guess yourself. Which Bradford did.

"Oh. I must have misheard."

"Well, I suppose you can come in."

Okay. Like a pitiful, stray dog, he followed them inside.

Inside it smelled like air freshener and ammonia. No butter smells, no turkey, no gravy, nothing cooking. They weren't cooking.

Bradford had stumbled dumbly into the same old trap.

"What are you cooking?"

"Oh, we'll just have a salad," his dad said.

"Just salad."

"Helena has to watch what she eats. It wouldn't be fair if the rest of us got to eat rich, buttery foods and she just had to sit there and be hungry."

"But it's Thanksgiving."

"Try to have some compassion, Bradford."

His stepmom had already retreated to her bedroom, so she didn't overhear this conversation. She needed to rest. And maybe, in a different universe, a kinder one, her absence meant that Bradford spent quality time with his dad, that they talked or played cards or tossed the football or watched an old western on TV, together.

But this Dad just said, "I've got an hour or so of work to get done before Thanksgiving dinner," as if boring salad even counted as Thanksgiving dinner, and then scurried away to his home office.

And he left Bradford alone, in the living room, with its off-limits furniture and untouchable rugs, bare walls, windows undressed, with a view of gray drear, bare branches, vast lawn, unused, its raison d'être the ostentatious display of wealth, like everything else.

He was suspended by indecision. To stay or go. To mollify or confront. To eat Thanksgiving salad for the sake of familial harmony or hightail it to a biscuits-and-gravy buffet. If he could find a good one.

He checked his phone and found something better: a two o'clock showing of *Peregrine* at the art house cinema on Ludlow, right next door to the Cheezy Mac Shack, open all day, serving the best fried turkey-mac-and-cheese balls in town.

Screw the salad.

Why bother with goodbyes? They didn't really want him there anyway. Bratty headed for the door. But before he escaped, his dad emerged from his office.

"Where are you going, Bradford?"

"I—I'm going to the movies."

"The movies?" His dad frowned. "Oh. Well, I guess, I was just coming to tell you, Helena's really not feeling well. The holidays are so disruptive. So, we thought, we should just cancel—"

"Right."

"Well... I hope to see you soon, Bradford."

Bratty meant to just leave, by himself, but maybe the look of disappointment on his dad's face made him change his mind. Maybe he harbored a blind, desperate faith in that other, kinder universe. Or maybe he thought he could remake this one.

"You should come with me," Bratty said.

"What?"

"To the movies."

"But I, well—"

"If Helena's sick, if you're canceling Thanksgiving, what are you gonna do, Dad? Sit here by yourself? You should come. They're playing *Peregrine.* You know, that old detective flick? It'll be fun."

His dad wanted to go. He had a wistful gleam in his eyes.

But he was so so so so so skilled at not doing what he wanted that how would he know what the fuck that was anymore?

No way would he actually go.

He said: "I'll have to check with Helena." Who wouldn't let him go, because it wouldn't be fair if they got a trip to the movies while she stayed home and felt sick.

While he checked, Bratty waited by the door, not holding his breath.

But then a minute later, his dad returned with coat hat mittens scarf and an hour later they were buying popcorn, drenching it with butter, watching the curtain pull back, the black screen turn ocean blue, the opening credits, Ricardo Merman as Detective Eddie Tides, and three hours after that they were sitting in a diner booth, stuffed full of mac-and-cheese balls, drinking beers, discussing the trajectories of their lives.

"If you could go back in time," Bratty asked, "if you could change something, what would you do different?"

"Why would I do anything different?" his dad said, because he was too steeped in his unchanging self, and attached to the conception of his singularity.

"Because— It's just like, to see how things would be. Or maybe, there was always something you wanted to do, but it seemed impractical, so you never did it."

"Huh." His dad took a sip of beer. "Okay. One thing. And it would never work out, because Helena, well... But if things were different, I always wanted a dog."

FLASHBACK

MIRIAM + JACK

A BABY was a miracle.

A baby was a gift from God.

A baby was the mortar, the parents the bricks, and now they were sealed together.

A baby was pure joy, until it woke up in the middle of the night, wailing. A sound that stoked panic, paranoia, a burgeoning fear that no night would ever again go uninterrupted.

But it didn't wake Jack. Oh no. When the monitor crackled, then erupted with desperate mewling, he didn't even stir. He slept with his arms splayed above his head, in a victory pose.

Miriam turned off the monitor. She rolled out of bed. Every movement tugged at her stitches, a tidy line where they'd cut the baby out. Every movement was agony.

But a baby!

Rory had a shock of black hair. A baby mohawk. He had tiny legs that liked to pedal, flappy arms, pajamas with mitts so he didn't scratch himself. He had a talent for screaming. He could scream for ten-twenty-thirty minutes straight. Pure joy.

He screamed until she stuck her sore teat in his mouth and then, like magic, he stopped. His legs pedaled as he suckled and she had to hold him back, away from her body, so the motion wouldn't pull at her stitches, and she worried that this forced space between them presaged a fissure, a family cleaved apart, by pain, by choices. It came down to choices, always. Even now. She chose not to hold this bicycling baby close. She chose to scroll on her phone, inattentive, as he drained her. *How long until a baby sleeps through the night?* she asked the internet, already anxious for this short phase in Rory's short baby existence to end. She wanted to jump ahead. To what?

He finished nursing. She changed his diaper, rocked him, kissed him, swaddled him, laid him in his crib to sleep. *Cry it out*, she thought, steeled to let it happen. But he didn't cry. Not even a whimper.

He was good. Lindsey was good. Not once had Lindsey ever poked her fingers in a socket or shoved a bean up her nose. Lindsey slept twelve hours straight. She slept through Rory's screaming. Miriam chose to check on her anyway. To see the rise and fall of her breath. To remind herself how good the good things could be.

When Miriam returned to her bedroom, Jack was awake. Up. Getting dressed.

She felt a wave of panic.

"What are you doing? What's wrong?"

"Work."

Panic.

"What? No."

"I got a call from the office. I have to go in."

"They called you?"

"The law never sleeps."

"It's five thirty in the morning."

"Which is technically morning."

"No. No, it's not. It's messed up. Stop defending them."

"Miriam—"

"You're supposed to be on paternity leave. Or did you forget?"

"I didn't forget. But there's this big deal we're trying to wrap up, and I've been involved with it the whole way through. They need me."

"*We* need you. *I* need you."

"I know," Jack said. "I don't like it either. But I've got to be flexible and dependable, if I ever want to make partner. So I need to do this. For our future. For our family."

He sounded so convincing. She could almost believe him. He believed him. And she was tired. Beyond the panic was an eon of exhaustion.

She slid into bed, *ow, ow, ow*. Cocooned herself in blankets. Took a last look at her husband, as he existed in this moment of their marriage. They were strong, weren't they? She could choose to believe this.

"Fine. Okay, Jack. I know it's important. But I just... I'm tired. And I want us to be together. But I'm tired."

He leaned down, kissed her forehead, turned off the light. She watched him leave the room, and in the dark, the shape of him looked foreign. His shadow looked like the shadow of someone else.

She closed her eyes. She told herself it would all be okay. He did what he did for his family, was the prevailing narrative. But sometimes, a narrative became so convincing, so consuming, that it eclipsed the truth.

She tried to sleep, but Jack's absence was palpable. She rolled out of bed, *ow, ow, ow*. She went downstairs, made a cup of tea, turned on the television. Roxster sat at her feet. He rested his head on her knee. He was solid and predictable. He was, at all times, his doggie self, beholden to no narrative. The truth was, she loved this dog, and she loved Jack, and years would pass before the narrative of their happy marriage would crumble and fold and she could only hope that something still stood amid the wreckage.

She browsed the movies and shows until something caught her eye. An image of a dog at the prow of a boat. His jowls flapped in the sea breeze. A man stood beside him, a strange man, leathery and bearded, in patchwork pants, a telescope in hand, a mystic gleam in his eye. She recalled something the man had said, long ago faraway, in the story of her childhood. *Be you, be true*, he'd said. Another rhyme, like all his silly rhymes, that might mean nothing, or that might be a vessel for the meaning ascribed by the person who heard it. *Be you, be true*. She turned the words over in her mind.

She conjured a memory.

Mr. Yay on her childhood TV.

He wrote those words on a scrap of paper. He sealed them in a bottle. He tossed them in the water, so they could sail across the distant ocean and be found, by the person who needed to hear.

THE BARTENDER

IMAGINE YOU are a bartender.

You work at a beach bar on the tiny island of Koh Lanta in the Andaman Sea. It is quiet, peaceful, perfect, everything you could possibly want in your life.

It is better than perfect, because there are beach cats. A whole happy crew of barback cats who supervise the mixing of drinks and entertain the customers and lounge in the sun, setting a good example for us all.

Imagine it is evening, off-season, quiet, no one at the bar except you and the cats.

And then, all at once, the cats start yowling, and you turn and see a man sitting alone at a table with a half-finished drink that you did not pour.

This man appeared out of nowhere.

Like he wandered out of the sea. Except he is dry, and somewhat drunk.

What's wrong with them? he asks you with a nod to the cats.

He is an older man, late middle-aged, gray hair. His clothes are too expensive. He has a watch tan line on his wrist, but no watch. Not anymore. His fingers are ringless.

Where did you come from? you ask him.

You already asked me that, he says, even though you haven't.

Koh Samui. But that was just last week. Before that, Ohio.

You do not know Ohio. You envision a vast land of highways and Buck-a-Bacons. A sea of corn. A crossroads.

Or, maybe, the crossroads is here.

It all depends on who you ask.

What brings you here? you ask him.

You already asked me that, too, he replies. *Maybe you want to lay off the, you know...* He makes a gesture that you recognize as *smoking a joint,* because maybe once or a dozen or a hundred times you did. Depends on who is asking. But you haven't smoked anything for a very long time.

My son... the man says, then trails off.

You refill the man's drink, and he gazes out at the darkening sea, and his eyes look unfathomably sad.

My son, he smoked weed. This sounds like it should sound judgmental, coming from a gray-haired man in a polo shirt. But it does not. It sounds wistful.

Where is he now? Your son?

The man shakes his head. *Nope. No sir. Not going to talk about that.*

He finishes his drink. Drink number *X*. Sometimes, the only way to face a feeling is to drown it first. He orders another. He invites you to sit down.

You ever hear of that old detective movie, Peregrine?

No, you have not.

With that actor, what was his name... Ricardo Merman?

Him, you have heard of. *Mr. Yay,* you say.

Mr. who?

Mr. Yay. From The Adventures of Mr. Yay?

The man says he has never heard of this show, but you don't believe him. Everyone has heard of Mr. Yay. Every American. Every Ohio dad had an Ohio son with a Captain Barksford lunch box and thermos. You know this to be true. Unless you have completely misunderstood what it means to be American.

Nope. No sir. Not him. Not his son. There was no such show, he says. He tries to prove it with his cell phone, but the reception is bad and his battery dies and you are both confined to your respective memories. You argue. Your argument becomes a conversation that goes on for several rounds of drinks and twists and turns and you would like it to keep going. You did not expect to like this man, but you do.

It is rare to make a new friend.

Ohio?

Yes.

It is far. Are you going back there?

I don't know. I... I quit my job. I don't know where I'm going next. I have all the time in the world.

That's never enough, is it?

Not unless you can turn it back, the man says. *Hey, let's stay in touch. I'll give you my number. If you're ever in the States...*

You find paper and a pen. He writes his phone number, and his name. *Brian Pierson.*

The moment he puts the pen down the cats yowl, all of them, all at once, and he is gone.

JUNE

STREET GOLF

IF TOM HAD NOT thrust his leg out, if he had not tried to catch the road with his foot, and lost balance, and swerved into that driveway, soared over cement, and crashed into the neighbor's front lawn, if he had sailed straight, he would have flown headfirst into a grove of trees. He would have knocked himself instantly unconscious, a blessing, because he wouldn't have heard his neck break or felt himself die.

He would be in the ground, instead of at the hospital, with two broken arms, a broken nose, and assorted other broken parts, including the wife part.

She wouldn't pick him up.

"She said if I wanted to come home," Tom told Jack over the phone, "I could ride my skateboard. And I would, if, you know..."

Holly was also day-drinking, which made it a bad idea to drive anywhere.

"And I'm busy golfing," she said, when the Miriam-Kate Meal Train arrived outside her house, bearing lasagnas. She had a nine iron and a wheelbarrow full of golf balls. She dropped a ball on the grass and swung her club. The ball sailed through the air and landed in the street.

"Maybe you should... not golf on the street," Kate said, as they set the lasagnas down on the porch.

"I have to golf somewhere." Holly pulled a bottle of wine from the wheelbarrow. She took a swig. "Now that we quit the country club. We couldn't afford it with all the medical bills."

This was true, in part. The other part, according to neighborhood gossip, involved afternoon margaritas, a puke-in-the-pool closure, and a golf cart joyride into the water hazard.

"You'll have more bills if you keep hitting golf balls into the street," Miriam said, glad that she and Kate had left their kids with Gonzago at Kate's house, where they wouldn't get hit in the head with a stray ball.

"Tom can pay them." Holly dropped another ball. She swung and missed. "He can have all the bills. I'll take the house, the cars, the wine. He can have the bills. That's fair, right?" She swung again. The ball narrowly missed a passing car.

Miriam glanced at Kate. Kate shrugged. Neither of them knew what to say to this version of their friend and her insouciant disregard for, well, everything. Holly picked up another golf ball, tossed it in the air, and swung her golf club like a baseball bat, which missed, but the momentum took her down. She landed on hands and knees. Fortunately, drunks were pliable. She popped back up, heedless of her now-bleeding lip, which she must have bit. She brushed the grass off her hands.

"I'll even let him sleep on the roof," she said. "That's fair. Isn't it fair?"

"It's—"

"I mean—"

"He clearly messed up—"

"Of course you're mad—"

"You should be mad, but—you have to—"

"What?" Holly yelled. She swung her golf club around. "What do I *have to do*? Because you know what? I'm tired of that, that, that stupid, unfair, unjust setup. Where Tom gets to be Tom. Hooray for Tom! Everyone, let's have a parade to celebrate my husband, Tom Waters, who gets to embrace his true self! Because that's what matters, right? Find your true self, follow your dreams, blah blah blah blah. Good for fucking Tom! Great for Tom! Because there is no cost, to Tom. Oh no, he gets to have his fun and follow his dreams, because I'm here to pick up the fucking pieces when they shatter. Tom gets to go skydiving because Holly is there to deal with soccer practice. Tom gets to break his arms because Holly is there to cook and clean and wipe his ass. Tom had money for a motorcycle because Holly saved money by doing things herself. Like cutting everyone's hair. Do you know who cuts my hair? Me! I'm the family barber!"

Holly had been wearing her wig, but she yanked it off and tossed it in the street. Her hair underneath had grown out into a pixie cut, dyed bleach blond.

"I'm the barber. I'm the cleaning lady. I'm the gardener, the cook, the organizer, the chauffeur, in addition to my fucking day job. And now I get to be the official ass wiper, the sponge bather, the bitch who cuts that lasagna into bites and flies the little airplane into my husband's mouth because he just really wanted to embrace his true self. *Fuck!*"

A tear slipped from Holly's eye, and it seemed to piss her off.

She grabbed the wheelbarrow handles, yanked them sideways, and dumped the entire stockpile of golf balls onto the lawn.

"Holly—"

"I'm so sorry—"

"If there's anything—"

Holly growled. "And you two!" She swung her club. Balls scattered. "You think you've got it different? You, Kate!"

"Me?" Kate squeaked.

"Look at you, bringing that lasagna. Who baked that? Bet it wasn't Fred!"

"Well, it's—it's got fermented nut cheese and homegrown kale—"

"That *you* grew."

"But Fred is— I mean, he takes the kids to school, and he feeds the goat, and—"

"And he's perfect, right? But which one of you gets to do yoga all day, and which one of you works a corporate job that *you despise*? Kate? And you—" Holly turned to Miriam. "You get to work and cover all the bills, but Jack gets to quit his job so that he can pursue his dream of being a detective."

"Well he did work really hard for a long time," Miriam said, suddenly defensive of her husband and his workaholism.

"Because that was what *he* wanted! But what about what *you* want? What do you want, Miriam? Kate? What the fuck do you want?"

Holly stared at them, and they stared back, at her, at each other, each struck by this articulation of a truth they'd all known but had never faced, not consciously. There'd been no time. Between the soccer practices and school drop-offs, the homework, the doctor visits, vet visits, dentist visits, holiday shopping, shoes that grew too small overnight, beloved plushies with torn ears that required emergency surgery by Doctor Mom, because Dad had never learned to sew, between dishes and laundry and cooking and planning and husbands, good reliable men who just needed to feel supported, challenged, essential, but who, above all, needed—and felt entitled—to fulfil their needs, there was no time for their wives to question what they wanted. There was only time to suppress and react. With drinking, with cigarettes, with a kombucha-brewing spree and a bulldozer to the front yard. With a golf club.

Two things happened at that moment.

First, Holly's front door opened, and Chad stepped out. He still had casts on both his arms.

"Hey, Mom?" He walked across the porch, down the stairs. "Hey, uh, Mom? My bedroom is doing that weird thing again, where everything gets fizzy and shifts around—" He stopped, seeming to register the scene before him, his mom with the nine iron, the kamikaze gleam in her eyes.

Then, as Chad took a step back, a car turned onto Ravenswood Drive. Jack's car. It pulled up outside the house. Jack and Fred got out. Jack got a wheelchair out of the trunk. Fred helped Tom climb into it. Tom waved, kind of. His arms, like his son's, were both in full-length casts, hand to shoulder.

"Hi, honey! I'm home!"

Holly ignored him. "You know what I want?" she asked her friends, but she didn't wait for them to answer. She turned and walked, casually, toward the motorcycle parked in the driveway. She lifted her golf club. She swung.

"Holly!" Tom cried. "Don't—"

Holly swung again. The headlight shattered.

"Holly! Stop!"

She swung again, with a crunch and a crack.

"Stop! Please! Holly! Someone, stop her!" Tom begged. He couldn't stop her, with his broken arms and fractured kneecaps. Holly pummeled the fender. She smashed the taillight. Fred and Jack took a few cautious steps toward her.

Miriam raised her hand. "Don't you dare!"

"You'll get hurt!" Kate added.

"Holly! Stop!" Tom yelled again, and he kept on yelling, as Holly battered chrome and dented metal, as she destroyed the gas tank, bent the exhaust pipe, pummeled the ignition, kicked the whole motorcycle over, and kept on going, swing after swing, and with each swing she cried out, all her fury and fear subsumed in a battle cry, her face a portrait of vicious, justified rage. She wasn't crazy. She wasn't even that drunk yet. She had been pushed to her limit by a man who loved to push the limits. She was caught in something larger, something that she couldn't explain. They all were. And as she demolished Tom's motorcycle, as Tom abandoned his futile pleas and fell quiet, Kate sat down on the grass, and she motioned for Fred to come sit beside her, and Jack waded through the golf balls, to Miriam, and when his arm brushed hers, she took his hand in her own, and together they watched.

On the porch, Chad began to cheer. "Go, Mom! Destroy it! Kick its ass, Mom!"

And she did. She swung and kicked and spit, and eventually she wore herself out. She sank down beside the wreckage. She wept.

Miriam turned to Jack. "I'm taking her. Kate and I are taking her."

"Where?"

"I don't know yet. Someplace . . . not here. You and Fred can take care of the kids. And Tom."

"But—"

"No buts. This is what's happening."

"How long will you be gone?"

Miriam shrugged. "As long as it takes."

Then she kissed Jack on the cheek and went to pick up the pieces of her broken friend.

HYPNOSIS

IT DIDN'T TAKE LONG to realize that they couldn't stay at the hotel. They'd checked in, single room, two beds. Miriam and Kate could share. They took Holly to the hotel spa, floated in the pool, went out for dinner, no drinks, watched a movie in the room.

"See, I don't need to drink. I'm fine," Holly said. "For now."

They fell asleep sober.

Holly woke screaming.

"No! No, please, no! Not him, not him, NOOOOOOOOOO!"

Miriam jolted awake. Kate was up already, at Holly's side, trying to make her stop.

"Holly, it's just a dream. You're okay. You're—"

"NOOOOOOOOOO! AHHHHHHHHHHH!"

"Holly!"

"AHHHHHHHHHHH!"

"HOLLY!"

Kate shook her. For a moment, she went limp. Then her eyes opened. She looked around the room.

"It's okay. It was just a dream," Kate said. "But you're safe now. You're here with us."

"It's not— I'm not— I can't—"

"You can," Miriam said. She climbed onto the bed next to Holly.

"It doesn't feel like a dream. I can't make it stop. I can't."

She couldn't go back to sleep unless she ransacked the hotel minibar.

"But it won't help," Kate said.

"It'll help me go to sleep."

"There has to be something else. You can't just drink until you pass out—"

"Can and will," Holly said. "Better than the dream."

"So you make it stop. Miriam's a therapist. Maybe she can—"

Miriam interrupted. "That's not— I'm not what she needs."

"So what, then?" Kate asked. "Do we just take her to rehab, or—"

"No," Holly said. "I mean sure, fine, take me, whatever. I'll take a vacation from taking care of Tom and Chad. But I told you, this isn't about booze. I'll still have nightmares. I'll still wake up screaming."

"Not rehab," Miriam said. "I was thinking of something . . . different."

Holly stayed awake all night. Miriam dozed off during one movie and woke up to another. Gray light filtered through the blinds. Kate did sun salutations in the corner. Holly looked haggard.

She looked even more exhausted two hours later, when they parked outside the *Psychic—Mystic—Fortune-Telling* shop. A new neon sign in the window said OPEN, but the door was locked. The front stoop was covered in cicada exoskeletons. The tree behind the building tittered with starlings. A vulture circled overhead.

"There's no one here," Holly said.

Inside, the lights flickered.

"She's here," said Miriam. "Go around back."

They walked around the side of the building. The avian

graveyard had grown. Limp flowers wilted on the tiny graves. The target window into which the birds had flown was boarded up, with a message spray-painted across the boards: BIRDS—DO NOT ENTER HERE!

"But it didn't work," the psychic said, appearing out of nowhere. "They fly straight at the boards. Like they can't even see 'em. Like they're still lookin' at the window."

"That's... sad," Miriam said.

"It's something. I like to think that they're still alive somewhere. But anyways, look at you." The psychic looked at Miriam. Her blue eyes flashed. "And you. And you. I thought you three might show up."

"Well, here we are."

"You see? I'm psychic. Come on in. Y'all want some root beer?"

"Um—"

"No thanks."

"I'm good, thank you."

They followed Destinia Amber Rose inside. None of them wanted Diet Fizz Wizard Root Beer, but she poured four glasses anyway. She invited them to sit on her velvet couch.

"You want to gaze into the crystal ball?" Rosy opened a shoebox and took out a round white rock, the size of a golf ball.

"That's the crystal ball?" Miriam asked. "It seems a bit—"

"Small? I know, I know. I used to have a bigger one, but there was too much to see in it and it always left me feelin' woozy." Rosy tossed the crystal ball to Holly.

"Um, what do I do?" Holly asked. "Do I just look at it, or—"

"Squeeze it real tight," said Rosy. Holly squeezed. "Tighter...

tighter... There, that should do." She plucked the crystal ball from Holly's hand. She held it up to the window, where the light shone through.

"Do you see anything?"

"Hmm." Rosy twirled a strand of her hair around her finger. "I see... I see... wheels?"

"Wheels?"

"I think... yes. Wheels. Small ones. Like on a skateboard."

"Oh my god," Holly said. "Seriously?"

"I'm a psychic."

"Yeah, but, that's crazy. My husband just—"

"Not *like* a skateboard," the psychic said. "That's a skateboard *for sure*." She shook the crystal ball like a cocktail shaker. She held it up to the light and gazed inside.

"Do you see anything else?" Holly asked.

"Nope. Nothing but fuzz. It's a neat gimmick, this crystal ball, but more'n half the time it doesn't work. An' then sometimes it'll only show you scenes from the future that you already know will happen for sure, like you goin' to the grocery or takin' a nap. But enough about that. Y'all ain't here to talk about the future anyway. Y'all are here to talk about the past."

"Well, no," Miriam said. "We're here because my friend Holly has been having these awful dreams. She can't sleep. She woke up last night screaming. And we'd hoped—"

"Oh, it's the past," Rosy declared. "The future don't assert itself like that. The future's more like... like a hair caught in the back of your throat. All tickly, but then you stick your finger back there to pull it out and you can't seem to find it. But what you described, waking up like that, that's the past. Only question is who it belongs to."

Rosy got up, walked into the other room, and returned with a fresh bottle of root beer. She popped the cap off. Foamy fizz bubbled out. She held her nose up to the fizz and sniffed. She took a long drink and set the bottle down on her shelf. Then she tossed the crystal ball back in the shoebox and, from the same box, pulled out a plastic digital watch, shaped like a cat's head with the hour framed inside a Cheshire grin, tied to a long piece of ribbon.

"Now take a drink of root beer," she told Holly.

"Um..."

"It'll work better if we both drink root beer."

"Okay, but... why?"

"The root beer's got specialized placebic properties."

"Placebic properties..."

"That's right," Rosy explained. "When I was young, I met another psychic. I didn't know much about bein' a psychic back then, but she showed how it was done. To properly harness my powers, she said, I'd need something with placebic properties. There are several such things, but I liked root beer the best. Cream soda'll do in a pinch. Now, are we all ready to get started?"

"I guess so?"

"All right, then," Rosy said. "Now sit back, make yourself comfortable. I'm going to swing my watch here back and forth, and—"

"Wait, that watch?" Kate pointed at the plastic cat-head timepiece.

"You was prob'ly 'specting one of them fancy silver pocket watches, right? But it don't matter what kind of watch. This one'll get the job done just fine. Now, I'm gonna swing the watch back and forth, and I want you to watch the watch, and listen to the sound of my voice. And that's it. You ready?"

Holly nodded. The psychic scooted her chair closer. She looped the ribbon around her finger. Slowly, she began to swing the watch back and forth. Holly's eyes followed.

"Okay, darlin'. Keep watching. Take a deep breath. Relax. Like you're sittin' on a porch swing on a summer day. You ain't got nowhere to be. Nothin' to do but swing. Watch the trees. Listen to the birds. Nothin' to do but relax. And when you're ready, when you're totally relaxed, you're gonna go inside."

As the digital watch swung back and forth, Holly's shoulders relaxed. Her jaw unclenched. Her gaze softened. She stared at the watch, but her mind was somewhere else.

"You ready?" the psychic asked. Holly nodded. "Okay. Now open the door and go in. You feel so relaxed, you just might take a nap. You know where your bed is. It's your house. But it smells different. Like lavender and lemon. It feels different, because now you can see what's really there.

"But first, close your eyes." Rosy's voice deepened. "You hear something. *Ding-dong*. It's a doorbell. You're not ready to answer it now. Not yet. But if you hear the doorbell again, you'll need to open your eyes and go answer right quick. You hear that doorbell again, you'll wake up."

Holly did not respond. Her eyes were closed now. Her face was serene, as if she'd fallen asleep, but she still sat upright.

Rosy set the watch down. "Inside the house," Rosy went on, "there's a door you need to open. You were afraid, but you ain't afraid no more. You're gonna find that door upstairs. So you go up. One, two, three steps, four steps, five, six now, seven, eight, nine steps, ten steps, eleven, twelve, thirteen, fourteen, you're almost at the top now, fifteen, sixteen, seventeen, eighteen, nineteen... there. You're there. Now walk down the hall. Do you see the door?"

"I see it," Holly said. Her eyes blinked open. Her voice sounded faraway.

"Open it."

"I... I don't want to."

"I know, hon, but you need to."

"It's all I have left."

"And you need to see it. You're gonna take a deep breath. Grab the doorknob. Turn it. Now open. All the way."

Holly's face was impassive, but tears welled in her eyes.

"I want you to describe what you see."

"I... It's Chad's room," Holly said. Tears rolled down her cheeks. "It was Chad's room. Now it's..."

"It's okay. You want to talk about it. You're ready."

"It's a shrine. It looks just like it did. On the day he died."

Kate gasped. Miriam held her hand. A steady waterfall of tears streamed from Holly's eyes.

"What day was that?"

"It was right before Halloween. Last year. October twenty-second. He was going to be Spider-Man. He loved Spider-Man. But then..."

"What happened?"

"It was Tom's fault. No, no it wasn't. It was—it was an accident. But it was Tom's skateboard. Tom was supposed to keep it hidden because Chad is—Chad was—Chad wanted one, and I told him no. But he found Tom's. And he... he... they said he died on impact.

The paramedics. When he hit the street. And he was gone when I got there, he was gone and I never got to say goodbye. I just . . . I can't let him go. . . ."

Miriam typed a note on her phone. *Chad is still alive.* She showed Rosy.

Rosy mouthed the words *I know*. Out loud, she said, "You don't have to let him go. But you have to fix his bedroom. Okay?"

Holly nodded.

"Put everything back where it goes. His shoes, he just kicked 'em off and left 'em there. But you put 'em in the closet. He left his dirty clothes on the floor. Now they're in the hamper. He's been sleeping in that bed every night. Now it's made. It's all clean. It looks just like it's supposed to look. I want you to look."

The tears stopped.

"It all looks how it's supposed to look. And what you saw before, that was . . . it was just a very bad dream. But it's over now. It's over. And now time is gonna move very quickly. Time is gonna speed past, till you reach the moment when you awake. You ready?"

Holly nodded.

Rosy counted down. "Five, four, three, two, one, *ding-dong. Ding-dong.*"

Holly blinked. She looked around, at Miriam, at Kate, at the digital watch on the table. She wiped her wet cheeks. "It was just a very bad dream," she murmured.

"That's right," the psychic said.

"But now it's over?"

"Now it's over."

"Holly—are you—" Kate started.

“I’m fine,” Holly said. “I’m fine. I just— I need a minute.” She stood up. She walked to the back door, opened it, and stepped out into the sunlight.

“Is she—”

“I think she’s fine,” the psychic replied.

“But—you know, I’ll just go keep an eye on her,” Kate said. She went to the door, then stopped and watched from there.

“Is she really fine?” Miriam asked the psychic.

“Are any of us really fine?”

“Point. But what you said, that it was just a bad dream—”

“Was exactly what your friend needed to hear.”

“But was it?” Miriam asked. Rosy stared at her. Into her. She reached for her bottle of root beer. She drank. She burped. Her eyes stayed fixed on Miriam.

“You know the answer, hon, as well as I do.”

“It wasn’t a dream.”

“Not just. Must have felt like a nightmare though, rememberin’ somethin’ like that. But the important thing is, the room is in order.” Rosy chugged the last of her root beer. “Now go on, get outta here. I got some things to finish up before the game starts.”

“Okay. What do I owe you?”

“Season tickets, in the infield box. Plus a lock of your hair, for my collection.”

“What—”

“Kidding. Sixty bucks. And next time you come back, bring me a case of the good stuff.”

MERMAN

WHEN MIRIAM GOT HOME, three days later—minus one friend (Holly had checked into rehab, not because of the drinking problem she swore she didn't have but because she needed a safe space to work through her reckless-husband rage), plus another friend who'd just bought her first deck of tarot cards, plus a friendship crystal (Kate and Holly had matching ones), a new fondness for kombucha, and the determination to figure out what she really wanted for herself, and pursue it, responsibly, and not with the rash abandon of *the husbands,* for whom were also purchased matching friendship crystals—she found her own husband on the front porch, looking detective-ish. Like he'd struck a private-eye pose and held it for her return. Back against the wall. Head bowed. Hat on, his face hidden by its shadow. Cigarette between his lips. Entirely authentic detective, except for the flip-flops, and his reaction when her car pulled into the driveway. He ran, arms out, shouting.

"Miriam! Miriam!" His face was pure glee.

She got out of the car. He flung his arms around her.

"Did you have a good time with Fred and Tom?" she asked.

"Exhausting. But guess what?"

"What?"

"I found him!"

"Who?"

"Mr. Yay! Who else?!"

"But he doesn't exist, officially, so—"

"I know, I know. Not him. But the guy who played him. Ricardo Merman."

"You found Ricardo Merman?"

"I found where he lives. It's only a few hours away. But I've already booked a hotel and packed our bags, so—"

"Wait, wait, wait, wait. You what now?"

"I booked a hotel, and—"

"No, I heard what you said. It's just, you want us to go there? Like, just show up at his house?"

"Miriam, I'm a detective. That's what detectives do."

"Okay but you know this is just a hobby, right? Jack? I mean, you're not making any money from your detective work—"

"But I am," Jack said. He grinned proudly. "I'm crowdfunded!"

"You're crowdfunded."

"Fred helped me set it up. We raised over twenty thousand dollars to help find Mr. Yay. And that was just last night!"

"Okay, that's . . . absurd. But what about the kids? And the dog?"

"They're all with Fred. They're building a little house for Gonzago's racoons."

"Okay, that's also absurd."

"But I told them you'd stop over to say goodbye. And then we'll go!"

An hour later she was in the car with Jack, driving east, windows open, jazz on the stereo, for ambiance. The city unfurled into strip-mall suburbs, dealerships, highway churches, motel-fast-food-gas-stops sandwiched with billboards for the best

Double-Wubble-Bacon for your buck, the buy-one-get-one Frosty Freeze-Whip, the Eternal Damnation for the unrepentant, the rapper known as Mr. Yay, live in concert, June 21.

"I'm changing the music," Miriam said.

"What? No! This is the detective soundtrack!"

"But that's a sign. Mr. Yay. Live in concert. Should we go? Maybe he's got answers."

She changed the music. She turned up the volume. The car rumbled with bass. Rap blasted from the speakers.

Hey, mama, yo dad
It's fuckin' time to kick back
'Cause you been workin' too hard
And work ain't the right track
To happiness
bliss, yo, you wanna get that
You gotta relax
Read a book, take a nap
Get smashed, shake that ass
Take a toke, a cap, a fuck
Yo, I ain't tryin' to be crass
I'm tryin' to be nice
'Cause the past is the past
And I just want to show
You a slice
Of this life
What it's like
When you live
Instead of tryin' to buy

A life that you'll never have
When you're always fuckin' busy
Bustin' your ass, yo—

"He's talking to you, Jack," Miriam said, and then she glanced over at her husband in the driver's seat and saw his lips in sync with the lyrics, his head bobbing along with the beat. He knew this song. She laughed to herself. She watched him, and beyond him the concrete landscape softened into fields and groves of green.

—but the past ain't the past
And whatever they say
That you're fat, that you're bad,
You're a waste, a disgrace
A lawn-gnome
The way you're always on grass
Well fuck them, and fuck that
'Cause the shit that you take
Yo, it ain't gotta last.
So turn your back
Raise above
Raise your glass
And relax.
Yo, raise your glass, and relax—

The greenery blurred and the fields became forests and Jack sang along with every song.

"Who are you?" she asked. "How do you know these songs?"

"They spoke to me. I heard them and I knew. Something had to change."

"Are you happier? As a detective?"

"I've never been this happy in my life. Not since before law school. Not since I met you. Except..."

"I'm glad for you. But I don't know if—"

"I know."

"—if I still love you."

Or if she wanted to. She looked at her husband, his hairy hands on the wheel, his skinny goat legs, his cultivated five-o'clock shadow, his eyes fixed on the road. He looked like the man she'd married. But he would never be that man again, if he ever was. He was an incarnation, a Jack of this time and place, as fleeting as the tessellating waves of a changing sea. Yet in him, in the slope of his jaw, the solace of his gaze, his lips pursed in agonized anticipation, there was the glimmer of a man who had swept her heart.

They didn't speak, but when the album ended she replayed it, and Jack rapped along. The highway became a winding road, and the road grew narrow and the trees grew tall, and beneath the shadows of their ancient boughs the light played in harlequin patterns and Miriam sensed that they were close. They passed a country house with an old red barn. A peregrine falcon circled in the air above it. The scene sent a shiver up her spine. The light had a strange quality here, hazy, foreboding. But Jack kept driving, up a hill, down through a valley, up again, and when the hill crested there was a clearing, in which stood a house.

The house had a wooden mailbox carved in the shape of a boat.

Jack parked beside it. He hopped out, opened the mailbox, and pulled out a stack of mail.

"Jack, stop! You can't just rifle through someone's mailbox."

That tampering with mail was a federal offense apparently didn't matter in the Detective Arts.

"It's him!" Jack held up an envelope addressed to Ricardo Merman.

"I could have guessed from the mailbox."

Jack sifted through the mail. "Look at these postmarks. Some of these were mailed months ago. March, March, April. No one's been collecting the mail."

"Maybe Ricardo Merman doesn't live here anymore."

"Maybe it's more than just that," said Jack. "Come on, let's go investigate the house."

He knocked first, but when no one answered, Jack picked the lock.

"Seriously?"

"I learned on YouTube."

"You know breaking and entering is a crime, right?"

"Only if you get caught. Besides, how else are we supposed to get in? And if we don't go in, we might not be able to solve the mystery."

They went in. Miriam shut the door behind them. Jack flipped the light switch. Nothing happened.

"The power's out."

The air was musty and stale. A winter coat hung on a hook by the door, above a pair of snow boots. No one had occupied this house for months.

The house was small and sparse, no sign of kids or animals, no knickknacks, no TV. Old movie posters hung on the walls—*Canyon of Arrows, The Lucky & Unlucky, The Last Train to Topeka.* There was a single bedroom in the back. It felt stifled and sad, and as they searched through drawers and cupboards for clues of the Real Mr. Yay, Miriam thought about the Mr. Yay of her youth, his enthusiasm, his vibrance, in striking contrast to her vision of the Ricardo Merman who had lived here. This Ricardo Merman had an expired passport with no stamps. This Ricardo Merman kept his kitchen stocked with canned tuna, canned corn, canned green beans, saltine crackers, instant oatmeal, white bread turned chalky-blue with mold. This Ricardo Merman had an album with pictures of his childhood pets—a spider, a squirrel, a blind dog. Here was a photo of the teenage Merman with a two-legged rat, his face still full of promise, his future, in that moment, undecided. He could have been the Mr. Yay she'd known, but he was not.

She wandered into the bedroom, into the closet. He had sweaters in navy and gray and brown, plain button-up shirts, khakis, slacks, nothing with color. Except, in the very back, a spot of red.

Miriam pushed the dull clothes to the side. The spot of red peeked out from the torn edge of a dry cleaner's bag. She ripped the bag further, down the seam, until it slipped off. Underneath hung a pair of wide-legged patchwork pants, velvet, handsewn, every square a brilliant color. Mr. Yay's pants.

She took them down from the hook. She knew from their texture that these pants had almost never been worn. The hems had no frays. The fabric had grown stiff from untouched decades. The buttons were bright and untarnished.

She held the pants in her arms, and a tear slipped from her eye, down her cheek, a single saltwater drop on pristine velvet.

She hugged the pants to her chest, and the tears came in a torrent, seasons and seasons of tears, for all that she remembered that had vanished, for all that wasn't, but might have been. She might have watched *The Adventures of Mr. Yay* with her kids, her and the kids and Jack together. She might have whispered, when she tucked them in to bed, *Silent like a starfish,* and they might have known what she meant. She wept, and she thought about her broken marriage, and the choices she could make, each choice casting an outward ripple that would shape each other choice, until the waves all crashed together, and cause was indistinguishable from effect.

She wept, and Jack heard her, and came. He reached for her, to hug her, then stopped.

"Do you want—"

She looked up at him. She could choose, to hug him or not. What did she want?

She looked down at the velvet, now splattered with tears.

She had met Jack because another car crashed into his and he crashed into her and from the start, things were broken. But a broken thing could be salvaged, pieced together, sewn into a patchwork brighter and better than the sum of its parts.

She nodded. "Yes."

He wrapped his arms around her. He held her close, the pants sandwiched in between them. *Yes,* she wanted *this* Jack. The other one, the workaholic, she might have left. This one had his flaws, but he deserved a shot. They deserved it. Miriam + Jack. Maybe not forever, but at least for now.

He held her, and she wept, and when her tears finally stopped, he said, "I found this."

He had a notebook, plain, lined, yellow and weathered, unremarkable, except for the writing inside it.

"What is it?"

Jack flipped through pages. Tiny scrawl covered every page. Each page had a date. The dates spanned decades, all the way up to the current year, March 21, the equinox, which bore the last entry:

I fear that I have lost myself. I had a dream, once, where
I put on those old patchwork pants I'd sewn and danced
across the deck of a ship, all the colors flowing around me,
and there were animals and children, and I told them how
they could grow up to be them, just them, because there
was nobody better. I felt inspired, and I inspired others.
But it was just a dream, I thought. And I was afraid.
I wish I could reach out, to myself. Don't be afraid,
I would tell him. Be as weird as you want to be.
It's too late for me, now. But for him, it's—

And then the message abruptly ended.

ROBERT KAI

A WEEK AFTER they'd returned home, Jack left mysteriously with the dog. A few hours later, he and the dog returned. He wouldn't say where they'd gone.

"I don't think keeping secrets is good for our marriage."

"I'm not keeping secrets," Jack said. "This is more like a surprise. Maybe. If it works out."

For days, he said nothing more. But he wore a goofy grin, and he replayed the album of Mr. Yay, the rapper, until the kids had memorized all the dirty lyrics, and he wore his pants loose and low on his hips, and he bought another bottle of Hennessy, and he held his cigarette between his thumb and forefinger, like a joint.

He was in this posture—Hennessy, cigarette, baggy pants, flip-flops and fedora, on the back deck, working on his detective novel—when the doorbell rang. Miriam decided to ignore it. The only people she wanted to see would text ahead. But the kids thwarted her plan.

"Mom!"

"Hey, Mom!"

"There's someone at the door!"

"I'll get it!"

"No, you got it last time! Mom, Rory got it last time!"

The lock clicked. The door opened. Miriam glowered at her kids.

"Hi there. I'm looking for a Mr. Jack Shipley, private eye."

"What's a private eye?"

"Who are you?"

"Kids!" Miriam approached the door. The kids scattered. Any human at the door was less interesting than the act of competitive door-opening. "Hi. You're looking for Jack?"

"The detective. Yes." The man looked thirty to forty-ish, though it was hard to gauge with his bushy beard. He was tall and lean, except for a small potbelly. He wore jeans and a sports coat over a T-shirt depicting a bubbling beaker, with the words SCIENCE, BITCHES! printed beneath. He had a dog on a leash, a corgi. "I'm SherLok Ohms. I'm here about Mr. Yay."

"Oh. Jack's around back," she said. "Follow me."

Miriam led the man and his corgi around the side of the house, to the back deck, where Jack deduced his identity.

"You must be SherLok Ohms."

"Indeed."

"But that's not your real name, is it?"

"Correct again. My alter ego. All electronic communications under my real name are being monitored."

"You're being monitored?"

"I have highly specialized and, um... potentially dangerous knowledge. About the nature of time and space." He said this in a serious voice, but his eyes had a mischievous gleam.

"Oh."

"I know that sounds crazy. But I assure you it's not. I'd monitor me, too."

"And how is it that you know you're being monitored?" Miriam asked. "I don't mean to sound skeptical, but—"

"Totally fine. I know, Conspiracy Chasers, RVK, tinfoil hats, it all sounds crazy." He stroked his bushy beard. "But one of my buddies from grad school designed the monitoring software. And he's got a program running that scans for anything, well, let's just say, anything he can use to make fun of me. Which I guess I deserve, after that prank I pulled with the bowling balls. But anyway, I'm off on a tangent. I'm here because you were looking for information on Mr. Yay—the children's television star Mr. Yay."

"As opposed to the rapper. That's right. Do you remember him?" Jack asked.

"I adored him," SherLok Ohms said, arms flapping excitedly. "I was fanatical about the show. I had all the merch—the Mr. Yay lunch box, the Mr. Yay bedspread, the Christmas album. I dressed up as Captain Barksford for Halloween, three years in a row. So of course, finding out that the show doesn't exist, well..."

"But we found his house," Miriam said. "Jack did. We went there."

"Ricardo Merman's house, you mean?" the man asked.

Jack nodded.

"Did you find any artifacts?"

"Artifacts?"

"I'm getting ahead of myself. I guess that's my fate, ha. Always ahead, behind, off on some tangent. But let me go back to the start. I'm an astrophysicist. My real name," the man said, offering his hand, "is Robert Kai. And my friend here is Samwise Corgi."

Lindsey and Rory, initially deterred by the adultness of the situation, had registered the presence of this dog. They crept across the deck and sat down beside it.

"Aww, he's cute."

"He's mostly good. Unless you've got cheese and you leave it unattended. Are you familiar with the Green Creek Observatory?"

"The telescope array?"

"That's right," Kai said. "A few months ago, in March—March twenty-first, the spring equinox, to be exact—I was at the Green Creek Observatory collecting data when I noticed something very odd. One of the things we monitor at the observatory is the rate of cosmic expansion. It should be constant. But for several months, there had been... blips in the data. And then on March twenty-first, it declined. Precipitously. This is not a thing that should happen. I recorded the data. I printed it out, as the decline was occurring. And afterward, I checked and rechecked. I ran calculations. I had all the equipment inspected. I reached out to other physicists at other telescope arrays. None of them had recorded the decline. What I had seen, what I'd recorded, made no sense. It was, quite literally, impossible. Unless, of course, it didn't happen."

Robert Kai smiled, and from a small satchel that hung from his shoulder he produced a piece of printer paper in a protective plastic cover, lined with numbers, dated March 21. He handed it to Jack.

"This," Robert Kai said, "is the record I made of the declining rate of universal expansion. It is also an artifact. A physical object that should not exist in this universe, and yet somehow, it does."

Something clicked in Miriam's mind. She looked at Jack. His eyes lit up.

"Meat loaf!" they both said, at the same time.

"We have artifacts!" Miriam explained. "We have two notes,

and they're identical, except one says 'meat loaf' and the other says 'pot roast,' but they can't both exist. I couldn't have written both of them."

"You couldn't, if you were the only you. But if there's more than one of you—if there's a whole multiverse teeming with versions of you, each one of you could write an identical or near-identical note. And if one of those notes ended up in a universe it didn't belong to—"

"It would be an artifact?"

"That's right."

"But how do you *get to* the multiverse?" Lindsey asked, as she scratched Samwise Corgi's head. "Because *she said* I was supposed to go. But I don't know how to go."

"Who said?" Miriam asked.

"The dark bird."

"That's— What's your name?" Robert Kai asked. He looked down at the child, a curious look in his eyes.

"Lindsey."

"Lindsey, what do you know about the multiverse?"

"I know it's got lots of songs," Lindsey said.

"Well, yes, that's true. It's got lots of everything. The place we live, we call the *universe*, and it's the only one. But the multiverse, or the meta-universe, is made up of lots of universes. Lots of Lindseys. Lots of Samwise Corgis."

"Lots of Roxsters?" Lindsey asked.

"Our dog," said Jack.

"Yep. Lots of Roxsters," Kai went on, talking to both kids and parents. "Maybe infinite Roxsters. And since there are so many of them, well, some of them are very, very different."

"Like a Roxster who's a cat?"

"Or a Lindsey who's a cat," Kai said. Lindsey giggled. "Or a Samwise Corgi who's bigger than an elephant. But among all these universes, there are also some that are very, very similar. Maybe so similar that if you moved from one to another—if such a thing was possible—you wouldn't even notice.

"Imagine that there are two universes that are very similar," Kai continued, stroking Samwise Corgi alongside the children. "Almost the same, in every way. Except in one of them, there's a children's television show about a silly dude named Mr. Yay who travels the world on a boat captained by a dog, and in the other universe, there is no such show. Imagine those two universes are like branches on a tree, growing alongside each other. Or—maybe it's easier to picture them as bubbles. They're separate. They should stay separate. But somehow, they collide. And for a while they become one bubble. What happens then?"

"They pop?" Rory asked.

"Well, hopefully not," Kai said. "They could though. Or it could be like nothing happened, and everything in each bubble is unchanged. Or they could separate, with each bubble bearing traces of the other. Artifacts, if you will. Or they could merge into a single bubble."

"Wait, so what happened, then?" Miriam asked. "Are you saying that a universe with *The Adventures of Mr. Yay* collided with a universe where the TV show didn't exist, and the two universes got all mixed up?"

"Basically yes."

"So which universe are we in?" Jack asked. "The redivided one? Or the merged one?"

"No way to know for sure. And it might not even matter. Though..." Kai glanced down at Lindsey. He frowned. "No, there's no way to know. Not yet, anyhow. It's all just speculation."

"So if this is what happened," Jack said, "that would explain why some of us remember Mr. Yay and some of us don't?"

"Precisely."

"And if Jack doesn't remember," Miriam said, "and I do, does that mean we're from different universes?"

"Or something like that," said Kai. "Keep in mind this is all just theory. It could be that each of you are from distinct universes, or it could be that you're the amalgamations of yourselves from both universes. No one entirely understands the effects of a collision like this. If that's what happened. Which, at this point, is still an unproved hypothesis. And it's entirely unclear how long it would last. I speculate there'd be a focal point, like the temporal crux of the collision, probably the day I recorded that data. And the effects could spread forward and backward in time from that point. Though like I said, it's all just hypothetical. But the circumstantial evidence supports the theory. As do the, well, the psychological ramifications."

"What do you mean?" Miriam asked.

"Imagine the effects on the psyche of having two minds crammed into one brain. Having conflicting memories. Or memories of things that, according to the world around you, never happened."

"It would cause confusion and distress," Miriam said. She thought about her friends—Holly's nightmares and alcoholism, Tom's reckless adventures, Kate and Fred's crunchy lifestyle shift. Jack's career change. Her own smoking habit. "And that could manifest in all sorts of ways. Stress, self-transformation, depression, addiction..."

"And you think people all over the world are all experiencing this?" Jack asked.

"Not just people," said Kai, "but yes. I am. I've been driving obsessively."

"Driving?"

"It started back in January. I'd get this itchy feeling, like I had to get up and go somewhere. I couldn't focus on my work. I couldn't seem to focus on anything. Driving seemed to relax me. No idea why, but it did. I've been taking long road trips. Every weekend I drive from Raleigh where I live to the beach, and sometimes down the coast. When I saw that you were here, in driving distance, I thought, hey, might as well."

"Wait, you said it started in January," said Jack.

"That's right."

"But the data you recorded, that was afterward, from March."

"Ah, yes," Kai said. "Like I said, it's not so much about after or before. It's more like... well, picture what happens when you toss a stone into a pool of water. There's a ripple outward, from where the stone hit. The event, the collision, if that is what happened, is the impact point, the temporal crux. And the effects would ripple backward and forward through what we perceive as time. And the farther we get from that impact point, the fewer the effects, and the less detectable they are. Eventually I suspect we will hardly even notice."

Robert Kai stayed for a while. They drank Hennessy and lemonade on the back deck, and theorized about the multiversal collision, and reminisced about Mr. Yay. Miriam and Jack shared their artifacts. They showed Robert Kai the notebook of Ricardo Merman, and the patchwork pants, which Jack had insisted they take from the house.

"Because he won't miss them," Jack said. "He disappeared."

"Ricardo Merman disappeared?"

"Him and Mr. Yay both. How does that make sense?"

"I... I'm not sure," Kai said. "I'll have to give it some thought. But if science ever solves that mystery..."

Jack the Detective invited Robert Kai to stay on the guest bed, but Kai had a camping hammock in the back of his car, and a telescope. He wanted to drive out, beyond the city lights, to where he could see the stars.

He left, and Miriam went inside, and a moment later, Jack ran in, grinning, ecstatic.

He squealed. "He got picked!"

"Who?"

"Roxster! Remember when I left the other day, with Roxster? They were looking for dogs, for the Mr. Yay concert—"

"Mr. Yay, the rapper."

"Yeah, they needed dogs for the show, and I took Roxster to audition, and they picked him! They said he was very good, and they liked that he only had three legs. And since he's in the show, we're getting free tickets!"

ALMOST SHOWTIME

THE TOUR BUS rode east from LA, through Vegas, Salt Lake, Denver, down through the bowels of Texas, north to Milwaukee, Chicago, and then they were home.

They picked up strays along the way: dogs, rappers, DJs, groupies, YouTubers, KlipSwatchers, parents and grandparents of kids who only ever wanted to be Captain Barksford when they grew up, friends of friends of friends of Tommy's who hitched a ride on the bus, or sailed along behind it. All creatures welcome, like in the show *The Adventures of Mr. Yay*. They met a woman who painted their portraits aboard the SS *Deliverance*. They met a theater troupe that performed remembered skits from the vanished show. They went to a Mr. Yay after-party stacked with Mr. Yays, hundreds of them, in patchwork pants and fake beards. They played a renegade set aboard a boat captained by a man in a dog suit. They collected dogs, dogs who traveled on from city to city, show to show, dogs who made a special one-time guest appearance and then went home. They stopped at an intersection in their hometown because Tommy saw a sign out the window, taped to a telephone pole. HAVE YOU SEEN MR. YAY? it asked. It looked like a lost pet sign, except instead of a pet's photograph, it had a drawing of a Mr. Yay and Captain Barksford on their boat.

The tour bus pulled up in front of a large house, a sterile, cavernous, soulless house where the young Bradford Pierson had learned what a bad little boy he was. What a brat he was. It was nighttime, the street dark. The black branches of moneyed trees reached out to a gold-flecked sky. The moon was diamond white. It had rained all day. Rain fell softly from a passing cloud.

The floodlights flipped on. Somewhere, an alarm went off, and a neighbor called the cops, just to report the unexpected appearance, in their serene and predictable neighborhood, of a tour bus, a fleet of cars, and dozens of fellows and ladies all dressed in the same colorful, oversized pants who now loitered in the middle of the residential street, passed bottles in brown paper bags, and kicked around something that looked, disturbingly, like a hacky sack.

While the entourage played and drank and walked the dogs and stretched their travel-weary legs, Bratty and Tommy drank a beer on the bus. *Liquid courage,* Tommy called it.

Bratty wasn't ready.

"Dude. What if I just, like, never talk to them again?"

"You could. Maybe you should. But you're here."

"Fuck it." He chugged the beer. He tossed the can. He clipped the leash on his dog. He and Tommy and the dog all climbed out of the bus. They walked across the soggy lawn. The front door opened. Bratty's father stepped out.

"Bradford? Bradford, is that you?"

"Hey, Pops!"

His dad left the door wide open. He approached, slowly, arms crossed, brow furrowed.

"What have I told you about dropping by unexpectedly?"

"I know. Helena doesn't like it. But—"

"And where did that dog come from? And what's the meaning of all this?" His dad motioned toward the convoy.

The Mr. Yays had busted out bongo drums. A cop car pulled up and two officers got out and someone offered them captain's hats.

"This ruckus."

"Well . . . s-so—" Bratty stuttered. The old fear washed through him.

He closed his eyes. He would not let it take him.

He heard a voice in his head. *Ride on, sailor! Across the briny deep!* He opened his eyes. He stood up tall. He looked at his dad, gaze steady. He spoke. "I'm on tour."

"Tour?"

"With Tommy."

"I don't understand."

"No. You never understood," Bratty said. "You always judged, but you never tried to understand. But I'll tell you anyway. Tommy is Mr. Yay. The rapper. I mix the beats. I guess you could say . . . we're both Mr. Yay."

He stared at his father. Brian Pierson. This sad old man, with his white hair, fret lines across his brow, bags beneath his weary eyes. This man who made him hate himself, as a boy. But now he was grown, and he only felt pity.

"But Tommy is— That's not a career. What about school?"

"I dropped out. To pursue my music."

"What? You can't just— That's not acceptable."

"It's not like you were paying."

"You are— I don't even know what to say! You make *rap music*?"

Rap was not a plan. Music was a pastime. The old man's face

grew red with rage. Then, behind him, in the doorway, Helena appeared. She did not greet Bradford or embrace Bradford or acknowledge him.

She said, simply, "Rap isn't even music. Rap is a waste of time."

Which reminded the old man that he had plenty to say. "She's right! Helena is right. You had real opportunities, and you chose to squander them. For what? Rap is just crude, dangerous junk and bass that'll blow your eardrums out. You can't quit school for something so stupid! What did I tell you, Bradford? You drop out of college? What do you think will happen? Your life will amount to nothing."

It was at this moment that the dog, Tux (Tux the Avenger, Tux the Destroyer, Tornado Tux), who had sat peacefully, patiently, at Bratty's side up until then, must have sensed the threat, or the bongo drums riled him, or the fates implored him. He sprung up. He lunged, so fast that the leash slipped from Bratty's hand. He tore across the wet grass, through a patch of mud, toward Helena, mouth open, drool streaming, and he growled, a primal tear-your-heart-out growl.

But he didn't attack.

She wasn't worth it.

He ran past her, into the house.

"No! Stop it! Do something! Stop it!" Helena screamed, but her sad, useless old husband stood there, stewing in uncertainty, his face already betraying regret for what he'd said, watching tragedy unfold.

Bratty and Tommy had their damp shoes, their lingering scent of beer and sweat and pot smoke, their bold vulgarity that made them generally unwelcome in the refined abode of Mr. and Mrs.

Pierson, and when they approached the door, the latter moved to block them, even as she kept screaming, "Stop it! Stop that awful dog!"

The dog (Tux the Gleeful, Merry Fairy Tux, Terminator Tuxy) looked happier than he had ever been in his life. With a broad smile on his face, tongue out, eyes gleaming, he sprinted through the house, across the pure white carpets, over the stark white upholstery, marking everything with muddy paw prints. And after a few laps, he darted out the door, past the humans, into a puddle, where he rolled, and got all his paws and fur all freshly muddied, and then went back inside again. Bratty pretended to try to stop him, but gosh darn if the jolly dog didn't evade his grasp. Tommy just stood there and laughed and laughed as the dog knocked over the lamp, shredded the throw pillow, crunched the remote in his formidable jaw, and covered every surface of the entryway and living room with mud.

Then, when Tux had enough, he sprinted outside, cleaned his paws off on the grass, and climbed back inside the tour bus.

He was a very good dog, and they all had a big show tomorrow.

INTERLUDE

A VERY GOOD DOG

IMAGINE YOU are a dog.

Imagine you are a golden retriever. A Very Good Dog. Except no one has ever told you. You drift around, from the street to the shelter, from pack to pack, like flotsam. You land in a house with humans who are not Bad Humans. They are indifferent. They are Very Busy Humans who do not have time to cuddle a dog or walk a dog or play with a dog, or cuddle or walk or play, and you are underfoot, and alone. You are alone and sad because you feel that something is missing. You can't say what. But you feel it.

You feel sad, except for when you have the dream. In the dream, you have an animal family. You have a jaunty hat. There is wind and water and sun, and you are beloved. You are Famous. Humans pet you and scratch you and shake your paw, and everyone says you are a Very Good Dog.

You know this is just a dream, because you cannot smell it. But you know it is more than a dream.

How do you know?

You have a dog's brain.

The universe is mysterious, and smelly, and one day, when you are back in the shelter again, abandoned, sad, and dreamless, you smell a smell and it is very particular and intriguing and delicious and your dog's brain knows this smell means something different.

It is a smell that reminds you of a dream.

It makes your ears perk and your tail wag, and your tongue flops out and you are hot and excited, buzzing, drooling, gazing out between the bars at the humans who appear in search of a dog, a Very Good Dog. You.

They want you.

They choose you. They hug you. They tell you, for the first time in your life, that you are a Very Good Dog. That you are going places.

They address you as *Captain.*

You must act as befits this title, and so you are on your best behavior when you meet the others. There are so many others. There is a pit bull type. There is an old dog with three legs. Some are friendly visitors, but others belong to the pack. You will belong to the pack.

You all play a game. There is music. There are salmon treats. You all get matching hats. Everyone claps.

You are all Very Good Dogs.

SUMMER SOLSTICE

MR. YAY CRUSHES IT

MR. YAY WAS BACKSTAGE. In a moment, the show would begin.

Mr. Yay the rapper shared a joint with the giraffe. Once, in a different universe, the giraffe had fallen overboard, nearly drowned, learned to swim. Once, in this universe, the giraffe had been an electrical engineer, had worked sixty hours a week, had wished that he could sail around instead. But he'd always been too afraid to stick his neck out.

Mr. Yay the DJ pulled up his patchwork pants. They hung low, lower now after all those runs with his dog. He examined himself in the mirror. His long fake beard. Black eyeliner for the ocean glare. A luster in his eye. He thought about *The Adventures of Mr. Yay*, how he'd watched it as a kid with Tommy, and later in high school, after class, how he'd cowered at the sound of the garage door, how he'd hated *hated hated* himself for being who he really was. Which was not much. Just a boy, ordinary but kind, who loved music. He thought about Mr. Yay before he became Mr. Yay, and how he had transformed, from bandit to sailor, with a detective interlude between. He thought about his dad, rewatching the same old Ricardo Merman westerns, working late into the night, unreachable, except for that one Thanksgiving when they had seen *Peregrine* in the theater and they had gorged on mac-and-cheese balls and there, in his dad's eyes, was that elusive glimmer. Things might have been different for him. They might still be. He thought about how fearful he had been, all those hungry times he snuck to the pantry, all the snacks he pillaged in the dark, the dread that they would catch him. *Silent,* he'd told himself. *Silent like a starfish.* He thought about the one time in his life when he'd sailed on a boat, Tommy's dad's boat, on that rare summer day when the boat got used. The silver-blue river rolled on all the way to the sea *and so should we,* Tommy had said. *Sail away, never come back.* They were just boys, barely ten years old. Young enough to believe that a dog could be captain.

But now they were Mr. Yay. Perhaps the boat was still there, green and fuzzy with moss, waiting for Mr. Yay to sail it away. And maybe Mr. Yay would. Mr. Yay was a carpe diem kind of guy. He was not afraid.

He had been onstage, to the side, out of the light. Tonight would play different. Tonight, backstage was packed. Other musicians had come for this show: rappers; DJs; a punk band called the Yay-Yay-Yays; the Fantabulous Queen of Sequin Pop, Nova Z'Rhae. Dozens of dancers stretched their legs, fixed their makeup, adjusted their costumes. They were dressed as lions and jaguars, bears and deer, rabbits, squirrels, turtles, wolves, human men in short shorts and women in skintight halters and miniskirts patterned with the colors of myriad nations, a multicultural assortment of salacious spandex, their skin glazed in glitter. Roadies prepped the replica ship, its wheels, its sails, its neon lights, its cannon, made to fire confetti into the crowd. A dozen dogs in captain's hats gathered on the deck, where the treats were stashed. All the dogs were up there, except for Tux, Tux the Loyal, Tux the Loving, the best dog friend a dude could have. Tux stayed by Bratty's side, as Bratty meandered the backstage crowd, to the edge of the stage, as he peered out, at the thousands who'd gathered that night, for Mr. Yay.

The stage overlooked a field, and the field was packed, shoulder to shoulder near the rail, knee to knee in the back, where people spread picnic blankets, drank beers, passed joints, and the smoke lingered in the still summer air, festive, ready for lasers.

Tommy's parents sat in the VIP section, safe from the crowds, sipping wine from tiny plastic bottles. Bratty's own parents weren't there, as far as he could see, even though he'd sent them tickets. They never would be there, and maybe it would always hurt. But he was stronger now, weathered. Fearless.

Tommy joined him then, at the edge of the stage, looking out.

"You ready?" Bratty asked.

"Who the fuck is ever ready? Tonight, this shit, it's gonna be crazy."

"It's been crazy. But this—"

"Yeah," Tommy said. He laughed to himself. "You remember that goose?"

"The goose?"

"The big one. Outside the apartment in the middle of the night. It was like, *Pop! Oh, hello, I'm a big, weird goose!* Did that really happen?"

"I think so."

"Crazy." Tommy paused. He gazed out at the crowd. "You know, I could imagine a million different things we might do. All kindsa things. Just imagine. Tommy and Bratty roaming the desert on some quest, throwing festivals, fighting zombies or formulating psychic drugs or running some huge evil corporation. Tommy and Bratty in space. A million different things, and every path would be fun, because we'd always be together. But this—you and me, making music. Damn. This is the best."

"It is," Bratty agreed.

"Are you ready?" Tommy asked.

"I am. But... let's give it a minute. Let it build."

They waited backstage, as the crowd grew, and pushed toward the stage, and more crowds gathered beyond the amphitheater, pressed to the fence, in the streets, on the rooftops of cars and buildings beyond, all there for a glimpse of Mr. Yay. The noise grew, from conversational thrum, to ruckus, to tsunami roar, deafening. Almost loud enough. But they would wait. Until it swept over them, until this riptide of fame and fate pulled them onto the stage, into the light. But they had a moment still. Bratty closed his eyes. He could see the waves rolling toward him, the vast sea, his life a tiny boat, captained by him, with his best friend, and This Random Dog.

Out in the crowd, in the field, a man carried two beers, poured to the brim. They sloshed over, onto his hand. On his finger: a ring. He couldn't explain how much it meant. He'd been a lawyer, a writer. He knew the power of words. But words were paltry, pale things beside this luminous creature, his wife.

He found her, handed her a beer, lit two cigarettes, one for them each.

"We're going to quit smoking," she said. "After tonight."

"Is that what you want?"

"Yes."

"Then we will."

They had a small blanket on a patch of grass, and for the first sips they sat. But they had to stand, as the crowd pressed in, as it got louder, rowdier, packed with doe-eyed teens in halter tops and bootie shorts, boys in baggy jeans, with joints and vapes and gold chains and name tags that all said HELLO MY NAME IS MR. YAY, and men in jeans painted with patchwork squares, men in pirate hats, shirtless men, nearly naked men with *Mr. Yay* scrawled a hundred times across their skin, women with doggie ears and doggie tails and sequined captain's hats, middle-aged women drinking tequila cocktails from water bottles, chanting, necking each other, old bald men funneling six-packs into beer bongs, slapping the bag, dancing hard, though the music hadn't started yet. They could all still feel it, the bass beat, in their bones.

It was the same beat they'd all heard, as kids, with their headphones on, volume up, to drown the volley of *shoulds* and *should-nots*, judgment disguised as direction, to fill the vacant space in their souls with music. It was the beat they heard on the breeze, as they hung their hammocks, because life was short, and hammocks were marvelous. It was the beat, the drop, the sound of work swept off a desk, clock punched, bird flipped, and no, you never looked back. It was a beat heard by those who chose a life of adventure. Who chose life and wouldn't let work get in the way. Who would entrust the dog with command, and not take themselves too seriously, because what were they really? A lumpy sack of bones, a crooked nose, a head-nest full of tangled brain-wires, a sense of passion and wonder and awe, 60 percent genetically identical to a chicken. A vehicle for music. The music, the beat, the words of Mr. Yay belonged to Mr. Yay before him, who sailed to distant lands, who vanished mysteriously and completely, who would live forever, in music.

The music started. Low at first. A steady beat. A dream of sound waves. Then, on the stage, a small boat appeared. A rowboat, a life raft, a dolphin, a seal, its shape changing with the shifting light. And on the belly of the seal, the dolphin's back, the boat, there was a young man with headphones, mixers, controllers, the power to build the beat, to shape it, to let it drop and build it up again. He stepped out to the edge of his small craft, into the light. He wore pants made of squares of color. He had a telescope. He looked out upon the crowd. He was not the rapper, but Miriam knew him. She had known him broken, and watched him grow strong.

The crowd cheered, clapped, waved their arms to a beat that got louder, faster, a promise of good times ahead, and then another Mr. Yay stepped out. This Mr. Yay wore the same patchwork pants. He walked across the waves of light, the stage projected to resemble water. His only equipment was the mic in his hand.

The crowd roared.

The music played. Mr. Yay spun beats. Mr. Yay rapped. For a handful of songs, it was just them, Tommy and Bratty, Mr. Yay and Mr. Yay. With each song, the crowd got louder, drunker, wilder. The punk band rolled out, the Yay-Yay-Yays. Shirts came off. Beautiful bare titties smiled at the stage. A mosh pit formed along the rail. A massive disco ball suspended from a crane appeared above the stage, and the Queen of Sequin Pop strolled out, in sequined pants and a crown of glittering shells, and she sang along with the crowd, and they went *wild*.

When she finished, the lights went out. A hush spread across the audience. A quiet moon rose over the field. A fog machine turned on. Then lasers.

Then the lights came back, and onto the staged rolled the boat, a big, glittering boat painted with the words SS *Deliverance*. A golden retriever in a captain's hat stood at the prow. Mr. Yay appeared on deck, in billowing velvet pants, a fake beard pasted to his chin, a microphone in his hand.

"Are you ready," he said, into the mic, in a voice like cream soda, "for adventure?"

The crowd howled, but their cries were subdued. They were letting it build.

The beat came back. Blue-green waves rippled across the stage. The dancers came out, the lions and jaguars, bears and deer, rabbits, squirrels, turtles, wolves, the glittered humans, the giraffe, Nova Z'Rhae in a mermaid suit, all of them swirling in unison.

Yo, my name is Mr. Yay
And it's time I tell my story
'Cause my name is Mr. Yay
Like the one that came before me
Yeah you know the one
Patchwork pants, long beard

Sailed the world
Never feared
What was different, what was strange
Cuz yo, he knew the truth
Being different makes us stronger
You be silly, you be strange
You gotta be the real you

The lyrics belonged to this new Mr. Yay. But mixed into the beat was a familiar tune, the theme music of the original show. Mr. Yay remembered them. The crowd remembered them. Not all of them at first. But the ones that remembered cried out. They raised their arms. They sang, as the song sailed on.

Yo my name is Mr. Yay
I ain't never sailed the seas
But like my namesake
I don't stress
Don't dress to please
Don't need to impress
Nobody but me

The theme music looped back, louder this time. More and more people remembered. Hundreds. Almost half the crowd. More than half. Even the ones who didn't remember felt it, a tsunami wave of glee, and they lifted their hands and tears streamed from their eyes and their voices joined together, building, echoing across the sea of people.

Yo my name is Mr. Yay
And yeah I love to play
With the ladies, video games
Get extra blazed
But that's all glaze
Cuz what I love most is rap
Music speaks to me
But here's a bit of history
From before I found my glory:
I was just a little shorty
When I came across the story
On the TV, of adventure
And acceptance, and freedom
From convention
And that show it never bored me
Yo, that show was fuckin' weird,
Which was great until you hear
What is weirder than weird
That Mr. Yay and his show,
That shit done disappeared!

The theme music circled back again, louder, guiding the beat. Everyone remembered now. On the stage, on the boat, more dogs appeared, all of them in captain's hats. There was a second golden retriever, a Great Dane, a husky, a pit bull. There was an old border collie with three legs, and beneath his missing fourth he had a peg, like a pirate. The crowd went berserk. They sang and spun and shook their arms and screamed with joy, elation, excitement for the Mr. Yay before them, and the Mr. Yay they remembered, from their past. Mr. Yay sailed on:

So I ask you the question
We all want to know
Mr. Yay was here
So where the fuck did he go?!

Miriam went back in time. To a moment when she clutched a plush Captain Barksford to her chest. To a moment when she held the puppy Roxster in her arms. She tasted salt. She was sobbing, sobbing, screaming, and it all came out.

On the stage, the dancers swirled, and the dogs ran laps across the deck. The lasers flashed. The fog rolled and everything turned hazy and sparkly and it was all so fucking beautiful.

Everyone lost it. The crowd screamed and cheered and wept and pushed, toward the stage, away from it. The dancers went freestyle. The lion scrambled up the hull. The giraffe leapt from the stage and surfed the crowd. The dogs zoomed around. Only Mr. Yay and Mr. Yay remained composed. The rapper raised the mic to his mouth. He chanted.

"Where is Mr. Yay? Where the fuck is Mr. Yay?"

The crowd chanted back.

Where is Mr. Yay?

Where is Mr. Yay?

Where is Mr. Yay?

Where is Mr. Yay?

The rhythm caught her, and Miriam found herself dancing,

spinning, yelling along with the crowd. "Where is Mr. Yay?! Where is Mr. Yay?!"

Jack was dancing, too. His eyes glistened with tears. His hands waved, and all around them the crowd roiled. Everyone was yelling. *Where is Mr. Yay?!* Everyone was moving, in all directions, all at once.

Where is Mr. Yay?

Where is Mr. Yay?

Where is Mr. Yay?

All around them, people went mad, or they'd been mad, and this was just the natural madness coming out. The crowd moshed and screamed and wept and danced and sang along, and the music kept playing and it was gorgeous and perfect, and suddenly too much.

Miriam reached for her husband's hand. He looked at her, and she knew he knew she was ready. He nodded. He held her hand tight, and together they weaved through the crowd, through fog and smoke and everyone jumping, dancing, the whole field moving all at once as they moved through it, all the way up to the fence, and past it, out the venue, into the packed streets, until the music faded and the crowd thinned enough that they could run, and they ran.

They ran together, hands clasped, still weeping, but also laughing, and it felt like it had that first night they met, when their lives crashed together, when Miriam knew who she was, and what she wanted. They ran until they couldn't hear the music anymore.

They stopped beneath a streetlamp. Jack looked at her, his gaze incandescent.

"What now?" he asked.

She kissed him, hard, on the lips. She kissed him, and she tasted anger, mistrust, frustration, but also adventure, mystery, fun. Love.

"Who are you really, Jack?"

The retired lawyer. The detective. Her husband. She kissed him again. Who was she? What did she want now? She bit his lip, not hard, but hard enough.

"Tonight?" he said. "I'm—"

From behind him came a jinglejangle sound. Dog tags. Then an old, three-legged dog with a fourth peg leg limped up, with the biggest grin he'd ever had in his life.

"Roxster!" Miriam laughed.

Roxster barked. Another dog appeared behind him, a smiling young golden retriever with a captain's hat.

"And look!" Jack said, as he crouched down to pet them both. "You've brought a friend!"

Fall Equinox

MR. YAY'S NEXT MOVES

THE FIRE CRACKLED and the crickets croaked and the wind hummed through the trees, and yet the forest felt still, and silent. *Silent like a starfish.*

Tommy stabbed a stick into a marshmallow.

"Like the storm has passed," Bratty said, mid-thought. He warmed his hands over the campfire. "And everything is calm and clear and you're all like, 'What the hell just happened? What was that crazy dream?'"

"Yeah," Tommy said, adding another marshmallow. He would add five, six, ten, eleven, as many as he could roast on a single stick.

In Bratty's lap lay a dog. His eyes were closed, his tail curled beneath him. On his face, a smile. Tuckered Tux. Tux the Cuddlasaur. Tux Once Random, but Random No More.

Tux the One and Only.

Bratty stroked the dog's head. He sipped his beer. He thought about the album. Their new one, launched today. He thought about all the people listening now, downloading, dancing, all the press, the buzz, the looming tour. The coterie of dancers and stagehands and groupies and dogs, back at the Compound of Yay, which was just a big warehouse on the desert edge of LA, but was also something so much more. From the roof, if you squinted just right, you could see the distant glint of an endless sea.

"You talk to your dad?" Tommy asked. He turned his marshmallow stick over the fire.

"Yeah. I..." Bratty had. About the album, the tour, the absolute certainty that at no point, in this or any other timeline, would he ever pursue a career in investment banking. But the conversation had faded from his mind, because it didn't matter. "It doesn't matter. Whatever he says, whatever he thinks, it doesn't matter. Because this life, making music, getting to share it, getting to kick it with you and Tux... this is the best life I could possibly imagine ever living. It's like, the craziest dream come true."

At that moment, Tommy's marshmallows erupted in flames. He yanked them back from the fire, fanning and blowing, until the embers turned to char.

"Perfect," he said, admiring the black and gooey mess. "Hey, you want to hear something really crazy?"

"Yeah."

"At the end of the tour, in Louisville, I was like, in the hotel trying to sleep, and all of a sudden there's this bird just flapping around inside my hotel room. At first I thought it was just in my head. Like I ate too many gummies and was just tripping out or whatever. But then the bird started talking."

"Wait, wait, what?" Bratty laughed. "What'd it say?"

"It said, 'if you build it, they will come.'"

"So... the bird is Kevin Costner—"

"No, no, no, *I'm* Kevin Costner. The bird is just—"

Bratty laughed again. "A hallucination. A dream?"

"I swear, dude," Tommy said. His voice sounded serious. But what was that wild look in his eyes? "I swear. It happened just like that."

ACKNOWLEDGMENTS

Once upon a time, many years ago, when I had a mutt named Mulder, and Nymeria the husky who lives with me now had yet to be born, my little brother Anthony, aka Delux, had a brief, glorious career as a rapper. At least, I thought he was glorious. I loved his albums, his music videos, his whole weird vibe. He never hit any lists or sold out any shows or really made bank from the endeavor. But he made me happy.

In some other universe, he might have made it big.

In this universe, as I write these acknowledgements, he is about to get married to one of the most amazing women I've ever met. Taylor Hughes, we all love you so much.

In this universe, instead of living more than a thousand miles away, in Colorado, where he lived during his rapper days, my brother lives in a house that he owns, only a mile from my house. On the weekends, we go out dancing and drink beer and play games with my kids, who get to grow up knowing their uncle. We throw the most amazing parties together. He doesn't rap anymore, though some of his lyrics live on in this book. He's a DJ now, and I get to hear him play at my book launch parties.

In this universe, I am living a better life than I could possibly have imagined, and it's because of all the people in it. I'm endlessly grateful for all of them.

In particular, and as always, I am grateful for my husband

Steve, without whom I wouldn't be sharing any books with you at all. I'm grateful for Ella Jane and Sammie, who always delight me. And for all my friends here in the Ridge, whose kids I've watched grow up, whose lives I get to share, y'all are awesome. Thanks in particular to Beth Sullivan, who first told me about the Berenstain Rift, which provided inspiration for this book.

Thank you to my superstar agent, Holly Root, whose insight and dedication is unparalleled.

Thank you to my wonderful editor, Adam Wilson, who has helped me hone my writing and make this a better book, and who selected this book from all he had to choose from. This is one of my earliest, first drafted long before my debut (though rewritten since). Honestly, I didn't ever think it would get published, but I am so glad it will be.

Thanks to my fantastic team at Hyperion Avenue—Jennifer Levesque, Amy C. King, Vicki Korlishin, Crystal McCoy, Raegan Cutrino, Daneen Goodwin, Greta Shull, Sara Liebling, Guy Cunningham, Sylvia Davis, Dan Kaufman—and to Amanda Hudson, for continuing to design such great covers for my books.

Finally, thank you all, readers, for coming along with me on another strange journey.